LOVE & OLIVES

ALSO BY JENNA EVANS WELCH

Love & Gelato

Love & Luck

From the *New York Times* Bestselling Author of *Love & Gelato*

LOVE &
OLIVES

∞ JENNA EVANS WELCH ∞

SIMON & SCHUSTER BFYR

New York   London   Toronto   Sydney   New Delhi

SIMON & SCHUSTER BFYR

An imprint of Simon & Schuster Children's Publishing Division
1230 Avenue of the Americas, New York, New York 10020
Text copyright © 2020 by Jenna Evans Welch
Jacket design and illustration copyright © 2020 by Karina Granda
All rights reserved, including the right of reproduction in whole or in part in any form.
SIMON & SCHUSTER BFYR is a trademark of Simon & Schuster, Inc.
For information about special discounts for bulk purchases, please contact
Simon & Schuster Special Sales at 1-866-506-1949 or business@simonandschuster.com.
The Simon & Schuster Speakers Bureau can bring authors to your live event. For more
information or to book an event contact the Simon & Schuster Speakers Bureau
at 1-866-248-3049 or visit our website at www.simonspeakers.com.
Interior designed by Tom Daly
The text of this book was set in Adobe Caslon Pro.
Manufactured in the United States of America

2 4 6 8 10 9 7 5 3
Library of Congress Cataloging-in-Publication Data
Names: Welch, Jenna Evans, author.
Title: Love & olives / by Jenna Evans Welch.
Other titles: Love and olives
Description: First Simon & Schuster Books for Young Readers hardcover edition. | New
York : Simon & Schuster Books for Young Readers, 2020. | Audience: Ages 12 up. |
Summary: When her long-estranged father invites sixteen-year-old Liv Varanakis to help
him film a documentary about his theories on Atlantis, she looks forward to reconnecting
but discovers he may have invited her to Greece for a very different reason.
Identifiers: LCCN 2020019092 |
ISBN 9781534448834 (hardcover) | ISBN 9781534448858 (ebook)
Subjects: CYAC: Fathers and daughters—Fiction. | Atlantis (Legendary place)—Fiction. |
Documentary films—Production and direction—Fiction. | Dating (Social customs)—
Fiction. | Santorini Island (Greece)—Fiction. | Greece—Fiction.
Classification: LCC PZ7.1.W435 Lu 2020 | DDC [Fic]—dc23
LC record available at https://lccn.loc.gov/2020019092

To Sam.

I will battle
one million Ender Dragons,
a hundred million Creepers,
twenty Cave Spiders,
and a Zombie Pigman,

for you.

Prologue

THERE'S THIS THING ABOUT ME THAT I DON'T TELL ANYONE. I haven't told my boyfriend or my stepdad, or any of my friends, but it's important to the story, so I think I'd better put it out there right at the beginning.

Two or three nights a week, I drown in my sleep.

Here's how it goes: I'm in the water, an oxygen tank strapped to my back, and I'm diving, my face pointed toward the ocean floor. The water is warm and a startling blue-green, but I hardly notice it because I'm too busy looking for something. *Searching* for something. I don't know what it is that I'm trying to find, only that I want it more than I've ever wanted anything.

Finally, I see something down below—a glimmer of light. It's bright and inviting, and without a second of hesitation, I kick harder, chasing it. The glow is centered around something, a small piece of metal that shines brighter the closer I get to it. But right as I reach my hand out to touch it, the light goes black, plunging me into thick, stunning darkness. And that's when I realize the worst part. My oxygen has run out. I panic, trying to claw my way to the surface, but it's so far away, and when I open my mouth to scream, water fills my throat and ears and—

You get it.

In my sleep I don't know what I'm looking for, but once I'm awake, and my cheeks are salty and my throat feels raw, it's all so obvious. *Painfully* obvious. I'm looking for the lost city of Atlantis. My dad's world. And even though I know I'm safe, that I'm lying in my bed, not at the bottom of the Aegean Sea, I still have to get up and find my dad's map.

The map is another one of my secrets. I keep it hidden in the top of my closet under the tower of sketchbooks I've been adding to since grade school, and though I've tried to throw it out at least a dozen times, I've never been able to. The map is hand drawn and overflowing with arrows and overlapping notes, some in Greek, some in English. There are even a few of my dad's characteristically quirky drawings, like a sea serpent wearing an eye patch and Poseidon napping in a hammock with his trident.

It's strange, though. When I open the map, I don't really see any of that. I see my dad. We're at our tiny kitchen table, his dark head bent over the map. His eyes are bright, because he's talking about our shared love of Atlantis. Child Me is hanging on to his every word, because back then I wasn't just Olive. I was *Indiana Olive*, the world-famous explorer.

Part scientist, part archaeologist, part deep-sea diver, Indiana Olive fought pirates and giant squids and greedy money mongers who wanted her treasure. She was brave and smart, and no matter what the ocean threw her way, she always had her dad next to her.

Until she didn't.

When my dad left, he left twenty-six things behind. A lot of them were throwaways, but I kept them anyway—a pack of his favorite cinnamon gum, a faded T-shirt, scribbled-on papers. I gathered them up and hid them in an old shoebox under my bed, and while my mom was at work, I'd bring them out, trying to make sense of them. Why had he left *these* things behind?

A few of them were easy to figure out. The T-shirt was scratchy. The gum, too cinnamony. But why would he leave his favorite shaving soap? And what about our map? He'd left it folded on my nightstand. Wouldn't he need that in Santorini—to help him find the lost city?

I made a careful list of all the items, and I looked at that list every single day for two years—which is how long it took me to figure out that my dad wasn't coming back for me. I don't like to say much about that time period, but let's just say that sometimes I think I know exactly what it felt like for the

Atlanteans to have their entire lives crumble and disappear.

After that, I stopped looking at the list. But it moved with us. From place to place, tagging along through all the school changes and apartment changes, all those lonely places that made up our post-Dad life. It was when we were living in Seattle, shortly after Mom married James, when she found the list: *26 Things My Dad Left Behind, by Indiana Olive*. And she wanted to talk to me about the last item—number twenty-six.

But, of course, I didn't want to talk about it. I wasn't Indiana Olive anymore. I wasn't even *Olive* anymore. I was Liv. And part of being Liv was never ever talking about my dad. I'd learned the hard way that telling people that your father left you for a mythical island that 99.9 percent of the world doesn't believe ever existed is not a great idea. In fact, it's best if you don't even tell it to yourself that often.

So, "no," I told her. I didn't want to talk about my dad. I didn't want to talk about my past. And I most definitely didn't want anything to do with that list. It symbolized everything that had hurt me, and everything that I no longer wanted to be.

My mom told me that important things don't like to stay buried, but then, thankfully, she let it go. It felt like a victory. We'd moved on, hadn't we? I had no use for golden cities and broken promises. I was no longer interested in cryptic clues. I'd declared that part of my life *over*. Case closed.

And then Atlantis came looking for me.

Chapter One

#1. HALF A PACK OF BIG RED CHEWING GUM

My dad chewed this all the time. One foil-wrapped stick after another starting right after his morning cup of coffee. He said it was the first thing he bought when he arrived in the Chicago airport from Greece, and the second he popped it into his mouth, he knew he'd made the right decision: any country that made gum like this knew what it was doing. He emigrated with almost nothing. Just his passport, a ratty backpack, a few hundred dollars, and a Greek accent so strong he said it took three months before he could successfully order a cup of coffee.

His philosophy for navigating the US with zero connections, zero money, and zero friends? "Jump and a net will grow."

He was always getting American idioms wrong like that.

I'M GASPING FOR AIR. MY LUNGS FEEL LIKE TWO FIERY balloons. The mailboxes and trees are starting to sway in my blurry vision. And according to the fitness watch my stepdad, James, gave me for Christmas, we've gone only 1.32 miles.

In the tradition of the great Master Yoda: a runner I am not. And today I couldn't even fake it.

"I need another break," I wheezed, doubling over to rest my hands on my bare knees.

My boyfriend, Dax, slowed his jaunty pace and sighed loudly, not because he needed the extra oxygen, but because this was our third break in less than fifteen minutes. I didn't have to glance at him to know exactly what his face looked like. Disappointed. Well, disappointed and gorgeous in that sun-kissed, fauxhawked, blue-green eyes kind of way. Because, *Dax.*

He rested his hand on my back, but the weight of it felt more incriminating than supportive. "Liv, we already had a break. I still have three more miles if I'm going to hit my training goal, remember?"

I did remember. And honestly, I wanted to run those three miles with him. Not only does Dax hate running alone, but last night he also accompanied me to an art exhibit in downtown Seattle that was all about the history of the Polaroid. He'd even turned off his phone so we wouldn't spend half the night being bombarded by texts from his legions of friends. So this morning, as a thank-you, I had planned to make it through his entire run without any complaining, which I can usually at least sort of do.

But unlike every other member of Dax's family/friend circle, I am not a runner. Or a biker. Or a cross-country skier. And I'm definitely not a morning person. I am an occasional Star Wars–quoter, a collage artist, and a friend to all houseplants, but when Dax and I first started dating, I'd casually agreed with him when he mentioned how much he loved running in the mornings, and here we were. Two years later the ruse was definitely up, but he was still dragging me along with him. He was nothing if not persistent.

Today felt extra hard. I was so *sleepy*.

And then the memory hit me in the face. Splashed me in the face. I'd had the dream last night. No wonder I had the stamina of an elderly sloth.

I blew the ends of my sweaty bangs out of my eyes and attempted yet another ponytail, but my chin-length hair was too short. Not even my hair wanted to complete this run. And now Dax was disappointed and hurt and . . . annoyed? I neatly shoved the nightmare to the back of my mind. Time to pull out SUPER! GIRLFRIEND! capable of averting all oncoming squabbles with the power of *flirta-tious diversion*!

I abandoned my ponytail holder, instead ruffling my hair into what I hoped was mussed perfection. "Hey, Dax, do you know what would be great for your conditioning? Running with extra weight. Something like . . ." I looked at the sky thoughtfully, then landed my smile on him. "Something like me!"

He groaned again, but a smile slipped through, and he bent down so I could jump onto his back. We took off at a steady clip, me clinging happily to his shoulders. Dax's shoulders were actually the first thing I noticed about him, mostly because I'd sat directly behind him in homeroom, and that first day I was so busy trying to fake the same bored look everyone else was sporting that I could barely focus on anything else.

He says my style was the first thing he noticed, which, to be honest, is the first thing everyone notices and is entirely by design. When I'd transformed from Olive to Liv, I'd scoured hundreds of style videos before finally landing on the ones that I thought I might be able to pull off—French-girl style. I'd cut off twelve inches of hair, binge-watched makeup-application videos, then spent a solid month looking for clothes that were neutral and effortlessly stylish. In the sea of Patagonia wearers, Parisian chic had made quite the splash.

And yes, I'm Greek American, not French American. But who's keeping track? Not me.

He took off at a jog, and I sank my face into his neck. During the summer, Dax spends twenty to thirty hours a week in a pool, and he wears chlorine the way other guys wear cologne. Dax technically goes to a private school, but to be on our water polo team, he has to have dual enrollment, so he spends part of the day at my school. Or at least he used to. As of two weeks ago he is officially a high school graduate, a fact that tipped my world slightly off-balance though I've been working hard to conceal it. "I love the smell of hypochlorous acid in the morning," I said.

"You smell like sweat," he said, giving my right knee a squeeze. "I can't run three miles with you on my back. Let's go back to your house."

"If you say so." I pressed my cheek into his. "We can make chocolate chip pancakes. The breakfast of champions. Not even your new college coaches can argue with that."

College. The muscles in Dax's jaw tightened, and I held my breath, already regretting the conversation that was about to happen. Unless he magically decided *not* to bring it up?

My eye snagged on a red-cheeked garden gnome planted in the flower bed of a yard we were passing, and I found myself praying to it out of sheer desperation. *Please, little garden gnome, please don't make me have to lie to my boyfriend today—*

"Did you contact Stanford about their high school day yet?" Dax interrupted. "Amelia says that's really important to the admission process. They want to see that you've put in the effort before they consider your application."

Thanks for nothing, garden gnome.

"Of course," I said. "Hopefully I'll hear back soon."

My voice sounded like it belonged to a lark or a sparrow or something equally chirpy. Not only was Dax going to Stanford, but half his family had gone there too, and his older cousin Amelia worked in the admissions office. It complicated things, a lot. And by *things*, I mean the fact that every time I'd clicked on the link that Amelia had sent me, I'd immediately gotten that panicked-for-air feeling that I get in my drowning nightmares. So, no. I had not applied to Stanford's high school day. But I didn't want to tell him now. Not when it was such a gorgeous summer day. Not when we'd had that great date at the art exhibit. Not when we were galloping through my neighborhood, my arms tight around him.

Dax started to say something, but luckily, a blur of lululemon activewear suddenly appeared in the driveway next to us, stopping the oncoming inquisition I knew was about to happen.

"Dax?" It was Maya Nakamura, a girl from Dax's graduating class, looking all kinds of sporty in her pink sports bra and leggings. Her long black hair was in a sleek ponytail, and she held a straining Labrador retriever by its leash. She was out for an actual, non-pressured run. Also, her abs were a thing to behold.

"Hi, Maya," I said, jumping off Dax to pet her dog, who was smiling through his slobber.

I knew Maya from parties and our SAT prep class. Dax knew her from kindergarten, which was how it worked for most of the people in his prep school—I'd learned quickly that rich Seattle was small Seattle. They clung to each other like barnacles. Today I was so happy to have a distraction that I was more than willing to pretend that Maya didn't have a raging crush on my boyfriend that had spanned a decade. In all fairness, who could blame her? He was *Dax*.

"Dax, I tried to call you last night," Maya said, ignoring me like she always does whenever she thinks she can get away with it. A lot of the girls in his graduating class are like that. They hadn't been particularly pleased when he'd started dating someone who went to (gasp!) public school. Not only had it taken him off the market, but they really didn't like to break ranks.

Maya's dad owned a Fortune 500 company, and she was the kind of girl who could run five miles in her sleep while also painting student rally posters and doing her hair for the homecoming dance. I'm not sure why anyone would attempt these things in their sleep, but you get it.

"Did you hear the news?"

"What news?" Dax grabbed the hem of his shirt and wiped the sweat from his glistening brow, exposing his abs. Ugh. Was he *trying* to torture her?

"I got into UC Berkeley! We're going to be, like, thirty miles from each other!"

"Really?" I jumped to my feet, wiping dog drool on my shorts. Despite the fact that mine and Maya's relationship existed primarily on Planet Awkward, I couldn't help but be excited for her. She'd been on UC Berkeley's waitlist for almost six months, and I'd seen how hard she'd worked on her SAT prep. This called for a celebration.

"Maya, that's incredible! You deserve it." I shot my elbow into Dax's ribs. "Isn't that great, Dax?"

He sprang dutifully into action. "Yeah, that's really great, Maya. You worked hard for that." He landed his arm around me. "Liv's trying for early decision at Stanford; hopefully she'll be there with us in a year."

Ugh.

Ugh ugh ugh.

"Oh. Really? You're thinking about Stanford?" Maya's expression fell for a moment, but her ponytail bobbed enthusiastically. "Well, that's great. Then you'll be together!"

Dax's gaze fell heavily on my face. "Maybe," I said. "I have a few schools I'm considering, and it's not like Stanford is easy to get into. Luckily, I have six months to decide where I want to apply. You don't have to make decisions this early, you know?"

Now Dax's body stiffened. But if Maya sensed the tension between us, she didn't let on. "Liv, I'm sure you'll get in anywhere; everyone knows your SAT scores were off the charts. Plus, you won that statewide art competition. For your, like . . . collage things? Right?"

Collage things. This was exactly the reason I didn't tell people about my art life. I hadn't even entered the contest in the first place; it was my teacher who had sent in my entry. "It wasn't that big of a deal," I said, doing my best to wave the whole *statewide art competition* thing off.

"Well, everyone else thought it was," she added, but she was looking at Dax when she said it.

My phone dinged. Text from Mom. Olive, are you home? I need to talk to you.

My heart lurched into my throat, but it took my brain a moment to realize why. *Olive.* She'd called me Olive. She'd been really respectful of my decision to go by Liv, and she almost never slipped up on that anymore. Also, it was 9:37. Shouldn't she be at work by now? Why wasn't she at work?

I felt another jolt in my chest, and suddenly my head was swirling, my thoughts racing by so quickly I couldn't snag a single one. *Is something wrong? Nothing's wrong. Keep it together, Liv. You're overreacting like usual. So what if she called you by the wrong name? She's fine—*

"Liv, you good?" Dax whispered. A small crease had formed between his eyebrows.

I nodded, doing my best to smile. Fine. I was *fine.*

Maya was still talking, and I focused on regaining my bearings in the conversation. "I can't wait. I wish summer was over already. I am so ready for college!" She smiled at Dax. "So, Balboa Island. You ready for senior trip?"

"We're ready," Dax said, slinging his arm around me again.

Maya's eyes widened slightly. "Liv, you're coming with us? That's so great!"

"My mom still hasn't decided," I said quickly. About thirty people from Dax's class were going to a classmate's beach house, which sounded chaotic and fun, but also . . .

I don't know. If I had to pin it down, I'd say that the ocean and I aren't the best of friends. I mostly like to admire it from afar, but Dax was already talking to me about this rock formation he planned to swim out to, and I was already coming up with a long list of excuses as to why I would not be swimming out to said rock formation. I *can* swim. I'm even scuba certified. It's just that I prefer *not* to drown in the depths of the murky sea. I still wanted to go. But not in the same way Dax wanted me to. It seemed to be a running theme these days.

"I'm going to make it work," I said confidently, and Dax shot me one of his dazzling smiles. A real smile. My shoulders loosened.

Maya hesitated, her grin turning sly. "Cool. Well, I guess I'll see you in Balboa, Couple Most Likely to Outlast High School!"

Aw. The infamous yearbook title.

"See you soon, Maya," Dax said, looping his other arm around me.

Maya turned, and we watched her and her dog trot off into the distance while I waited for Dax's customary denial. He didn't disappoint.

"Nothing's going on with her," he said quickly.

"I didn't *say* anything was going on with her." I fell into him, so he had to catch me. "Why do you keep telling people I'm applying to Stanford? I'm only a junior."

"Senior," he corrected, setting me back on my feet. "In three months, you'll be a senior. And I said you're trying for it, not that you're going for sure. Besides, what do you have against us going to the same school?"

"Nothing." I shut my eyes for half a second. Because, yes, the thought of wandering around campus and dorms and parties with Dax and zero parental supervision made me want to click my heels together and sing. But something about it made me feel a swirl of panic, too. Dax's dual enrollment meant that we only went to the same school part of the time, and already he dictated most of our social life. Maybe that had worked at first, when I didn't know anyone at my high school. But once I began making my own friends, it had started to feel a bit . . . constricting. He didn't love when I spent time with other guys (understandable), and it was hard to balance all of my own activities and schoolwork with going to his games and spending time with his school friends. Life had been so busy that I'd even had to drop soccer this year (I played goalie, of course, less running, all the social benefits) so I had enough time to balance everything.

Not that I was complaining. I was wild about Dax. Bananas about Dax. The real problem with Stanford is that it wasn't *Rhode Island School of Design*.

RISD. Thinking about it made me want to swoon into a field of lilacs or burst into spontaneous song or whatever it was people did when all their dreams come true. But I needed to wait for the right moment to tell Dax, and today was clearly not it. For Couple Most Likely to Outlast High School, we sure fought a lot.

I took a deep breath, mentally prepping for a conversational U-turn, when my phone dinged again. Another text from Mom. This time a bit more aggressive. Olive, please come home NOW. I really need to talk to you.

Olive again?

"Who is it?" Dax asked, glancing at my phone.

I quickly tilted it away from him. "Mom."

Dax wiped his face on his shirt again. "Thought she was at work?"

Instantly, my stomach turned to origami, and I had to force myself to relax. Worrying about my mom is an automatic reflex. That tends to happen when you lose one parent—you automatically worry more about the other one. Not that she ever gave me reason to worry. She probably needed someone to watch my little brother is all.

"Come on. Let's go make pancakes," I said.

I climbed onto his back again, and we were mercifully quiet for the next few minutes. We had made it to the last few feet of my driveway when Dax pointed to the mailbox. "You should check. Amelia told me they'd send out the invitations by mail."

"Dax," I groaned, tumbling off his back and making a big show of going boneless. I'd learned it from my five-year-old brother, Julius. He was a master at becoming an invertebrate should the situation ever demand it. "Does the mail even come on Saturday?"

"Of course it does," he said in that authoritative tone he sometimes gets. "Let me check." He reached for the mailbox, but luckily, a small, Julius-size ninja chose that exact moment to drop from a nearby maple tree, landing directly on Dax's head.

"Only the ninja can defeat the ninja!" Julius yelled, clamping down hard.

"What the—" Dax yelled, spinning around, his arms outstretched. "Julius, I thought we agreed you had to give me fair warning!"

"The first priority to the ninja is to win without fighting!"

I quickly peeled Julius off Dax. Today he'd gone all out in the costume department: a mask, two plastic katanas, and our mom's black bathrobe. "Is Mom okay?"

"She's okay," he said, looking at me blankly. "Why?"

My body relaxed slightly, and I put my hands on his shoulders. "Remember what Mom and James said? You aren't supposed to ambush from trees anymore."

"Or maybe not from anywhere?" Dax added hopefully, and Julius smiled indulgently at him. Dax had always been one of Julius's main targets, and so far all attempts at a ceasefire had been met with resistance.

"Oh no." I pushed Julius's mask off his face. "Is that my

new eyeliner?" His eyes were ringed with a gold shimmer that I'd recognize anywhere. Urban Decay Goldmine. I'd bought it for Dax's graduation dinner. "Julius! That was thirty dollars at Sephora!"

"The ninja must be cloaked in secrecy!" He pointed a katana at me. "Liv, I was in the tree because Mom told me to come looking for you. You got a postcard in the mail. It's really dirty and the writing was weird. Mom's face got scrunched up when she saw it."

No.

"A postcard?" Dax whirled on me excitedly. "That must be the invitation."

The dread hit me in an icy wave. My entire body went numb. *You see!* my mind shrieked triumphantly. *Something* is *wrong!*

"Let's go look!" Dax said, grabbing my hand and lacing his fingers through mine. "Come on."

My mom's text scrolled across my brain. *I need to talk to you.*

"Let me go. . . . Wait here, okay? Stay with Julius?" I untangled my fingers from Dax's and headed for the front door. I was going for brisk power walk—think *mall walker on a mission*—but it turned into a sprint about six steps in. I had too much adrenaline not to.

"*Now* you run," Dax called from behind me.

I didn't even try to respond. There was only one person who sent me old postcards with weird writing. Only one. And it definitely wasn't Stanford Admissions.

I had to get that postcard and hide it before Dax or anyone else saw it.

Chapter Two

#2. FADED T-SHIRT THAT READS HERMES GREEK DELIVERY, YOU ORDER, WE FLY

During his first few months in the US, my dad worked as a deliveryman. That wasn't by default; it was by design. He said New York City is a wild beast, and, like all wild beasts, the only way to truly tame it is to look it in the eye and then ride your bicycle all over it. (Don't overthink it; it doesn't make any sense.) The day he arrived in NYC, he knocked on the door of every Greek restaurant he could find and within three hours managed to find both a job working as a deliveryman for a deli on 56th Street and a room to rent in the deli owner's aunt's cousin's house. He's always been good at making himself at home.

MY MOM MUST HAVE HEARD ME COMING, BECAUSE WE nearly collided in the entryway. Luckily, I was able to reroute in the nick of time, performing an involuntary triple axel in order to circumvent her belly. She was officially in the stage of pregnancy where her bump entered the room first, and no one was ever prepared for that.

"Liv!" She grabbed my shoulders, steadying both of us. "Slow down."

Her feet were bare, but she was dressed to go into the office, in the maternity version of a power suit. My mom is a corporate attorney, which is a lot less *Law & Order* and a lot more staying late way too many nights in a row trying to meet deadlines and coming home smelling like stale coffee. But still, it's pretty impressive. Especially when you consider the fact that she attended law school and passed the bar exam as a single parent.

I wanted to take a moment to catch my breath, but there was no time. "Julius told me I got a postcard. I need to hide it from—"

"Hi, Mrs. Williams!" Dax's voice rang out into the entryway. He wore a katana-wielding Julius on his back and a winning smile. Too bad it wasn't actually going to win my mom over.

"The enemy of my enemy . . . ," Julius prompted, widening his eyes at us.

"Is my friend," she said automatically. "Hello, Dax."

He pushed straight through her lackluster tone. "How are you feeling today?"

"Oh . . . you know," she said, gesturing vaguely to her stomach. "Very with child."

Julius jumped down, then poked his katana directly into my left rib cage. "Did Mom show you the postcard yet? The writing on the front wasn't even like the alphabet. It was like all those squiggly things."

"Squiggly things?" Dax gave me a confused look.

I shrugged. *Who knows?*

"Liv, it's like different writing. Like a *secret code*—" Julius insisted.

"Why don't you two go have some cinnamon rolls?" my mom interrupted, deftly deflecting Julius. She was great at that. "Dax, would you like one?"

Whenever she says his name, my mom's face goes the tiniest bit rigid. She will never ever admit it, but she doesn't like Dax. I've tried to get her to say it before, but the most she'll say is cryptic things such as "Life is long and first loves are short" or "It can be easy to lose yourself in your first rela tionship." Which is ridiculous, coming from someone who met, married, and got pregnant from her first relationship by twenty-two. It was similar with James. They met, and she was pregnant and engaged within six months. My mom is the falling-in-love type, and you'd think that would make her more sympathetic to my case, which, admittedly, is less falling and more diving. But still.

"Love one. Thank you, ma'am," Dax said.

She smiled at him, but a tiny crease appeared on her forehead, the one I officially coined the Dax crease.

"Dax!"

All three of us jumped. My stepdad is less of a speaker and more of a boomer. He's so tall that he makes my mom look short, with big hands, a friendly face, and a loud voice that gets louder whenever he's around people he likes, and he definitely, unequivocally likes Dax.

He's a lawyer like my mom is, and the only time I've ever seen him in a bad mood was after he lost a case that he'd spent more than a year on. But instead of yelling and stomping around like my mom and I would have, he channeled his energy into doing the kinds of healthy things that magazine articles always tell you to do. First he replaced all the light fixtures in the dining room, and then he went for a thirty-mile bike ride. His level of healthiness is a bit frightening.

James clapped his massive hand on Dax's back and nearly sent him sprawling.

"Hi, Mr. Harrison," Dax said dutifully, recovering his footing. He shot me a *help me* look, but I pretended not to notice. Dax had no idea how much he needed James as an ally in this household.

"How's the water polo season? Your father?" James boomed. "And I heard about Stanford. Your dad is pleased as punch."

"Thrilled," Dax said, sending me a meaningful stare.

James leaned against the wall, folding his massive arms over his chest. Today he wore a white golf shirt and a pair of slacks. "Think you'll play goalkeeper at Stanford? That is one tough-looking position."

"It is challenging, sir." Dax's shoulders relaxed, his spine straight. Sports were his comfort zone, and he was used to people congratulating him on them. According to the photographs and trophies his mom displayed all over the house, he'd been excelling at them since elementary school.

I took the opportunity to edge toward my mom. "Where is it?" I whisper-demanded.

I put my hand out, hoping she'd slip the postcard to me covert style, but instead she grabbed my hand. "We'll leave you two to talk," she called, pulling me into the foyer and all the way down the hall to the nursery.

The hallway was cool and quiet, and when we stepped into the nursery, the only sound was the muffled noise of our next-door neighbor mowing the lawn.

"Um . . . why are we in here?" I asked, looking around at all the half-finished projects. A stack of boxes sat next to one wall, along with a partially constructed dresser and several piles of baby clothes. *Boy* baby clothes. Julius #2 would be here before the end of the summer, and thinking about it made me tired already.

She turned, almost whacking me with Julius #2, and I had to jump backward to miss him. "You hid the postcard, right?"

She nodded but took a moment to lower herself into the rocking chair, which had been delivered last week.

"Sit, please," she said, gesturing to the box containing the stroller. But I stayed standing. She seemed to be gathering up the words the way a storm gathers up the elements. What could possibly require this much of a buildup? Not the postcard. Was it something else?

Wait.

"Is it Grandma?" The words shot out of my mouth.

My grandmother is a fairly new addition to our lives— well, my life anyway. My grandparents weren't a huge fan of my dad or the fact that their debutante daughter had fallen for a Greek immigrant. Marrying and procreating with said Greek had sealed the deal. It makes it a little awkward, being the procreated and all. My mom and her parents had an on-again, off-again relationship for years, but once my grandfather passed away, Grandma had started to come visit every few months or so. I think she was lonely. A couple of weeks ago, she'd had a fall. Maybe it was worse than we thought.

"No, it isn't Grandma." She pointed to the cardboard box again. "Sit."

This time I complied, watching her smooth her completely wrinkleless skirt over her knees. Her cheeks were flushed pink, and when she met my eyes, I saw that she was nervous. It set my stomach ablaze. "Olive, an invitation came in the mail today. I wanted to wait for the right time to discuss it, but it's a bit time sensitive, and I think we need to talk about it right away."

A time-sensitive invitation? Now I was completely lost. Also, up to my neck in anxiety. "Mom, I thought this was about another postcard."

"It is." She reached into her blazer pocket . . . and there it was.

A postcard.

A tattered, rumpled-looking postcard that appeared to have battled all manner of elements and hardships before landing on its unwilling recipient.

Me.

She held it up so I could see the front of it. Julius had been partially right. It was an overexposed photograph of Greek temple ruins with large Greek writing overlaying its English counterparts. WELCOME TO BEAUTIFUL GREECE!

It was so kitschy and earnest that it was almost cute. And even if it hadn't said GREECE!, I would have known who it was from. There is only one person I know who would track down a tattered, poorly printed postcard, dress it up with a fortune's worth of postage, and send it halfway across the world.

Nico Varanakis. Noted Atlantis hunter, absentee father, and my new, unwanted pen pal.

I slumped over on my box, all of the anxiety seeping out of me to make way for something new. Sadness? Emptiness? I'd gotten the first postcard almost six months ago, completely out of the blue. I hadn't heard from him in years, and suddenly I had a postcard with a chatty one-liner written in his familiar crabbed handwriting. *Hello from Beautiful Santorini. Wish you were here!*

It was possibly the worst opening line in the history of opening lines, other than *How was the play, Mrs. Lincoln?* Since then, I'd been getting postcards every few months or so, and they were all pretty similar. Misprinted or vintage-looking postcards from Greece with a few quick lines that would have made sense if he were on vacation, but in our context made absolutely no sense.

And no, I didn't respond to them. I read them, cried alone somewhere, and then tore them up and threw them in the trash. But after the last one, I'd decided to stop doing even that. The postcards made my nightmares worse.

"I don't want it," I said, getting to my feet and yanking at a thread on my T-shirt.

My mom nodded understandingly but held it out anyway. "Honey, I think you'd better read this one."

"Not this time." I tried to back away, but she was on me before I knew it, shoving the postcard in my hand. My mom moved a little *too* fast for a pregnant woman.

"Mom . . ." I stalled.

"Now."

Ugh. There was no fighting her. I flipped the postcard over carefully, instructing my heart not to do that thudding thing it always did whenever my dad was involved. I took a deep breath, reminding myself of my ground rule: *Nico Varanakis no longer has anything to do with my life.*

Olive,

Great news! I'm working on an exciting project, and I could really use your help here in Santorini, Indiana Olive. How does June 15th sound? I have already e-mailed your mother the plane ticket.

Baba

My heart didn't have a chance.

Instantly my hands began to shake, my vision going blurry around the edges. "Liv?" my mom said, her voice worried, but she sounded far away.

I staggered for my cardboard box, but my mom intercepted me, planting me in the rocking chair and smoothing my hair back from my forehead.

"Liv. Breathe," she ordered.

I was breathing, but I was breathing *too much*. "Mom—" I tried. My hands were shaking so hard that the postcard began flapping around. I couldn't really see the words anymore, but I couldn't stop looking at it. Not only was it in his scrawly chicken-scratch writing, but he'd also used my old nickname. Indiana Olive. The one I hadn't heard in more than nine years. And he'd signed using the Greek word for dad, a word I'd once said about a thousand times a day but now hadn't said in years.

My head felt—

I felt—

"Liv, look at me!" my mom said. I locked my dark eyes with her blue ones and *whoosh*, I was connected again. My breath was even. It was a postcard. *Only a postcard.* Card stock and ink and a few colorful stamps. Nothing more, nothing less.

"Okay?" she said, reaching out for my arm.

"Okay," I said evenly.

"Good." She exhaled, her arm on mine. "Liv, I know it's very sudden, but I think it's a good idea."

What? Her words hit me like an icy bucket of water. *Stay calm*, I ordered my brain. There was no way she meant that. "Mom, you're joking, right? There's no way I'm doing this. June fifteenth is like . . ." I searched my brain quickly. "It's like a week away." I shoved the postcard at her. "Besides, he said 'Indiana Olive.' What if it's about Atlantis?"

A ghost of a smile appeared on her lips. But as quickly as it came, it disappeared. "Of course it's about Atlantis," she said. "It's always about Atlantis."

Not following, I gripped the postcard so tightly I felt it crinkle in my palm. "But, Mom, Atlantis is a hoax. Why would you want me to get dragged down into Dad's delusions again?"

"Delusions" was the wrong word. Pain flashed across her face before she smoothed it away, moving into lecture mode. "Liv, I don't care about Atlantis. I care about you. Despite what your seventeen-year-old brain is telling you, you don't have all the time in the world. One day you'll wonder where all that time went."

Her eyes met mine again, and the resolve in them frightened me. Now I knew exactly what was going on. She was thinking of her relationship with her father. They'd been close for most of her childhood, but after my dad entered the picture, things had turned rocky. He'd died before she had a chance to make things right with him.

She looked at me pleadingly. "Besides, I think you'll actually really like this project."

A vague, uncomfortable suspicion crept up on me. "Mom, how do you know what the project is?"

She took a deep breath. "I've been talking to him."

"What?" I yelled. My hands were shaking again, the postcard flopping around. It all felt too . . . *much*. "Are you being serious?"

The ends of my mom's shoulder-length hair brushed my arm as she stood next to me, her voice steady in my ear. "Yes," she said firmly. "And I promised I wouldn't tell you what the project is. Honey, he's in a great place in his life. I talked it over with Ali, and she thinks this could be a good idea. I know you've been having the nightmares again. I can hear you all the way downstairs—"

"You told Ali I'm having nightmares again?" I yelped. Now I sounded like Julius when confronted with the prospect of a bath. Ali is my mom's best friend from childhood and an adolescent psychologist. She lives in Maine, and I can always tell when they've been spending a lot of time on the phone together because my mom will use phrases like "assertive anger expression" and "self-defeating patterns." If she'd called Ali about me, then she really was worried.

Ali was the one who had suggested that my mom and I get scuba certified as a way to combat the dreams. Maybe if my waking mind knew the ins and outs, my dreaming brain could calm down. I'd thrown a massive fit, but we'd done it anyway, taking a certification class at a local pool and then completing our certification on a family vacation to Mexico. Once I got over the panic part, it hadn't been too bad; I had actually really enjoyed the feeling of freedom that came from breathing underwater. But my dreaming brain had not gotten the memo. Dreaming Liv drowned. Every. Single. Time.

She cupped my hands in hers, the band of her diamond ring pressing into my wrist. "This could be a good chance to reconcile, put some things to rest before you go out on your own."

"Reconcile?" I sputtered. In our context, what did that even mean? We were not two warring countries needing to work things out. We were two countries who no longer had anything to do with each other.

Her face softened. "Also, honey. Your list. I keep thinking about your list."

"*Mom.*" I twisted away from her. Now I was angry. That list was private, and I had asked her not to talk about it ever again. I was about to remind her of that when a James-intense knock made us both jump.

"Ellen?" James boomed. "Liv? Dax says you have a tennis court appointment with his sister at eleven."

"Ten forty-five," Dax said, clearly right next to him.

Without meaning to, I made a face. Dax's twin, Cora, is not my favorite person in the world. Her name is cute, but she's always stomping around in her ugly combat boots and glaring at people with her blue-green eyes. I'm almost 100 percent sure that she can see straight through me. That she knows that up until recently, I had never fit in anywhere.

But Dax claims that Cora wants to get to know me, and so we've been meeting up with her and her best friend for weekly tennis matches, a sport she excels in—mostly because she's intent on murdering the ball—and I fail. Under the circumstances, tennis sounded laughable. Claustrophobia coiled its grip around me.

"We'll be out in a minute. You two go have more cinnamon rolls," my mom called.

"I can't go. Mom, I can't go." I sounded like I was hyperventilating again, only this time I had to keep it down. And I wasn't sure which place I was talking about. The tennis club? Greece? Both? I had plans after tennis to meet up with my friends to pick out what we were all going to wear at my school's end-of-the-year bonfire, which I was hoping to talk Dax into attending with me. Nowhere in my plans was there *fly to another country to confront the thing that hurt you most.*

She pushed the bangs out of my eyes. "Honey, I really think you could use some time away. I'm worried you're getting caught up in . . . distractions."

Distractions? A second surge of anger surfaced, this one big enough to bring me to my feet.

"Mom, this isn't about Dax," I said.

"No, it isn't," she agreed. "This is about you. You don't have to forgive your father, and you don't have to help him with his project. But you do need to go."

Panic built, hot and fast in my chest. "Mom, *no*. I can't."

"Yes. You can," she said evenly. Her blue eyes met mine, and for a moment it felt like it did in the devastating years right after my father left, when it was the two of us, bumping into each other in one of our cramped, noisy apartments. We'd been through a lot together.

She set her cool hand on top of mine. "Ten days. You have to go for ten days. You don't have to do anything you don't want to once you get there. But I do want you to go."

Anyone listening in would assume she was making a request, but I knew my mother, and this was not a request—it was a nicely worded demand. My mom was what you'd call *determined* on a good day and *stubborn* on all the rest. She had to be. We wouldn't have made it through the bad years otherwise. I knew that if she said I was going to Greece to spend ten days with someone I never thought I would see again, looking for a city the world didn't believe ever existed, then that was exactly what I was going to do.

"But . . . senior trip. And I have plans with my friends, and . . ." I looked into her eyes and I knew. No matter what I said or did, I was going to Greece.

My entire summer shifted on its axis. Gravity lost meaning. I was falling, *plummeting*, with nothing to stop me or break my fall. End-of-year parties? Balboa with Dax? Any semblance of normal?

Gone. And all because of this ratty bit of paper. I stared down at the postcard, anger burrowing deep inside me as I read the line that felt worst.

I'm working on an exciting project, and I could really use your help here in Santorini, Indiana Olive.

Since when did he ever need my help? That was a game we used to play, and the fact was, in real life when I'd actually needed him, he hadn't been there. He'd let me down. Even if he sent me a million postcards, that fact would never go away.

They could make me go, but they most certainly could not make me like it.

Chapter Three

#3. CLOTH NAPKIN FROM CONSTANTINE'S FINE DINING, STOLEN EITHER BY MY MOTHER OR MY FATHER, DEPENDING ON WHO YOU ASK

My dad had moved out of the deli owner's aunt's cousin's house and into an apartment with two of the chefs from Hermes, and he had to pick up a second job to make rent. A restaurant made sense—he could practice his English. Plus, the more he played up his Greekness, the bigger the tips were.

One night he was assigned to a table that housed a University of Chicago student named Ellen Williams, who was spending the summer working as an intern for a local politician. She was tall with long blond hair and the kind of laugh that made you look twice.

My dad said she spilled the pitcher of water on him on purpose. She said he was misremembering, though she'd always have a tiny gleam in her eyes when she said it. And, honestly, I wouldn't put it past her. In the photos of them from that first summer—there aren't many—my dad was handsome, with thick dark hair and his overeager smile, and my mom was so happy she looks dizzy.

A SHORT LIST OF RULES GIVEN TO ME BY MY MOTHER regarding my trip to Santorini, Greece—a place I did not want to go to in the first place:

1. Call her morning and night.
2. No talking to strangers.

    Impossible, seeing as every single person on that island will be a stranger, including, at this point, my own father. I literally don't even know what he looks like these days. And the last time he saw me, I had a Frida Kahlo–esque unibrow and was usually wearing a fake microphone headset because I believed myself to be in active training to become a Disney Channel star. And yes, all photographic evidence of this period of my life has been destroyed.

3. No talking to boys at the airport, regardless of how cute they may or may not be (see rule two).

    According to her, these boys may actually be part of an elaborate crime circle with plans to kidnap me and reenact that Liam Neeson movie. And I don't exactly have a gravelly voiced ex-assassin for a father. I have an absentee Atlantis hunter for a father.

I told her that the fact that this rule was even on her list was proof that I shouldn't go. Mom said that Santorini is actually very safe and that I'll be fine. But how does she know? Despite having once been married to someone from Santorini, she's never set foot on the island.

4. Should I at any point feel in danger of any type of neglect or harm, then I am to phone her immediately and she will fly me home.

   This one came with the following caveat: in order to activate the *Get out of Jail Free* card, it must be a grave emergency, not just uncomfortable silences or challenging conversations. *Grave.* Again with the morbid.

5. Take some time to "find myself."

   Or, in other words, take some time away from *Dax.* Of course, she didn't come out and say this directly because she's trying not to be her parents, which might actually be the goal of every person who ever lived. They desperately did not like her boyfriend, and look what happened there. She dropped out of school, married him at Chicago City Hall, and got pregnant with me. Live and learn.

   And for the record, I resent being told to "find" myself. I'm not lost. I'm right here.

6. Give my dad a chance.

(No comment.)

7. Wear sunscreen.

Really. That made her list of rules.

I had one rule for her: *go along with the story I came up with for Dax.* The last thing I wanted was Dax—and everyone at school—knowing that my father was on a decades-long search for Atlantis, a city that he 100 percent, unflinchingly believed was real, despite the fact that only a few internet weirdos seemed to agree with him. The thought of everyone knowing made me feel weak in the knees, and not in the good way.

I was Liv now. The Liv who got invited to parties, and prom, and put on the nomination ballot for homecoming queen, and I needed to be the person everyone thought I was. That probably sounds shallow, but when you feel invisible for most of your life, feeling seen starts to matter. That's who I was now. Not Indiana Olive, and *definitely* not the daughter of a man whose lifework put him in the same category as a UFO hunter with maps and charts and a pile of books on alien abduction. End of story.

So instead, this is what I told Dax: *My Greek father is an amateur archaeologist! He studies ancient civilizations! How weird I never mentioned that! I know it's last-minute, but my mom is making me go!*

"Amateur archaeologist" was a bit misleading, but it sounded a lot better than "professional myth chaser."

This is what Dax said: *I can't believe you aren't coming on the senior trip! My friends will be so disappointed because they like hanging out with you so much, and I'm so disappointed because I was dying to spend a week on the beach with you!*

Or at least I'm sure that's what he'd say if he were still speaking to me. Which, after my last-minute cancellation of our trip, he wasn't. Dax likes to have a plan, and me skipping his senior trip had thrown everything off. Also, in the stress of the past few days, I accidentally let slip that I may have *forgotten* to apply to high school day, and it had been exactly as dramatic and earth-shattering as I'd imagined. According to Dax, our relationship was at the very end of a list jammed at the very bottom of my very messiest bag. In other words, every other aspect of my life came before him.

That wasn't true. But the fact that I couldn't tell him why this trip was such a big deal most definitely did not help my case.

And now I was here. On the plane. Trying to breathe as I regretted literally every decision that had led me to this moment. In less than an hour I would be in Greece. *Greece.* Why hadn't I fought harder against my mom? It wasn't like she'd physically carried me onto the plane. I could have run away. I could have . . . Oh no.

I'm going to throw up.

I wanted to put my head between my knees, but the Santorini-bound plane was way too tiny for anything, much less sprawling panic attacks over the unfairness of being an almost-adult who doesn't actually have control of her own life. I couldn't even be that mad at my mom. She was so *pregnant* and so sure that she was right—so sure that for a moment there I'd begun to believe her too. *Maybe I should give my dad a chance. Maybe this is a good idea.* But . . . no. Clearly we'd both suffered a lapse in sanity.

Almost unconsciously, I grabbed one of the in-flight magazines out of the pocket in front of me and automatically began yanking out interesting-looking images to add to the envelope I keep stashed in my bag. My art teacher, Ms. Martinez, said that cultivating your mind to constantly collect images is the important part of being an artist—not that I'd call myself an artist. Well, not *yet*, but if I wasn't drawing, then I was cutting out images and stuffing them into envelopes I carried everywhere with me. Think of it as visual hoarding.

Right now it was also acting as a much-needed calming technique. A distraction from all the rippling ocean I'd been flying across for what felt like an eternity. I was probably the first person in aeronautical history to be happy to have *not* been assigned the window seat. There was so much *ocean* out there.

I focused on my hands again. This was airplane number three, and ever since Seattle, each airplane had gotten progressively smaller and smellier. Add to that, I was on hour twenty-three of no sleep, unless you count the twenty minutes that occurred after takeoff from New York City (airplane number two), which was right before the woman sitting in 28B spilled her entire coffee on my T-shirt. Her *hot* coffee. And then, in penance for not only burning me but also making me smell like a human Starbucks, proceeded to show me twenty-plus photos of her bulldog, Winston Churchill. At least I was on my final flight.

A picture of a packed swimming pool went into an envelope. Then a boy with a dog on a leash. A father giving his daughter a piggyback ride. She was looking down at him, smiling like his shoulders were the most stable place in the world.

Ugh.

I shut my eyes tightly, but my dad's scribbly handwriting appeared behind my eyelids. *I could really use your help here in Santorini, Indiana Olive.* With what? What could he possibly need *my* help with?

I abandoned the magazine and pulled my phone out of my backpack again, in case a text from Dax had managed to find me over the Atlantic. But no, there was only the one he'd sent me last night when he was supposed to come over but had apparently been too busy. Sorry, can't make it. See you in two weeks.

Those periods looked passive-aggressive. Could punctuation be passive-aggressive? And then there was my overly-bouncy-full-of-nerves text back. Two weeks will pass in no time. Miss you already, hope you have an amazing time in Balboa!!! Then I panicked and added a bunch of mushy-looking emojis that made me hate myself more every time I looked at them. No wonder Dax hadn't answered. He was probably in the process of rethinking every minute of our time together.

Looking at the wasteland that was our text history made me feel like an elephant was enjoying a leisurely afternoon tea right in the center of my chest, so I shoved my phone away and attempted to soothe myself by looking through my backpack. Sketchbook. Pencils. Watercolors. Makeup. Water bottle. Journal.

I'd definitely pushed the limits on carry-on baggage, but I'm kind of weird about my stuff. Dax jokes that I'm a pack rat, citing the fact that every inch of my room is packed full of things, including twelve plants and a mini garden of succulents, but it's not that I don't like to throw things away. It's that I like to keep things.

"*Eísai kalá?*" The voice sounded in my right ear, and I sat up very quickly, coming face-to-face with a kind smile and a whole lot of eyelashes. My seatmate. He was in his mid to late twenties, wearing purposely nerdy black glasses and a concerned expression. His entire left arm, or at least what I could see of it, was engulfed in a tattooed rose garden that under regular circumstances I would have been obsessing over. And while I'm sure my skin was currently a shade resembling dead fish, his dark skin was luminous, his hair coiffed. He clearly wasn't having a mid-flight breakdown.

"*Eísai kalá?*" he said again, but this time his voice was less confident. He pointed at the seat-back pocket. Was he offering his magazine to my nervous clutches?

"I'm sorry, I—I don't know what that means," I stammered. At least that solved the Greek language dilemma. I'd been wondering if I'd remember all the Greek I'd known as a child. The answer was definitely no.

His face broke into a relieved, brilliant smile. White teeth as far as the eye could see. "Oh, thank God, you're American." His accent had a hint of the Midwest in it. Minnesota? Chicago? You'd think I'd know, having been born there and all that. "I thought you must be Greek, and I was trying the one phrase I know. Are you feeling ill? I have a vomit bag if you need one." He gestured to his seat-back pocket again.

"I'm not sick. Or very Greek. I'm . . ." I searched for a word. Petrified? Horror-struck? "Nervous."

He glanced at my pile of torn-up magazine pages, and I quickly shoved them into their envelope, my face burning.

"Aerophobia," he said. "It's a wonder we aren't all affected by it, seeing as we are literally hurtling through the air in a large sardine can that could plunge to the earth at any given moment. Do you ever think about that? How we could plunge to the earth? Oh my God, don't think about it."

He widened his eyes at me behind his round glasses, and I felt a smile creep onto my face. Pointing out looming danger may not be a standard way to calm a nervous flier down, but it was working for me. Also, talking felt good. Very good. "I actually don't mind flying. It's more about what will happen when I get there."

He leaned in, as if in preparation for a bit of juicy gossip. "Oh?"

If juicy was what he wanted, I could definitely deliver. "I'm here to visit someone. It's a bit . . . complicated."

"A boyfriend," he pronounced.

I shook my head. "No. My boyfriend is back in Seattle. It's . . ." Was I really going to tell this stranger? Yep, I was. Rule number two on Mom's list—*No talking to strangers*—was but a fleeting memory. I couldn't help it. After all the lying I'd done to my friends and Dax this week, I was the emotional equivalent of an overfilled balloon. "It's my dad. He lives in Santorini, and I haven't seen him since I was eight."

He studied me for a moment, waiting for a punch line.

When none came, his eyes softened and he quickly dropped the eager look. "Rea-lly," he said, dragging out the syllables. But it was a kind rea-lly. A gentle rea-lly. A knot inside of me loosened. He paused a moment, then carefully put his hand out. "I'm Henrik."

"Liv." His hand was warm and sure in mine, and for a moment I felt steady.

He tilted his head toward the window. "About your dad, that's a big deal." He was looking me straight in the eyes, which sent a tiny ray of hope surging through me. Was this a mythical person who wouldn't shy away from talking about the fact that my father had abandoned me? I'd always wondered if they existed.

And he was right. My history with my dad was a big deal. The *biggest* deal. Or at least it used to be. And now I had a no-strings-attached opportunity to talk about it. "Do you want to hear the weirdest part?"

He nodded, and I went for it. "My dad is an Atlantis hunter. He thinks that the lost city was in Santorini, and he's been looking for it for most of his life. That's why he left. One day I went to school, and when I came back, he was gone."

I'd been keeping those words away for so long that they felt rusted and cobwebby. There was a long pause, and this time the expression on Henrik's face was clear. Bewilderment. "The lost city of Atlantis? Are you talking about the golden city?"

"That's El Dorado." I shook my head, a million facts crowding my mind. Despite my attempts to shove it all into a dusty corner of my brain, I knew almost everything there was to know about Atlantis. I'd known a lot before my dad left, and after he left I'd studied it for years. The fact that I'd once prided myself on being a walking Atlantis encyclopedia was humiliating. "Atlantis is the one that sank."

Henrik sat up excitedly, bumping his tray table with his knees. "That's right. I saw a movie about it. It's an underwater city, right?"

"Well . . . not exactly," I said.

Henrik's was a typical response. People thought they knew about Atlantis, but they didn't really. Not the way I did. They didn't have ownership of it the way my father had. *Did.* Whatever. But most of the adaptations went way off script, which was impressive considering how ludicrous the story was to begin with.

I could already see the questions bubbling up for him. I'd get the basic premise out there, give him the facts, and then we could move on from it. "Atlantis was a city built on an island by the sea-god Poseidon. The people who lived there were half god, half human, and they were some of the wealthiest and most advanced people to ever live. Their island was shaped like a circle, and it was made out of alternating rings of land and water." I formed a ring with my fingers, then pointed to the center. "There was a temple in the middle full of golden statues. The people had everything, like plants and exotic animals, and their own type of precious metal, cool buildings, all of it. But instead of being grateful for what they had, they made plans to conquer the rest of the world. So the gods decided they were ungrateful and ordered the ocean to swallow the island whole. The people were never heard from again."

Jazz hands. Atlantis in a nutshell. A tale about a mythical people that reminded me so much of my father, it stung. We hadn't been enough for him either.

Henrik was still staring at me. Not in judgment of my explanation or my still waggling fingers, but in surprise.

"It's a myth," I said, as though that wasn't obvious. I dropped my hands to my lap. "A morality tale. Be grateful for what you have or the gods will get you."

My voice came out as bitter as 28B's coffee, but instead of being put off by it, Henrik adjusted his glasses thoughtfully, leaning in closer. "But people still look for it. Your *dad* is looking for it."

"People have been looking for thousands of years, but no one has ever found any definitive proof."

Atlantis theories were literally all over the map. Point to almost anywhere on the globe and you could bet that at some point some Atlantis hunter had decided it was the only possible location of the lost city. Antarctica, the Sahara desert, the Amazon jungle . . . In the (tiny) world of Atlantis hunters, these were all viable but hotly contested theories. Expeditions had been sent out. Scientists had been summoned. Even the *Nazis* had looked for Atlantis. They thought that the Aryan race must have descended from the demigod Atlanteans. I know. Gross.

"So why does your dad think it's in Santorini?"

"Well . . ." I was beginning to regret telling Henrik. We were going way too far down the rabbit hole, but this is how it went with Atlantis. The more people heard, the more they wanted to know. I got it. I'd been that way once too. "Santorini is actually one of the main theories of Atlantis because the island has a lot of similarities that match up to the legend. My dad's been trying to find proof of it for as long as I've known him."

He rubbed his chin thoughtfully. "So your dad is an explorer."

I couldn't help the laugh/snort. Explorer. That was a much nicer word than I'd heard hurled at people like my dad over the years, and probably more than my dad deserved, but I felt my shoulders soften anyway. I could tell already that Henrik was the sort of person who gave people the benefit of the doubt. My dad had been like that too. Or maybe he still was like that? I didn't know anymore.

"Something like that," I managed.

Henrik's face erupted into a smile. "Well, you don't have to explain it to me. I have one of those in my life too."

My eyebrows shot up. "An Atlantis hunter?"

"Worse. He's an archaeologist. *Academia.*" He whispered the last word, and I burst out laughing, which made Henrik laugh too. He had a ridiculous, honking kind of laugh, and the man sitting in front of us turned to glare, but Henrik ignored him, so I did too.

I wiped my eyes, enjoying the bubbling feeling of laughter. It had been a while since I'd had such a nothing-to-lose conversation. "That's what I tell people my dad does, because the truth is too embarrassing."

Henrik took off his glasses and polished them on the hem of his T-shirt with a flourish. "God bless the seekers. They're hopeless really, aren't they? My boyfriend works on the Minoan excavation sites, and it mostly amounts to him sifting through dirt and getting worked up over old chunks of pottery."

The bubbles in my chest turned to stone. "Did you say *Minoan?*"

"What?" Henrik asked, registering my surprise. "You've heard of them?"

"Uh, yeah." I knew more about them than any normal American teenager really should. The Minoans were a Bronze Age civilization who once had a strong presence on the Greek islands and who also happened to have a starring role in my dad's theory. "My dad believes that the Minoans were part of Atlantis."

"Ohhhhh," Henrik said. "I see. Advanced island civilization that was completely destroyed by natural forces. According to Hye, the Minoans were really ahead of their time. Do you think . . . ?"

"Ta-da. You are now officially an Atlantis hunter." And I was now officially done talking about Atlantis. Time to change the subject. "Is your boyfriend Greek?"

Henrik shook his head. "American. He spends the summers in Santorini and the rest of the year teaching archaeology in Austin, Texas. I'm the director of a special ed school in Boston, but we spend our summers together."

"How long have you been dating?"

"Three years. We've mastered the art of the long-distance relationship." He said it casually, and I felt hope swell up in me. Dax and I didn't have to go to the same school to date, did we? People made long-distance relationships work all the time. Maya's voice rang in my ears. *We'll only be thirty miles apart!* Providence, Rhode Island, was three thousand miles from Stanford. But we'd make it work, wouldn't we?

Henrik glanced pointedly at the pile of images I'd pulled out of the magazines. "So what's all this?"

"Oh . . ." I hesitated, then quickly shuffled the pile together. "I collect images. For collages and as reference photographs. I draw and paint and . . ." My overstuffed envelope looked even more ridiculous than usual, and I quickly shoved it into my backpack. "It's no big deal."

"So you're an artist."

The zipper on my backpack got stuck, and I wrestled with it, keeping my eyes down. "Sort of. I'm in high school now, but I'm thinking about going to art school. I mean, probably not, but I like to think about it, I guess. I'll probably end up studying something completely different."

I sounded about as confident as a snowball on the beach, and when I met Henrik's eyes, he was smiling. "But you're only sort of an artist?"

I couldn't decide if I should nod or shake my head, so I did both. "Yeah?"

"Well, I can't think of a better place for a *sort of* artist than Santorini. It's absurdly beautiful." He nudged me lightly with his elbow. "And, Liv, I know our relationship only goes back twenty minutes or so, but I already know you're going to be fine here. More than fine. Santorini is magic. Whatever you're looking for, you'll find it."

His tone was a mixture of confidence and kindness, and I felt a whisper of something descend over me. Hope?

Maybe Henrik was right. Maybe I *was* going to be fine.

But then my eyes drifted to the window and I realized with a jolt that I was no longer looking at the ocean. I was looking at Santorini. That brown strip of land contained my father. My *father*. All good feelings evaporated.

Chapter Four

#4. MAP OF SANTORINI

Out of all the items my dad left behind, I think this is the one that gave me the most trouble. The map was the crux of my dad's belief in the Santorini-as-Atlantis theory, and proof of all the work he'd put into it. Along with being alarmingly accurate as far as modern Santorini goes (I've checked it against other maps), it illustrates all the ways that Santorini matches the description in Plato's writings.

My dad literally spent years marking up all the clues and even overlaying a drawing of what Atlantis had once looked like with "concentric rings of land and sea" all matching up with the way the island system actually looks today. The map felt like my best proof that he would come back: He wouldn't leave behind his life's work, would he? Then one day it hit me. People don't usually leave behind *their life's work, but they also don't usually leave behind their families.*

There had never been anything "usual" about him anyway.

THIRA INTERNATIONAL AIRPORT SEEMED LIKE A BOASTFUL name for one small building and a handful of runways enclosed by a chain-link fence. It wasn't even big enough for a Jetway, and it most definitely didn't seem big enough for the reunion that was about to happen. The cabin was sweltering, but my teeth wouldn't stop chattering.

The flight attendants herded us to the middle of the plane to exit on a mobile stairway, and all the previously asleep people suddenly had the energy of wild mastodons, elbowing and shoving their way through. Henrik gave me a tight squeeze, asked for the millionth time if I was okay, then wrote his phone number on one of my magazine scraps before making a beeline for the door.

I, on the other hand, spent an inordinate amount of time gathering up my headphones and books and pictures, and when I finally looked up, I realized I was about to be the last one off and had to hurry to join the trail of people. As I stepped off the plane onto the stairway, my legs went wobbly. *I am standing on Greek soil.*

Well, technically I was still twelve feet above Greek soil, but I could smell the ocean. And jet fuel, and . . . something sickly sweet and rotting. Garbage? Banana peels baking in the sun? I tried to squint into the distance, but everything beyond the airport was hazy in the humidity. A complete unknown.

Once I'd tottered down the metal steps, a small transport bus drove us an insultingly short distance to the baggage claim building, and we filed out, making our way into a crowded room with linoleum floors. People were gathering their things quickly, then heading for the exit. And then it all became *very* real to me. My dad was behind those walls. What was I going to say to him? Why hadn't I spent the past twenty-three hours figuring that out?

My chest burned. I needed to find a way to buy more time. My mind snagged on to a single possibility. Maybe my bag would be lost! That would require time at the lost desk, lots of time standing around arguing with airline agents, some emergency calls to my mom . . . but then, *boom*. My Louis Vuitton suitcase came thumping out of the shoot and began making its merry way around the track, completely oblivious to my plans.

Maybe I'd freshen up first.

The bathroom hosted a full-length mirror that seemed to have no problem *telling it like it is*. I looked like a transcontinental zombie. Pale, and splotchy, with limp hair, dark circles under my eyes, and a profoundly freaked-out expression. Plus, the coffee stain on my shirt was starting to look sentient, like it was ready to sprout hairs and walk away.

This was not the new and improved Liv I wanted my dad to see. This was pitiful.

I leaned in closer until my bloodshot eyes were a few inches from the mirror. They weren't my dad's deep brown eyes, or my mom's blue. They were my very own, big and a brownish-green color that refused to fall into any of the neat categories provided on my driver's license application. The rest of my features are classic Greek and can be a bit intense if I don't play them right—big lips, slightly cleft chin, and an aquiline nose. And even though I have my dad's dark olive skin, I did somehow manage to inherit my mom's freckles—a chaotic smattering across the bridge of my nose that I pretend to be annoyed by but secretly love. The first time I met Dax's sister, she asked me if my freckles were real or tattoos. Right. Like my mom would *ever* allow that.

I leaned in even closer, this time assessing the full picture. How had I changed since my dad last saw me? Well, my body for one. I was five-seven, almost five-eight now, and my legs were almost as long as my mom's. Also, my hair. Up until a few years ago I'd always worn it long. Now it was chin length with bangs right above my eyelashes. I loved the haircut for the main reason that it kept my stick-out ears covered. Those hadn't changed one bit since he'd seen me last, despite the number of hours I'd spent wishing they would.

What if my dad walked right past me? What if he was

waiting at the airport for eight-year-old me and then I walked out and he was disappointed? *No.* The thought snapped me back to reality, and I met my own eyes angrily in the mirror. He didn't *get* to be disappointed. He was the one who had left me. If he didn't recognize me, it was his own fault. All I cared about now was making sure he knew how okay I had been without him.

I wheeled my suitcase into one of the bathroom's stalls and dug through my clothes for a moment before pulling out one of my go-to outfits: black skinny jeans, a cropped tank, and delicate leather sandals. Casual but pulled together. I had about a million variations on this outfit, and every time I put them on, I felt sophisticated and important, like a Parisian art student running late to class.

I changed into the clothes, found my favorite gold earring studs, shakily applied some makeup, and brushed my hair until my bangs fell smooth and glossy. By the time I finished applying my eyeliner, I felt infinitely better. What was I worried about? Liv Varanakis could handle anything.

I gave my reflection one last look, then squared my shoulders and marched out the bathroom door and into the baggage claim. My feet carried me forward toward the doors, my heart hammering with all its might, and then I stepped out into the open air and . . . nothing.

Well, not nothing. In front of a two-way road sat a dirty

curb, a bus stop, and a small storefront lit up with a bright orange sign that read AIR CANTEEN. A few people trickled past me, heading for the taxi stop or waiting cars. But my dad?

Not here.

Unless I wasn't recognizing him? I'd thought about how much I had changed, but what about him? Was it possible that he was unrecognizable? I scanned the crowd, desperately hunting for some characteristic that would pin a passing person as my dad. Old lady. Young dad carrying a baby. College-aged boy wearing headphones.

No one who could possibly have been my father at some point in time.

For a moment I was free-floating, suspended above my emotions, but then I came crashing down. Hard. *My dad isn't here.*

What was left of the crowd was disappearing, dispersing into cars and cabs, leaving me as the sole buoy. I turned in a slow circle, my worry escalating to full-blown panic. My throat felt tight and constricted, and already I was sweating.

Keep it together, Liv. People are sometimes late. Had my dad been a punctual or a late person? Punctual, I think. But that didn't mean he had somehow forgotten about me. He'd sent the ticket. My mom had confirmed with him. He was expecting me.

But he did forget about me once before.

The air was suddenly too thick to breathe. I fought against the humidity, trying to slow my lungs, but I was already light-headed. I couldn't help it. I staggered over to one of the Air Canteen's rickety chairs and managed to haul myself up onto it. I was shaking so hard I could barely keep a grip on my suitcase handle. Was I cold? I couldn't be cold. Not in this heat. So why was I shaking this hard?

I fumbled for my phone. Should I call my mom? James? What could they do from all the way on the other side of the ocean? Would Dax answer if I called? I pulled up his number and was about to hit call when a male voice pierced my fog.

"Olive?"

I spun around, phone in hand, and when I saw what was behind me, I almost screamed. A camera lens stood less than two feet away, staring at me with its enormous, unblinking eye. It even had a giant light attached to it.

"Wh-what . . . ?" I stammered.

The camera continued. "I'll take that as a yes. Olive, how does it feel to be the daughter of the man who is about to rock the archaeological world with proof of Atlantis?"

Finally, my brain caught up to me, and I scrambled to my feet, knocking over my suitcase in the process. Obviously, there was a person connected to this camera. Because cameras don't *randomly interrogate people outside of airports*. But it had taken me much too long to figure that out. Was it stress or sleep deprivation? My mom's rules flashed to mind. She hadn't said anything about what to do if a friendly voiced cameraman suddenly appeared, but I was pretty sure staying on the offensive was my best move.

"Why are you filming me?" I demanded, regaining my literal and figurative footing. "Who are you?"

"Which one do you want me to answer first?" The camera lowered slowly, and when I saw the person behind it, I nearly toppled over again.

The boy was Greek, close to my age, with skin several shades darker than mine and thick black hair. He was slim, just short of skinny, and wore a black T-shirt tucked sloppily into a pair of black jeans and a worn pair of Adidas, also in black. His hair—half curly, half knotted—was at least twice as thick as the average person's and shoved back away from his forehead. Usually that much hair would take center stage, but not in this case, because his *face*.

Huge eyes, barely contained eyebrows, a very straight nose, and lash lines so dark they rivaled the ones I'd spent a solid five minutes drawing on.

He was the kind of good-looking that doesn't ever have to try to be good-looking. And he *clearly* was not trying. There was something infuriatingly careless about him, like he'd rolled out of bed and left the house without looking in a mirror. As if he was so good-looking that he didn't have to bother with mirrors. Were those crumbs on his T-shirt? And would it kill him to tie his shoes properly?

Now he was staring at me, too, like I was as much of a surprise to him as he was to me. "What?" I demanded.

He shook his head slowly, his hair falling into his face like he was auditioning for a shampoo commercial. Was this guy for *real*? "You . . . look really different in your pictures."

I stopped thinking about his hair, likely because I now recognized that I was in imminent danger. My mom's rules flashed to mind. Had she been *right*? Was this an attempted kidnapping? He seemed way too laid-back and awkward for that. Also, kidnappers would probably tie their shoes, because of the *getaway*. I stood as tall as I could, trying to look as threatening as possible. We were close to the same height. With high heels, I'd have him.

"What pictures?" I roared.

It worked. He stumbled back slightly, shaking himself loose from whatever trance we were under. He smiled and stuck his hand out. "Your dad's pictures." He took a moment to compose himself, then aimed a smile at me. "The prodigal daughter returns. I've heard so many things about you."

He'd practiced that line, you could tell.

His English was precise with a sliver of an accent, so small you could forget it was there. I obviously needed to ask him who he was, but I was still trying to untangle any part of this situation, and I stared at him. Also, what *things* had he heard?

Suddenly his gaze landed on my suitcase, and his jaw dropped. "Is that yours? It's behemoth."

Who uses the word "behemoth"? It made me think of my English teacher. But when I followed his gaze down to my suitcase, I could see his point. When I was packing, it hadn't seemed all that large, but here on the tiny stoop, it did in fact look monstrous, and it was heavy, too. I'd tried to do a summer-in-Paris capsule wardrobe, but then the whole mystery project thing kept tripping me up. Did I need running shoes? Dresses? I ended up packing everything and then unpacking half of it, then packing it all over again.

Then there were the art supplies. Oh, the art supplies. At the last minute I'd panicked and packed literally every brush, sketchbook, and pencil I could fit in there. And then . . . well, I couldn't even explain it to myself, but I'd brought the box of my dad's stuff. I had no idea what I was going to do with it (Return it? Throw it into the ocean in a fit of rage?), but it felt weird to leave it in my closet while I traipsed across the world. My suitcase was more piñata at this point, but it was my piñata. This random boy had no say in what I brought with me.

"I'm here for ten days," I said, grabbing the handle defensively.

"Yes, but how are we going to get it on that?" He pointed to a beat-up-looking black motorcycle that was propped precariously next to what appeared to be a NO PARKING sign on the curb. "I can stash the camera by my feet, but—" He gave my suitcase another judgmental look.

That did it. "Who *are* you?"

His face split into a smile, revealing slightly overcrowded teeth. And somehow that imperfection took him from merely good-looking to next-level attractive. I quickly averted my eyes to avoid my retinas being burned up by the pure level of attractive beaming from his person.

"Olive, I'm *Theo!*" He said it like he was a one-name celebrity. Like it should mean something to me. "Your dad had a few things to get in order, so he sent me to pick you up. He asked me at the last minute, so I had to rush here. I almost didn't make it."

So that cleared things up . . . not at all. But before I could tell him that, his face brightened. "I have an idea for our luggage problem. Watch my camera?" And then he and his sloppy shoelaces ran into the crowd, leaving me blinking into the evening sun.

What was going on here? I toed nervously at the camera and wished Henrik would appear, but his boyfriend must have whisked him away immediately, because he was nowhere to be seen. A moment later Theo reappeared, speaking rapidly in Greek to a barrel-shaped man whose mustache made him look vaguely like a walrus. For moment I was transfixed.

I'd forgotten how much I loved the slippery, rolling sound of Greek. It always made me feel unsteady. Homesick. "Olive, this is Yiannis," Theo said.

"*Yasou!* Welcome to Santorini," Yiannis boomed. "I take your bag." To prove his point, he lunged for it.

"What? No. Absolutely not." I tried to block his access, but Yiannis the Walrus seemed adept at handling reluctant clients because he simply sidestepped me, then scooped up the bag, hoisting it onto his shoulder, and then strode for the curb.

"Stop!" I yelled, but Yiannis was not stopping. "Where is he going?"

"To Oia. He's a cabdriver, and he already has a fare driving there. He's going to bring the baggage to us, free of charge." Theo was clearly very proud of this solution and offered me a smile that charmed and enraged me all at once.

"This is *not* okay," I said, my hands balling helplessly.

Theo rested one hand on my shoulder. "He's happy to. More than happy to. Your dad's done so much for him."

I slid out from under his hand. "That's not what I meant."

"I do for father. Your father," Yiannis yelled, beaming at me over his shoulder. "Nico, he is good. Take care, yes?"

"No!" I said. But my earthly belongings disappeared into the back of a dented-up taxicab anyway. What was happening right now?

"That was lucky," Theo said, scooping up his camera and heading for the curb. "Now come on. We're in a really big hurry."

"Who are you and where is my dad?" I yelled after him.

"Olive, I told you, he's running late and—"

That did it. "Stop calling me Olive!" I yelled angrily. "It's Liv. I go by Liv."

This time Theo stopped, really stopped. His forehead wrinkled as he studied me. Part of me wanted to apologize for yelling, but a bigger part of me felt completely justified, so I held my silence. He approached me hesitantly, like one might a potentially rabid raccoon. He peered at me earnestly, forcing eye contact. "But your dad always calls you Olive."

Anger ricocheted through me, forcing me back a few steps. "What do you mean 'always calls'? I haven't talked to him since I was eight."

"Since you were eight?" Theo's eyes widened. "But the postcards . . ."

My heart thudded. He knew about the postcards? I suddenly felt flayed open. Vulnerable. Why did this guy know so much about me? "Postcards aren't the same as talking." *Another exceptionally insightful comment by Captain Obvious.*

But Theo didn't laugh. He studied me for another beat. Then he stepped forward, his eyes softening with concern. "Your dad has a surprise for you, and he had a few details to finish up. He wanted to be here, but he wanted to get your surprise ready more. Will you please come with me? We have to go all the way up to Oia, and we can't be late." He gestured toward the motorcycle again, clearly hoping that I'd start moving.

But I was stuck on the word he kept saying. *Oia.* That was the name of the village on all the postcards. Only Theo said it EE-uh, not OY-uh, like I'd thought it was. Suddenly I felt ridiculous. How did I not know how to pronounce the village that my father had been from? Had my mom even known how to say it?

Oh no. Mom. Her rules popped into my head again. *No talking to boys at the airport.* This was the definition of talking to boys at the airport. She had actually prepared me for this scenario. *Don't let strange boys give you a ride.* But she hadn't told me what to do if my dad had *sent* said boy, or what to do if said boy sent small jolts of oxygen to my brain every time I looked at him.

Okay, not oxygen. More like . . . electricity? This was getting weird.

I took a deep breath, wrapping my fingers around the straps of my backpack. At least I still had my backpack. "How am I supposed to know you're not like that guy on the movie *Taken*."

Theo's eyebrows shot up. His eyebrows apparently did half of his communication for him. "I'm sorry?"

Judging by his tone, he was massively amused, a feeling I did not share. I stepped forward, feeling emboldened. "You know that movie where the girl goes to Europe and gets kidnapped and her dad's an ex-CIA agent?"

Theo's expression morphed to horror, which mostly involved his eyebrows shooting up even higher. He stepped forward like he was going to touch my arm, then must have realized that that was exactly what a kidnapper from *Taken* would do, so he stopped himself. "...What? Oh my God. No. I told you, I'm a friend of your dad's. I work for him."

"You're going to have to prove it," I said, adjusting my posture to match my confident tone. *Spine straight, shoulders back, make eye contact.* James called it the power stance.

Theo looked genuinely stumped. "How?"

Good question. For a moment I was stumped too. Then a solution presented itself. "That's on you."

"*Pismatara*," he mumbled to himself. "Like Nico." The word sounded vaguely familiar. Stubborn? Proud? I bristled, but I couldn't exactly call him out on something I hadn't understood.

"So?" I said. Watching him flounder for an answer was surprisingly gratifying.

His eyes shot up to mine, and he spread his hands out triumphantly. "I knew about the postcards."

True. "Well . . . ," I countered.

He pointed at the curb. "And that's his motorcycle. Could anyone else in the world possibly own that motorbike? It was scrap metal when he met it."

I looked over Theo's shoulder, giving the automobile my full attention. The motorcycle had clearly been through some kind of catastrophe, and along with a rusted frame and a duct-taped seat, the muffler looked jerry-rigged on. So, so my dad. He could fix anything with anything.

"Something else," I said, but I was starting to relent.

Theo's face twisted, drawing attention to his lips. I mean mouth. "Tell you what, you can ask me any question you want about him."

"And you'll know the answer?"

He nodded confidently, already looking relieved. "Guaranteed. I've spent a year with your dad now. I know everything about him."

A surge of jealousy moved through me. An entire year? Who was this guy, his stand-in son? Now I wanted to stump him. I took a deep breath, thinking hard. It's difficult to come up with intimate details about someone you haven't seen in about a million years, but finally I landed on something. "What does my dad have tattooed on his inner forearm?"

Theo smiled proudly, raising one finger. "A compass. With some numeric coordinates on the outside."

Correct. It was actually the coordinates of a small coffee

shop in Chicago where my mom first told my dad she was pregnant with me. He said you have to mark the moments that change everything, and to him that had meant a tattoo. And yes, that was seriously depressing to think about.

I folded my arms over my chest. "What are the numbers?"

His eyebrows rocketed. "Seriously?"

I shrugged.

"Um . . . Forty-one point . . . eight? And eight-something . . . west?" He looked at me hopefully.

"Close," I said. It was actually 41.8786° N, 87.6251° W. I can't even remember my mom's cell phone number, but I can rattle off the numbers tattooed on my dad's forearm. I remember staring at them when he'd read to me at night and thinking, *There we are.*

"Also, I know you were born during a snowstorm and your dad kicked a guy out of a cab to get your mom to the hospital on time," Theo said hopefully. Or was it smugly?

Great. Two minutes in Greece and the memory-lane thing was already getting old. I needed to take control of the situation. Fast. Now that the fight was draining out of me, I was starting to get woozy. I really should have tried to sleep on the plane. I took a deep breath. "Fine. But I need you to know that my stepdad is a Krav Maga master, and he's taught me how to take down anyone, anywhere. Also, if you try to film me again, I'm going to freak out."

Theo laughed, and the sound of it surprised me. It was a deep, goofy-sounding belly laugh, and it instantly set me at ease. Well, mostly at ease. "Seattle must be rough."

"Not really," I said, thinking about our manicured lawn, the way our modern house stood giant next to all the other massive houses in our community. Seattle wasn't rough; it was everything that had come before Seattle that was rough.

Theo tilted his head toward the curb. "Ready now? Your dad will be so upset if we miss the surprise."

I turned to look at the spot where Yiannis's cab had once stood. "What are the chances my suitcase will actually make it to Oia?"

"Sixty-forty," he said confidently.

I laughed, and he must have liked my laugh too, because he smiled. Huge. And when our eyes met, it sent me into spirals of panic, because his face should be carved into stone or painted on a tapestry or something. Faces didn't *look* like that.

"Let's go," he said, gesturing to his motorcycle, and this time I followed. Hopefully I wouldn't be spending a lot of time with him. Theo was trouble for me. I could feel it in my bones.

Chapter Five

#5. A PIECE OF BRIGHT BLUE SEA GLASS, COURTESY OF THE AEGEAN SEA

Technically my dad had given this one to me, but I'd always considered it more of a loan than a gift. He told me it was the only piece of Santorini that would fit in his suitcase, and it moved from place to place with us. I loved the ocean back then, and every chance we got we'd bike the few miles to North Avenue Beach and comb the sand for treasures, but I never found anything nearly as pretty as the Aegean Sea glass.

Unless we were talking about Atlantis, my dad had almost never talked about Santorini. The most that I could ever get him to say was that it was very beautiful and sometimes he missed it. As far as the sea glass went, I guessed that when he went back, he didn't need it anymore. There were probably beaches full of beautiful things.

I STARTED OFF WITH A RESPECTABLE THREE INCHES between mine and Theo's bodies, but that three inches lasted all of two seconds, because the moment I was semi-settled, Theo took off in a blaze of glory, and my main job was to keep myself attached to him.

The motorcycle was unbelievably noisy, all kinds of grinding gears and clicks and rattles, and the very real possibility that some type of Mediterranean rodent had been caught in the spokes. But even if it weren't so loud, I doubt we would have spoken much. Theo was too busy trying to break a land speed record, and I was too busy trying to swallow Santorini whole.

After all the hours I'd spent looking at my dad's map, a part of me had thought this place would feel familiar, but knowing about the island had done exactly nothing to prepare me for the reality. I'd already known that Santorini was shaped like a crescent, a big half-moon with a bay cradled in its curve, but I hadn't realized that the island was small enough for me to actually see that moon with my own two eyes.

And then there were the cliffs. Red and jagged, filled with sprawling villages of whitewashed houses and churches, all glaring white with pops of pale yellow, baked pink, and the occasional cobalt-blue roof. Every so often, Theo slowed down enough to yell out the names of places we were passing through.

"Fira!" he screamed as we zipped through a small town with a clogged main street and a McDonald's coexisting with traditional Greek architecture. "Old Harbor!" He pointed to a wide blue expanse of sea hosting cruise ships so far down below that they looked like Battleship pieces. Every residential area we passed through had something to love. Small winding streets of donkeys wearing colorful blankets with tinkling bells, and miniature churches with blue domed roofs sprouting crosses. I kept having this stupid jet-lagged thought: *Santorini really does look like this.* And then the other thought: *Theo smells really good.* Like a lemon tree. He may not have brushed his hair, but his cologne or aftershave or whatever it was, was so fresh and citrusy smelling that whenever he leaned back to yell out a location name to me, I unconsciously inhaled.

We had passed Fira, and were climbing a narrow, winding road when Theo's opening line really sank in. *How does it feel to be the daughter of the man who is about to rock the archaeological world with proof of Atlantis?*

Had he really used the word "proof"? Because if there was one thing I knew about Atlantis hunters, it was that they didn't throw that word around lightly. Now I was dying to ask Theo, and my heart raced as the motorcycle climbed higher and higher.

And right when I had decided that this was my new life,

that I was going to buzz around on a clunky mini motorcycle taking in unthinkable beauty for the rest of my life, while attempting not to enjoy the smell of the driver's cologne, Theo pulled sharply into a dirt parking lot, kicking up a cloud of dust and sending me smashing into him.

"Oof," I said.

"Oia!" Theo announced. "We're here."

"Warning. A little warning would have been nice."

Where is he? As I frantically scanned the parking lot, my heart began the traditional Greek dance known as *Complete and Utter Meltdown.* The ocean was to the right, and to my left was a makeshift bus stop, a fruit stand, and a dense maze of bright white buildings. Two boys stood talking in front of a car, and a woman sat in a folding chair on the porch of a souvenir shop.

He wasn't here. *Again.*

"Your dad is meeting us somewhere else. At your surprise," Theo said, acknowledging my unspoken question.

Right. I sighed, ignoring his outstretched hand as I stumbled off the motorcycle, my legs wobbly while I took in my surroundings. "Theo, what did you mean back at the airport?"

"Huh?" Theo was stashing our helmets under the seat of the motorcycle, and when he turned and smiled, my stomach performed a series of backflips that would concern me if I were not currently in a firmly committed relationship. Or at least *hoped* I was in a firmly committed relationship. Should I call Dax? My fingers itched for my phone, but I shoved the thought away. Dad first, then I'd deal with Dax.

I adjusted my backpack straps, feeling their reassuring weight on my shoulders. "Back at the airport, you said I'm the daughter of an Atlantis hunter who has *proof*."

"I didn't say that," Theo said quickly, but his eyebrows flew up, completely giving him away. He'd be awful at poker.

"Yes, you did."

His face broke out into a wide smile. "Fine, I did. But your dad wants to be the one to tell you about it."

He had to be joking. "But I'm talking proof, proof. *Actual* proof."

Theo walked up close to me, and my body temperature went up a couple degrees, exactly like it had on the motor-cycle. To be safe, I stepped backward. "*Scientific* proof."

"Is there another kind? But I'm not telling you any more. I don't want to spoil it for your dad."

My heart lurched. "Does the proof have something to do with the 'mystery project'?" I was careful to insert air quotes.

Theo threw them right back at me. "The 'mystery project'? Not entirely." He flashed me a smile that could wipe out an entire city. Easy. But even if I hadn't had a boyfriend, I wouldn't have allowed myself to dwell on that smile, because this guy was clearly as delusional as my father was. I wasn't falling for it.

"Where's my dad?" I asked.

"You ready to run?" Theo was holding his hand out for me to take, and I caught myself right before I put my hand out.

"Did you say run?"

"Yes, here. Let me take your backpack for you." When he saw my expression, he grinned. "Your dad never lets me carry his either. Did you know you two have basically the same backpack? His is older, but still."

We carry the same backpack? I gripped the handles tightly. I was a tiny bit obsessive about my backpack. My mom had found it for me at a consignment shop the year before she married James, and I'd been using it ever since. It was latte-colored, the leather worn to perfection, and its square shape was exactly the right size for my art supplies. Did my dad carry art supplies in his too?

I shoved that thought out of my head, turning back to Theo. "I'm not running."

"But . . ." Now he looked crestfallen. "It's the only way we'll make it in time for your dad's surprise," Theo said. He was clearly starting to get tired of repeating this fact to me, but I wasn't about to give in.

My last run with Dax flashed to mind and I shook my head. "I don't run. Ask my boyfriend." My voice broke a little on that last word, which was embarrassing and also kind of telling.

"Suit yourself. But trust me, it will be worth it." Then, before I could decide if Theo was worthy of trust of any kind, he turned and ran for the maze of buildings. Not power walking, not a brisk jog—a dead sprint. The buildings immediately swallowed him up, and then it was just me in a dirt parking lot, with no luggage, a severe jet-lag-induced headache, and no clue where I was supposed to go.

I'm actually really fast when I want to be.

Oia managed to simultaneously look exactly like all the photos I'd seen online, and not like them at all, because photos couldn't do it justice. The village felt grittier and prettier and smaller and somehow even more charming than still images could capture. Or at least, that's the impression I was getting; I was mostly trying to keep my eyes on whatever scrap of Theo was still in my view, and that wasn't easy.

At first Oia all looked the same. The buildings all had a similar theme—low, white, and angular—but as we ran through the narrow corridors, the buildings began to distinguish themselves. We passed a small church with blue candy-striped poles out front, and then a grocery store full of things that I vaguely remembered my dad buying from the shops in Chicago's Greektown: soft nougat, canned octopus, sun-dried figs, sesame bars, and jars of Nutella. Tourist shops displayed their wares on open patios—everything from stuffed donkeys to original artwork. But most of all there was *white*. The buildings, churches, and walkways all glowed a stark white in the late-evening sunlight, broken up by the occasional bursts of fuchsia bougainvillea flowers and the bright blue of Greek flags. There were no cars in Oia, and that was a good thing, because where would they possibly fit?

Pedestrians—tourists, judging from their rapturous gazes—clogged up nearly every inch of walking room. Half of them were dressed stylishly in flowing dresses and summer suits, and the rest looked like they were straight off the beach. They moved in slow, dazed clumps, cameras in hand, stopping to take photos of small churches and charming doorways and stepping over all the shaggy lumps of dogs lounging inconveniently in the middle of the sidewalks. They were unbelievably annoying—the people, I mean; the dogs, I wanted to scoop up and carry to wherever we were going—but I would be taking photos and staring too, if I weren't desperately trying not to get left behind.

Theo dodged down streets and careered up steps, while I ran behind him, my sandals slippery on the marble walkway, my backpack bouncing heavily. By now I wished I'd taken his hand; it would have made a lot more sense. Not even Dax could argue with that. Right at the moment when I felt like my heart might explode, Theo skidded to a halt. I attempted to stop, but my sandals were no match for the worn-down marble, and Theo caught me by the upper arm to keep me upright. I was a sweaty mess and breathing like I was making a jailbreak.

"Welcome to Atlantis," Theo said.

"Atlantis?" I wheezed. I turned slowly, taking in this new set of surroundings. We'd run to what had to be the west side of the island and were now a stone's throw away from the edge of the cliffs. The caldera—the bowl-shaped bay partially enclosed by the island—spread bold and glittery below us, a much smaller island bobbing in its center like a heavy rubber duck. To our left, the rest of Santorini curved around into a backward C, and to our right, the marble path extended a tad more, ending in what looked like the ruins of a castle. We were at the very top of Santorini, but it felt like we were on top of the world. No wonder this place was so crowded. *Welcome to Atlantis.*

I turned back to Theo. He didn't seem at all out of breath; instead he was glowy and healthy looking. "You mean because Santorini is the origin of the Atlantis myth?" I asked, finally catching my breath.

"Myth?" He squinted at me. "No, welcome to Atlantis bookstore."

He pointed, and suddenly I became aware of a spit of a building sitting right in front of all that spectacular view. Not just any building, but an entire inside-out bookstore. It was tiny, maybe about as wide as my bedroom back home, and looked like it had been carved into existing rock, its facade dominated by two whitewashed staircases, one leading up toward an open terrace overlooking the ocean and another leading down to an arched door painted shiny gold. Murals of Atlantis colored the external walls, and every possible nook and cranny had been fitted with wooden shelves that overflowed with books and quirky hand-lettered signs, all in English. I ♥ UNRELIABLE NARRATORS. And DINOSAURS DIDN'T READ AND NOW THEY'RE EXTINCT. COINCIDENCE? An excellent, excellent point.

The mishmash of color and images and writing gave the whole bookstore the appearance of a life-size collage. My fingers itched for my pencil and sketchbook. I didn't know what I wanted to draw first, but I knew I wanted to capture everything.

And then I saw it. Above the door, painted in gold and in handwriting I would have recognized anywhere:

Welcome to
the Lost Bookstore of Atlantis.
What was lost is now found.
(Open daily from first coffee to sunset)

The force of that handwriting knocked the breath out of me. Before I could stop myself, I hurried over and reached out to touch the letters, feeling the rough texture of the building under my fingertips. Underneath the words was a hand-painted map of Santorini—a shape I could have drawn in my sleep.

I looked up at the writing again, my breath catching in my throat. *What was lost is now found.* Was it really that easy?

"First impression?" Theo said, his voice muffled. I turned to see he had the camera out again, zoomed in way too close on me.

"Not again." I attempted to dodge out of the camera's view. If I had my back to the writing on the wall, then it didn't hurt as much.

Theo kept the camera trained on me, entirely unfazed. "Does the shop remind you of anyone?"

"Are you really asking me that?" I asked, folding my arms self-consciously. With a camera on me, I had no idea where to put my hands or where to look. Besides, it was a question that obviously didn't need answering. The bookstore was whimsical and weird and so charming it sucked the breath straight out of me. This was the brick-and-mortar version of my dad. And by that, I mean it was sending me into spirals of panic.

I wanted to demand that Theo stop filming me, but instead I pointed to the bookstore's door. "Is he in there?"

"Yes. Give me a minute to prepare." Theo set his camera

on the ground, fiddled with it for a moment, then aimed it at me again. "Ready. I'll stand here while you knock."

He had to be joking. But when I turned to look at him, the camera's RECORD light was on, and he gave me a thumbs-up over the top of it. "Ready," he said.

"Theo, *no*. This is not happening." I tried to dart away, but several tourists on the walkway had taken notice of the camera, and now a small congestion of people blocked my escape.

"What do you mean?"

I hurried up next to him. "You aren't *filming* our reunion." It wasn't a crowd exactly, but the knot of people standing behind Theo was starting to make me feel woozy. "What are you, my paparazzi?"

"Paparazzo," he corrected. "Olive, this is an important moment. You said it yourself. You haven't seen him since you were eight."

"*Liv*," I reminded him. My voice was beginning to sound panicked.

"It's important for the story," he said.

So far, he hadn't said the name *Liv* once. "This isn't a *story*. This is me seeing my dad."

"Everything's a story. And you're going to want this, believe me." He readjusted the camera on his shoulder. "Okay, you go knock."

"What? I'm not staging this—" But before I could fully

panic, there was fumbling at the door, and then there was no time. My breath came in hot and quick, a rushing filled my ears, and then the door flew open and . . .

Not my dad.

Not unless he'd aged a solid seventy years since I'd seen him last.

The man was bright-eyed and well dressed, with wrinkled cheeks, thinning hair combed carefully to the side, and this sort of overall dapperness that made me think of the Frank Sinatra vinyl record covers James had displayed on the wall in his home office. The man had the same thick eyebrows and large eyes that Theo had, and he was holding a small cake covered in white frosting petals.

"*Kalispéra!*" the man said. I wasn't sure if I was relieved or disappointed. Was my dad ever going to show up?

"*Kalispéra,*" I said back. I'd said that word all the time as a child, but today it felt thick and too heavy on my tongue. *Good evening.*

The man let off a string of Greek, losing me instantly, and Theo answered, gesticulating toward me. The only thing I understood was *Olive.*

"Olive, this is my grandfather, but you can call him Bapou." He said it from behind his camera, which was still firmly aimed at me.

"Bapou? Like . . ."

"The Greek word for 'grandpa' is Papou, but I said it wrong when I was little and it stuck. He also wants me to tell you that he speaks really great English, and I can tell you with 100 percent certainty that that is not true. Proceed with caution."

Bapou beamed at me, and I felt the full awkwardness of the situation. "It's nice to meet you, Bapou," I said uncertainly.

"Beautiful! Welcome to Santorini!" Bapou said, jabbing one of his fingers at me enthusiastically.

He was massively likable. "Thank you," I said, trying to return a smile that was half as friendly as his. "That's a beautiful cake."

Bapou scrunched up his face, and Theo translated, which earned me a dazzling Bapou smile. Like grandfather, like grandson. Bapou raised the cake toward me in a toast.

"Theo? Theo, is it you?" Suddenly the entrance was rushed by another person, and then there were two of them crowding the door.

Also not my father.

Most *definitely* not my father.

The woman was short and curvy, with golden-brown skin and dark hair pulled up into a topknot with thick bangs fringing her dark eyes. She wore a vintage pair of dad-style Levi's that had been cuffed at the ankle, a faded Rolling Stones

T-shirt, no shoes, and a red lipstick the exact shade of fire-houses and Red Hots candies. I was immediately obsessed with her.

"Olive!" she shouted, spreading her arms wide. "Welcome to Atlantis! I can't tell you how happy I am to finally meet you." Her voice was deep and throaty, and her accent was so similar to my father's that my homesickness snowballed into something much bigger and more hollow feeling. Longing? Pain?

"Call me Liv," I croaked.

She hurried up the stairs and gave my outfit a quick once-over. "Iconic," she breathed. "You have perfected the art of French makeup, my little Greek trickster! And I should know. I spent ten years in Paris."

Gulp. It was like she could see straight through me.

"Olive, this is my mother, Ana," Theo said from behind his camera.

"Your mother?" I managed. Ana looked too young to be anyone's mother, much less Theo's. But now that he'd said it, I suddenly saw their matching big eyes and lips. "It's nice to meet you. Is my dad . . . ?" *Here? Ever going to show up?* I wasn't sure what to say. Luckily, Ana jumped in.

"Of course. Your father stepped away, but he will be back soon." Ana caught sight of Theo's camera, and her expression turned sour. "Theo! Respect! I told you not to—" She finished her sentence in Greek, her tone sharp.

Theo half-heartedly lowered the camera, but it was up again the second she turned around. Whatever she said didn't have any impact on Theo, because the camera stayed firmly in my personal-space bubble, and Ana must have been fully aware of his stubbornness, because she didn't push it.

"Olive, we must get you to the roof for your surprise. Hurry, please. And I will meet you there." She rattled off something to Theo and he nodded; then she hurried back down the steps to the bookstore.

Finally, Theo dropped the camera to his side. His eyes were bright with excitement, exactly like his mom's, and without any consent on my part, my stomach twisted with excitement too. I knew my dad's surprises. Whatever this was, it would be a big deal.

"They want you to close your eyes. I'm going to guide you up." Theo's voice was authoritative, this time not giving me a choice. I put my hand tentatively in his and he grinned, flipping my hand over to inspect my cuticles. "You bite your fingernails, like your dad does."

"I don't," I said, pulling my hand back. Olive had been a consummate nail biter. Liv was not. But when I inspected my nails, he was right. I'd chewed my blue-gray polish to bits. When? On the plane?

"Is my dad up there?" I asked.

"No. Your hand, please, Olive," Theo said.

"Liv," I said, but it was entirely without hope. I put my hand in his, and once Theo was convinced that my eyes were closed, he led me stumbling up the terrace steps (Was this really necessary?), walked me a few paces, and then turned me until I felt the breeze from the ocean wafting up the cliffs. Footsteps started up behind me, and my heart quickened until I heard Ana's voice. "Where is Nico? We can't wait any longer."

"Let's begin," Theo said to her. Then his voice was near my ear, sending a tickle down my spine. "Ready for your surprise? Open your eyes."

I opened my eyes, with no idea what to expect, and what I saw—

Well, it delivered.

The top level of the bookstore was a rooftop patio about the size of our dining room, with a short ledge separating it from the cliff and the sprawling vastness of the caldera. Bookshelves lined the patio's perimeter, and strings of light bulbs snaked around and between them. Jewel-tone cushions lay scattered under a small wooden pergola, and flowers and plants blossomed from repurposed tomato cans all along the ledge. But all of that shied in comparison to what was happening over the ocean.

While I'd been taking in the bookstore and Theo's family, the sun had dropped toward the horizon and in the process transformed into something entirely different. Instead of a bright splash of yellow, it had condensed into a dense orange ball, its edges hot and defined. Sunlight splashed against the white cliffside buildings, reflecting in a spectrum of blazing oranges.

The sunset was too bright to look at directly, so I turned my gaze to the caldera. The water was still, but several large boats were booking it toward the sun, leaving silvery snail trails in their wake. One of them let off its horn, and the full, lonely noise reverberated around the caldera, culminating in a spot right below my rib cage. A chill moved through me, as sudden as a breeze.

I tried to say something, tried to react, but I couldn't. All I could do was stare, transfixed. The sun dropped slowly, elegantly, like a lady sinking into a curtsy, getting redder and denser as it sank, inch by inch, into the ocean. It was almost too beautiful. Behind me, the island was quiet, the crowds holding their breath like I was.

When the final pinprick of red had melted away, there was a large whoosh of cold, salty sea air, which sent my hair flying, then one delicious moment of silence, followed by the entire island bursting into a wild, unfettered applause.

It was the only appropriate response.

"Beautiful! Welcome to Santorini!" Bapou yelled, patting my shoulder.

"Happy you trusted me?" Theo said. He'd put the camera

down and was smiling at me like he was somehow respon-
sible for the sunset. Which I guess he was, or at least for the
fact that I'd seen it.

I was about to ask him if Santorini's sunsets looked like
this every night, when a hushed voice carried up the steps,
stopping me cold. "Ana! She's already here?"

"With Theo," Ana said.

I didn't only recognize that voice with my ears. My cells
recognized it. I knew its weight and timbre. I could smell the
cigarette smoke in it, hear the pop of the cinnamon gum. I
had been unconsciously listening for that voice since I was
eight years old.

My body turned without me having to tell it to, and then
there he was. Flying up the stairs with a wrapped package
tucked under one arm, a spray of fuchsia flowers in the other,
out of breath from running, his eyes focused on me.

Nico Varanakis.

My dad.

Chapter Six

#6. HALF A TUBE OF WINSOR & NEWTON OIL PAINT

Most kids grow up learning colors like red, yellow, orange, and green. I grew up knowing color names like burnt umber, sap green, and Prussian blue.

I found this one behind the scuffed bookcase where he'd kept all his art supplies, and I didn't even have to look at the name to know which color it was. Gold ochre. When I opened it, there was only a smudge of color inside, and I dabbed it onto my wrist, like perfume.

I like to pretend I didn't get my art from my dad, but of course I did. I don't remember even deciding to be an artist. My dad was always drawing or painting, so I was too. I thought it was what people did. It was what we did. I tried to quit art once, take up the flute or dance, something that didn't remind me so much of him, but I couldn't. I don't have any way to see the world other than the one he left me.

SEEING HIS HANDWRITING HAD SHAKEN ME, BUT THIS WAS an actual emotional earthquake. I couldn't move. Couldn't even blink. If I blinked, he might vanish again. Was my heart still beating? Was oxygen circulating through my body?

There'd been no need to worry about not recognizing him. If anything, he looked *more* like himself, like a cartoon caricature, the volume turned up extra high. He was wearing exactly the kind of thing I remember him wearing—an old leather jacket, worn sneakers, and gray jeans. Theo was right about the backpack. His was a darker leather, and more of a rucksack style, but it could have been my backpack's older cousin.

The salt-and-pepper in his hair was new, but it hung tousled on his forehead, the way it always had, and his olive skin gleamed in the evening light, exactly the way I remembered. And even though I knew I couldn't actually smell his cigarettes from here, my throat itched anyway.

My dad. In real life. A possibility I'd given up on years ago.

I couldn't read his expression. The flowers hung from his side, and his eyes were fixed on me. What was going on in his head? Was he noting all the ways I'd changed? Had his heart climbed to his throat—making speech impossible—the way mine had?

Blood began pounding in my ears, and when I couldn't stand it anymore, I stepped forward. "Dad?"

My voice acted as a starting gun. Before I knew what was

happening, he dropped the flowers, then closed the space between us in less than three steps, and then I was mashed up against him, his arms tight around me.

"You're here," he said into my hair, like he couldn't believe it. "Olive, you're here." I was so much taller now, my chin was almost to his shoulder—we'd missed so many heights in between. I inhaled, and his jacket smelled exactly like it used to—a mixture of salt water and aftershave and that cinnamon gum.

I closed my eyes, and for a moment my feet hit surface. I was eight years old. He hadn't left me yet. Everything was still okay.

"We have a lot to talk about, honey," he whispered, and my eyes snapped open, the spell broken. After all this time, what *wasn't* there to talk about? I yanked backward, adrenaline rushing through my body, and suddenly it was like I was seeing him through someone else's eyes. Dax's, or Cora's, or maybe even my stepdad's. The old, worn-out clothes; his glasses, which he probably hadn't updated in twenty years; the flowers on the ground.

The look of confusion.

Ana ran to scoop up the flowers, then took my dad's backpack from him. Theo still had that stupid camera pointed at us, and the weight of our audience suddenly felt enormously heavy.

"Olive?" my dad asked, his eyes wide with concern.

I was still backing up, edging my way toward the ledge. "Thank you for inviting me," I managed, my voice stiff.

Thank you for inviting me? After all this time, that's what I'd said? I wasn't thankful that he'd invited me. I was resentful. And confused. But right now I felt mixed up. A whirlpool of emotions threatening to suck me in.

My dad opened, then closed, his mouth. Like he knew he should say something, but he didn't know what. *Join the club.*

"Over here," Theo called from behind the camera, breaking the tension.

I turned toward him and realized that while my dad and I had been staring at each other like emotionally distressed owls, Ana and Bapou had been busy. A small table pushed up next to the wall of the bookstore had been set with a vintage-looking lace tablecloth, and Bapou's cake sat in the middle, now decorated with pink candles. The bouquet of flowers and my dad's wrapped package sat carefully arranged across a smattering of gold glitter. It was simple and elegant, especially against the bookstore's whitewashed wall. I took a mental snapshot, storing the image away.

"What is this?" I asked, but according to the blood pounding in my ears, I already knew.

"It's a birthday party," my dad said, smiling. "Come on over."

Theo zoomed in with the camera, and Ana swatted at him as we stepped over to the table.

"But . . . my birthday was last month." I turned to look at him, but managed to stop halfway. He knew when my birthday was. I'd turned seventeen. I'd had a huge pool party, and half the school had been there, shoving each other into the deep end and eating catered sushi, which James had insisted on. He said you only turned seventeen once. But I seemed to be doing it twice.

And my dad knew when my birthday was. He'd sent me a birthday postcard, which I had refused to read.

"I figured I have a few to make up for," he said quietly. "And I'm guessing you've never had a sunset birthday party. Oia has the best sunsets in the world. I thought it would be the perfect way to begin your trip."

"Ta-da," Theo sang. "And your dad wasn't at the airport because he was signing for your gift at the post office."

My gift?

"They promised it would be here two days ago," my dad said. "I'm sorry I wasn't there. I really wanted this to be . . ." He trailed off, but my mind filled in the word. *Perfect. Magical.* Both.

And now I had something else to contend with. I turned to look at the wrapped package, my heart pounding loudly. It was a smallish flat rectangle, wrapped in plain brown paper with a piece of twine twisted around it. But I already knew one thing about it: unless my dad had changed radically, whatever was in there was perfect and exactly what I'd wanted.

"Go ahead, love," Ana said, her voice excited. She either knew what it was or had at some point been the recipient of one of my father's gifts.

I edged toward the table, feeling almost seasick I was so nervous. Suddenly I realized that the specks of gold weren't glitter; they were hundreds of tiny cutout gold stars that had been sprinkled over the table. *Magic is in the details.* My dad's words. He must have spent hours on these.

Was everyone else holding their breath too? Bapou beamed happily at me.

My dad stepped up next to me. "Do you want to open your present?"

I didn't, but it wasn't as if I had a clear exit strategy, so I nodded reluctantly. My dad handed me the package, and I carefully slid my finger under the paper, my heart beating a little faster. Inside was a smooth wooden box, held together by gold hinges and a gold clasp. A word had been etched into the top of it, and when I turned it over to read it, I couldn't help myself—I gasped. SENNELIER. I abandoned all pretense of calm, my fingers clumsy as I hurried to open the lid.

And there they were.

Fifty brilliant oil pastels nestled into soft, protective foam.

Each one pristine. Each so rich and bright, they could have been on display in a candy shop. They weren't just any oil pastels; they were the pastels that other pastels idolized—the oil pastels I'd wanted since the first moment I picked up a paintbrush. The colors were unlike any I'd seen before. Lemon yellow, cerulean blue, viridian green, Chinese orange.

My fingers were itching to pick one up. To start layering them over all the half-finished collages in my sketchbook, to begin sketching the scene in front of me, blending the pigment with my fingertips, or maybe a palette knife. But I couldn't do that now because I had to say something. Anything. The silence had stretched on for too long now, and nervous energy wafted toward me from the rest of the birthday party.

My dad stepped in closer, his voice quiet. "Henri Sennelier owned an art supply store in France near the apartment of Pablo Picasso. He made custom materials for artists, and one day Picasso asked for something particular. He loved the ease of crayons, but he wanted pigments that could cover anything—wood, glass, metal, everything. So Henri Sennelier made these." He reached out, pointing to the crayons in the lower right. "The shop is still there. It's fourth generation now, right across from the Louvre."

The thought of Picasso walking into an art supply store and requesting these made my heart ache. Of course, he was the genesis of these. I'd never seen anything like these colors.

I picked up the ochre color and ran my finger over its waxy point. Even without using it, I knew how it would melt into the paper, layering until the color was perfectly saturated.

"Nico went to Paris to order them," Theo burst in, his camera still angled at us. I shifted nervously. "He found a flight and went."

"Theo, hush," Ana said, but she had a huge smile on her face.

I shot a nervous glance at my father. He'd flown to Paris for these? Even without a flight, these pastels probably cost more than his entire bungee-corded-together motorcycle. Did he have the money for these? One glance at his clothes and I knew the answer. No. No, he did not.

"But . . . why?" Before I could stop myself, my eyes had met his. I forgot what his smile felt like. It was like a thousand birthday candles, all full of wishes and lit up for me. It made everything else pale in comparison.

He flourished his hand at the set. "Your mother said you love Paris. And art."

"I do," I said. "But . . ."

When I didn't finish the sentence, his expression turned hopeful. "And I think you will like Greece equally as much."

"She *will*," Theo cut in, his voice exasperated. Was agreeing with my dad Theo's entire job? "Now will you tell her the best part already?"

"Theo!" Ana warned again.

My heart skipped. The best part? Wasn't this the best part? "What . . . ?"

My dad's smile grew. "Some of these colors . . . I had them custom-made for you."

"That's why he had to go to Paris," Theo said. "He had to meet with the Senneliers."

What? My heart thudded. Fell? My gaze whipped back to the set, and instantly I knew which ones my dad had commissioned. The final three. I knew because they didn't fit in with the rest of the set's carefully arranged rainbow progression. I knew, because something about their intensity reminded me of my father.

My hands shook as I carefully pulled the pastels from the box, rolling them in my palm until they were label-side up, the pigment names marked in tiny script. The deep cobalt I'd seen on the church's domes was *Santorini blue.* The rich turquoise echoed in the tide at the bottom of the cliffs was *Ammoudi mood.* And the final one? The chocolaty green that I'd seen in every mirror and every rippled reflection for my entire life?

Olive's eyes.

I heard a deep, shuddering exhale, and it took me a moment to realize it had come from me. My breath felt heavy, the pastel stick featherlight in my hand. He'd gotten it exactly right. How had he gotten it exactly right? I couldn't look at him. Couldn't look at any of them.

"Beautiful! Welcome to Santorini!" Bapou said. He pointed to the table. *"Toúrta!"*

At last, a Greek word I recognized. *Cake.* I spun to look at it, this time giving it more than a cursory glance. Was it . . . ? Yes, it was. My heart swelled. Every year on my birthday my dad had made a big show of finding the most perfect oranges in the city, which he pureed whole and added to the batter. The finished product was coated in a thick tart yogurt, drenched in honey syrup. Bapou had added a ring of crushed pistachios and orange slices arranged into a flower. We'd called it Sunshine Cake. I hadn't had a slice of it in years, and the mere act of looking at it made my mouth water. Traitor.

How does he always do this?

My dad stepped forward, gesturing at the pastels, his hand a few inches from mine. "The first two are to help you with your art while you're here. The third needed to be a color."

This was too much. My heart was swelling up like a balloon. Any minute now I was going to rise up on the tips of my toes and drift out over the caldera. Only their gazes were keeping me anchored. The three of them crowded together, a nervous family. Their faces shone expectantly. Well, their three faces plus Theo's camera.

Bapou cocked his head, and Ana shot my father a nervous look. The camera was steady.

"Olive, is it all right?" my father asked quietly.

The correct answer was that it was far from all right. It was perfect—the gift, the party, every detail had been magical. But another truth was bubbling to the surface, crowding out every other thought, stifling my voice. *He can't do this.*

He couldn't fix the last nine years with one grand gesture, no matter how perfect it was. He couldn't erase all those empty years without him. He didn't *get* to do this.

But when I opened my mouth, I didn't say any of that. Instead, I burst into tears.

Some girls cry and it's a pretty, delicate act, capable of inspiring grand gestures or at least a pack of tissues.

I cry and people panic.

At first they all thought I was weeping tears of joy over what was, clearly, a transformative moment, because they all exchanged a knowing glance. A silent high five. But as soon as it became apparent that there was an actual river of snot happening, they switched into disaster mode. My dad rushed over to me, examining me like he was trying to figure out if I'd twisted my ankle or had been stung by a large Santorinian bug. Bapou began repeating his English phrases even louder. "Welcome to Santorini! Beautiful!"

Theo got excited and swooped in closer to keep filming, and Ana nearly tackled him to get him out of my face. "Theo, *stamáta to*!"

"Mom, this is great footage! This is real—" Ana said something sharp in Greek and dragged him away by the scruff of his neck.

"Olive, do you not like this set? Because I saw on your social media that you've been working on self-portraits. I thought you could use this color."

He'd seen my social media account? My brain started buzzing, too loudly for me to hear the rest of what he'd said. I'd started it last year on a whim so I'd have a place to put all of the work I was doing, but my following hadn't even reached triple digits yet. It had never occurred to me that my dad could be one of them.

I wiped my eyes, stepping back from the table, the gift, the whole party. I took a deep breath, and finally, finally some words came out. "Dad, I go by Liv now."

They were the wrong words. Of course they were. No one had told me what to do if I was ever in this situation.

Hurt, confusion—something—flashed across my dad's face, but he replaced it quickly. Smoothed it over with acceptance. Understanding. He nodded. "Liv. That's beautiful. Very sophisticated." His smile was back, but he was looking away, giving me some emotional space, which obviously I needed. But still. *Ouch.*

"Hmm." The noise came from behind the camera, which had reasserted itself. Embarrassment swilled through me, powerful enough to navigate me through my emotion. *Okay, Liv. Time to pull this together.* Ana had started bustling around, snatching up the wrapping paper and string, like the world's most awkward scene wasn't playing out in front of her, and Bapou was carefully repositioning the cake, spinning it so the candles were perfectly centered.

I cleared my throat, stepping back from my dad. "Sorry about that, everyone. Thank you very much for this nice surprise. But I haven't slept since I left Seattle, and I'm feeling really jet-lagged."

"Don't apologize for your feelings," Ana said, her voice ferocious. "Never apologize for those."

Theo lowered the camera, and when I saw his expression, I wanted to throw something at him. His eyebrows were up, a smirk of a smile aimed at me. I'm sorry, but was he enjoying this?

My dad carefully replaced his backpack, gesturing for me to do the same. "Of course. Let's get you settled in." He turned for the stairs, and I hurried after him. Despite my anger, a part of me refused to let him out of my sight.

While I'd been having my mini breakdown on the terrace, the sunset-viewing party had thinned, the crowds disappearing down the rabbit holes of the village. Even the dogs were on the move, and one particularly fluffy one sidled up to my dad, resting his dandelion head on my dad's knee before continuing his amble down the street.

I prepared to make the trek to my dad's house or apartment or wherever it was he lived, but instead, once Theo was dispatched in search of my suitcase, Ana and my father led me down into the bookstore. My legs were shaky on the steep steps, but I was anxious to see what was inside.

It didn't disappoint. "O-oh . . . ," I stammered as Ana flicked the lights on. If the bookstore was charming on the outside, it was downright bewitching on the inside. My dad beamed at me.

"Like it?"

He couldn't really have been asking, because there was no way anyone had ever seen the Lost Bookstore of Atlantis and not liked it. The space was dollhouse tiny, with a small, semicircle-shaped room making up the bulk of it. An arched doorway led to a second space that was more closet than room, and both had high, domed ceilings covered in brightly colored murals. Ingeniously built bookshelves hugged the curved walls, and hundreds, maybe thousands of books were nestled tightly together—a mixture of shiny new paperbacks and worn leather hardbacks. Small cards stuck out at intervals to indicate what each section was. MYSTERY. HISTORICAL FICTION, and one large card that read ROMANCE!!!

And the *smell*. I inhaled, feeling my muscles loosen. I'd never consciously realized that old books had a smell, but of course they did. It was old leather with hints of vanilla and must, and a dash of something else. Magic? Pixie dust? I walked to the center of the main room, turning slowly so I could see every inch of it. The late-evening light filtered in through two high windows, dust motes swirling like ballerinas, and I suddenly had an overpowering desire to spend my life savings on new books and then fall down on a soft surface somewhere and read the kinds of things my literature teacher was always trying to talk us into. Charles Dickens? Emily Brontë? Bring it on.

"Well?" my father asked. He looked much more confident in this space. He filled it up. Staring at him among all his books made me feel like I was going to crumple up and cry again, so I quickly turned my gaze upward to the domed ceiling, where a constellation of stars had been painted. "How long has this been here?"

"The space, probably a hundred years. The shop, one." He smiled at me. "Although Ana has dreamed of opening a bookstore in Oia since she was a little girl."

Ana gave an aggravated sigh, but her eyes sparkled. "Is it a dream or a nightmare? Running a bookstore on a small island has not been easy. Even finding a building felt impossible. You should have seen this place before your father began his work. It was nothing but a hollowed-out cave. I've needed him every step of the way. His genius is literally on the walls."

"It would have been nothing without your vision," my father said, deftly sidestepping the compliment.

"I love how it smells," I said, spinning again.

"Book air is the best air," Ana said, reaching for a pile of mail on a small desk and sifting through the letters. "If I could, I'd bottle it up and dab it on my wrists every morning."

"You could sell it and make a fortune." My dad's dark eyes met mine. "It's only the old books. When the paper in old books breaks down, the compound smells like almonds and vanilla flowers. The new ones smell of paper and glue."

"You would know something like that," Ana said. Her voice was soft and sweet, and when I turned to see the admiring smile she was aiming at him, my senses were suddenly on the alert.

Was Ana his girlfriend?

I felt a pang in my chest, followed immediately by frustration. A part of me had believed that despite the fact that he had left us, there was no way my dad had moved on from us. But of course he had. It had been nine years. Who knows how many other relationships he'd been in?

Either way, I needed to know. I walked over to a bookcase, trailing my fingers along the spines. "So you two know each other from . . . ?"

"Childhood," my dad said. "We both grew up on Santorini."

"And now you're . . . friends?" I laced the last word with a question, but my dad didn't bat an eye.

My dad nodded. "Yes, dear friends."

"We are friends and business partners," Ana said, looking pointedly at me. I glanced at her and she gave me a little wink.

My dad chimed in. "We reconnected a few years ago. Ana had been away from the island for many years, but she came back to care for Bapou and we devised this plan. She used to work for a design company, but she said her job didn't have enough soul. She wanted to spend the rest of her life around books."

"Romance books," she clarified. "I wanted it to be an all-romance-novel bookstore. I even had a name for it, 'The Red Knickers.' Luckily, your father talked me out of it. He said a Greek island bookstore catering to English-speaking romance readers might be a bit *too* niche."

She tossed a handful of papers into a small metal trash can, then turned to me. "Do you know what I love the most about this place? You are never quite alone when you are in a bookstore. So many voices are jammed into one place, it is impossible to feel alone. While you stay at the bookstore, feel free to read anything you'd like."

"Wait, while I *stay* at the bookstore?" I spun around, looking at the tiny space. "Is there an apartment or something?"

"Better," Ana said, her red lips stretched into a smile. "Nico, show her."

My dad reached up and under a long bookshelf lining the upper edge of the ceiling, and I heard a little *click*. The shelf swung forward, revealing a hidden pocket of space just large enough to house two suspended platforms, each featuring a twin bed with a set of shelves at its foot. A dinner-plate-size window sat in the middle, and an attached ladder lay folded in the space between the beds.

"A hidden bedroom?" I said.

"Guess who designed it," Ana said, but there was no need to respond. Only my dad would come up with something like this.

He unfolded the wooden ladder, bringing it down to the floor, and I clambered up until I was at eye level with the beds. Both had been neatly made with crisp white sheets and hand-knit blankets, but the wall space above the one on the left was covered with maps and handwritten notes, most in Greek. Thick, scientific-looking books in French, Greek, and English had been shoved into the shelves, alongside a small stack of black T-shirts and jeans. A worn pair of Adidas sat on top, identical to the pair Theo was currently wearing. My heart drummed in an infuriating way.

I pointed to the opposite side. "Is that bed for me?"

My dad nodded. "Well, it could be. I rent out a room from a local family—"

"Room? It's more of a shoebox." Ana's voice was disdainful, but she smiled affectionately at him.

"—and you are welcome to stay there with me," he said, "but I think this may be more *comfortable*."

The inflection on the last word made me zero in on his expression. He'd jammed his hands awkwardly into his jacket pockets, and he rocked back on his heels, his face wiped clean of emotion except for a faint hint of worry. I was clearly supposed to be reading between the lines of the situation, but whatever was there was completely illegible. Which one did he want me to choose?

"You are also welcome to stay with me," Ana said. "But Bapou is also there and insisting on treating our apartment like the industrial kitchens he used to work in. It makes for a rather chaotic environment. Theo likes it here best. It gives him some quiet time to think. And with all the work you three will be doing, you will likely want some space to rest." She raised her eyebrows at my dad, and a small smile broke through the worry on his face.

Right. The work.

The birthday party and all my jumbled feelings had distracted me. I jumped off the ladder, landing with a thud on the bookstore's woven rug. "Dad, what's the project? Mom wouldn't tell me."

My dad's face lit up again, forcing me to avert my eyes.

He was the sun and I was Icarus. If I flew too close, I'd get burned. "Like I said earlier, we have a lot to talk about. But tonight you need to rest. Ana, could you give us a moment, please?"

"Certainly." She scooped up a pile of paperback books, then scurried into the next room. "I am here when you need me."

I doubted that anywhere in the bookstore was out of earshot, but my dad waited ceremoniously until she had disappeared into the next room before speaking in a low voice. "I understand you have only just met Theo, but I've known him for a long time, and I trust him completely. If you feel at all uncomfortable, I am happy to make other arrangements. But I thought this might be . . . fun."

I hesitated. Sharing a bedroom—er, platform—with a boy I didn't really know was not exactly comfortable, but what about this situation was? And no, Mom would probably not be happy with this, and Dax would definitely not be happy with this, but technically it did not violate my mom's rules. She had never said *Do not share a bunk room with a Greek boy you meet at the airport.*

Also, the bookstore felt like a friend. A harbor in the proverbial storm I was about to pass through. I *wanted* to stay here, and it had nothing to do with my bunkmate.

Okay, it had a little to do with my bunkmate. But mostly because I wanted to pepper him for information about this mystery project and maybe look at the way his eyelashes fanned out over his face for a few seconds longer.

Completely joking about that last part.

I turned to my dad, resolve lacing my voice. "I'll stay at the bookstore."

His relieved smile felt like a punch to the gut.

Mystery solved. He'd hoped I'd choose the bunk room. Meaning, we were both more comfortable with the idea of me sharing a bedroom with a stranger than we were with the idea of sharing a roof over our heads. Eight-year-old me would never have believed how far my dad and I had drifted apart.

Chapter Seven

#7. ADJUSTABLE VENDING MACHINE RING, AKA MY MOM'S ENGAGEMENT RING

When my mom's internship ended, she left NYC, and my dad did too. He found a room in an apartment and a job waiting tables at a restaurant in Chicago's Greektown. He spent his days working on his English while serving tourists spanakopita and dolmades, and his evenings with my mom. She was studying all the time, so he went with her to the library, where he drew or practiced English.

He proposed to her on the last warm day of October. They'd decided to take a walk to the Navy Pier and stopped to watch the Ferris wheel next to a cache of vending machines. My dad put a quarter in, and when a ring popped out, she said yes. They'd only known each other 139 days. She was pregnant with me by then.

I once asked her if Dad was part of her plan, and she said that plans are for buildings, not people, but that's not what I'd meant.

THE BOOKSTORE'S BATHROOM WAS ANOTHER SURPRISE, mostly because it was housed in an underground cave. To get to it, Ana led me out the bookstore's sunken entrance and through another door built directly into the rock under Oia's main street. Inside, the cave was divided into two sections: One was a walled-off bathroom featuring a tiny sink and shower, a toilet, and a maddeningly small mirror. The other section was storage, stacked high with crates full of books and flyers.

The shower was really an overactive spigot sticking out of the wall, and using it required choosing which part of your body you wanted pummeled while you contorted in acrobatic positions. But a shower is a shower. I stepped out feeling on top of my game again. So what if I'd sobbed uncontrollably my first night in Oia? That didn't mean I couldn't have this whole situation under control.

I scrubbed every inch of makeup off my face, then did my best to check out my face in the mirror. My eyes were a bit swollen, and I had deep circles under them, but overall, not bad. Theo still wasn't back with my suitcase, so I grabbed the pajamas Ana had left outside the bathroom door and slipped them on. They were gorgeous lace-trimmed shorts and a matching tank made of a buttery soft fabric, and I relished the feeling of the night air on my bare arms and legs as I crossed out of the cave and back into the bookstore.

Ana or my dad had propped open the window in the bunk room, and I stretched out on top of my covers, extending my arms over my head until I filled up the entire space. It felt so cozy and hidden up here, like a tree house or a submarine. Julius would trade his best nunchucks for a night in this place.

Thinking of Julius instantly made me think of Dax, and my stomach turned. He must have texted me back by now. My dad had left my backpack and the box of oil pastels propped up on my set of shelves, and I scrabbled through my backpack, finally locating my phone at the bottom of all my things. I had a text from James's phone. **LIV ITS JULIUS IT IS OK TO LOSE TO OPPONENT BUT NOT OK TO LOSE TO FEAR.** Then about thirty emojis, mostly ninjas.

Surprisingly relevant.

But from Dax? Nothing. So, like the Queen of All That Is Pathetic, I wrote to him again. **Made it to Oia!!! Talk soon?**

Ugh.

Looking at all those exclamation points made me want to throw myself into the depths of Ammoudi Bay. I texted Julius back, **I MISS MY NINJA,** then looked around, my eye snagging on the maps on Theo's walls. I tumbled forward on my bed, trying to get a good look. There were several, but the main one was a colorful map of the world, with cities and countries marked with pushpins. A series of sticky notes surrounded the tattered edges, and each had a number plus a string attached to one of the cities. It must be a plan of some sort.

I was preparing to jump the gap to get a closer look when the door below me opened, and Theo's voice stopped me mid-crouch. "Olive?"

Busted. I tumbled back onto my bed. "Up here," I said, cringing at how perky my voice sounded. "Are you coming up?"

His footsteps made their way to the ladder. "That depends. Are you going to cry again?"

I was prepared to hit him with a snarky comment, or at least one of my pillows, but luckily, a piece of the Sunshine Cake suddenly appeared at my eye level, set on a white plate with a small fork, followed by Theo's smiling face. "Joking. I know that was a train wreck up there, but you *want* a piece of this cake. Believe me."

I deeply resented the train wreck bit, but I also deeply wanted the cake, so I took the plate from him. Theo finished climbing up the ladder, carrying his own slice of cake, then settled cross-legged, his back to the wall. And then he looked at me. *Stared* at me. Which would have been terribly uncomfortable, except I had the cake to keep me busy. I took a bite, involuntarily closing my eyes. Sunshine Cake had always been delicious, but Bapou had managed to elevate it to the next level. It was bright and buttery, with a hint of cinnamon in each melting bit. It made up for a lot of today.

I opened my eyes to see Theo smiling at me. "Good?"

"Anyone ever tell you that your Bapou is a genius?"

His smile deepened. "Everyone. He's the best baker in Santorini. He may not remember how to take his medication or pay his electric bill, but he can bake any Greek pastry you can think of without having to look at a recipe. It's a miracle. All your dad had to do was describe the cake, and he made this. Well, this and six other test cakes. Your dad really wanted to get it right, and we all agreed that this was the best version."

Six other test cakes?

He was still staring at me. Studying me. Like if he looked long enough, he might figure something out. My cheeks suddenly felt warm, which meant my rosy splotches were starting to appear—the ones I got whenever I was embarrassed. I dropped my head and took another bite before gesturing to the bunks. "I invaded your space."

"Huh?" He was still staring.

I pointed to the bunks with my fork. "Your mom said you like the peace and quiet of the bunks; me being here will ruin that. I invaded your space."

He grinned, his arms folded smugly over his chest. "Aggressive. Olive the Conqueror has *invaded*."

"Liv." I threw my pillow at him and he caught it with one hand, then tossed it back.

"I don't mind sharing the bookstore bunks with you. But I do have a question."

His voice was serious, and I stabbed my cake nervously. ". . . Okay."

A line appeared between his eyebrows and he leaned forward, resting his elbows on his knees. "What's the problem with you and your dad?"

I nearly choked on the cake in my mouth. "What do you mean?"

"Your dad has always talked like you two were very close. But it seems like you don't know a lot about each other. I thought you'd at least know about the bookstore. And then at the birthday party . . ." He made his hand into an airplane and then crashed it into the bed.

I grimaced. That was about right. But didn't Theo know you were supposed to avoid talking about people's awkward situations? I folded my arms tightly across my chest, a self-conscious version of his posture. "That's pretty personal. Not sure I know you well enough to talk about that."

A smile broke over his face and he sat up, gesturing to the tiny space between bunks. "I think we're past politeness. Might as well get to know each other fast, right? I mean, you're wearing my mom's pajamas."

He had a point. A very strong point. Also, it had felt so good to talk to Henrik on the flight over; how would it feel to talk about the situation with someone who actually knew my father?

I exhaled. "Fine. I haven't seen my dad since I was eight."

"Why not?" He leaned forward again, elbows on knees, chin in hands.

Theo's gaze felt worse than his camera. I quickly averted my eyes, staring at the open window. "Because he abandoned my mom and me so he could look for Atlantis."

"Abandoned" wasn't my word. It was James's word. I'd overheard him say it to a colleague once. It had stung, but sometimes that's what the truth does. *Hurts.*

I waited for the word to do its magic. People usually get this horrible pitying look, or start scrambling for something comforting to say, but not Theo. Similar to Henrik, when I mentioned my personal drama, he didn't even look uncomfortable. Rather, Theo had the nerve to seem *intrigued.* "Who told you he left you for Atlantis?"

My face went hot. "No one had to tell me. It's pretty obvious when someone leaves and doesn't come back."

"Hmm." Theo went back to studying me, and I felt the overwhelming need to defend myself. Who was he to ask me all these personal questions?

"Where's your dad?" I blurted out. Instantly, I was horrified.

What if Theo's dad was dead? What if Theo didn't have a dad at all?

But this didn't disturb him either. He shrugged casually. "In Singapore, probably making his new fiancée as miserable as he made my mom."

I instantly deflated. I wanted to tell him that my parents were divorced too, but he obviously already knew that. There was another long moment of silence. "Sorry."

He shrugged. "It's fine. He wasn't very engaged in my life even when I did live with him, so it isn't all that different. He's from Le Bugue in France." The French name rolled off his tongue as easily as Greek did, and I felt a stab of jealousy. The best I could do was sort of understand some Greek words, and here he was fluent in at least three languages. I was beginning to think his English might even be better than mine.

"Which language do you speak the most?"

He looked up at the ceiling. "Well . . . I swear in French, talk to my grandfather in Greek, but feel most comfortable in English. Whenever my dad was around, he insisted we speak English together."

My cake was down to crumbs. Theo noticed and passed his plate across the gap to me. I didn't have the dignity to refuse.

As I dug in, a smattering of a language I didn't recognize floated through the window. Croatian? Russian? I leaned toward the window to see a group of people taking photos of the bookstore. If I'd stumbled across it, I would have taken photographs of it too, or pulled out my sketchbook and recorded as many details as I could. I turned back to Theo. "Is Singapore where you lived before Santorini?"

"Briefly. My dad's a management consultant for multi-national corporations, so he moves every few years. We've lived everywhere."

I stopped eating. Intrigued. "Everywhere where?"

He looked up at the ceiling. "Singapore, Melbourne, Tokyo, London, Munich, Amsterdam, and LA. We were in LA the longest. Almost three years. Then we were in London for two. My mom and I moved to Santorini after they got divorced. We've been here for a year."

I was impressed. I couldn't help myself. "So that's what your maps are about. Those are all the places you've lived!"

Oops. Busted myself on snooping. But he didn't seem to mind. "Plus all the places I want to live. My ultimate goal is to be an adventure filmmaker. Travel around and make films of it all."

Well, that explained the camera. I felt my view of him shift ever so slightly. He may be a little pushy, but he was adventurous, and he had a plan. I couldn't help but admire his confidence. It made my wishy-washy art school plans look kind of pathetic.

"Interesting." I took one more bite of his cake, then set it aside. "LA. So, besides your dad speaking it when you were together, is that why your English is so good?"

"My English isn't good. It's perfect, Olive," he said, dropping a heavy Greek accent on the last word. "Also, I watch a lot of American TV. If you want to learn English, all you have to do is watch nine thousand hours of situation comedies."

"It's Liv," I corrected him.

Theo shook his head. "Sorry, but I don't think I'm going to remember that. Olive has been imprinted on my brain, and besides, you don't look like a Liv."

My head snapped up in indignation. "What? Yes, I do," I protested.

He shook his head. "No. You really, *really* don't. How about a nickname? I'll call you . . ."

"Absolutely not—" I started, but he barreled past my objection.

"Kalamata!" He stabbed the air triumphantly.

"Kalamata?" I groaned. "Kalamata, as in the type of olive?"

His eyes widened in mock surprise. "Is it? Oh, you're right. It's actually my favorite variety of olive. What a strange coincidence."

"So what you're saying is that you'll still be calling me Olive, but in a different way." I was annoyed, but not as annoyed as my voice made me out to be. Kalamata wasn't the worst nickname ever invented.

But this was ridiculous. And so was the fact that I was smiling.

He shook his head. "I won't be calling you Olive. I'll be calling you Kalamata. It's completely different."

"Well, I forbid it," I said, trying to sound queenly and in charge. It didn't work.

"And I forbid you to forbid it. My bunk, my rules."

"*Your* bunk?" I said, but now we were both smiling. My stomach did a happy sort of spasm. Was he flirting with me? And worse, was I flirting back? Suddenly I thought of Dax again, and my stomach twisted but for an entirely different reason. He had to have texted by now.

I quickly grappled for my phone, but when I looked at it, the only notification was from my mom. You make it? I turned and glared out our shared window. After the sun's dramatic exit, night had lowered as swiftly as a stage curtain. Where was Dax?

When I came to, Theo was watching me with one eyebrow raised. I hastily shoved my phone under the pillow, my cheeks hot again.

"So back to your relationship with your dad," Theo said, like this was a normal conversational jump.

"Are you always this interested in other people's lives?"

"Always," he said firmly. "I want to be a filmmaker, remember? Also, you interest me."

His voice was harmless, amused almost, but then our eyes met over the gap for a few seconds longer than was strictly necessary and heat flushed down my neck. Whatever it was that was swirling between these bunks, I needed to put a stop to it. Immediately.

"I have a boyfriend," I blurted out.

"Yeah, you mentioned that."

"I did?"

He nodded nonchalantly. "Yes. When we pulled in to Oia. You said, 'I don't run. Ask my boyfriend.'"

He actually did a fairly spot-on impression of my voice. Also, he sounded calm, borderline dismissive, which made me feel stupid. I had obviously misinterpreted his intentions. So that was a relief. Or at least I think that feeling was relief. It was definitely at least in the same *family* as relief.

He pointed to my lap. "Is that why you keep checking your phone? He's texting you?"

"Uh . . ." I realized how uncool the truth would make me sound, but I was too tired to come up with anything. "I'm waiting for him to text. We're sort of . . . not speaking."

I waited for some kind of commentary or way-too-personal questions, but nothing. Just more of that curious look. "What's your boyfriend like?"

"Dax? He's . . ." My stomach sank as I thought over the past week. He'd been annoyed, and distant, and honestly, sort of petty. But he'd always struggled with last-minute changes in plans, and besides, he'd really been looking forward to me going on his senior trip with him. Whenever I was terribly disappointed, I felt grumpy too. It was understandable. It also hadn't helped that I'd clearly let him down on the whole college visit thing. "Well . . . he's really focused, and good at everything. Everyone likes him a lot."

"Everyone, huh?" A slow smile spread across his face, revealing his crowded bottom teeth. Why were those so obnoxiously charming? "Well, I should probably tell you that I have an ex-girlfriend. A serious ex-girlfriend. But we're still friends. Just the kind that don't talk to each other."

I surprised myself and him by bursting out laughing. "Does the 'still friends' thing ever work out?"

He was clearly pleased by my laughter. "Not in my experience, which honestly is pretty vast."

"Heartbreaker. So why did you and Ex break up?" Nosy, but according to Theo's logic, we might as well get over any fake boundaries.

"I moved."

I waited for more of an explanation, but he only blinked at me. "So what? You don't do long-distance?"

"Not anymore." His voice was a dead stop. As in, *I'm not*

talking about this anymore. Unacceptable, given the fact that he had grilled me about my relationship with my father. I looked him straight in the eyes. "Why *not* anymore?"

He held my gaze for one point three seconds, which was exactly the right amount of time for me to see a glimmer of sadness lurking there. It was honestly unnerving. It disappeared almost as quickly as it arrived. One eyebrow went up. "That's pretty personal. Not sure I know you well enough to talk about that."

He was way too good at imitating my voice. I even heard a hint of Chicago in there, which I hadn't realized I'd carried with me. I raised my eyebrow in return, but I had a feeling I wasn't as good at it. And besides, I wasn't going to chase down Theo's sadness. Whatever had happened looked personal and painful, and I knew all about personal and painful. "Well, remind me not to tell you anything ever again," I said, purposely making my voice playful.

"You will," he said. "I'm a filmmaker. People can't help but tell me their stories."

"*Future* filmmaker," I corrected.

"Mmm," he said, flipping off the light. We lay down in the darkness, but the conversation didn't feel over. Moonlight pooled onto both our beds, and I felt hyperaware of him lying across the gap.

"Sorry about your girlfriend," I whispered.

"Sorry about your dad," he said. "I guess I don't know that much about your relationship, but I do know he's always talked about you nonstop. I assumed you were best friends."

"Just the kind that don't talk to each other," I said, echoing him.

He laughed, then was quiet, and the darkness pressed in on my thoughts. Before I'd understood that my dad was never coming back, I'd talked about him nonstop too, to anyone who would listen. Now it felt like I spent all my time trying to get people to *not* ask about him.

He's always talked about you nonstop. Did Theo mean *always*, or did he mean since my dad had started sending me postcards? Was that when he'd had a sudden change of heart? The thought made my chest turn thick and heavy.

And sleep? Forget it. I'd been dying for a bed for what felt like days, but now that I actually had one—and a comfortable one at that—my mind was racing too much to relax.

After an interminable two or three minutes, Theo popped up on one elbow. "Kalamata, do you want to listen to French rap?"

I popped up on my elbow too. "French people . . . rap?" Wow. I sounded very educated. Theo laughed.

"Of course they do. I mean, yes, rap originally started in the 1970s at block parties in New York City"—he said this as if it were completely common knowledge—"but it's spread since then. The French caught on a little bit later, but they're great at it. Plus, I don't know what it is about French rap, but it's like chamomile tea. I sleep like a baby when it's on. You in?"

His face was a shadowy outline, but outside lights had caught his eyes. He was even good-looking in the dark. "I'll give it a try."

Theo sat up, then began messing around with speakers and cords, and suddenly a horrible thought sent me upright. If we were going to share a room, then I was going to have to warn him about the dreams. The problem was that I'd never told anyone about them, and there was no way he wouldn't ask me questions. But still, I had to do it. I grimaced, then took a deep breath. "Hey, Theo, I need to give you a heads-up. I have, um . . ." I hesitated before launching the right word at him. "Nightmares."

He paused, moonlight glinting off the speaker in his hand. "Nightmares?"

"Yeah, bad ones. And I yell or . . . cry sometimes. Not a big deal, but I wanted you to know so it doesn't freak you out or whatever." My voice was supposed to be nonchalant, but it wasn't cooperating. It was sort of shaky and high and all-around weird.

Ugh. *This* was why I never told anyone about them.

Theo stayed still, as if soaking in the information. "Okay. What should I do when it happens? Wake you up?"

That one stumped me. I went to great lengths to avoid sleeping in front of other people, so the only people who had ever seen it happen were my mom and a couple of my friends from school. "Um . . . I don't know. No one's ever done that before. I usually wake up on my own. So maybe leave me alone?"

He set the speaker down. "Got it. And don't worry, the soothing sounds of Busta Flex have a way of solving all problems."

French rap began playing loudly through the speakers, and he adjusted it before crawling under his covers. I felt relieved but also a little surprised. Why hadn't he asked me what my nightmares were about? And if he had, would I have told him?

Probably not.

I closed my eyes and focused on the music. Theo was right. It definitely wasn't bedtime music, but something about it was oddly calming. The words and sounds all blended together, and the underlying beat cleared out all the worried thoughts from my head. Hopefully I wouldn't be such an emotional mess in the morning. And at least I had Theo to help me navigate this with my dad. Regardless of how relentless he was, he felt like a good ally.

I was in the process of trying to figure out how to thank Theo for steering me through the day when he said, "Olives are so fascinating. Did you know that the largest type of olive is the donkey olive, and the smallest is the bullet olive? Also, that they can be black, purple, green, brown, or pink? Or that the average olive tree lives somewhere between three hundred and six hundred years? I did some light reading up on them while I waited for Yiannis to bring out your suitcase."

I couldn't help the smile that crept over my face. "You still can't call me Olive, Theo."

He threw one hand in the air. "Who's calling you Olive? I'm merely reciting some *interesting facts*. Also"—I heard him take a deep breath—"do you think you can trust your dad? Because I do."

Nope. I wasn't going there. Not tonight. "Good night, Theo," I said forcefully.

And then we were quiet for real.

Chapter Eight

#8. TWO PHOTOGRAPHS OF MY MOTHER, TAKEN WITH VINTAGE POLAROID 600 CAMERA

According to family lore, my mom had decided to be a lawyer at the ripe old age of seven, after settling a dispute on a playground. She was on track to start law school, but after she had me, my parents decided to work for a few years instead. One of their jobs was with an estate clean-out company. My dad turned out to be great at estate sales. Once he found my mom a Givenchy dress exactly like the one Audrey Hepburn wore in Breakfast at Tiffany's, and another time he found me a hand-painted miniature tea set, where each cup was shaped like a different songbird.

The cameras, he bought for himself. He said that if they were good enough for Andy Warhol, then they were good enough for Nico Varanakis. I remember him taking dozens of photographs of my mother, but these were the only two I found. In the photographs, she's wearing a sundress and

*a wide-brim hat, and she's smiling a deliriously happy smile
that I've never seen in real life. When he left, I think he took
that smile with him.*

I THOUGHT THERE WAS NO WAY I'D SLEEP. EVEN WHEN I'M
not six inches away from a decidedly intriguing boy who was
decidedly not my boyfriend, I'm a terrible sleeper. Along with
the whole night-drowning thing, I talk and laugh and even
cry in my sleep, and once I woke up on our front lawn in the
middle of a cold snap wearing nothing but pajama shorts and
an embarrassing T-shirt my mom and James got me on their
anniversary trip to Paris that says I'M LE TIRED.

But in the weird bookstore tree house with Theo's French
rap blaring? I didn't merely sleep. I reposed. I *slumbered*. From
the moment I closed my eyes to the moment I opened them,
I don't think I moved a single inch. I was snug, my blankets
tucked around me in a warm cocoon, and the music had been
turned down to a low thrum. Theo's bed was already empty,
his sheets pulled up and tucked in neatly, his pillow fluffed to
perfection. Despite his messy appearance, he apparently kept
his environment very neat.

Dax! my brain yelled as my eyes roamed Theo's things,
and instantly my chest tightened with anxiety. Had he texted
me yet?

I rolled over and grabbed my phone from where I'd

stashed it on my shelves. Messages from my mom. Lots of messages from my mom. While I'd been reenacting a scene out of *Sleeping Beauty*, she'd been pummeling me with texts for almost an hour now.

Liv, call me.

Liv, call me this instant.

Are you alive?

I am turning Julius loose on your Urban Decay eye shadow palette.

3 . . . 2 . . .

I sighed heavily and hit dial, rubbing the sleep out of my eyes. When was the last time I'd felt this rested? My body was so happy it was humming. Also, the light filtering in through the window was a warm, sunny yellow, and when I inhaled, I caught a whiff of salt water. Maybe I could get used to island life.

"Liv?" My mom answered on the second ring. She sounded slightly out of breath, and there was a familiar steady *thwack-thwack-thwack* in the background.

"Mom, are you on your treadmill? What time is it there?"

"Almost ten p.m. The Stench called an early meeting and I had to miss my morning run."

The Stench was my mom's private nickname for her law firm's managing partner. Along with a sordid history of taking credit for work he hadn't done, he wore heavy colognes, took long, sweaty runs during his lunch break, and liked to let his damp running clothes accumulate in a bag situated near his office door. He'd also once—and this was possibly his greatest offense—*microwaved a plate of halibut and Brussels sprouts in the room next to her office.* Normal Mom hated The Stench, but Pregnant Mom had an active bounty on his head.

I leaned back against the wall, preparing for one of her stories. "What did he do now?"

"I won't get into it, but it involved tuna fish." She made a gagging noise that didn't sound entirely under her control.

I stifled a laugh, and I heard her adjust the speed on the treadmill, probably an increase. My mom never missed her daily run. Ever. Not on weekends or vacations, or even when she was sick. Not even during her pregnancies when every-thing made her throw up and she had to wear a heavy-duty torture-device-looking belt thing that made sure her belly stayed supported. As annoying as her strict habit sometimes was, there was also something comforting in knowing exactly where she was. I could picture her in her running shorts, her blond hair in a tight ponytail, her pale skin glowing with sweat. People never assumed we were mother and daughter, likely because we looked so different from each other, and also because you would have to pay me close to a million dol-lars and hire a pack of vengeful hippos to chase me to get me to participate in one of the half-marathons she was always signing up for. But I digress.

"Liv, why didn't you call to check in last night? I was so worried."

I hesitated, studying the way the sunlight coming through the window played over my legs. Part of me wanted to keep being angry at her for sending me here, but the fact was—the fact had always been—she was the one who had stuck with me. It counted for a lot.

I took a deep breath. "Dad had this little party set up for me, and then when I got to my bed, I was so jet-lagged that I fell asleep." I looked over at my shelf. My oil pastels sat looking at me, and maybe it was my imagination, but I got a whiff of their waxy scent.

Her voice softened. "He threw you a party?"

"For my birthday. He gave me a custom oil pastel set from an art shop in France. And he timed my arrival with the sunset here. It was . . ." I tried to make it sound like it was no big deal, but thinking about it made my eyes feel like they were going to well up again, and the last thing I wanted to do was make her cry too. Best to stick with the facts. "He'd gone to a lot of work."

Despite my efforts, she definitely heard my emotion, because there was a long pause, followed by a series of beeps as she hit stop on her treadmill. "He was always good at birthdays," she said, and now it sounded like maybe she was battling her own emotions. For a couple of seconds, I felt that old familiar ache stretch between us. We'd held that feeling between us for a long time, and no matter how badly it ached, I'd always had her to back me up on it. Not having her here to experience this with me felt wrong.

"Did he tell you about the project yet?" she asked.

"No." I didn't even try to pry it out of her. No matter how many times I'd asked in the week leading up to my trip, she hadn't said a word. All she'd said was *I think you'll enjoy it.* My mom was a vault like that.

"How's the bookstore?"

I slapped my arm down onto the bed. She knew about the bookstore, too? "Mom, how long have you and Dad been talking?"

"Six months," she said.

"Six months?" I knew it shouldn't feel like a betrayal, but it did. We'd shared the loss of my dad together. Why hadn't she brought me in on this?

"Do I even know you?" I tried to make it sound jokey, but it came out serious sounding, and when she spoke again, she matched my tone.

"Liv, I'm sorry to have kept this from you. But I thought it would be best if we approached things with your dad slowly. I wanted to know how he was doing before I allowed him to initiate contact."

Initiate contact? This wasn't an alien encounter. And was that what the postcards were about? A plan to make my dad's reappearance look completely out of the blue? My head immediately went fuzzy with anger, but she quickly jumped in, distracting me from it.

"How amazing is Oia? I looked at photos online all day."

She knew how to pronounce it correctly, which I guess made sense. "It's gorgeous," I admitted. "Lots of dogs and people. And all the buildings are painted white."

"It keeps the houses from getting too hot in the summer. How's the bunk room?"

I gripped the phone tightly. "You know about that, too?"

"Your father was worried that you might be uncomfortable with the setup. I told him I thought you'd be fine with it. After all, you do have a brother."

"Who's *five*," I said in disbelief. Since when was my mom so chill about boys? Even though I got the sense that she trusted me, I had a Cinderella curfew at home. *Midnight, not one minute later*, and ever since I'd started dating Dax, we'd had what I now called our monthly Safe Sex Summit, in which she asked if I had any questions, reviewed how to give and receive consent, and offered to take me to Planned Parenthood to discuss birth control options. I ran my hand through my snarled hair. "Mom, you sent me to Greece with explicit instructions not to talk to any boys."

"But this is one your father knows very well," she said smoothly. "Do you feel safe around Theo?"

"Well . . ." She had me there, because the truth was, I did feel safe around Theo. Something about him felt . . . trustworthy. "Yeah, I do," I admitted.

"Good," she said, like that settled things. Her voice lowered a register. "I really think you can trust your instincts. Is he cute?"

I threw my non-phone hand up in disbelief. Who *was* this person? "It doesn't *matter* if he's cute."

She didn't even try to disguise the smile in her voice. "I'll take that as a yes. It might be fun to have some time with another teen. He can show you around. Introduce you to the local scene."

"The local scene? Mooooooom." This was definitely all about Dax. She wanted me to get to know some other boys in hopes that I would forget all about the one back home. I was about to call her out on her anti-Dax campaign—when I noticed an envelope taped to the bookcase door with the word KALAMATA written across the front in all caps. "Mom, I'll call you back."

"Tonight. You'll call me tonight," she said merrily. "Now, go enjoy that island. And remember to *wear your sunscreen*."

I honestly couldn't handle it.

Inside the envelope was a single sheet of paper, and when I unfolded it, it took me several moments to figure out what I was looking at.

OLIVE VARANAKIS

Dubois Productions presents:

FINDING ATLANTIS,

a National Geographic documentary

ON LOCATION:
Day 1 of 5

Nea Kameni Island, Santorini,
84700, Greece
28 degrees C / 23 degrees C
Sunrise 6:04 a.m. ~
Sunset 8:42 p.m.

GENERAL CALL TIME:
8:00 A.M.*

Shooting (on location)—
10:00 a.m.
Lunch—12:30 p.m.
Est. Wrap—5:00 p.m.

---

*Meet at the Lost Bookstore of Atlantis for orientation
meeting and transport to location.
(Nomikos Street, Oia, 847 02)

FILMING NOTES:
History of volcanic eruption

ETC. NOTES:
Dress for sea/volcano

*** ALL CREW EXPECTED TO MEET ON TIME,
NO EXCEPTIONS ***

No way.

This was a *call sheet*. I knew because I'd seen variations of these strewn around Dax's house whenever his dad's production company was working on a new film. Dax had explained that call sheets were daily schedules used to tell the crew where they needed to be and what they needed to be doing on each day of filming.

We were making a movie? Not a movie. A *documentary*. For . . . I scanned the paper again and almost fell over. *National Geographic*? Could that be true?

I stared at it for a good thirty seconds. I mean, it *looked* true. This whole thing looked exactly like the call sheets at Dax's.

My heart thundered in my chest as I scanned the paper again. *Dubois Productions*. The logo was a simple circle with a film reel through the center. Yes, the film was about Atlantis. But this looked legitimate. Also, my name was at the top of this call sheet. Did that mean I was going to be a part of it?

Excitement flared in my stomach. I mean, yes, this film was about my least favorite topic, but it was a *film*. Experience on a film set would look incredible on my college applications. I'd read online that RISD preferred when applicants had experience in multiple artistic fields—

Okay. Now I was getting ahead of myself.

I glanced over the notes. General call time was eight a.m.,

and I needed to be dressed for sea/volcano? What did that mean? I checked my phone. 7:57.

Three minutes?

My intent was to burst into action, but the latch was closed on the bookcase, and despite how easy Theo had made it look when he'd closed it last night, it took me several moments of fumbling to figure out the latch, probably because my hands were so shaky. First you had to get a good grasp on the handle, and then you had to slide out a lever, which stuck a little, and push while leaning out over the gap, and then my arms slipped and—

Gravity.

As I plunged gracelessly to the earth, a few things immediately became clear:

1. The Lost Bookstore of Atlantis was not the early-morning nest of tranquility I'd assumed it to be. It was, in fact, a thriving place of business.
2. The bunk room must have superior soundproofing.
3. This was going to hurt.

The sound of my body colliding with the floor ricocheted through the tiny room, forcing every eye my way. The trio of Japanese women I'd landed in the center of had clearly not been expecting a pajama-clad American to tumble into their midst, because they let out a trio of high-pitched shrieks.

Luckily, I'd crossed that threshold where you're so embarrassed that you don't actually feel pain, so instead of lying there in a tangle and checking my bones for fractures like I should have, I jumped to my feet and made a big show of straightening the books. "So sorry. My bed's up there and I'm not used to it yet."

"Ehhhh?" the woman closest to me said, tugging at the strap of her colorful sundress.

"Bed." I crossed my arms over my pajama top. Also, what did my hair look like right now? "Sorry, everyone. Carry on."

She gave me a pitying look. Then she and her friends hurried away, casting backward glances at me.

"Olive Varanakis, live and in person," a deep, rumbly voice boomed. I spun around, coming face-to-face with an Indian man in his early to mid twenties. He was tall and lanky, with long giraffe eyelashes, terrible posture, and tragically Shaggy-esque facial hair. His T-shirt said BOOKMARKS ARE FOR QUITTERS, and he wore a red name tag that read GEOFFREY THE CANADIAN, which despite being oddly descriptive only brought up more questions.

"Are you an employee?" I asked, suddenly realizing I wasn't wearing a bra. What time was I going to have to get up around here? Six? Seven?

"Yes. I'm Geoffrey from Canada." He tapped his badge.

"There used be a Geoffrey from Wales. He was only here a few months, but it really made a mess of things. Theo's the one who made the tag for me. A bit of a joker, that one."

"Ah," I managed. Customers were still staring at me, and I risked one hand to attempt to smooth my hair. Judging by their stares, I'd definitely bypassed the just-rolled-out-of-bed mussed look and jumped straight into the wind-tunnel-meets-electroshock-therapy look. "Well, I'd better . . ." I edged toward the cave, but Geoffrey reached for my hand and pumped my arm enthusiastically.

"So sorry I missed your party. My girlfriend, Mathilde, had a show in Athens last night, and I didn't get in until this morning. She's a principal ballerina with Greek National Opera. They work them like dogs over there. No, like *hedgehogs*."

Was that meant to be a joke? "Ah, the industrious hedgehog," I managed, and he blinked at me.

Change of plans. Maybe if I let him talk, he'd give me my hand back? "Your girlfriend's a ballerina? How interesting." I edged my bare feet toward the door.

Geoffrey's arm stopped moving, but he held my hand firmly in his. "Olive, have you ever been in *love*?" His voice had gone wistful and serious, and I froze before slowly turning back to him. Was he kidding? He didn't look like he was kidding. But who asks a question like that to a brand-new acquaintance? Also, why was his hand so damp?

"Hey, Geoffrey, I actually go by Liv. And I have a boyfriend—"

"Mathilde is the peanut butter to my jelly," he interrupted, blinking his giraffe eyelashes. "The cream to my coffee. The dragon heartstring to my walnut wand."

His walnut *what*?

"Um," I squeaked.

As if drawn by my horror, Ana miraculously appeared at my elbow, whisking me away. "'Walnut wand' is a Harry Potter reference," she whispered. "Geoffrey is our assistant manager. He's great with books, terrible at social interactions. Give him some time. He will grow on you."

Ana wore a simple shapeless black dress that would have looked like a garbage bag on anyone else but came across as chic and effortless on her. A long pair of earrings that looked suspiciously like fishhooks dangled from her ears, and she was wearing a different shade of red lipstick today, darker but equally vibrant.

"If possible, you look even more beautiful this morning than you did last night," she said, echoing my thoughts about her. She ruffled my bangs. "So chic! You were made for this messy look."

She was probably being overly nice, but I felt my embarrassment dissipate anyway. "I wasn't expecting the bookstore to be this crowded. Or even open."

"We open early during cruise ship season. I should have warned you. Aside from the fall, how was your first night?"

"Great." I shook my head, still in disbelief over how rested I felt. It was so *novel*. Suddenly I remembered the call sheet in my hand and held it out. "Is this real?"

She snatched the paper from me, then sighed heavily. "Oh, Theo. I see he has officially ruined the surprise."

Excitement flickered in my chest. It would not be stopped. "That's what the mystery project is? We're making a movie?"

"A documentary." She glanced up at the vintage yellow school clock tacked above the door. "I believe your dad is planning a special team breakfast where he will tell you everything. Theo is waiting on the roof, but don't let him talk you into a rush. We're on Santorini time, and that means *enjoy*."

She winked one of her long-lashed eyes at me, a move she was clearly born for, and then sashayed back into the crowd. It was probably disloyal of me to think, but if my dad hadn't at least tried to date her, he was a fool.

I liked the sound of a "team breakfast." And despite the fact that I had no idea what she meant by "Santorini time," I definitely didn't want to keep a team of people waiting for me. How many crew members did it take to make a documentary? And did my dad really want me to help out? I hurried into the cave, where my suitcase sat in the tiny space looking like the overstuffed monstrosity that it really was. Had I seriously thought I'd need all this stuff? It was a Mediterranean island, not an arctic expedition. It was amazing what twenty-four hours could do for perspective.

I splashed water onto my face, applied my best five-minute makeup, brushed my teeth, and attempted to reassemble my bangs into something less feral-looking. Now, what to wear?

Volcano hunting was not the sort of thing my capsule wardrobe covered, but after churning everything around in my suitcase for a while, I finally went for my two favorite items. A pair of worn-in-just-right cutoff shorts and my favorite striped tee, both of which I wore as often as I thought I could get away with. At the last minute I added a simple pair of gold studs and my initial necklace, the one I'd made in a summer jewelry-making class. *L.* Now I felt like myself.

I briefly considered going without my backpack, but that was beyond my capabilities as a human, so up in the bunk room I carefully packed it with the bare necessities: a handful of pencils, my current sketchbook, my phone (still nothing from Dax), and my sunscreen. Finally, I closed the bunk room carefully behind me and burst out onto the street.

Oia was calm and relatively spacious in the morning, a scrubbed-down version of what I'd seen the night before. The streets contained only a few tourists and the sun glimmered across the white surfaces, making the marble walkway sparkle.

The day was going to be hot, but for now we were tiptoeing around the edge of the sun, the breeze from the ocean keeping the air comfortable.

Looking out over the white angularity of the village, a wave of melancholy hit me. *This is where my dad has been.* All that time at home I'd never known how to picture where he was or what his life could be like without us, but now I knew. Of *course* he was from an eclectic village perched on the edge of the sea—why wouldn't he have left our tiny apartment back home for this? But what about us? Hadn't we been worth more than a village?

Before my feelings could hijack me, I readjusted my backpack and climbed the steps to the roof, forcing myself to even out my breath. There might be other crew members up there.

Up on the terrace, the remnants of my birthday party had been cleared and swept away, turning the rooftop back into an open-air bookstore that held exactly none of the stress I'd felt the night before. Sunlight bounced off the colorful book murals on the wall, and customers browsed the bookcases or sat reading in the nook. It took me a moment to spot Theo, and when I did, my stress levels soared. Theo clearly had no fear of heights, because he sat on the edge of the rooftop, his legs dangling over the side of the cliff, laptop on his lap, giant headphones encasing his ears, completely engrossed in whatever he was watching.

As a general rule, I try to avoid sending people sprawling to their untimely doom, so I approached cautiously, gently touching his shoulder and speaking in a quiet voice. "Theo, I got the call sheet."

"Kalamata! Finally!" He swung his legs around, spinning to face me. He was dressed in an outfit almost identical to the one he'd worn yesterday—sneakers, a black T-shirt, and black jeans—but today his hair was contained by a baseball cap. His camera lay at his feet.

His *camera*. Of course he had his camera with him. And then I saw the word stenciled onto his shirt: CREW.

I grabbed his hand and pulled him to his feet. "Are we really making a film?"

His face split into a smile. "So you *do* get excited about things, Kalamata."

I bit my lip, forcefully suppressing my smile. I didn't want to give Theo the satisfaction. "I'm late. Did we miss the call time?"

Theo shook his head. "We moved back our call time so you could get some sleep. Your dad thought you needed it. Especially after I told him you were snoring like a wildebeest."

My face went red hot. "I do not *snore*." But did I? I'd worked so hard to make sure no one ever saw me sleep that I actually had no idea if that was true or not. I'd have to check with my mom.

He rested his hand reassuringly on my shoulder. "Yes,

Kalamata. You really, really do. Did you meet Geoffrey the Canadian?"

I liked the weight of his hand on my shoulder perhaps a little too much, so I quickly moved away, focusing my eyes on the water. "Yes. I actually sort of belly flopped out of the bunks. I took out a stack of books on my way down and heavily traumatized a few customers." The ocean was a bright glimmering turquoise, and all the sunlight bouncing off it already hurt my eyes. I was going to need to add sunglasses to my backpack. All this light would be great on camera.

"Well *done*," Theo said, surveying me with new respect. "Did Geoffrey talk about his pretend girlfriend?"

"Pretend?" I shifted my gaze back to him. "No, he told me about this girlfriend who's a ballerina. Her name was . . ."

"Mathilde?" Theo sighed heavily. "Of course he told you about her. She isn't real. Every few days he leaves to go visit her on tour, but no one has any idea what he is actually doing. My guess is a lot of weed."

I turned to see if he was kidding, but his face was completely serious. "He has a made-up girlfriend? Why?"

Theo flipped his hat around, turning the brim to the back, and let out an exaggerated sigh. "If you figure it out, let me know, will you?"

"But . . ." I trailed off, staring down at the bookstore. This place was getting stranger and stranger.

When I turned back to him, Theo was taking in my outfit. "Is that what you're wearing?"

I stepped back, gesturing to my shorts and shoes nervously. "Uh, yes. This is what I am currently wearing. Why?"

He shook his head so hard that the tangled ends of his hair flew around. "No, I mean, you look amazing, but I'm not sure how great sandals will be for hiking the volcano."

"We're *hiking* the volcano?" I asked, my eyes flicking uneasily toward the water.

He snapped his fingers. "I forgot! I have a present for you." He unzipped his backpack and tossed me a T-shirt rolled up like a burrito. "Sorry if it's too big. I didn't know what size to make you."

I shook it out and held it up, rubbing the fabric between my fingers. CREW. The shirt was too big, but I could make it work. "Does the whole crew wear these?" Excitement was building in my chest.

Theo shrugged happily. "All two of us. Your dad wears his usual clothes. If he's on camera, he tries to dress up more."

"What?" My heart sank, all delusions of grandeur slipping out of my grasp like an errant balloon. If there were only two of us, then this wasn't a real movie. This was . . . I don't know. A potential YouTube video? A home movie? Whatever it was, it was amateur. "All two of us," I repeated, not bothering to keep the disappointment out of my voice. "There isn't a crew."

"What? We *are* the crew," Theo said, putting his hand back on my shoulder. "I handle the camera and most of the editing. Your dad has been doing the writing and on-camera work. When your dad said he needed help this summer, he really meant it."

I held up the call sheet weakly, not ready to give up on the dream. "Let me guess. You're the one who went to all the work of typing this up for me?"

"Part of my job," he said. "I'm an early riser, and I like to print them out at the bookstore very first thing. It keeps us on task for the day."

"And Dubois Productions is . . . ?"

He smiled. "Me. I'm Theo Dubois."

That did it. My last remaining threads of hope slipped out of my grasp. My dad hadn't suddenly gained credibility. His plans were as homemade and unattainable as they'd always been. A sick feeling twisted in my stomach. This was why people laughed at him. And why was Theo playing into it? He acted like he cared about my dad. Did he not realize that my dad was going to get hurt?

I swallowed, hard. "I guess I hoped this was a bit more . . . legitimate."

Theo turned to me, his eyebrows bent into a question. "More legitimate?"

"Yes, I . . ." *I thought more people believed him. I thought I*

wouldn't have to feel so stupid about having once believed him.
That was the core of it. A shudder worked its way down my
spine. There was no way I was going to open that can of
worms in front of Theo. "Never mind. Let's go talk to my dad.
I'm sure he'll explain it."

But less than twenty-four hours in and I already knew
Theo wasn't the letting-it-go type. As I'd predicted, he stayed
right where he was, putting both hands on my shoulders,
his eyes meeting mine. "Kalamata, it's *National Geographic*.
How much more legitimate can you get? Besides, technology
is so good these days, you don't have to have a giant crew
to make something worthwhile. All we need is my camera,
drone, and GoPro, and a program to edit with. We're *more*
than equipped."

I took a risk and met Theo's eyes. His jaw was set, and
his eyes were intense. Focused. He meant it. Despite his
unwavering belief in my dad, Theo didn't seem delusional. He
seemed smart. And committed. And possibly even talented.
But I wasn't going to jump back on board without some solid
reasons.

"But you're saying the film is for National Geographic,"
I said cautiously. "What does that mean? They've hired him?
He's hoping they'll hire him?"

Theo dropped his hands, adjusting his hat. The heat was
already starting to warm things up, and he had a thin layer

of sweat on his upper lip that shone in a surprisingly pleasant way. "They're doing a series on explorers, and they want a mini episode on Atlantis. Your dad and I have been putting out content since earlier this fall, and they found us on his YouTube channel."

Yes, my dad had a YouTube channel. And yes, ever since it appeared a few years ago, I'd lived in constant fear that someone from my school would find it. But National Geographic had reached out to him? I let that sink in for a minute, allowing the news to simmer in my chest. Theo was right. Regardless of how small our crew was, National Geographic was National Geographic. It was one of the most well-known names in the science and exploration fields. If the documentary was successful, it would show everyone, me included, that my dad wasn't as delusional as we had all thought he was. And that felt . . .

Well, it felt like standing on top of a Greek island on a hot summer morning with the chance for vindication unfurling in the sea air. It felt like freedom. And relief. And a reason for everything my mom and I had been through.

And by that, I mean it felt *good*. Very, very good.

But I had one more question. "What about money? Is this like volunteer work, or is he being paid?"

Theo blinked uncertainly, and I realized I must sound like a complete money-grubber. I held up one hand. "I want to know if National Geographic has enough skin in the game to back it.”

Skin in the game was a phrase I'd heard James use about some of his corporate accounts, and I wondered if I'd need to explain it to Theo, but he nodded, his face still a question. “I think so? I mean, it isn't a huge amount of money, but it's enough to get the film made and have some leftover to fly a certain someone to Santorini.”

My heart leapt. Money was good. “So . . . it's real.”

“It's real, Kalamata.” He was still studying me. “Did it need money and a backer to be real?”

“No,” I said, but my head nodded yes, so that was all kinds of confusing.

“Kalamata—”

“Forget it. How do you want me to help?” I interrupted Theo. We didn't have time to dissect my motives. We were making a *film*.

Theo hesitated for another moment; then a smile overtook his face. “Kalamata, I want you to be my director of photography. Someone to make the shots look good. Your dad thought your art experience would make you a good cinematographer, and after looking at all your work online, I think he's right. You know how to put things together.”

“You mean my collages?” They were hardly the same thing. And I'd heard the word “cinematographer,” but that didn't mean I had any idea what it *meant*.

"And your paintings," Theo said. "They're so good."

"Thanks, but . . ." A pit formed in my stomach. They may be giving me too much credit. What if I let down the entire project? "I don't know if I'm the right person for this. Shouldn't he hire someone with actual experience?"

"You're the right person. Your dad knows it, and I know it too," he said confidently. "Also, did you know that the oldest producing olive tree is on Crete? It's four thousand years old and is still producing olives. And have you ever thought about all the different ways to use olives? You can use their oil, bake them into bread, put them on pizzas. . . . They're just so versatile; they make everything better."

"Theo!" I groaned, but I was smiling again.

He gestured to the T-shirt. "After you change, I'll take you to your dad's office. Sound okay?"

Instantly I tried to picture my dad in a suit and tie, carrying a briefcase the way James did, but my mind refused to conjure up *any* image. "My dad has an office?"

He grinned, flipping his hat brim forward again. "I think it's safe to say that there are a lot of things you don't know about him, Kalamata."

"It's mutual," I said.

Chapter Nine

#9. WORN COPY OF PLATO'S TIMAEUS AND CRITIAS, MY DAD'S NOTES PENCILED INTO THE MARGINS

Most kids would have no idea what this book is, but most kids don't have my father. It's one of Plato's dialogues, basically a written-down version of a conversation, and the main source of everything we know about the city of Atlantis.

My mom worked evenings usually at restaurants, so for a long time it was only my dad and me at night. He'd make our favorite dinners—buttered noodles for me, sausage and vegetables for him. And then we'd read Plato, keeping a dictionary handy for the words we didn't understand, until my mom came home and it was time for him to head out to whatever overnight job he was currently working.

For my second-grade talent show I did a dramatic

*recitation of my favorite line of Timaeus and Critias: "And
in a single day and night of misfortune all your warlike men
in a body sank into the earth, and the island of Atlantis in
like manner disappeared in the depths of the sea."*

*The kid who went after me played "Twinkle, Twinkle,
Little Star" on his violin, and the one after that did a
tumbling routine. Shocking that I never fit in.*

I ANTICIPATED ANOTHER RUN, AND I WAS RIGHT. WHILE
the rest of the village was leisurely starting their mornings,
drinking coffee and finishing up their crossword puzzles, or
whatever it was Greeks did first thing in the morning, Theo
took off at a pace slightly below hurtling, twisting down Main
Street with me in tow. He stopped twice, once to leap over
and then pet a furry heap of a dog, and another time to film
a church bell that began to ring. Finally, he slid to a stop in
front of a small two-story building with an empty pastry case
in the window. The name MARIA'S was scrawled in gold let-
tering over the door, and a delightfully buttery smell wafted
out from the edges.

"Where's his office?" I asked, checking out my reflection
in the window. I'd changed into a pair of sandals without
heels and attempted to knot my CREW T-shirt at the side
so it didn't look like I was wearing a gigantic muumuu, but
it had only partially worked. I looked decidedly un-Liv-like,

and not at all like someone working on a serious documentary, but the hopeful balloon swelling in my chest was hard to ignore. *National Geographic.* This was exactly the kind of thing we'd dreamed about. *Is this really happening?*

Theo knocked on the door. "You're looking at it. From five a.m. to eight a.m. he has the entire upper floor."

The balloon deflated slightly but managed to persist. "So not a *real* office," I said, but Theo ignored me and rapped on the glass.

Within seconds a gray-haired woman wearing a polka-dot blue housedress appeared at the door, letting out a puff of warm, sugary air, which made my sugar-loving soul all kinds of happy.

"Meet Maria," Theo said.

"O-live!" she sang. She had crinkly cheeks and dark, shiny eyes.

I was swiftly giving up hope on being Liv here. "*Kaliméra*," I said. Saying a Greek word felt a little less awkward than it had the night before, but I still felt embarrassed in front of Theo. I shot a covert glance at him. My accent must be terrible.

Luckily, the bar was set extremely low for me. Maria cheered at my attempt, then erupted into Greek exclamations and patted my cheeks half a dozen times before leading us inside.

Inside, the room was dim, with chairs stacked on top of

several wooden tables. The shutters were still drawn, and a mop sat drying in one corner. Maria pointed up at the ceiling and smiled at me. "Your father," she said. "Your father, he is . . ." She looked at Theo, then said a word I didn't understand.

"Special," Theo said.

Ah. That was one way to put it. "Thank you, Maria." Anticipation raced through me. I was about to see my dad. Again. "Upstairs?"

"Yes!" Maria sang.

As we made our way to the steep wooden staircase, disappointment suddenly clouded my mood. "His office is a closed bakery?" I asked Theo. It's not that an actual office would magically restore my confidence in my dad, but it maybe would have helped.

"Maria has a refrigerator and two ovens that she should have replaced ten years ago. He keeps bringing them back from the dead. In exchange she lets him work here."

This was all so familiar. "Like Yiannis the cabdriver. He said he owed my dad a favor."

Theo glanced back at me, one hand on the railing. "You know your dad. Everyone owes him a favor because he's constantly solving their problems. Some of the people in Oia jokingly call him the mayor. He makes things run around here. If anyone has an issue, they go straight to your dad."

Well, that hadn't changed. Every time we'd ever moved into a new apartment or neighborhood, it usually took about twelve minutes before he was inspecting someone's disposal or fixing a kid's bike, which inevitably led to us having dinner invitations for a week straight. He also had the unique ability to make it feel like you were the one doing *him* a favor, which made people love him even more. He'd had loyal devotees everywhere he went. Why had I expected Santorini to be any different?

As we made our way to the top, my hands suddenly felt shaky. *Dad.* This was sighting number two. Was I ready?

No. But my feet kept moving anyway.

As my nerves increased, the dimness evaporated into sunlight. The upper level of the bakery was an open-air patio featuring several small wooden tables and an exquisite view of the caldera. A light breeze ruffled a set of canvas curtains tied to the rooftop's railings, and the air smelled fresh and salted.

"Welcome!" my dad called, and I spun around to see him standing at a table. My heart flipped like it had yesterday. Seeing him was so *disorienting.* This morning he wore a faded long-sleeve shirt, board shorts, and a wide hat that made him look like a Greek version of Indiana Jones, which was massively embarrassing but also sort of worked. He'd staked out two tables, and stood surrounded by a ridiculous amount of ragtag gear, including an old dented tackle box, a monstrous backpack, a cooler, a snarl of extension cords, plus a stack of notebooks and several large maps. The maps . . .

Pain washed over me in a tidal wave, and I had to look away. "Good morning." I was surprised to hear my voice come out normal.

"Good morning, Liv." He said "Liv" carefully and precisely, like he'd spent last night practicing it. Hearing him call me by my new name did nothing to improve the mixed-up feeling in my stomach. "How did you sleep?"

"Like I mentioned, she snored like a wildebeest," Theo said. "It was almost as bad as you."

"I do not snore," I protested, whirling on Theo. He'd somehow managed to get his camera out without me noticing, and he was filming me. *Again.* I swatted at the camera, but he shuffled back a few steps, his grin appearing underneath the viewfinder.

"You do. Just like your dad," Theo said. "I had to turn up the music."

"You have yet to capture any proof of my snoring," my dad said. "And until I hear it with my own ears, I refuse to believe that Liv does either."

"Liv" sounded a tiny bit more natural the second time. And I liked that he was backing me up on the snoring thing, but I hadn't come halfway across the world to talk about how well we had or had not slept. Time to get down to business.

I held up the call sheet. "Congratulations on the documentary, Dad. It sounds really . . ." I took a deep breath, fumbling for a word. "Promising."

Promising? Not quite the right word.

But my dad's face lit up anyway, his smile so bright I could hardly bear to look at it. Energy rippled through him, and I could tell he wanted to come hug me. Instead he tapped his fingers against the edge of the chair. "Thank you, Liv. And what I said in the postcard is true. I really do need your help. Our deadline is tight, and we could use some extra eyes on the overall visuals."

"I'm not sure I can help with that, but I can try." I hesitated, then my curiosity spilled over. "So, what is the documentary about exactly? The Santorini theory?"

Saying that aloud made me feel light-headed. Post-Dad, learning that most people thought Atlantis was a hoax had felt like dismantling gravity—painful and disorienting—and now here I was treating it like it was something to be considered.

His face suddenly went serious. "Partially. I have some new theories and evidence to add, and I want to explain the entire thing to you, start to finish."

Evidence. There was that word again. My heart was galloping now. What was with all the suspense? "Okay . . ."

He gestured to the chair. "Why don't you sit down? As

the Greek philosopher Plato said, 'No important endeavor should ever be attempted without coffee.'"

I couldn't help the laugh. "Plato did *not* say that."

He smiled his crooked smile, and the familiar look made my chest feel warm. "You're right. *I* said that. But it's true, isn't it? And my guess is that you've graduated from stealing sips of grown-ups' coffees to a cup of your own."

He'd guessed right. And besides, I couldn't argue with that kind of logic.

"I'll get Maria," Theo said. He'd somehow managed to make me forget he was there, and when I spun around, the camera was still aimed at us.

"Don't you need a release form or something?" I asked. "Because you do *not* have my permission."

Theo grinned, then darted for the stairs, taking his camera with him.

And then . . . it was just us. For the first time in almost nine years. A thick and uncomfortable silence seeped into my dad's makeshift office. I tried to ignore it by fiddling with my shirt and pretending to check out the view, but who was I kidding? This could not be more awkward. My dad seemed to be struggling for words too. Finally, he pointed at my shirt. "I see Theo has given you a uniform."

I nodded, my move embarrassingly exaggerated. "Yeah. And typed up a call sheet. Is he always so . . . ?"

"Intense?" My dad smiled. "The best ones always are. He cares a great deal. About this project."

"And about you," I blurted out, stating the obvious.

"Yes."

Another long, awkward silence.

"So . . . what's all this?" I slid into my chair and looked down at the map, but I regretted it immediately. It was almost an exact replica of the one I had buried deep in my suitcase. I may be nine years older and in an entirely different country, but looking at the map's worn-out edges took me right back to our kitchen table all those years ago. No wonder he hadn't taken the map with him. He hadn't needed it.

"Oh," I whispered. My heart was in my throat.

My dad attempted to meet my eyes. "Look familiar?"

Duh, I wanted to say. No matter how much I didn't want it to be, the map's image may as well be burned on the back of my eyelids.

Luckily, Theo and Maria appeared, coffees in hand.

"Maria! *S'efcharistó!*" my dad said, jumping up to give her a hand.

Maria clucked happily, passing me a doll-size cup that nearly made me laugh. *This* was my Plato-prescribed coffee? Was I supposed to take it like a shot? Sip it slowly? I looked at Theo and my dad for clues. They both seemed to be having a spiritual experience, sipping slowly and reverently, so under Maria's watchful eye, I went in for a large sip.

Wrong move. I coughed, loudly, and Theo had to whack me on the back a few times. "Kalamata, breathe!"

It tasted like melted cedar and was more bitter than anything I'd ever tried. If this was what my dad was used to, no wonder he'd always called American coffee "weak as a kitten."

"Sorry," I managed. "Down the wrong pipe?"

Maria looked at me in concern. "Very good, yes?"

"So good," I managed. I put the cup to my lips, but the second she turned away I set it down, leaning in to Theo. "Please tell me this is not what all coffee tastes like in Greece?" I whispered.

His mouth dropped open. "Of course it is. Boiled instead of brewed, the way it was intended to be made," he said, not bothering to whisper. "And don't you dare offend Maria—she has ties to the Greek Mafia. Cross her and you'll sleep with the fishes." He held up two fingers, pointing from his eyes to mine.

"Nice *Godfather* quote," I said, shooting a look at Maria. He was joking, 93 percent sure. Still, I brought the cup to my mouth again. Sip number two went just as badly, and I couldn't help the face I made. Luckily, Maria and my dad were deep in conversation and didn't seem to notice.

"Okay now. You work!" Maria suddenly shifted toward

me, giving my shoulder one last squeeze before leaving us—the *crew*—alone. My gaze went right back down to the map. I couldn't help it. Up close it was pretty clear that this was Map 2.0, or our first map's older, smarter sister. The island had been drawn in much more detail, and instead of all the scattered, sprawling writing, the margins had been sectioned off and filled with neatly written Greek characters. And not a single serpent cartoon in sight. His theories had obviously evolved. And I had not been a part of that.

A big, heavy door swung shut on me. Rejection. After all this time it shouldn't hurt like this, but it did. It really, really did. I felt a sudden, confusing homesickness for our original map. And by this point, my anticipation was killing me. Had his theory really evolved? If so, how?

Curiosity and I wrestled for a few moments before I, as usual, lost. "Okay, what is this all about?" I blurted out, gesturing to the map.

My dad set his cup down, his eyes soft. "Let's begin at the beginning. Liv, how do we know about Atlantis in the first place?"

Liv again. Every time he said it, I had to regain my balance. I forced my eyes to his. "We know about it because of the Greek philosopher Plato."

He slid a sketchbook out into the center of the table and lightning fast drew a cartoon version of Plato, complete with a beard, toga, and large book, then looked up at me seriously.

I stifled a laugh. His theories may have evolved, but his drawings hadn't. They were exactly the same, with big goofy Ping-Pong-ball eyes and small noses. I'd missed seeing his renditions of the world.

He looked up from the pad. "Good. And who did Plato hear it from?"

A quiz. And fortunately—or unfortunately—I knew all the answers. I wanted to pretend I hadn't thought about them in years, but the truth was, I had. All the time. "Plato heard it from Solon, who was a famous Greek politician and poet."

"Not quite," Theo said. "Solon lived two hundred years before Plato, so he never told him in person. Plato knew the story because it had been passed down orally from Solon, who had gone to Egypt and learned about it firsthand from the Egyptian priests."

"Right," I said, barely containing my sigh. They had to realize how ridiculous this was. It was like a convoluted game of telephone.

My dad, of course, continued. "And why do we, as people of the twenty-first century, know this story?"

"Because of Plato's dialogues," I said, making sure to beat Theo to the answer. Then, before Dad could ask, I added, "Plato's dialogues were fictionalized conversations used to discuss philosophical topics." *Timaeus and Critias* had sat on my nightstand the way *Charlotte's Web* or *James and the Giant Peach* sat on other kids' bedside tables. And yes, I did have a very weird childhood, thank you very much.

"Excellent. Almost everything we know about Atlantis comes from Plato. Who was Plato?" He capped his pen, then looked at me expectantly.

Who was Plato? Was this a trick? Now they were both looking at me. Last year my history class had studied Plato, and every time the teacher said his name, it had felt like she was referring to an old family friend. It had taken me almost a month to stop flinching when she brought him up. I'd gotten a 99 on my final paper, with a note from my teacher that read *Excellent in-depth understanding of topic.* I'd actually held back.

I dropped my eyes to the cartoon. "He was a Greek philosopher who lived in Athens. He founded the first university in the world. A lot of people consider him the most influential philosopher of all time."

I felt, rather than saw, Theo and my dad share a look. I'd either passed or failed. I couldn't tell which.

My dad added a scroll to Plato's right hand, then gave his beard a few extra squiggles. "What else is he known for?"

I hesitated, and Theo chimed in. "He figured out a lot of scientific truths about the Earth. He was one of the first to say that the Earth isn't flat and that the planets orbit the sun and not the other way around."

Earth not flat. Planets orbit sun. Most influential. My dad scribbled it all at the top. He looked up at us. "Plato studied under Socrates, and later he taught Aristotle. He also founded the first institution of higher learning in Western Civilization. He was one of the most well-known philosophers of his time, and his theories are still taught all over the world. All of this is impressive. But I think there is only one qualification that truly matters." His eyes met mine. "Do you think we can trust him?"

The question startled me, and I flinched, then shot a look at Theo. He'd asked me this exact question in regard to my dad right before bed last night. *Do you think you can trust your dad?* So much for Theo *not* reporting to my dad on our conversation.

"Well . . . ," I hedged. My dad's dark eyes were still on mine, and for a moment I imagined myself saying what I really thought. *Atlantis is a made-up story that an old philosopher told to scare people into avoiding being rich jerks. It was a parable, meant to caution the people of Athens to not be greedy about money, knowledge, and technology. It was never meant to be considered truth. No one was ever meant to try to find it. No one was meant to upend their* lives *over it.* But his eyes were so bright. I forgot how bright they got when we were talking about Atlantis. And when I opened my mouth . . . well . . .

"I'm not sure," I mumbled.

I know. Pathetic. It was almost genetically impossible that

I had descended from a lawyer, and a good one at that.

My dad broke our gaze, then blinked. Once, then twice. "That's okay. In fact, that's more than okay, because it's part of what I'm trying to establish in the documentary."

"Think of it this way," Theo said, setting his elbows on the table and leaning in toward me. "In Plato's time, Solon was one of the most famous and well respected people in history. Everyone knew who he was, so Plato would have been very careful about getting his story right. Also, Plato said a lot of things about the story of Atlantis that show how fantastical he thought it was—how big it was, the elephants, all of that. Why would he express doubt about his own made-up story?"

I hated to admit it, but it was an interesting point. Luckily, a rebuttal quickly came to mind. "But did Plato ever say it was true?"

Theo's eyes lit up. "We have twenty-two documented moments of Plato telling the audience, point-blank, that the story is not a fable; it's *true*."

Twenty-two? That seemed like a lot of work for a lie. Also, Theo would be excellent on my school's debate team. Judging by the way his voice had gotten all fired up, I had a feeling that if I didn't stop him, I might be stuck at this table all day. Time to put an end to this.

I held up one hand. "Fine. What if Plato was telling the truth? Then what?"

A smile spread across my dad's face. "Then we get to talk about Santorini." He flipped to a fresh page of the sketchbook and quickly sketched the island of Santorini. "Theo, what did Plato say specifically about Atlantis?"

Theo straightened in his chair, his smile matching my father's. "He said that an island containing an advanced civilization was destroyed in the space of a few short days. The island was oblong, and it contained rocks in three different colors: white, red, and black. During the destruction, there were floods and earthquakes, and afterward, the sea was impassable."

My dad gestured to the island, aiming a kind smile at me. "What shape is this?"

"Oblong," I admitted. But Santorini's shape didn't prove anything. There had to be hundreds of oblong islands on the earth. What were the chances that my father had been born on the correct one?

Next, he marked three spots near the bottom of the island and scribbled out their names. *Red Beach, Black Beach, White Beach.*

"Wait," I said. "Those are actual places here?"

He looked up, pen still in hand. "Absolutely."

"Also, a hot spring and a cold spring," Theo said. His camera was out again, and he fiddled with the switch. "That's also in the dialogues."

"Most importantly, there's the town of Akrotiri," my dad said. He marked a spot on the lower section. "The Minoans were a highly advanced civilization that lived on Santorini more than three thousand years ago. Unfortunately, their entire civilization was wiped out when Santorini's volcano exploded."

My heart sped up—but only slightly. Yes, the dominoes were lining up, but I'd been on the false-hope train before. I ordered myself to calm down. "Advanced how?" I said, not bothering to hide the skepticism in my voice.

My dad began sketching again, and when I craned my neck to see what it was, I couldn't help a smile. It was a toilet. With eyeballs. "They were advanced because they had toilets?"

He met my grin. "Not just any toilet. The world's first toilet. And literally a thousand years before anyone tried it again. They had them up on the second and third levels of their multilevel homes. The houses even had technology allowing them to be earthquake proof."

"Or at least they did until a large volcano accompanied by floods destroyed their oblong-shaped island," Theo said, making his eyes go all big and scary.

Interesting.

I hadn't known much about the Minoan piece. Or the technology piece, or—

No, Liv. Stop.

"So you think that the Minoans are the real-life Atlanteans?" I meant for my question to sound sarcastic, but intrigue slipped over me, warm as sunshine. I forgot what it felt like once you were in my dad's clutches. He knew exactly what to say. To slowly let go of the doubt swimming inside your brain. And I couldn't help it. He was towing me out. Angling bait.

"Yes," my father said firmly.

"But, Dad . . ." I hesitated. "There are, like, dozens of other theories about where it could be."

"More like hundreds," Theo said. "Morocco, Malta, Spain . . ."

"Right. And I'm sure that all of those places fit the criteria of Plato's descriptions. So why are you so sure it's Santorini? I mean, besides the reasons you've already given me."

It did seem sort of convenient that my father happened to be born on the location of what he believed to be the "correct" theory. Not to mention, a tad biased.

My dad nodded. "Well, location for one. Plato said that Atlantis lay beyond the Pillars of Heracles, which most historians interpret to be the Strait of Gibraltar. That fact alone negates most of the theories out there." He shuffled some papers to produce a map of Europe, then pointed to the spot between Spain and Africa. "It's where the Atlantic meets the Mediterranean Sea. In Plato's time, the Pillars of Heracles represented the dividing line between the known world and unknown world."

"Okay . . . ," I said again, making sure that everyone could tell I was not buying it.

"Nico, tell her," Theo urged. The energy wafting off him hit me full force, and I turned quickly to look at him.

"Tell me what?" I asked.

Silence. My heart began pounding loudly, and I turned to look across the table. "Dad, tell me what?"

My dad hesitated, but when he looked up, his eyes were calm. Focused. "I think I know where the center of Atlantis is located."

There was a long pause in which I waited for a punch line, but none came. Because . . . he believed this. His eyes were eager and too enthusiastic. They looked at me as if he had said something earth-shattering. Or at least *believed* he had. Nope. I wasn't biting. I'd been down this road too many times. "Right . . . ," I said, averting my gaze. "Let me guess, in the center of Santorini?"

Theo shook his head impatiently. "No, he means actual underwater ruins."

Of course he did. I barely contained the facepalm.

I looked away, unable to meet my dad's hopeful expression. I was too embarrassed. For him and his enthusiasm and what I knew to be his absolute 100 percent belief that he was right. "You have an actual *location*?"

"I've narrowed it down to a half-mile radius." My dad hesitated before leaning back in his creaking chair. "For the past few years I've been working with a British Egyptologist at the University of Oxford to connect details from the Egyptian *Book of the Dead* to Plato's dialogues. Her name is Dr. Bilder."

There were Atlantis hunters at Oxford? My face felt hot. "So where is it?"

"There." My dad lifted his arm, and it took me a second to realize what he was doing. He was *pointing*. I let my gaze follow his finger out toward the south end of the caldera. "Near that small island. Aspronisi. We think the temple is within a half-mile radius of it."

I squinted out at the caldera, but it was too bright and I wasn't sure if I was looking at the right place. This made no sense, even for him. "But, Dad." I cupped my hands over my eyes, letting them readjust. "If it's right there, why has no one found it yet?"

"No funding," Theo answered quickly. "No one seems to want to spend the money to actually look for it. That's why we're selling our theories to National Geographic via the documentary. If we can get enough excitement generated around it, then maybe the government will actually invest in an underwater excavation."

"But . . ." I gripped the table, wishing with my entire heart that this whole thing would disappear. "Dad, have you seen it? Any of it?"

Slight pause, then his eyes flicked from the caldera to mine. "I've seen what could be underwater formations, but it's hard to tell if they're natural or not. The problem, of course, is that the volcano erupted in the sixteenth century BC, so it will be difficult to see underwater evidence without proper equipment."

His voice was authoritative and so sure. The implications of it made me want to throw myself into a giant volcano. An *active* giant volcano. Why couldn't he hear how ridiculous he sounded?

I slid a bit lower in my chair, my head turning, trying to make sense of what I was hearing. "So . . . we really are looking for Atlantis." It seemed with my dad, nothing had changed. "We aren't . . . making an informational piece about Atlantis?" My hand waved over the documents: the maps, the scribbles, the notebooks, the drawing. "We are literally going to go out there and look for Atlantis?" My wild treasure-hunting father was still here, in all his tattered glory.

"We're looking for proof of Atlantis," my dad corrected. "We've already found Atlantis; it's Santorini."

Ugh. He was so sure he'd found it. *Found* it. For a second, I pictured Dax, my friends, listening to the whole con-versation, seeing the piles of notebooks, the images tacked to the wall, the declaration of discovering Atlantis. I could hear their laughter, could feel them rolling their eyes. They'd think he was delusional, like I did.

"But if I can find evidence of the Temple of Poseidon," he continued, "then all other theories will be laid to rest."

"Lofty," I managed, and Theo gave me a concerned look.

"Wouldn't have it any other way," Dad replied, winking at me.

I settled into my chair, letting my eyes wander out to the aqua-colored water, the depth and mystery of it. Here's the thing—it wasn't actually that hard for me to imagine that Atlantis was out there. All I had to do was pretend I was eight again. I could see it—the Temple of Poseidon, my dad finding it, all of it. I let my mind roam, thinking about Theo's argu-ments. Had Plato really claimed Atlantis was real twenty-two times? If so, who's to say proof wasn't down there? If an Oxford Egyptologist was involved and on board with this theory, then maybe . . .

OMG.

Get it together, Liv. It was time to stop this daydream in its ridiculous tracks. People didn't find proof of Atlantis for the same reason that they didn't find proof of Santa's workshop or the tooth fairy. Atlantis didn't *exist*.

And that's when I saw it—the last glittering shard of belief. Regardless of all the pain I'd been through, some stubborn, embarrassing part of me still *wanted* to believe. It had worked its way into me like a glass splinter, so subtle and transparent that not even I had noticed it. I plucked it out, then cocked my arm back and hurled it into the calm blue depths of the caldera.

Metaphorically, of course. We were still having breakfast.

Chapter Ten

#10. ONE PALOMINO BLACKWING PENCIL

My dad always said that when you're living lean, you need to make sure you have a few luxuries to keep you rich in spirit. My mom's luxuries were monthly trips to our neighborhood's fanciest patisserie and her favorite cashmere scarf. My dad's luxuries were memberships to the Art Institute of Chicago and his favorite pencils. Palomino pencils, to be exact, specialty pencils with lead so smooth and dark they might as well have been chocolate. They've been made since the 1930s, and writers like Steinbeck and E. B. White swore by them. They were even used by the creator of Looney Tunes to draw some of the first sketches of Bugs Bunny.

They weren't terribly cheap, but he wasn't stingy with them. I always had one in my backpack and one on our little desk for drawing, and I can't remember him ever telling me to make mine last or to be careful not to

*lose them. He told me that there are two categories of
people: those who know why you'd want to spend $25
on a box of luxury pencils, and those who can't have it
explained to them. I didn't have to ask which category I
was in, because I already knew I was in his. I was always
in his.*

THEO AND MY DAD WERE BOTH STILL STARING AT ME. MY
coffee had gone cool and I felt a bit seasick, like we were
already out on the water, not looking at it from a safe distance. I'm not sure they'd followed me on that entire emotional journey I'd been through, but I needed them to stop
staring at me. Now.

"What do you say, Liv?" my dad finally asked. "We could
really use some help making this look professional. You have
the eye. I've seen your artwork."

Small hiccup in my chest. I had to stop thinking about
him perusing my social media. It felt like a clash of two worlds.

"It isn't the same as working on a film. I really don't have
the experience," I finally said.

Theo clapped one hand on my shoulder. "You're seventeen. Of course you don't. But how do you think people get
experience? They fake it. That's what I'm doing with filming."

"And you are doing wonderfully," my dad said. "Liv, I'm
not asking you to do anything beyond your capabilities. But

I know you have an eye for beauty. You always have."

An eye for beauty. That was something only my dad would say. And to be honest, he wasn't wrong. When I looked at things—paintings or pictures or outfits or even entire rooms—it was like I could see what needed to be fixed to bring it into alignment. To make it harmonious. It was why I liked collage so much. I could see what was meant to go together, even if no one else could.

"Not to mention the fact that you know a lot about Atlantis," Theo added. "Your dad said you used to recite parts of Plato's dialogues as a party trick. We could film that—"

"No!" I said, rubbing my forehead. Thank goodness Liv had picked up some *new* party tricks, because quoting philosophers wasn't going to cut it at my high school.

"Only if you want to. There is no need otherwise," my dad said quickly.

I sighed, then tried to disguise it, then sighed anyway. "Where will they air it?"

Theo mistook my question for excitement. "Online, and possibly on TV. It's part of a series about explorers, and your dad is slotted for episode four, right after El Dorado. Although I'll be honest, I don't think that El Dorado team has much going for them. A lost kingdom made out of gold? *Ridiculous.*"

A laugh burst out of me. I couldn't help it. Why could Theo make me laugh so easily?

My dad was smiling too. "The world is made up of people who try for things and people who sit on the sidelines watching them. Every one of those explorers has my support."

As far as I knew, he'd never sat on the sidelines of anything. "God bless the seekers," I said, echoing what Henrik had said on the plane about his archaeologist boyfriend and my dad. I settled into my chair and took a few deep breaths of the sea air in hopes of calming my mind. It sort of worked. "And what if we don't find anything? What then? Will they still air the show?"

Underlying question: *When your theory is wrong and you look like an idiot, is everyone going to see?*

My dad shook his head. "I don't think they're expecting any actual evidence. They want good, solid storytelling. They want to give viewers a taste of what it would be like to look for the city. Deep down, everyone's an explorer, aren't they?"

"Not everyone," I blurted out, but relief hit me, fast and hard. National Geographic wouldn't air something that made him look like a complete kook, would they? I mean, he'd definitely come across as eccentric, but there was no way around that. Maybe this wasn't the worst way for Dax and everyone back home to find out about my dad. And besides, if I was on the team, cinematograph-ing or whatever it was they wanted me to do, maybe I could keep it all from getting *too* embarrassing.

Suddenly I realized I was nodding, my body agreeing even before the rest of me did. I was finally taking the bait. Sort of. Besides, what else was I going to do while I was here?

"So?" Theo said, raising his perfect eyebrows. If they weren't so gorgeous, I'd be sick of them.

I exhaled. "Okay."

"Okay?" My dad's eyes carefully moved to mine.

I shrugged nonchalantly, disguising my racing heart. "I'll help. But don't expect too much."

"Yes!" my father exclaimed. I could tell he wanted to fly around the table and hug me, but he restrained himself. *Yep.* Too soon for that.

"That's great news, Kalamata," Theo said, clapping me on the back again. "Because here's the kicker. We have just over a week to complete the filming and then get all the editing done. And that includes the dive."

Dive? *Heart-beating-too-fast.* "Wait. We are diving?" I glanced out at the water, and it was the entirely wrong thing to do. Panic gripped me. "But I thought you said you would need government funding to find anything underwater."

My dad nodded. "We need to get something on camera. Something simple. I'm still determining the best spot with

Dr. Bilder, but I'm not expecting much besides interesting footage. I can only afford one day of diving."

"If that," Theo said. "My mother will have a conniption if you try to do a serious dive."

My dad's smile disappeared so quickly you'd think the gods had ordered it to be so. What was that about?

"Because it's too expensive?" I asked.

"No, because of safety," Theo said. My father shot him a look.

"But, Dad . . . you're a master-level diver, aren't you?" That was one thing I knew for sure about my dad. He'd grown up diving—said it came with island life—and one of his many jobs had been at a diving center, where he'd taught certification classes. The fact that my absent dad could have been the one to teach me to scuba dive had been just one of many uncomfortable thoughts I'd had to contend with during my own certification class.

His smile reappeared, washing away the concern. "She worries. I'm not supposed to dive much anymore. Complications with asthma."

Asthma? I stored this tidbit away. Yet another thing I didn't know about him. "Since when do you have that?" I asked.

"Since I decided to smoke for twenty years," he said with a shrug.

Theo leaned forward. "It isn't that serious. His doctor said it was fine if he was careful and didn't go past recreational limits. Mom's overly protective."

"And headstrong," my dad added.

"Like Kalamata," said Theo.

"Kalamata?" My dad glanced at me, and I felt my face go hot.

"Instead of Liv," I blurted out. "Like the type of olive?"

"I told you it has nothing to do with that," Theo corrected me. "You just *look* like a Kalamata."

"Nobody looks like a Kalamata except for a small fruit that has been cured in brine," I said.

Theo's eyes lit up. "Olives are a fruit? What an interesting fact."

A small smile pulled at my dad's face, and I quickly looked away. "Did you really say we only have a week to film and edit? Is that even possible?"

"It's a long shot," my dad said. "But we're trying anyway."

He hadn't changed at all. Not one single bit. *All Hail the King of the Long Shot.*

Theo leaned into me, his bare arm touching mine, before raising his coffee to my dad. "Kalamata? Ready to begin filming?"

"Ready."

And by that I meant, *Not at all.* I could not, in fact, even picture a scenario in which I would be ready for this, but that didn't exactly matter because here I was, in Greece, sucked into a project that had nothing to do with me.

Also, it would maybe be best if Theo would stop touching me. As team members, I found it highly unprofessional and more than a bit distracting.

Just over a week is a lot of time to, say, be stuck on a desert island with no potable water, or to sit on the couch watching Hallmark's Countdown to Christmas in the same ratty pair of sweats. But it is not a long time to film a multi-location documentary, even if it is only supposed to be about twenty-five minutes long. Even I knew that, and I knew virtually nothing about filming.

Of course, Theo was prepared. More than prepared. Once my dad had gone to try to convince Maria to let him pay for our coffee (according to Theo, they'd been having this argument for over a year now), he sprang into action.

"Welcome aboard," Theo said, setting a shiny red binder on the table and sliding it over to me. OLIVE VARANAKIS was across the front of it in black marker, but he'd crossed out the Olive and written KALAMATA.

"This was before I realized you had an aversion to your given name," he said.

I gave him my best withering look, then flipped it open to the first page.

SHOT LIST

NEA KAMENI/VOLCANO

OIA/FIRA

AERIAL SHOTS OF CALDERA + ISLAND SYSTEM

BEACHES—RED BEACH, WHITE BEACH, BLACK BEACH

VOLCANIC HOT SPRINGS

AKROTIRI—MINOAN CIVILIZATION

ASPRONISI/WHITE ISLAND

UNDERWATER SHOOT: TEMPLE OF POSEIDON LOCATION!!

I didn't even have to know what all these places were to know how much work we had ahead of us. Also, the fact that that last one had made it onto the list made me want to curl into the fetal position and stay there until someone promised me it was all going to be okay. I settled instead for a heavy sigh, slumping down even further in my chair.

"You okay?" Theo asked, looking at me worriedly. "Because it would really be better for the film if you were okay."

I couldn't tell if he was joking or not. I pointed to the handwritten paper. "Do you always write in all caps?"

"Always. It's how you can tell I really mean something."

I pulled my phone out of my pocket. Nothing. Still nothing. Being in my dad's world was like stepping into Oz: nothing made sense. I was desperate for a lifeline from home.

"Don't tell me he still hasn't texted," Theo said. I was a little bit glad for the disbelief in his voice, but it also made me feel defensive.

My eyes shot up to his. "He's on his graduation trip. He and his nine hundred best friends are packed into three cars road-tripping to California. He's driving, so he hasn't had a lot of time to call or text."

"That explains it," Theo said. Except I'm pretty sure he didn't mean it. I averted my eyes to the binder, running my hand over the reality of what I had agreed to.

"Theo, I have no idea what I'm doing, with the film," I blurted out. "You know that, right?"

"Kalamata, no one knows what they're doing. It's called *life*." A philosophical answer that Plato would have been proud of, and not even remotely helpful to me. I was on my own—point taken.

While Theo flipped through his binder, I googled "director of photography," which I'm pretty sure disqualified me for the job immediately. According to the first article that popped up in the search engine, I would be in charge of framing, lighting, makeup, costume, and color correction. I started to google those things, but all the descriptions made my head spin, so I took deep cleansing breaths like my school's yoga teacher had taught me and watched Theo scribble notes.

I was on my own. My dad's words came to mind. *Jump and a net will grow.* Maybe he was onto something there. I did have one idea almost right away. After my dad had lost the coffee-paying war, I brought up what he was wearing, and he went back to his apartment to look for a shirt that fit the specifications I'd given him—solid color or simple pattern, not white, preferably from this decade—while Theo and I ran back to the store, this time at a more reasonable pace because in the thirty minutes we'd spent at Maria's, Oia had filled with chaos. The streets were flooded with tourists, some of them dragging bulky suitcases and almost all of them looking pleasantly lost.

Most of the businesses had opened, which meant store owners shouting back and forth to each other across Main Street in voices that sounded angry but were accompanied by smiles. Even the dogs were up and trotting around friskily. The whole scene felt hot and festive—and like a headache in the making.

"Is it always this crowded?" I asked as we moved through a particularly stubborn pocket of slow movers. Theo was clearly used to the tourist situation. He shoved his way through without a second of hesitation.

"Oia is a sponge. All summer long, cruise ships come in, it swells to max capacity, then sunset hits and everyone runs back to their stateroom suites. Good for business, bad for everything else. Wait until you see the shop. It should be packed by now."

"Nice metaphor," I said.

"I liked it," he said, combating my sarcasm with a brilliant smile.

As we rounded the corner to the bookstore, I texted my mom. Dad told me. He wants me to be something called director of photography. I don't even know what that means.

She must have been watching her phone as closely as I was, because she wrote back immediately. It means you make the whole thing look good. That's a perfect job for you. Trust your instincts. The world is run by people who have no idea what they're doing.

Me: That's what Theo said.

Mom: He's smart. Then she sent me a bunch of links to articles with titles like "Visual Element: How Cinematography Tells the Story" and "Taking Your Film from Good to Great," followed by a horribly cheesy meme with a gopher wearing star sunglasses that read GOPHER YOUR DREAM, then added, Think how great this project will look on your RISD application (!!)

She was simultaneously the worst and the best. And, in a shocking turn of events, clearly not in favor of me applying to the same school as Dax. I shot Dax a quick text. How's the drive? Yes, it made our lopsided conversation look even more lopsided, but making contact made me feel slightly better. I shoved my phone back into my pocket.

Theo was right about the bookstore. The word "packed" didn't begin to do it justice. The terrace was completely full of people, and the inside was elbow to elbow. Geoffrey the Canadian stood at the register, ringing people up like his life depended on it, while Ana flew around the shop, answering questions and shoving romance books at unsuspecting customers. Bapou was holding court in the worn armchair, and when he saw me, he jabbed his cane at me and yelled, "Beautiful! Welcome to Santorini!"

"Thank you!" I yelled back.

When she heard me, Ana nearly threw a stack of romance books in her haste to get to us. "Did she say yes? Liv, did you say yes?"

I gestured to my new T-shirt and my cherry-red binder. "I said yes."

Her face transformed with happiness, and she gripped my upper arms so tightly it almost hurt. "The moment they were accepted into the series, he wrote to you and your mother. He said that no discovery would be right without you and that he thought you'd love this. And he'll need your help. He really, really will."

For a moment the floor dropped out from under me, and I felt it—that old pain flaring up in the same familiar spot.

I'd never understood the term "heartache," because I'd always felt my pain in my throat, a tightening that made me wonder if I'd be able to breathe. Had he really said that no discovery would be right without me? If so, what had changed between nine years ago and now?

I stepped backward slightly. "But this is *his* dream."

Her face tightened in concern. "Well, of course," she said, "but—"

Luckily, a customer came up right at the moment, giving me a chance to escape. I fled for the bathroom/cave and quickly locked the door behind me, taking a moment to settle myself.

All of this with my dad was so confusing, it was probably best if I stuck with the things that did make sense. We were making a documentary, and it was my job to make it look good. I could do that.

As the newly minted DP of the project, the only thing I could think of to do was survey my makeup supplies to figure out what I'd brought that would help my dad look his best on camera. I obviously didn't want him to look like he was wearing makeup, but a little coverage might be helpful. I picked out a few items and stuffed them into my bag.

Up on the rooftop, Theo was attempting to shove a shocking amount of equipment into his backpack: video camera batteries, lavalier microphones, a tangled heap of cords, and more notebooks than even I had. Dad had changed into a white button-up and khaki pants and traded in his ball cap for a brown, wide-brim hat. He was also completely loaded down with equipment.

When he saw me, he pointed to the hat. "Liv, what do you think? Is it too much?"

I shook my head. "It gives you an Indiana Jones kind of look." And was probably exactly what National Geographic was hoping for. *Flawed but hopeful explorer, confident that his every dream lies just around the bend.* Well, they'd found him.

Theo reached for my dad's largest bag. "Let me get that, boss. You shouldn't be carrying all of this."

My dad attempted to swat him away, but Theo persisted until he had it slung over his shoulder.

"Ready, Liv?" my dad asked.

I nodded. Then he and his ten thousand remaining bags turned and lunged for the stairs, because never in a million years had my father done anything slowly. No wonder he and Theo got along so well. But all the energy in the world didn't make getting down to the dock any easier. It was quite the ordeal.

First, we had to march down the marble walkway through town looking like a parade of bag ladies in matching T-shirts. Not only did every tourist we passed by stop to stare at us, but it felt like every single local we encountered—the people putting out their wares, shop owners, random old women with grocery bags—not only knew my dad, but seemed to have something important to say to him. Three different men ran out to talk to him, each one asking him for some sort of mechanical advice, while two different women stopped him to marvel over me and do the cheek patting thing that Maria had done. By the time we reached the edge of town, my back was already slick with sweat and I was ready to keel over. I'd take running with Dax over this any day.

Main Street ended at a partially crumbled structure built out of dark, mossy rock, making it stick out among all the white like a fly on a wedding cake. Its roof, if it had ever had one, was long gone, and it stretched out to the very edge of the cliffs. Whatever it was, it had what must be the best view in Oia.

"What is that?" I asked, slowing to look.

"Watchtower of a Venetian castle," my dad said. "It was built in the fifteenth century to protect the inhabitants from pirates. A large portion of it collapsed in the 1956 earthquake."

"The fifteenth century?" I stood on my tiptoes to take a look. The castle made the oldest building I'd ever seen back home look like a toddler.

"I used to play in it as a boy. Now it's a great place to watch the sunset or for brides to do photo shoots." As if to prove his point, a veiled bride suddenly stepped out from behind the wall, a photographer trailing after her. My dad tilted his chin and smiled. *"Kaliméra!"*

I was momentarily distracted by the idea of my father as a child, scampering around the ruins of a castle, so it took me a moment to realize that my dad was talking to yet another person.

A dark-skinned man with a thick beard stood painting in the center of the tower, and when he noticed us, his face opened in a wide smile. "Nico! Is today the special day? Will you find Atlantis?" His accent wasn't Greek, but I couldn't quite place it. Spanish? Portuguese?

My dad reached out to shake his hand, his face lighting up. "Possible, always possible. But I have an even more important question for you. Is today the day you will finish that painting?"

"This masterpiece? You're lucky if I finish it before the end of summer!" the artist yelled.

"Liv!" My dad beckoned to me, and I made my way over, attempting to peel my T-shirt from where it was already stuck to my back. It wasn't terribly hot yet, but the way the sunlight reflected off the white surfaces made me feel like one of the fried pastries I'd seen in Maria's shop window. Theo stayed with the bags, his camera perched on his shoulder. I was beginning to feel like a reality-TV star.

"Liv, this is Hugo. He has been working on the same

sunset painting for almost five months. Hugo, this is my daughter. She is an artist too."

"Sort of," I said, but I was already itching to get a glimpse of the painting.

Hugo gestured for me to look, and I hurried around to see. It was a large canvas, and so far Hugo had done his underpainting and blocked in midtones, darks, and lights. It wasn't a lot to go on, but the balance felt right. Besides, looking at it gave me that humming feeling I always got when one of my art pieces was going to turn out well. The humming feeling hadn't been wrong once, and now whenever it is absent, I immediately abandon the project rather than make myself suffer through it. My art teacher was always going on and on about how predeciding whether or not a piece was going to work out would keep me from evolving, but I disagree. Why waste time on something that would ultimately let you down?

"Well?" Hugo said.

I refocused. "Are you painting the view?" I asked, leaning over to look down the cliffs. A large rock sat within swimming distance from the coast, and from here I could see the blue dome of a miniature chapel nestled on its smoother upper layer.

Hugo squinted at the painting. "I am trying. But I find myself more and more unhappy with it."

I shook my head. "Don't worry. It's in the ugly phase, but it will all come together."

My dad made a small noise in his throat, and Hugo's eyebrows shot up in amusement. "You are calling my work ugly?"

"No." I shifted my weight to one foot. The stone underneath me was so hot that I could feel it through my sandals. "All paintings have an ugly phase. Once you get your form and color in there, it will be all right. I can already see that you have something here."

Hugo stared at me, and for a moment I worried that I'd overstepped my bounds, but then he smiled so wide that I could see every single one of his teeth. "Nico, you told me your American daughter was talented and beautiful, but you did not tell me she had excellent advice!"

"I have undersold her," my dad said. He was literally beaming with pride, which I didn't want to be happy about, but honestly, I kind of was.

"Thank you, Olive," Hugo said.

"Liv," my dad corrected quickly, and Hugo scrunched his face up into a question. "She goes by Liv," my dad said again.

Suddenly I realized something. Everyone on this island knew my name. How much had my dad been talking about me? And more importantly, *why*?

"Liv," Hugo corrected. He slapped my dad's back heartily. "This guy. Your father. He is something, isn't he?"

My dad was most definitely something, but I didn't say that. I had no idea how to answer that, and to be honest, I felt a little shaky about the fact that not only had my dad clearly told everyone about me, but that his life had so clearly gone on without us. He'd come back here and become a local celebrity. Had he even missed us?

The sun was stark and hot against the relentlessly blue sky, but a dark cloud passed over my mood. Of course his life had gone on; I just wished it didn't hurt to know that for a fact. "It's nice to meet you," I finally said.

"And you as well. Now, I must return to my *ugly phase.*" He winked at me, then turned back to his easel, while I bee-lined for where Theo stood with the bags. Theo's role on this trip was becoming more and more clear. *Buffer for my feelings about my dad.*

"Ready for the StairMaster nine thousand?" Theo asked me, pointing. It was a staircase. A big one. And suddenly all the gear we were carrying felt twice as heavy.

"Is there an elevator?"

"Ha," Theo said cheerfully. "You could take a donkey, but I'm morally opposed. A lot of them aren't treated well, and they aren't meant to carry tourists and their gear up and down hills all day. We need to get down to the beach."

"Come!" My dad darted for the steps. He was like a Russell terrier—relentlessly full of energy—and Theo was exactly the same. At least it kept my mind off the fact that we were headed for—drumroll—the ocean.

The ocean and I . . . We're not *terribly* friendly. First, my nightmares. And second, according to the Discovery Channel programs Julius loved to watch, there were lots of scary things lurking under the watery depths. Squid with ten-inch eyeballs. Sharks with twenty-five rows of teeth. Fish with translucent skin and no faces.

So, yeah, an island was not the best idea for someone who liked to dream about drowning every chance she got. But I could handle a boat. Right?

Right, Liv.

The staircase went on for absolutely ever, twisting and turning as it spiraled its way to the beach. The steps were steep and uneven and in terrible shape, with weeds sprouting through the spaces that had crumbled. The handrails didn't look particularly reliable either, which was tricky, because the wind had figured out how to rush straight up those steps and blast me in the face at random intervals. Within minutes, every muscle in my legs had managed to take on the consistency of marmalade, and my shirt had gone from being stuck to my back to completely drenched. I was the last one to reach the bottom, which, with my slippery sandals and wobbling legs, was not graceful.

Theo was waiting at the bottom, all cued up to film my descent. "Don't fall," he said. "That would suck, and also, how embarrassing would that be on camera?"

I made the worst face I could at him, regained my footing,

and took a moment to look around. "This is the beach?" I asked.

Our "beach" was beautiful, but about as conventional as my father. Instead of a stretch of sand leading to water, there was a tumble of black volcanic rocks plus a few docks with water sloshing over the top of them. The water near the shore was ringed in a light emerald color, and it faded into a deep cobalt the farther it got from land. Small tide pools had formed between the rocks, and if I were feeling braver, I'd probably want to explore them.

"Beautiful, yes?" my father said, exhaling.

I turned back to look at my suddenly still father. He was the calmest I'd ever seen him. How had he managed to live without the ocean? Was that one of the reasons he'd left? He couldn't handle city life anymore? Did parents leave their children for large bodies of water?

Liv, stop it, I reminded myself. *This isn't about figuring him out.* This was about surviving my time here and then getting out. *Do your time, keep things surface, and everything will be fine.*

"Beautiful," I pronounced. I even smiled back. See? Not complicated at all.

I followed Theo and my dad past several seaside restaurants, one with a string of coral octopi strung laundrylike on a line, until we reached a dock with three small boats tied to it. No one had to point out which one we would be boarding for me to know. It was the one that looked like it had been MacGyvered together out of hopes and dreams and a whole lot of duct tape. I looked at it skeptically, ignoring the panic rising in my throat. Was duct tape an appropriate material to use on a boat?

"Is this thing . . . ?" I turned to see Theo filming me again. "Theo!" I snapped.

"I have to film your first interaction with the SS *Atlantis*."

"Clever," I deadpanned.

Theo aimed his camera at me again. "One of many. Scientists and researchers may not take Atlantis seriously, but they love to name their spaceships and boats after it."

I scowled into the camera, and Theo gave me a thumbs-up.

"She's a lot sturdier than she looks. Also fast," my dad said, looking at the boat fondly.

I very much doubted that last part. But when he held out his hand, I stepped on shakily, the boat unsteady under my feet. Theo loaded in behind us, and the fact that it managed to hold all three of us felt like a tiny miracle. Once I wasn't too freaked out to walk, I made my way to the back and crash-landed on the crackly leather seat, the broken edges digging into the backs of my legs. Theo slid in next to me. His eyes, normally deep brown, looked caramel colored in the bright sunlight. I couldn't tell who looked more excited: Theo or my dad.

"How *Nico Varanakis* is this boat?" Theo said, waggling

his eyebrows at me. Apparently the two of us had a catch-phrase. *Great.*

"It kind of reminds me of my car," I admitted. "No one will drive in it with me because the back windows don't roll down and it smells like Parmesan cheese."

"I *love* Parmesan cheese," Theo said, widening his eyes.

"Michalis!" my dad yelled, waving to a man on the dock. In return, the man held up a very pink, very fresh-looking octopus, and my stomach heaved, more from the rocking boat than the octopus. It had probably been passed through my DNA, but I had a serious appetite for seafood. James always joked that there was nothing the sea could cook up that I wouldn't at least try. He was right. My dad and I had eaten fish every chance we got.

Also, did my dad know *everyone* on this island?

"Ready?" Dad called from the steering wheel, but he didn't wait for an answer. The motor started with a horrible coughing noise, and I gripped the edge of my seat as we slowly backed out of the marina.

"Please don't kill us," I mumbled below the drone of the engine.

"Huh?" Theo said, cupping his ear.

I shook my head, still gripping the seat like my life depended on it. *This* was life with my dad. One minute, you were having coffee. The next, you were out on an expedition. Off into the wild blue yonder and all that.

Breathe.

What was there to worry about? It's not like I was an active aquaphobic carrying nine years of emotional baggage onto a boat held together by duct tape.

Oh, wait.

You've got this, Olive.

LIV! I meant Liv.

This place was already getting to me.

Chapter Eleven

#11. *SILVER PUTTY KNIFE*

I don't remember if this was the apartment in Albany Park or Edgewater Glen, but I do remember the wallpaper—yellow and white with big red cabbage roses that had faded to a dingy pink. One night, my dad decided we couldn't live with that wallpaper anymore, so he stayed up all night stripping it with a bucket of wallpaper remover and his putty knife. He said that as soon as we were done, we'd paint a huge mural of anything we wanted—rainbows, mermaids, dragons, anything. I spent all evening drawing my ideas in my sketch pad.

But that night when my mom got home from her shift at a hotel, I could hear them arguing. She said he shouldn't have done something like this without consulting the landlord. I couldn't understand why my mom was upset—didn't she see he was making our place better?

We didn't stay long enough for him to finish the job.

MY DAD'S BOAT NOT ONLY LOOKED A BIT LIKE HIS motorcycle's long-lost cousin, but it moved like it too. Once we were out of the harbor, my dad ramped up the speed, and soon we were cutting through waves, bouncing up and down with Theo and me clinging to our seats as we raced toward the central island. Behind us, Oia spilled out over the sides of the red cliffs, looking more and more inconsequential the farther out we got.

"Are you nervous?" Theo asked, his voice close to my ear.

Was I that obvious? I discreetly dug my fingernails in a little tighter, anchoring myself. "No. Why?" I asked shortly.

He met my eyes, and the corner of his mouth went up. "Because you're clawing my leg?"

"Oh—" I looked down and realized that instead of gripping the edge of the seat like I thought I was, I'd been accidentally clutching part of Theo's pleasantly muscular thigh, which was all kinds of embarrassing.

I yanked my hand away. "Sorry. I guess maybe I am kind of nervous?" I glanced down at the water, and the way it whipped past us made me dizzy.

Theo's forehead creased. "On *this* stalwart vessel? Kalamata, you have nothing to worry about."

I grinned, because I couldn't help it, and the tightness in my chest eased. "I haven't spent a lot of time on boats." Translation: no time. I could swim, but I preferred my water chlorinated and three to six feet deep, preferably while lounging on one of our many inflatable pool toys with a can of Diet Coke sweating on the ledge next to me.

"Also, the ocean and I don't get along that well." My hair was flying in the wind, and every time I spoke, half of it ended up inside my mouth. I wasn't entirely sure why I was being so open about all this. Peer pressure?

"Really?" Theo said. I shrugged, and his face went from joking to serious.

"Look at him." Theo gestured to my dad, whose back was to us. He'd kicked off his shoes and stood rocking back and forth slightly, swaying to the sound of the instrumental music blaring from the boat's ancient-looking stereo. "Your dad could safely navigate anything. I think he's part merman. You're completely safe."

"You're right." My dad did look completely at home. Seeing him in his natural environment felt confusing—regardless of me knowing this side of him, he'd obviously been this person all along. He'd built a bookstore and could drive boats; what else could he do that I didn't know about?

Theo patted my arm encouragingly. "Let me know if you need to claw my leg again. I'm more than happy to help out."

I slugged him, then looked out at the water to hide my smile. Theo was great at distracting me from my worries. It was like his superpower. I leaned back and did my best to relax. So long as I didn't focus on the rippling depths below me, I was fine. Better than fine. It was a gorgeous day, the breeze making the scorching sun downright hospitable. I rolled up the sleeves of my T-shirt and turned my face up to the light. As soon as we docked, I'd abide by number seven of Mom's rules, *Wear sunscreen.* But for now, I wanted to lie here like a raisin and soak up as much sun as possible.

After a while my dad slowed the boat, turning down the music so he could give me a quick geography lesson over the sound of the wake. He explained that Santorini is actually made up of five islands. There was the main island of Thira, which was the largest by far. Next was Therasia, which sat opposite of Santorini and was maybe an eighth the size of it. According to Theo, it housed an abandoned village, a colorful church, lots of smartly adorned donkeys, and a few hundred residents. My dad said the island was like a time machine; it had managed to lag behind the rest of the islands.

Next were the volcanic islands, Nea Kameni (our destination) and Palea Kameni, the small islands I could see bobbing in the middle of the caldera. And finally, there was Aspronisi, or the "white island," a tiny splotch of land that didn't always make it onto maps, and which Theo told me was constantly rumored to be for sale. Grouped together, the islands formed the circular shape that got Atlantis hunters so excited.

I wouldn't say I was foaming at the mouth, but I was eager to see more of the islands.

Nea Kameni means "new burnt" island, and as soon as we arrived, I knew exactly why. It looked like the surface of Mars. The island was small, maybe a mile or so in diameter, and almost perfectly round with the occasional blast of sulfur rising up from the surface. After the chaos of Santorini, seeing such a barren space was jarring. My dad turned off the motor and we drifted quietly into the small dock. The vibe of the place was completely different from Santorini. It felt quiet and honestly a bit eerie.

I looked at it skeptically. "So this is the volcano that wiped out"—I almost said *Atlantis* but quickly caught myself—"wiped out Santorini?" Could something this small really wipe out an entire civilization?

Theo stepped up next to me, his sun-warmed arm brushing against mine as he tossed my dad the dock line. "No way. That volcano is long gone. It exploded once it downed Atlantis."

He said "Atlantis" so casually, it kind of killed me. "Then what is this?" I asked, gesturing to the island.

"Nea Kameni is evidence of the volcano," my dad said. "You see all of this?" He moved his hand to encompass the island and caldera. "This entire bowl-shaped area is what was left behind the last time the volcano erupted. It is flooded with water now."

Suddenly I grasped Santorini's circular shape. "You're saying this entire group of islands is a volcano?"

"All of it," Theo said calmly. We'd reached the dock, and Theo clambered fearlessly over the side of the boat, carefully pulling us in.

Despite the heat, I felt a chill move through me. "But ... it's not active, right?" I looked back at Santorini. From here the villages were small splotches of white, the buildings clinging stubbornly to the cliffs. It all looked so fragile. People didn't build their lives on places heading toward destruction, did they?

My stomach lurched. That's what my family had done. Had my mom ever sensed what would happen in her marriage? That my dad would one day up and leave, with no explanation?

My dad looked over from his gear, oblivious to my inner turmoil. "Dormant. It's a sleeping volcano."

I exhaled, picturing the volcano dolled up in a nightcap and fuzzy slippers. That sounded a lot less scary. "Meaning it won't erupt?"

Dad raked his hand through his hair, making it stand on end, before putting his hat back on. "Not likely. Our most recent natural disaster was an earthquake in 1956. Nothing compared to a massive volcanic eruption, but it did take out a couple thousand houses and damage the economy for quite some time."

Brilliant. My father had apparently felt that living along-side an active volcano was less dangerous than living with his wife and daughter. We weren't *that* bad, were we?

Something my mom had told me more than once flashed into my mind. *It wasn't about us.* But how could it not be about us? It was our *family*.

Not even one cloud marred the sky, but I felt the sun darken slightly anyway. It was time to get moving. I needed somewhere to put all the anger roiling through me. I quickly collected my backpack, then stood, stretching my back as I tried to keep my balance in the rocking boat. Heat seemed to be rising from the water.

"Let's hurry," Theo called, shifting impatiently from foot to foot on the dock. His hair was messed up from the boat, and he was so excited that his body looked electric. "We want to get this done before the mobs arrive."

"What mobs?" I asked. My dad held his hand out to help me off the boat, and I took it reluctantly before stumbling onto the dock. Theo quickly grabbed my elbow, right-ing me.

"People who are drawn by the cameras," my dad said, but a glint of a smile appeared on his face.

"It isn't the cameras; it's *you*," Theo said to my dad. He turned to me. "You'll see, Kalamata. Once he starts talking about Atlantis, people swarm. It makes filming difficult.

But that's why I knew we had to make this documentary. Everyone wants to know about Atlantis."

So the documentary had been Theo's idea. I guess that made sense. But at what point had my dad decided to include me?

"But who will find us here?" I asked skeptically. Nea Kameni did in fact look burnt, and besides a handful of other small boats, it also looked completely abandoned.

"It is a popular destination," my dad said.

I was going to have to take their word for it. So far, I wasn't terribly impressed. Besides the view of Santorini, Nea Kameni seemed to be nothing more than a heap of black rocks with a pathway leading up from the dock. Also, the air smelled vaguely like rotten eggs, which was not my favorite thing.

Once the equipment had been distributed, my dad started up the path, a spring in his step. I was about to follow after him, already regretting my shoe choice, when Theo put his hand on my arm. "Can I talk to you for a minute?" he asked.

His half whisper sent a shiver down my back, and I reflexively stepped backward. What could he have to talk to me about? "Okay?"

"Nico!" he yelled up the path. "You go find a filming spot. We're going to get a few landscape shots." My dad waved, and as soon as he was out of sight, Theo reached for me, our fingers touching briefly.

Physical contact with Theo felt . . .

Never mind how it felt. I met his caramel-colored eyes and was surprised by the question in them. "What's up?" he said.

I was the one who was supposed to be asking that question. I stepped back nervously. "Sorry?"

"What's up with Atlantis? More specifically, *you* and Atlantis." He ran his other hand across his sweaty forehead. "Every time it comes up, you get this miserable look on your face."

Busted. "I do not," I said, but my face was turning red, both from embarrassment and surprise. How could Theo— someone I just met—read me so well?

"It looks like this." He made a face, lowering his eyebrows and tightening his mouth. I had to admit that it looked surprisingly like me. He even reached up and brushed his invisible bangs back just the way I did.

Show-off.

I fought the urge to mess with my hair and instead folded my arms over my chest. The breeze was gone, and it was way too hot for an interrogation. "Are you sure you want to be a filmmaker? Because you'd probably make a great actor."

"Documentarian," he said. "And you're dodging the question."

I was hoping to distract him, but he didn't take the bait. "I even have proof on camera. At the airport you looked like you wanted to hit me when I brought it up. Do you not believe in it?" His voice was relaxed, like it wasn't a completely loaded question. For most people it wouldn't be. But for me? Well, whether or not Atlantis existed had already determined way too much of my life.

I dug my fingernails into the sides of my arms, trying to ignore the fury igniting in my chest. "Does that actually matter?"

He dipped his head, his eyes still focused on mine. "Of course it matters. I want to know what you think."

Maybe it was the sulfuric smell invading my nostrils, but something hot and angry welled up inside me. "To clarify, you are asking me if I believe that once upon a time there was a magical city that angered the gods and was swallowed up by the sea?" Theo leaned back as if to dodge my tone, but I kept going. "And despite thousands of people looking for it for thousands of years, my *dad* is going to be the one to find it?"

At first Theo didn't do anything. Then he grinned and nodded, impressed. "You're a skeptic. Interesting."

I shook my head hard, sending my bangs straight into my eyes. *Skeptic* sounded wishy-washy. Like someone who was leaving a little space open just in case it might be true. And the anger boiling in my chest left no space for something like that. "No, I'm a realist. Meaning, I only believe in things that are actually substantiated. That have proof."

Now his eyes relaxed, his eyebrows rising knowingly. Honestly, those eyebrows had their own *dialect*. "Got it. Name something that we have proof of?"

Huh? Frustration tumbled through me. "Um . . . like gravity."

His lips pulled into a smile that was equal parts triumphant and smug. "We don't have proof of gravity."

Now it was my turn to stare at him. How delusional was he? "Um, hello? Yes, we do."

He shook his head, his smile growing. "No, we have *evidence* of gravity. And *evidence* of electrons. There's a difference between evidence and proof." He crossed his arms over his chest. "Isn't your mom a lawyer?"

Smug just seemed to add to his charm. I honestly wanted to pull my hair out. "Theo, what are you talking about?" I groaned.

He held his hands up. "You're right, Kalamata. We *don't* have proof of Atlantis. I don't know if Atlantis, like, the utopian Atlantis, really existed, or if it's just a story. But I do know that one of the most well-respected minds in history was adamant about it having existed, and that despite all the problems with it, people have been drawn to the story for centuries. There's something to the legend."

His point was ridiculous, clearly. But it also had an undeniable sort of logic. This was the problem with Atlantis. It was so magical and unattainable that it wrapped its tentacles around your mind and refused to let go. "I still don't believe in it," I said.

"You don't *have* to believe in Atlantis, Kalamata," he said, stepping in closer. "But it's better if you're at least open to the possibility."

His bottom lashes were all clumped together, and the ends of his hair were slightly damp, which should have been revolting but definitely was not.

I needed to stop thinking about this boy's eyelashes. I shook my head. "Sorry, Theo. It's nothing against you. But believing in Atlantis is just not a possibility for me." Not anymore.

He hesitated, then lifted his chin to meet my eyes. "I've been thinking about what you said last night, about your dad leaving you for Atlantis. I think sometimes things look a certain way, but we don't always know for sure that they *are* that way."

"Excuse me?" My heart was hammering, and it took every ounce of strength I had not to yell at him. "Not following you."

He leaned forward, and I couldn't help but notice that morning light was Theo's friend. His eyelashes cast a shadow on his cheeks, and his eyes looked darker and deeper. As if he could read my mind, he smiled, his lips parting slightly. "For example, you think I'm good-looking, right?"

I nearly choked on my own saliva. "Theo! Boyfriend, remember?"

A boyfriend who still hadn't called me back. How many hours had it been now? But *still*.

He adjusted his hat. "Wait . . . you have a boyfriend?"

"Theo!" I groaned, and he grinned at me.

"Bad joke, sorry. But hear me out. Theoretically, if you didn't have a boyfriend, you likely would have noticed that I'm attractive, the same as I've noticed you're very, *very* pretty."

OMG.

Did he really just say that? My cheeks were bright flames, and the island spun ever so slightly. "Theo . . ."

He grinned and waved me off. "Relax. I'm a complete gentleman. Fully respect you and your boyfriend . . ." He trailed off, raising one eyebrow.

"Dax," I said.

"Dax. The point I'm trying to make is that just because your dad believed in Atlantis doesn't mean he would leave you for it. The same way that just because you and I are clearly attracted to each other doesn't mean that either of us is going to act on it."

Wow. My body decided to fulfill every stereotype it possibly could. Heart racing, palms sweating. Also, was I smiling? *Ugh.* I was. I could only guess what shade of red my face was. Vermillion. Scarlet. Ruby. Everything he was saying should have sounded cocky and arrogant, but it didn't. It just sounded sort of matter-of-fact. Sort of . . . *true.* "Theo, I have no idea how to follow this conversation."

His smile went lopsided. "Sorry, I get that a lot. My brain works fast. And my mom says I connect things that other people don't. Maybe it's a trilingual thing? Anyway. The real deal is that I think you have your dad all wrong."

I shook my head. This was exactly like last night. Why did Theo think he knew anything about me and my family? Also, he couldn't really be open to Atlantis being real, could he? I mean, it was one thing for my dad to go for it. He'd been raised before the internet, and as far as I could tell, the story had sunk deep down into his bones and caught ahold of him. But Theo? He had a screen in front of him 24/7. He could actually research things. "What about you? Do *you* think Atlantis is real?"

He studied me for a beat, his eyes thoughtful. "I'm excited about making a documentary. And I don't think we have to decide one way or another whether Atlantis is real." He gestured to the wide expanse of the caldera. "I would say that most stories, including the ones we tell ourselves, have a nugget of truth in them, and I think Atlantis is no different. Is it possible that there was some massive, destructive event in history that inspired the legend of Atlantis? Of course. And Santorini definitely matches up with it." He met my eyes again. "Besides, what's the harm in believing?"

What's the harm?

Had he really just said that? The *harm* was that believing could rip you away from your family, sending you halfway across the world on a delusional treasure hunt. The harm was that you could become so obsessed that you missed your family's birthdays, homecoming dances, and thousands of bedtime stories—

STOP. I slammed on my emotional brakes, screeching to a halt. I was over this. Whatever my dad had or had not done, that was over. I had moved *on*. I blinked angrily a few times, steadying myself, and when I looked up, Theo was still watching me. Though studying me was more like it. He might as well have had a camera on me, he was clearly picking up my every move.

"So?" Theo's eyebrows went up in amusement. "Do you think you could at least be open to it? Because we really need your help. Also, I think you need to tell your dad how you really feel about Atlantis."

And there it was. The final straw. "I'm sorry, are you telling me how to interact with my dad?"

"No. Yes? No." He shrugged his shoulders up and down in confusion. "I don't know what the right answer is."

If I weren't so angry, I probably would have noticed the undeniable cuteness in Theo's fluster. "I'm going to take a breather. I'll see you up there." I whirled around, head held high, and marched briskly up the path toward the crater.

My whirl/march wasn't nearly as dignified as I'd hoped. Not only had my eyes gone blurry with angry tears, but Theo had been right about footwear—sandals were not ideal for a hike up loose volcanic rock.

So that sucked.

As I staggered up the hill, I moved fast, trying to burn off some steam, which was fitting, because that was exactly what this island seemed to be doing. The island was mono-chromatic, with just a few sprigs of yellow plants and flowers offsetting the rock, and in some spots, succulents bloomed in dizzying patterns. It was also releasing steam into the air. So yes, *active* volcano. I could see it with my own eyes. Theo and my dad had chosen a great place to film; it was so stark and strange that it was beautiful.

I could hear the crunching of rock galloping from behind me. Theo. I sped up but immediately slipped and had to throw my hands out to stop myself.

"I overstepped my bounds," Theo said in an out-of-breath voice once he finally caught up.

"Big-time." I controlled my voice, made sure it was strong and sturdy. I was Liv. I didn't let the topic of my father affect me like this anymore.

He bit his lower lip, his eyes on mine. "I'm sorry. I just really care about your dad."

The intensity of his voice caught me off guard. I stopped walking, then slowly turned to face him. "Theo, I appreciate that you care about my dad—"

"And you," he interjected.

Whatever. He didn't even know me. I shook my head. "Sure. But you can't give people advice when you don't know them. What if I tried to give you advice about your family?"

He seemed to actually consider this. Take it in. "True," he said. "Very, very true." He shoved his hands into his pockets. "You know what? You're right. I messed up. I do care a lot, but that wasn't a good way to show it. I'm sorry. I really want to be your friend."

I'd known him for less than two days now, but I already knew this was true. He did care. Also, I needed an ally in Theo.

"It's okay," I said, my shoulders relaxing. "Let's just try to have a good filming day."

"Thanks, Kalamata." He looked up at me hopefully. "On an entirely unrelated note, did you know that the olive branch has historically been used as a symbol of peace? The United Nations even has it on their flag. Isn't that *interesting*?"

I'm pretty sure it was physically impossible to stay mad at him for long.

The crater was a large, well-formed indentation with a lip circling its edge. I found my dad crouched on one side holding a handful of soil and speaking rapidly in Greek to a small family who stood around excitedly asking him questions. No doubt he was explaining the surface manifestations of geothermic activity or the mineral composition of the volcanic rock or some other scientific facts he seemed to have been born knowing.

When we came into view, his face lit up. He gestured to me, and I heard the Greek word for "daughter." The couple beamed, and I attempted a smile back, but it felt wrong.

The woman made her way over to me, holding her sun hat on with one hand. "Very good. To work together. Very good."

"Atlantis!" her husband said, smiling large as he raised one fist into the air.

"Yes, thank you." It was the only response I could think of. No one here seemed to think my dad's Atlantis hunting was out-there. It almost made me wonder if I was the ridiculous one. *Almost.*

"See? His fans find him," Theo said from behind me.

While Theo and my dad set up the camera and tripod, I made my way around a part of the crater that was filled with small yellow flowers, which was charming among all the black rock. The crater kept sending up puffs of sulfur into the air, and I couldn't help but think how much my mom would hate the smell of it.

When I circled back, Theo had already set up the tripod and was positioning my dad to stand in his view of the sheer cliffs of Santorini, and the solid white buildings on top looked like a light dusting of snow.

"Okay, Director of Photography, where do you think we should film?"

It took me a second to realize my dad was talking to me.

"Um . . ."

"He's going to talk about the destruction of Atlantis." Theo had his camera out on his shoulder now, hat turned backward.

"Okay, destruction. I'm guessing we want . . . drama?" They looked at me hopefully. Which spot would be best? The sun was a bright hot circle above me, and I squinted around nervously. Why did they think I could do this? The couple beamed at me encouragingly. This was obviously making their day.

What made the most sense? Santorini in the background? The crater? And where would the light be best?

"Think of it like a painting," my dad suggested. "Something to frame the subject."

I spun around, letting my eyes follow the perimeter of the island. "Well . . . I don't think you can pick a bad spot. It's all beautiful. And the lighting—" I stopped, because there it was. A view so perfect it was almost comic.

"There," I said. I took off, heading for the view, while Theo, my dad, and the couple hurried after me.

The spot was made up of the same dusty rock as the rest of the island, but a divot in the rock had formed a small cove, and beyond the rock the ocean faded from bottle green, to turquoise, to deep cobalt, with Santorini floating in the distance. Patches of brick-red succulents coated the ground. It was the color that did it. It was just so satisfying.

"Perfect," my dad pronounced, and the couple clucked their approval.

While Theo set up his tripod, my dad changed into his fresh shirt and took his place. Theo and I studied him through the viewfinder. It felt easier to look at him that way. Like looking at the sun with sunglasses. He gave us a thumbs-up.

"What do you think?" Theo asked me.

I looked up at my dad. "No hat. It's giving you weird shadows under your eyes. Also, you're kind of shiny."

"It is my curse," my dad said. "And the walk was very hot."

We were all sweating. The woman took off her hat and fanned herself with it. Regardless of his credibility, I didn't want my dad to look like a sweaty tourist. I adjusted my backpack on my shoulders, remembering the makeup I'd brought, plus the blotting sheets I always kept in the bottom of my bag. The proverbial sweaty apple had not fallen far from the tree.

"Hey, Dad, okay if I put a little makeup on you?"

His face shone even more. "Makeup? Of course."

I walked up to him, digging through my backpack before coming up with some concealer, ChapStick, and a brow gel. My dad smiled at me, and I thought I caught a whiff of nervousness. "Layer it on, Liv. Do you think you will need a paint roller?"

"No, definitely not." Up close, his face did look weatherworn and a bit puffier than I remembered. "I'll have you dab your face; then I'm going to do some light coverage and cover up some sun damage and the circles under your eyes. Then I'll try to tame your brows a little."

"May the gods be with you," he said with a smile. I passed him the blotting sheets, and then we got to work.

It felt strange to be so close to a face I'd thought about so often, but I tried to put that out of my mind and focus on doing a good job. My hands shook slightly as I carefully applied concealer onto his cheeks. We were almost eye to eye now—my mom's height had given me a boost—and as I patted the makeup into his skin, it reminded me a bit of when he used to let me put shaving cream on his face. Also, our skin tone was *exactly* the same, and when I put my hand to his face, his whiskers were as sharp and as scratchy as I remembered.

ABORT MISSION! my brain screamed. *RUN AND TAKE COVER SOMEWHERE.*

Given the circumstances, it was a reasonable course of action. But I was almost positive that the only thing more awkward than being this close to my dad was running away from him in panic, concealer in hand, so I forced myself to stand still, biting hard on the inside of my cheek.

Focus on the job, Liv.

He was right about his brows. They didn't want to take creative direction from anyone. I didn't get it all perfect, but when I finally stepped back, he did look better. Well rested and camera ready. Professional.

"Thank you," he said quietly.

"Wow, good job," Theo called from behind the camera. "That made a big difference. Okay, boss. You ready?"

"Ready." My dad nodded, and I moved behind Theo to watch.

"Does he need cue cards or something?" I asked.

Theo snorted. "You are joking, right? Okay, everyone. Quiet, please." Then he counted down, going silent on the *three, two, one.* And then all eyes were on my dad, even mine.

"It's the year 1646 BC. You're asleep in your home, your loved ones around you, when you hear something outside, a deafening eruption. Welcome to phase one of one of the largest volcanic explosions in history." His voice was loud but calm, and he gazed intently into the camera, his eyes focused.

"Phase one was the volcano's warning shot—frightening,

but not devastating to the island's many residents. Ash and pumice burst into the air, leaving behind seven meters of debris. Phase two was a massive explosion of lava, which darkened the sky and brought tremendous heat and lightning.

"Phrase three devastated the island. Pyroclastic flows, a powerful combination of hot ash, gases, and lava, sped over the ocean's surface, decimating everything in their path. Anything not covered with ash would have been vaporized and destroyed."

He gestured to the caldera. "And then phase four, the volcano's now empty magma chamber collapsed, forming a large bowl. As ocean water flowed in, steam and pressure built, culminating in the grand finale, a massive explosion, many times that of an atom bomb. The displacement of so much water created tsunamis, with waves sixty feet and higher that traveled five miles in all directions. And finally, there were the earthquakes." He stepped forward, his eyes intense. "This was the destruction of Atlantis. As Plato said, 'There occurred violent earthquakes and floods; and in a single day and night of misfortune all your warlike men in a body sank into the earth, and the island of Atlantis in like manner disappeared in the depths of the sea.'"

His voice had taken almost a singsong quality, but now it solidified. Clear and ominous. "Imagine, in the space of three days, an entire city, an entire civilization, decimated. Not a single bone or body was left behind. This was the destruction of Atlantis."

His eyes traveled away from the camera, finding mine, and their intensity glued me to the ground. "What was lost is now found. Welcome to Atlantis."

Chapter Twelve

#12. MEN'S HERRINGBONE SILK TIE AND POCKET SQUARE, NAVY BLUE, STILL IN THE BOX

I loved everything about Atlantis, but the part I loved most was what my dad called Celebration Planning. It was as much a part of our Atlantis hunt as nailing down its exact location.

Though we already knew where Atlantis was, it was now a matter of saving up enough money so we could go to Santorini to prove our theory.

And once we found it, the celebrations would begin. Our picture would be on the front page of every newspaper in the world, and there would be a parade with fireworks and marching bands, me waving from the top of a shimmering float. The entire world would know my name: Olive Varanakis, the girl who discovered Atlantis. The president of the United States would hold a ball in my honor. I wasn't sure what I would wear for such an occasion, *but my dad knew: he'd wear his silk tie, the one he'd purchased during the few months he'd worked at a men's tailoring shop.*

Included on our list for party planning: a ten-foot chocolate fountain, three bedazzled elephants, and a conga line that would stretch at least twenty blocks.

It never occurred to me not to believe him. He had the tie already, didn't he?

IT WAS EASY TO WATCH HIM THROUGH A CAMERA LENS. I didn't have to worry so much about what had or hadn't worked between us. I could see him as anyone else would: someone who was interested in Atlantis, not someone who had *left* me for Atlantis. It was a monumental difference.

My body did not care in the slightest that I had made up my mind about how to react to my dad. I could blame the heat and sulfur for the light-headedness and stomachache, but I couldn't mistake my galloping heart for anything else. *Excitement.*

Despite the fact that she likely hadn't understood any of it, the woman standing next to me sighed, then nudged me, beaming up at me happily. I couldn't do anything but smile back. The entire thing had been magical. And those final words, *what was lost is now found* . . .

Well, they had sent chills spiraling down my spine.

He hadn't looked at his notes once. He hadn't even paused. And he'd quoted Plato like he was someone he met up with once a week for coffee. Listening to him, I latched on to every word, every rise and crackle of his voice. He had completely sucked me in. One minute I'd been sweating it out with the rest of the residents of modern Thira, and the next I was transported back in time to the moment when it had all changed. I had heard the panic of the Minoans waking in their beds, confused, then running for their lives. I'd smelled the sulfur. I'd felt the impending rush and terror of the tsunamis. I'd *been* there.

"Wow," I whispered.

"Told you," Theo said, not even lifting his eyes from the screen. I glanced behind me and realized that—exactly as Theo had said—a small crowd had formed, a group of tourists who must have seen the camera and quietly made their way over to us.

A few of them lobbed questions at my dad, and he smiled graciously, then began answering them one by one, as Theo and I crowded around the camera to watch it play back to us. The shot looked incredible—balanced and interesting—and even without sound I could already tell that the camera had captured his intensity. He looked natural, confident, and completely in his element. My dad, apparently, had been born for film.

"Wow," I said again, but the word was pitifully inadequate, an ember compared to an aerial firework.

Theo met my eyes. "In the words of every victorious winner in the history of Greece, *I told you so.*"

I punched his arm but couldn't help smiling. "Has it all been this good?"

"Better. I think he was nervous because you were here. Usually he moves his arms around more and it gets even more intense. He was a bit, as the Americans say, *off his game.*"

"What do you think, Liv?" Dad called, managing to disentangle himself from the crowd. "Did it look okay?"

My heart was swelling in my chest. I'd seen only ten minutes of footage, but already I knew that the documentary had the potential to be life changing.

Part of me wanted to downplay his performance, but I couldn't do it. Not if I wanted to maintain even a scrap of integrity. "Dad, you were amazing. National Geographic is going to lose their minds."

"You think so?" My dad's eyes lit up hopefully. "Well, you really helped out. I felt more confident with the makeup and better clothes. . . ."

I dropped my eyes, ignoring the warmth spreading through my chest. I didn't *want* to like compliments from him, but here I was, liking them anyway. "That was nothing."

"And you knew how to set up the shot," Theo said, like it was me who had made that magic happen. As if my tiny adjustments had made all the difference. The truth was, my dad could have delivered that speech standing under a freeway overpass wearing a chicken costume, and he still would have sounded credible and captivating.

Regardless of what the postcard and Theo had said, my dad didn't need me. He had his own magic. He always had. No one was going to care if Atlantis was real or not, not when it was told that way.

A quote my English teacher kept tacked to her classroom wall sprang to mind. *Never let the truth get in the way of a good story.* To my dad, it was both: the truth and a good story. And the rest of us? We had no choice but to be swept up by the current. Resistance was futile.

I adjusted the strap on my backpack, unable to stop the urgency swirling through my center. "Where to next?"

Theo wanted to get it all perfect, so even though my dad's execution was close to flawless the first time, we ran through the shot several times before tourist boats started showing up and people began gathering around to watch my dad. The good news was that having a large audience brought out my dad's inner storyteller and made him even better. The bad news was that they were noisy. After two American tourists came up mid-shoot to ask what we were working on, Theo gave up and we hauled our gear back to the boat.

We spent the rest of the day finding spots to send up Theo's drone for aerial shots of Nea Kameni and Palea Kameni. At lunch we ate out of my dad's red tackle box, which was actually full of thick cubes of feta cheese so salty they made my tongue hurt, hearty slices of the best tomatoes I'd ever eaten, and a crusty loaf of bread that we tore off in thick hunks. Whenever we got too hot, my dad killed the motor and announced it was time for *aragma*, which Theo explained as the "fine art of chilling, Greek-style."

The Greek in me was a huge fan.

Dad turned up the music and passed around sodas from his magical tackle box, and then he and Theo dove into the ocean while I sat on the stern with my feet in the water, trying *not* to think about all that cool blue depth. It was honestly a bit torturous. By midafternoon I was so hot I thought I might burst into flames, but no matter how deliciously cold and refreshing the ocean looked, it was too terrifying to even consider. Santorini was clearly not the place where I would make friends with the ocean, but maybe we could be casual acquaintances?

By the time we pulled back into the dock in Ammoudi Bay, I was sunburned, exhausted, thirsty, and—albeit grudgingly—completely lit up by how magical the day had been. My mom had been right about the island—it was stunning in this sort of ramshackle, mishmash way that I'd never encountered before. And despite how awkward things were between my dad and me, we had Theo as a buffer. Anytime conversation veered toward shaky territory, he was there to make a joke or turn up the music. Being here felt strangely . . . easy.

It was so easy, in fact, that I'd somehow managed to forget all about my problems with Dax, a fact I was alerted to the moment our boat bumped dry land and an army of text messages began invading my phone.

Liv, can you talk?

Liv, you there?

I'm still up, call me when you can.

Santorini was ten hours ahead of California, which meant Dax had been texting me in the wee hours of the morning. Hope skipped through me as I scrolled through his texts. Did this mean he was ready to move on from the whole high school day fiasco? Was he regretting not saying goodbye to me in person?

I'd stopped right in the center of the dock, which was creating a minor traffic jam as my dad and Theo tried to unload the gear. "You look happy," Theo said, his hot shoulder brushing against mine as he moved past me.

"I am," I said. "I need to make a phone call. Okay if I catch up with you later? You can leave some of the gear for me to carry."

"We can manage." My dad set his hand on my shoulder, his stance steady on the bobbing dock. "Will you be able to find your way back up to the bookstore?"

I glanced up at him and startled at how wilted he looked. His dark circles had reappeared, and his shoulders had rounded under the weight of the equipment. Filming and being out on the water had obviously taken a lot out of him.

"Dad, you look tired," I said, momentarily forgetting about my phone.

He smiled, pushing his hat back on his forehead. "Documentaries are a young man's game."

"Let me help you with that, boss." Theo grabbed one of my dad's bags from him. "How old are you anyway? Like, forty? What was it like to have a pet dinosaur? Did it ever bite you?"

"Are you hearing this?" my dad asked, but he had a big smile on his face.

"I'm hearing it." And I was positive that Theo was the only person in the world who could get away with it. "See you up there."

While Theo and my dad disappeared up the walkway, I followed the path running alongside the water's edge, carefully stepping over volcanic rock, daring myself to veer in and out of the tide pools and rippling puddles. The water closest to the shore was ringed in light turquoise, and so clear that I could see the jumble of rocks underneath. Eventually, the small rocks morphed into larger rocks, and I found myself climbing over boulders until I reached the end of the path, a large smooth rock overlooking the bay.

I took a deep breath and hit dial. Dax answered on the fourth ring.

"Liiiiiiv," he said, dragging my name out.

"Dax!" His cheerful and completely normal voice made me so relieved that I nearly toppled off my rock. I pulled my legs in to sit cross-legged, steadying myself. "How are you?"

"Missing you. We got a flat two hours out of Portland and ended up spending half the night at a rest stop, so it took forever to get here. How's my girlfriend?" His voice was bright and warm, and the relief turned my muscles to jelly.

"Good. Really good." I exhaled, a smile overtaking my face. "You sound . . . different. Less angry?"

"Well . . ." He exhaled. "I talked to my cousin, and she said that missing high school day isn't the end of the world. The majority of students they accept don't participate in those events, so you still have a very good chance of being admitted. I even talked to her about the art program. She said they have a really strong art history department, so I reached out and requested some brochures from the college. They should be here by the time you get back."

I absentmindedly kicked off my sandals, resting my bare feet on the sunbaked rock. This was so Dax. *Step one, identify problem. Step two, solve problem. Step three, celebrate.*

I didn't want to study art. I wanted to *make* art. But his voice was full of sunshine, and it was thoughtful of him. Besides, was now really the time to tell him I had other plans for college? No. The conversation could wait until I got home. "Thank you, Dax. That was really considerate."

"No problem. I know it's really nerve-racking to apply to Stanford. I felt the same way. If you want, I can help you with your application."

I closed my eyes, rubbing my temples in a way that reminded me of my mom. Where did I go from here? "Um, Dax . . ."

"How's the dig?" he asked, skimming over my hesitation.

The dig? It took my brain a moment to figure out what he meant. He was talking about my lie. The one where I lived in an alternate universe in which my father was a history professor working on an archaeological dig.

"*Great*," I said quickly. I probably should have researched my story a bit more. I tucked a strand of hair into my mouth and bit down. "It's good. Kind of boring. Lots of people digging things up and categorizing them—" I silently face-palmed. I had no idea what I was talking about. Everything I knew about artifact digs came from movies. Also, what if I got caught lying to him again?

Suddenly a brilliant idea landed on me. I could spin the conversation toward the film. Then, when the real project came out, it wouldn't be such a leap. "Dax, guess what? National Geographic is getting involved with some of my dad's studies. We're working on a documentary."

"Liv?" A girl's voice broke in. "Liv, it's me. Sophie."

"Uh . . . hi, Sophie," I said, thrown off by the change.

"You're on speakerphone," she said. As if to prove it, I suddenly could hear all kinds of ambient noise. Yelling, laughing . . . water running. "Alec is here too."

"Hi, Liv," Alec called.

"Hey." I rested my head in my hands. Alec was Dax's best friend and Sophie's boyfriend. The three of them had been friends ever since kindergarten, and as soon as Dax and I got together, Sophie had immediately started calling to invite me to parties and sleepovers. "Why is everyone up so early?"

"You mean up so late. We stayed up all night and now everyone's going out to breakfast and surfing, then we'll sleep. The drive was so *long*, but Balboa is awesome, and Matthew's dad's place is so nice. There are three hot tubs and, like, thirty beds."

A bunch of noise and shouting in the background drowned Sophie out, and my brain scrambled to fill in the scene. Soda cans everywhere, bright beach towels, a lot of skin.

I gripped the edge of my rock, staring out into the quiet, wild surf. My little beach was something like seven thousand miles away from them, but right at this second, it felt more like seven million.

"Liv, why didn't you tell me you weren't coming? Are you really visiting your dad in Greece? I didn't even know you *had* a dad."

"Um . . ." I let out a noise that might have been a laugh, but I wasn't quite sure. Was that meant to be a joke or . . . ? But she didn't elaborate, which meant I had to fill in the space. "Well . . . a lot of people have dads," I said weakly. "Guess mine never came up."

"True," she said, smoothing over my awkwardness. Her voice went low and conspiratorial. "Well, hurry back. Girls in bikinis are circling Dax like sharks."

My heart leapt into my throat, and my fingernails pressed into the rock. "What girls?" My voice sounded tiny and jealous, and I hated myself for it.

She laughed, and I imagined her tossing her long dark hair. "Mostly seniors," she said. "Did you hear Maya got into UC Berkeley?"

"Yeah," I said weakly. "Is she there?"

"She and Dax drove together. I mean, there were two

other people in there, but still, she demanded to drive in his car so they could drive past their schools on the way." She laughed, but none of this sounded funny. "Don't worry about Maya. Everyone knows that Dax is smitten with you."

She paused, waiting for me to either laugh or agree, but I couldn't muster up any kind of reply. Would Dax still be smitten with me if he knew I had no intention of following him to college?

"Thanks, Sophie," I finally said. "Would you mind handing the phone back to Dax? I need to tell him something." Anxiety was building so hot and fast it rivaled the sun glaring off the ocean.

"No problem. DAX!" Sophie yelled, not bothering to move the phone and nearly decimating my eardrum. I waited, my heart pounding, but a moment later it was still her on the phone. "Sorry, I don't know where he went. He disappeared."

I squeezed my eyes shut, willing myself not to imagine him disappearing somewhere with Maya. Maya, who he had apparently spent half a night at a truck stop with, and who actually would be going to school with him. My hands were shaking, but I called on all the powers of Liv, forcing my voice to sound calm, bored even. "No problem. Tell him to call me, okay? When you find him?"

"Sure. Talk to you soon!" She hung up, and then it was just me and a whole lot of silence.

This is bad. Very, very bad. I shoved my phone into my pocket and stood up to stretch my legs. I was already sore from all the walking we'd done today, but my body wouldn't let me hold still, so I began jumping from boulder to boulder, winding my way toward the water.

Down here I had a great view of the subject of Hugo's painting. The rock rose solid and dark out of the water, waves crashing all around it. It was clearly a popular swimming spot, because along with a few left-behind pairs of goggles and towels, a small ladder had been hammered into the side of the rock.

I wandered around the beach, praying that Dax would call me back, but after half an hour, I gave up. He wasn't going to call me, and I was going to have to deal with the fact that I couldn't tell him the truth until I got back. It made more sense to tell him in person anyway.

It took me almost twenty minutes to heave myself all the way back up the steps, and by the time I got to the top and assimilated with the early-evening foot traffic, I was a complete emotional mess. All I wanted was to go to the bookstore, hide out, and read for a while. But when I saw the shop, I knew that wasn't an option. If anything, it was busier than it had been this morning, bursting at the seams with a still lively looking Ana conducting the crowds like a circus ringleader. My dad and his mounds of gear were nowhere to be seen.

Squeezing my way through the shop, I saw Theo up on a ladder, helping a customer reach a book. "Kalamata!" he yelled as soon as he saw me. He turned around, completely ignoring the waiting customer to get to me. "Are you okay? You've been gone awhile."

I shook my head and was horrified to realize that tears were springing into my eyes.

He hurried down, abandoning whatever task had taken him up there. "What's wrong?" He put his hands on my shoulders, steadying me.

I shook my head again. I needed a distraction. Anything to keep me from thinking about Dax. "Can I help out in the shop?" I blurted out.

Theo's forehead wrinkled. "You want to work?"

I nodded quickly, swiping at my eyes. "Work, volunteer, apprentice, whatever. I need to stay busy."

He studied me for another moment, then cleared his throat, deepening his voice to a more formal tone. "In that case, I have some good news for you. Geoffrey the Canadian has stepped out for his customary afternoon call to his favorite fake ballerina, so we are shorthanded. However, we don't hire just anyone here at the Lost Bookstore of Atlantis. I'm going to have to conduct a quick interview. What are your qualifications?"

I bit the inside of my cheek, surprised to find myself suppressing yet another smile, even through my stress. "Well . . . I've read books. Lots of books. Also, I once owned a toy cash register." I pointed to the counter where Ana was ringing someone up. "And I occasionally watch my step-aunt's pet gerbil when she goes out of town for the weekend."

"Impressive," Theo said. Bapou was cheerfully poking a customer with his cane, and Ana swooped in to stop him. Theo turned to me. "Well, those three facts alone make you more qualified than half the people who have worked here. Congratulations, Kalamata. You're hired."

Chapter Thirteen

#13. SANDALWOOD SHAVING SOAP

I don't know if this was a gift or if he bought it for himself, but he used it the way my mom used her perfume, sparingly and only for special occasions. It was in a glossy wooden container, and I always knew when he and my mom had plans because it would appear on the bathroom counter and I'd wait for the deep, earthy smell to come wafting into the living room.

He always stopped shaving when he lost one of his jobs, and by the time I was eight, I'd lost count of how many times that happened. He wouldn't say he lost them either. Instead he'd say, "Where should we go tomorrow, Olive?" and I'd know.

AFTER SUCH A RIGOROUS INTERVIEW PROCESS, I WAS happy to learn that Ana had no qualms about integrating me into the Lost Bookstore of Atlantis typhoon. Within minutes, I was straightening merchandise, helping the newly returned Geoffrey at the cash wrap, taking credit cards, and steering people toward a plethora of heaving bosoms in the jam-packed romance section. Every so often there'd be a lull, and my mind would start to wander back to Dax and the college dilemma, but within seconds a customer would ask me a question, or Theo would corner me to conduct a spontaneous employee performance review, and I was back to gliding across the surface, all thoughts of Dax submerged somewhere down below. Perfect.

By the time we shooed the last of the customers out the door, the sun had already condensed into a heavy orange globe, and we only had time to grab sweatshirts and a couple bottles of water before making our way up onto the roof.

After feeding us a rushed, standing-up dinner, Ana had taken Bapou home, and Geoffrey had mumbled something about ordering flowers for Mathilde, so it was down to Theo and me. All the hiking and book hauling and time on the water had left me so exhausted that every single muscle in my body hurt, and I sank into one of the wooden chairs. The caldera shone bold and glittery below us, and I sighed, taking in the view.

"Well, that was a boring day," I said, propping my feet up on the ledge.

"You did a hell of a job in there, Kalamata." Theo took

the seat next to me and turned to face me, leaning his cheek against his chairback. He didn't look at all tired from the bookstore rush. If anything, he looked energized. He and Ana didn't seem to run out of steam. "I'd like to promote you to part-time unpaid employee."

"I accept."

"Good, because I made you something." He reached into his pocket, then handed me a small plastic disk with a pin on the back. My very own employee name tag. NOT OLIVE.

"You think you're so funny," I said, laying it faceup in my palm. "How did you make this?"

"I *know* I'm so funny," he corrected. "We have a name tag machine in the cave. I think we went through, like, thirty different interns last summer, so my mom went ahead and bought her own name tag maker."

"Brilliant." I carefully clipped it to my CREW shirt, right over my heart, and he gave me a thumbs-up. My skin was itchy from sea spray, and my hair hung in salty clumps. I couldn't remember the last time I'd gone this long without looking in a mirror. Something about Oia made me not care.

"Do you think my dad will come back to the bookstore tonight?" I asked, glancing backward. The sunset crowds were starting to get amped up, lots of voices and laughing.

Theo shook his head. "Probably not. He's been running pretty hard ever since he found out you were coming. Plus, he really throws himself into the filming. I think he needs a night off."

"Fair," I said.

We were quiet for a moment, Theo holding still for a miraculous few minutes as we watched the sun continue to dip. It had barely kissed the top of the ocean when Theo reached over and poked my arm lightly. "What happened with lover boy? Did he call?"

I kept my eyes on the sunset. "Uh-huh."

"And?"

"Things are . . . betterish."

"Betterish?" I felt his gaze swivel toward me. "Kalamata, I'm sorry, but I don't think that's proper English."

I sighed. "He was mad at me, but now he's not. So that's good." My voice fell an inch shy of convincing, and I felt Theo focus in. Even when he didn't have a camera, it felt like he had a zoom feature.

"Why was he mad at you?"

The sun had created a golden path along the water, and my eyes stung as they traced the rippling line. I wasn't about to tell Theo about RISD, but I could tell him the rest. "I was supposed to go on this trip with him and his friends, but I had to cancel last-minute to come here."

Pause.

I risked a glance over at him and was met with a look of

intense credulity. "He's mad because you canceled a trip to come spend time with your father who hasn't seen you since you were eight?"

Harsh. Hearing the words out of Theo's mouth did make it sound unfair.

I quickly folded my arms across my chest, turning back to the water. "It isn't only that. I think I'm generally a disappointment to him."

I'd never said those words before, had never even quite formed the idea, but I recognized them to be true anyway. It was just a heaviness I felt sometimes. Was the sunset shaking something loose in me?

Out of the corner of my eye, I saw Theo's eyebrows go up. "Why would he be disappointed in you? You're awesome. I mean, yes, you snore, and you have this weird thing about your name, but I've spent twenty-four hours with you, and I can honestly say I've only been sick of you for one of them."

"Theo." I groaned.

"Fine, two. But really, why would he be disappointed in you?"

"He probably isn't. Forget it, okay?" A wave of anxiety passed through me, and I quickly shifted the spotlight. "What about you? Tell me more about what happened with you and your girlfriend."

He cocked his head slightly. "Not much besides what I told you. I moved, and she's still in London."

I waited for more of an explanation. "So what happened? Long-distance relationship didn't work out?"

He'd already answered these questions, but I was desperate for a distraction. Thinking about it made my stomach twist. Once Dax left for college in the fall, we'd be in that same situation. If we made it through the rest of the summer, that is.

He shook his head. "Like I said, long-distance doesn't work for me."

"Lots of people make it work, though." There was a hint of desperation in my voice. Regardless of where I chose to go to school, Dax and I would definitely spend the first year apart.

Theo shook his head again. "When my parents were together, we moved every year or two. At first I tried to maintain my friendships, but after a while I realized I was always missing someone, and it made it hard to actually enjoy wherever I was at the moment. So now it's an ironclad rule of mine—no long-distance friendships or dating. It's not worth the agony of trying to make them last."

"Present-moment living," I said, thinking about my yoga class at school. It did make a sad kind of sense. "So . . . once I leave Santorini . . ."

"You're dead to me," Theo said glibly. "That's that. We will never speak again."

I laughed, but I felt an odd twinge in my chest. "Good to know."

He shrugged. "I like to be honest. And Demy, she knew the score too. It was fun while it lasted, but once I moved, trying to stay together would have ruined all of the good memories. It was time for her to experience university. I'm sure she is dating and enjoying herself, and that's the way it should be."

He sounded so *mature*. My stomach turned, thinking about Dax leaving for college. Would he want to start dating other people, enjoying the college life? And what about when I told him that I didn't plan to follow him there? "Meaning she was okay with it?"

"Um . . ." He blinked his eyes sheepishly.

"Oh right. You're still friends, just the kind that don't talk to each other," I said, repeating what he'd said the night before. I looked at him for a moment longer. It was strangely satisfying to see him avoiding *my* eye for once. "Theo, come on. Did you *actually* like her? Because my BS meter is running pretty high right now."

His lips parted in a smile. "Kalamata, I'm not lying. I'm telling you the truth. I liked her very much. She was funny and smart. But what's the point? Best case, we would spend a few months pining away for each other—"

"Pining away?" I said incredulously. "What is this, the 1950s?"

He ignored me. "—talking on the phone late into the

night, then the expensive trips back and forth, and then the calls and visits would eventually become less and less frequent, and then the jealousy, and the fights . . ." He gave a lusty sigh. "You see? Disaster."

I raised my eyebrows at him. "It sounds like you have firsthand experience with this."

"I will neither confirm nor deny. But it's a good rule, Kalamata. Enjoy the moment, then carry the memories with you as a souvenir. It's my life mantra. Can you try it for me?" He lay his head back against his seat again, his eyes finding mine. The bright orange sky reflected off his skin, making his eyes look even darker, and for a moment I wondered if he was hinting at something. Was he hoping I'd enjoy the moment here with *him*? Was this a fling suggestion?

Goose bumps moved down my arm.

"Theo . . . ," I started, but right then the sun hit its point of no return and the crowd behind us burst into applause as a gale of wind hit the island.

"You see? Like that." Theo gestured to the now purple sky, his hair flying into his eyes. "Enjoy the moment. I'm going to go check on Bapou. See you soon?"

"Sure," I managed. He jumped up and disappeared down the steps, leaving me disoriented and a bit off-balance. Theo obviously wanted to be friends, nothing more. Why did I keep thinking otherwise?

* * *

It was too stuffy to hang out in the bookstore, so once I'd shaken off all the confused feelings Theo had stirred up, I went for my sketchbook and oil pastels. The oil pastels were even better than I'd imagined—vibrant and satisfyingly smooth, like butter at exactly the right temperature. For the next hour or so I sat sketching, enjoying the quiet and watching as the cliffside lit up, light by light in the darkness. I was working on a shadowy outline of Ammoudi Bay when Theo appeared.

"Let's go see the blue domes."

I kept my eyes focused on my sketch pad. "You mean the ones on the cliff? I saw them from the water this morning." According to the postcards and artwork displayed along Oia's main street, the small white church with cobalt-blue domes was like the village's mascot. That image was everywhere.

"But have you seen them up close? Or at night?"

I shook my head. "Would seeing them involve walking? Because I think I'm done with that today."

He placed his hand over my sketch pad, careful not to actually touch my work. "Kalamata, people come from all over the world to see Oia's blue domes, and you're going to see them at night. I'll carry you if I have to. Also, I'm confiscating your phone so you don't check it all night. Come on."

* * *

Santorini at night had a completely different personality: cool and moody with an unruffled quiet that made me feel like I should tiptoe. The only sounds were the ocean and occasional voices and clanking silverware drifting over from the top of rooftop restaurants.

Nighttime made Oia extra confusing, too. If you didn't pay close attention, it was easy to get lost in all the twisting, narrow alleyways. Most buildings were the same height, and besides Main Street there didn't seem to be much planning involved in how the town was laid out. The constant white made the whole thing worse, but Theo marched confidently forward, sure about where we were going.

We walked down the main corridor before Theo turned right at a ritzy-looking jewelry shop and onto a slender pathway, and soon we were winding our way through the mishmash of buildings arranged on the cliffs. The houses built directly into the cliffs were more like small caves with miniature shuttered windows and doors that most adults would have to duck under. The path serpentining through them was confusing, full of jagged turns and mismatched steps and dead ends.

"This place is a maze," I said, keeping my eyes on the varying steps as I followed after him.

"By design," Theo said, glancing over his shoulder at me. "Pirates used to be a big threat, so people on the island painted their houses white so that from a distance their town would blend in with the landscape and the pirates hopefully wouldn't notice a new place to loot. And then if the pirates did show up, only the locals would know their way around the alleys, which made it easy to confuse the pirates and buy them some time to escape."

Distracted by his history lesson, I slipped on a particularly uneven step, but caught my balance once Theo's hand gripped mine. We didn't say anything and he didn't let go; he didn't even look at me. Instead he clasped my hand tighter, continuing down the path. I let him, because the slippery path had turned lethal, and because my heart felt rough and ragged and holding someone's hand made me feel a little bit better.

Theo kept explaining. "Then, when pirates weren't such a big deal anymore, and the Ottoman Turks had invaded, the white and blue became an act of rebellion. The Turks wouldn't let them fly their flags, so they painted their houses the color of their flag."

"Rebels," I said, glancing up at the hillside. Oia had a sleepy beauty to it, but its history gave it a lot more energy. That made sense. My dad had always been the ultimate rebel—he didn't care what anyone thought—maybe part of that had come from his hometown.

Theo's hand was warm and sure in mine, and I kept waiting for him to let go. He didn't, and I didn't pull away either.

Regardless of the way it was making my checks heat up, it felt steadying—emotionally and physically.

I kept getting glimpses of the blue domes as Theo led me expertly through the maze, finally coming to a stop in front of a silken rope draped with a sign that read PRIVATE. Beyond it the domes stood full and commanding, lit up by spotlights in the darkness, the cobalt blue popping against all the white. Theo was right. They were gorgeous.

He carefully dropped my hand, and I shoved it in my pocket, clenching my tingling hand into a fist as we stared for a moment in silence.

Photos hadn't done the domes justice. Paintings hadn't either. Nothing did except being here. I exhaled slowly. "Okay, you win. This was worth it."

"Told you."

I turned to look at some of the dark shuttered windows nearby. An enclosed patio housed a hot tub, and someone had left two wineglasses on a nearby ledge. A few of the houses were lit up, but most were dark and silent. "What are these?" I asked.

"Cave houses. After my parents divorced, my mom's original plan was to invest in a few of these and rent them out to tourists. But then she reconnected with your dad and they came up with the whole bookstore idea." He pointed at the cave house closest to us. "Cave houses used to be where the poor people of Oia lived, and now it's the opposite. Guess how much one costs today?"

I glanced at the one nearest us. It looked smaller than anywhere my mom and I had lived, with two small windows and a patio big enough for a chair and a tiny side table. "I have no idea."

"Three million dollars."

My mouth fell open. "Seriously?"

"Seriously," he said. "People want the Oia experience. And it's all about the tourists here. Your dad's idea to open a bookstore for tourists was kind of brilliant. It was like the one thing Oia was missing. And bringing in the Atlantis angle made people even more excited about it."

Theo was right, of course. The idea was brilliant. If it weren't for his Atlantis hunting, my dad probably would have been a very successful businessman. I felt my mood drop slightly. "Do you like living in the bookstore?"

He shrugged. "I don't *not* like it. And once my grandfather moved into our house, it was too crowded. I need some space. Plus, it's nice to never run out of reading material."

My phone dinged from Theo's pocket, piercing the quiet. I thought I was going to have to fight him for it, but he handed it over without looking at the screen. It was a text from my mom. I'm not entirely clear why we got you the uber-expensive phone plan if you're going to repeatedly ignore my calls. Are you safe? Are you eating your weight in feta? Julius wants me to ask if you've seen any Greek ninjas. How's filming?

I laughed but was suddenly overwhelmed by a wave of homesickness. I missed my little ninja brother and my mom and James. The longest I'd ever been away from them was when I went to art camp, and that was only three days long.

"Dax?" Theo asked, his eyes on my face.

I shook my head, the heaviness settling over my chest again. "My mom. I think she's been trying to call me today."

He studied me for a moment. "I know I've already been stomping all over your boundaries today, but is it okay if I ask something personal?"

"Do you ever ask things that *aren't* personal?" My laugh was way too high-pitched, and I gulped it back quickly.

His eyes widened teasingly, and he bumped his shoulder against mine. "I'm not a *monster*, Kalamata. You can say no and I'll stop talking. Promise."

"Promise?" His eyes took actual effort to look away from. People would pay for those eyelashes.

"Cross my heart." He drew an exaggerated *X* over his chest.

I was tempted to shut his question down, but my curiosity wouldn't let me. Theo clearly had more to say about my boyfriend situation, and I was at least a *little* interested in what that was. Also, and I wasn't going to look too deeply into this, I was still feeling a little flustered from holding Theo's hand, and I needed to put that behind me.

I squared up in front of him, and a breeze moved over us, ruffling our hair. "Fine. What is it?"

He bit his lower lip, then leaned in slightly. "Have you ever asked him why he left?"

My brain shuffled in confusion for a moment before landing on the answer. He wasn't talking about Dax. He was talking about my dad. *Again.*

My cheeks flamed up and I moved backward, as far as I could, careful not to lose my footing. "Theo, I told you already. He left because he was looking for Atlantis."

Theo moved with me, his eyes pleading. "But have you actually ever *asked him*? Have you ever asked his reasons? Because something doesn't seem to add up. Your dad doesn't seem the type to leave you."

Nope. Not happening.

"Well, he *did.*" Why was Theo not getting this? "Look, I'm happy to be here hanging out with you and seeing the domes and everything. But I'm officially finished talking about this." Why was Theo so adamant about defending my father? Even if we took Atlantis out of the picture, my dad *had* left my mom and me. Regardless of his reasons, his actions had been loud and clear.

He hesitated, raising his hand to meet mine. "But your dad doesn't seem—"

I shook my head angrily. "Theo, I'm saying *no*. You promised."

The word had a visceral effect on him. He froze, then dropped his hand. "Okay. Sorry."

I waited incredulously through a few seconds of silence. "Okay?"

He shrugged his shoulders. "You're right. I promised. If you don't want to talk about it, then we won't. But some people are worth second chances. Not all people. Just some people."

"Theo—"

He held up his hands. "I'm done. I'm officially done. I won't bring up your dad again."

"Promise?"

"Promise."

"Thank you." Despite his track record, I knew I could believe him. We wouldn't be talking about my dad again. So where was the relief?

We stared at each other for a moment, our faces lit up by the domes. The sound of the ocean below was spa-like, but I couldn't shake the sense that something was coming after me. One wrong step and this all would come crashing down. Also, was it possible that a part of me had liked having someone ask me all those tough questions?

The silence stretched out until I couldn't take it anymore. I took a deep breath. "Let's get out of here before any pirates show up."

And before I start thinking about your eyelashes again. There was something about Theo that made it hard to look away.

Chapter Fourteen

#14. THUMBNAIL SKETCH OF AMMOUDI BAY

One day my dad and I were working on my homework at the library, and I asked if he had a picture of the place he'd grown up in. He said no, but he could draw it for me. He drew it quickly, then slid the paper over to me. It wasn't a house or an apartment like I was expecting. It was the ocean, a rippled coastline leading to cliffs in the distance.

"But where did you live?" I asked.

"There," he said, pointing to the drawing.

I didn't get it. But before I could ask again, he stood and asked if I wanted to go out for a rainbow sprinkle ice cream cone, and the laws of childhood proclaim that nothing shall trump ice cream, especially not if rainbow sprinkles are involved.

I was surprised when I found the drawing on the top shelf of his closet. I'd assumed he'd tossed it out as carelessly as he'd drawn it. Instead, he'd filled it in, *shading the water and defining buildings on the cliffs. It was beautiful, but it didn't look like a home.*

THE NEXT FEW DAYS PASSED IN A BLUR OF FILMING, sunscreen, and bumpy moments with my dad, smoothed over by the presence of Theo. We fell into a routine—wake up early, gather our obscene amount of equipment, head for the boat, work on our shot list, then rush back to Oia to help out at the bookstore until close, followed by sunset, dinner, and editing/drawing on the patio until we were too tired to keep our eyes open. Lather, rinse, repeat.

This was doable. It was very doable. Not only had Theo stopped talking about me making up with my dad, but my dad also seemed to be content with keeping things surface level as well. It wasn't comfortable by any stretch of the imagination, but I could handle it for another week or so.

Dax was texting me again—relief—but I found myself not hovering around my phone like I usually did. There was no way I was ever going to admit this to my mom, but she had been right. While I liked my social life back home, it was also really nice to be away from the noise and chaos and pressures and simply *be*. More than once I realized that I'd accidentally left my phone in the bunk and spent entire blissful days out on the water with no worries about what was going on in Balboa. It had been a while since I'd felt this free.

Despite the emotional ruins my dad and I were tiptoe-ing around, the days picked up speed, probably because they were so full. Theo and my dad were both perfectionists about the content of the shots, and I was a perfectionist about how everything looked. It turned out that I did have a knack for filmmaking. Once we'd reach a location, I'd look around, trust-ing my eyes to land on the perfect place to film. It was like a tiny bell rang and I *knew*. I'd also gone out shopping for my dad's on-camera wardrobe, and even convinced him to update his glasses, which had improved his appearance immensely.

Most shots we redid three or four times, which was a prob-lem, because no matter where we were, people flocked to the camera, curious to listen to whatever topic he was expounding on that day, or to chime in with their own theories of Atlantis. I honestly had no idea that the general population was so intrigued by Atlantis. If the documentary turned out as well as I imagined it would, it could be a huge success.

We also filmed the cliffs on the inner edge of Santorini, showing the way that the ash and pumice from the vol-cano explosion had created multicolor layers of rock. Layers you could actually see. At one point my dad said that if you wanted to touch Atlantis, all you had to do was touch that lower layer, and the line was so good that I dragged him over and made him say it again, but with him actually touching the rock. It honestly made me feel a little emotional to watch him do that, and when no one was looking I reached my hand out and touched it fast. Not surprisingly, it didn't feel like Atlantis. It felt like rock.

On day four of filming, I woke up from a dream about the water. And for once I wasn't drowning. When I opened my eyes, daylight streamed through our shared window. As usual, Theo's bed was already empty and neatly made, a pile of books on his pillow.

I stretched my arms happily over my head. I don't know if it was the French rap or the absolute exhaustion, but ever since arriving in Oia, I hadn't had a single nightmare.

By now I was an expert bunk navigator. I took my time sliding open the bookcase, carefully peering out into the store. Empty. Perfect. I lowered myself to the floor.

After quickly showering in the cave, I found my sturdiest pair of sneakers and made my way up to the roof to find Ana and my dad with steaming cups of coffee in their hands, speaking quietly in Greek. It was a cool morning, the early-morning fog still wispy on the horizon, and when I heard their voices, I instinctively slowed.

Ana spoke hurriedly, her tone nervous, and it sounded like my father was trying to reassure her about something. What was this about? For a moment I tried to eavesdrop, but they were speaking too quickly, and I couldn't untangle more than a few words in Greek. I was peeking around the corner when

Dad caught sight of me and jumped to his feet mid-sentence.

"Liv!"

Busted.

"Morning, Dad. Are you feeling any better?" I asked, joining them on the terrace.

My dad put everything he had into the day's work, and by the time we made it back to Oia, he was usually so exhausted that he'd skip dinner and head straight to bed. This morning his coloring was back to normal, and his eyes were bright again, which was good because we had a lot of filming to do.

"A good night of sleep cures almost everything," he said, smiling. "I heard Bapou made his famous moussaka."

"It was incredible." My mouth watered at the thought of it. Bapou's moussaka was made with thinly sliced eggplant, richly spiced lamb, and a savory béchamel sauce. After a long day of work, it had felt like I'd died and gone to an oregano-scented heaven.

"Ready for Egyptology day?" I asked. Today we were going to film the ins and outs of my dad's theory of Santorini-as-Atlantis, and after I'd decided on the interior of the bookstore as the best location, Theo and I had stayed up all night setting the scene. We'd cleared off the desk and placed a few of my dad's maps on the wall, and then I'd spent almost an hour arranging books and knickknacks to make it look like we were in the office of a trained Atlantis expert. Even I had to admit that it looked great, and Ana had agreed to make a rare exception to her *Open after first coffee* rule. The bookstore would open at noon.

My dad's shoulders fell in resignation. "Liv, I am so sorry, but we have a bit of a . . . conflict."

The word "conflict" snapped me out of my thought process. That and the sharp look Ana gave my dad.

"What do you mean?" I asked.

He shrugged apologetically. "I'm so very sorry, but I've had something come up on the main island. I need to take the next ferry to Athens. You will have to do today's filming without me."

"But . . ." I stumbled. "How? Today is about you and your theory. We can't film it without you. I already set up inside the shop."

His mouth dropped into a frown. "I know this is inconvenient, and I am very sorry. I've already spoken with Theo, and you two are going to do as much of the work as possible, and I will pick up from where you left off as soon as I return this afternoon."

I was so confused. We had just a few days left, and losing even one of those days meant we likely wouldn't make our deadline. He knew that better than anyone. Also, was he really going to leave right in the middle of my visit? The floor shifted like it had back at the airport when I'd realized my dad wasn't there, and suddenly I was holding my breath.

Breathe, Liv. You aren't eight years old. He can't leave you again.

I straightened my shoulders, shaking my panic loose. "What's going on in Athens?"

Another look between Ana and my dad "Well . . . ," he started.

"Business, always business." Ana sighed. "Your father unfortunately has to do a lot to keep the bookstore afloat. There are complications with the business license."

The business license? "But . . . haven't you been open for over a year?" I asked, looking around.

"Complications," Ana said again, rolling her eyes. This morning she wore a mustard-colored maxi dress with lace inserts, and her feet, like usual, were bare. She must have done a fresh pedicure, because her toenails were bright pink.

My dad set his hand on my shoulder. "I'll be home this evening to catch up on filming. And afterward, would you like to join me on a sunset cruise? You really should see the sunset from the water while you're here."

I was still trying to recover my footing, reconfigure the day in my head. If he had to leave, he had to leave. We'd make it work. I'd take a picture of the set and we could re-create it when he came back. "Will Ana and Theo come too?"

He shook his head. "I thought we could be on our own tonight."

My stomach lurched dramatically. So far, our visit had been buffered by work or Ana and Theo. Without them, what would we talk about?

"There will be a small group on the cruise," he said quickly, as though he could read my mind. "A friend of mine owns the yacht. We will have dinner, music; it is a lovely evening."

I glanced out at the water. I'd seen boats out chasing the sunset across the caldera every night, and despite the potential awkwardness, it sounded . . . nice. "Okay," I said cautiously.

He pulled his backpack up onto his shoulders. "Wonderful. It's a bit of a dress-up event, although nothing too fancy. I'll pick you up at a quarter to six?"

Had I really signed myself up for a daddy-daughter date? I definitely had. I nodded, my nerves allowing no room for my voice, and he gave me a quick hug, then disappeared down the steps, taking off with his usual speed.

THIS IS A BAD IDEA, my brain alerted me helpfully. It was much too late to back out, and now I had to spend all day worrying about the cruise.

"So sorry to ruin your plans today." Ana watched as my dad disappeared down the street. "Our business permit has been a pain in our side. Hopefully today he will get it resolved."

I nodded, but I couldn't help the feeling that sat there.

Yet again, my dad was putting his priorities above our plans, leaving me to deal with the fallout. But the most difficult part to deal with? Wishing I didn't care so much.

Ana told me that Theo had gone for a swim, so while I waited for him to get back, I camped out on the terrace. I'd planned to get fully ready, but I'd gotten sidetracked by my sketch-book, so I was still in my pajamas, trying to draw the blue domes from memory while I listened to Geoffrey talk to a British customer near the entrance of the shop. She'd asked for a beach read, and he was making the case for *The Grapes of Wrath*.

"Sometimes the bleak is what makes the beautiful stand out," Geoffrey said. "Without the darkness, would we even notice the stars?"

It must be a bad Mathilde day.

"I don't think the American Great Depression is what I want to read about on holiday. How about a rom-com? Something light?" The woman was beginning to sound desperate.

"How about *Anna Karenina*?" Geoffrey suggested instead. "Now, *there's* a love story."

I hadn't realized Theo was back until I heard his voice over my shoulder.

"That's really good," Theo said, his wet hair dripping on my sketch pad. "Oh no!"

"It's fine," I assured him, brushing off the water. "It's a throwaway sketch. And it's only good because of the oil pastels my dad got me. They're amazing." I held it up in the sunlight to get a better look.

"That's like saying a meal is delicious because it's served on a pretty plate," Theo said, falling into the chair next to me. "You're too modest."

I shrugged, then flipped my sketchbook shut and turned toward him. "Can you believe that my dad went to Athens today? We went to so much work to set up the bookstore last night."

"No one starves to death *per se*," I heard Geoffrey say from down below, still pleading his case as his customer murmured her reply.

Theo's gaze had slid out to the caldera. "The business license has been a real problem."

I was still wrestling with my feelings about it. My dad hadn't abandoned our plans. He'd had something come up. My reaction to it was ridiculous. "That means we're losing a whole day. Aren't you worried?"

"A little. But what can you do? Owning a business in Santorini definitely has its struggles. They've had to cut through a lot of red tape to keep this shop going, and your dad is on a lot of the paperwork." He crossed one ankle over his knee, and I watched him jiggle his foot anxiously, his eyes still fixed absentmindedly on the water.

I stared at his moving foot. Wondering where the bluntly honest, straight-to-the-point Theo disappeared to. But of course he worried about his mom and her shop. I could understand that. Lucky for me, I knew exactly how to get his mind off his mom's shop. I glanced back toward where Geoffrey's voice was coming from.

"You're saying you aren't interested in the Dust Bowl," Geoffrey said. "How about Orwell's *1984*?"

The customer huffed. "Are you joking? That novel is a dystopian tragedy. Beach read. I want a beach read."

I dropped the pastel I was holding into the box, then tapped Theo's foot lightly with mine. "As director of photography, I would like to make a suggestion. Actually, no. I'd like to make a *decision*."

Theo's eyes moved smoothly over to mine, and one eyebrow went up. "So first you don't want the title, and now you're power hungry?"

I waved him away. "Listen. Today's filming was supposed to be all about establishing the credibility of my dad's theory. Which made me wonder about the idea of hiring a narrator who could help do that."

Theo wrinkled his forehead. "What do you mean?"

"*Lord of the Flies*?" Geoffrey's voice boomed. "*The Bell Jar*?"

"Have you ever *been* to the beach?"

I sat forward on my chair. The idea had only been

half-formed when I started, but now it was picking up speed. "Don't you think my dad's theory would sound more legitimate if the facts were coming from someone other than him? For most of the film, it's him explaining and telling the story. But what if we had a second voice in there, sort of backing him up? And a narrator could also tie the scenes together and explain where my dad is and what we're filming. My dad wouldn't have to talk the whole time. We could show him in action. Wandering around the islands, looking philosophical and broody."

Theo's eyes lit up, and he sat forward. "Kalamata, that's brilliant!"

Go away, butterflies.

"You're *good* at this."

I calmed my reddening cheeks and poked his arm. "Don't act so surprised. We need someone who sounds really good and authoritative to give my dad's ideas more gravity. Someone who sounds like he knows everything. Someone like Movie Trailer Voice-Over Guy. You know who I mean? He's the one who does all the promos for American movies." I pitched my voice as low as possible. "In a world . . ."

"Agreed. Movie Trailer Voice-Over Guy would be perfect. But do you really think he's hanging out on some small Greek island?" He looked back and forth dramatically.

"But sometimes you don't *need* hope," Geoffrey's voice insisted.

I smiled. "Come with me." Theo followed me down to the bookstore, where Geoffrey now stood beaming at his phone. His customer must have fled.

"Hi, Geoffrey," I said.

He gestured to his phone. "Three missed calls from Mathilde, all while I was helping that customer."

"Geoffreyyyyy." Theo groaned, but I stepped on his foot, effectively shushing him. We weren't here to debate the existence of ballerina girlfriends. We were here to—as I'd read on one of the many filmmaking websites I'd been perusing lately—*elevate our film*.

"Hey, Geoffrey the Canadian. I have a question for you. . . ."

Geoffrey the Canadian was an excellent voice-over for several reasons: not only did he have an inexplicably perfect voice, but said voice was cheap (we only had to buy him a granita from a stand near the bus stop), and Ana was willing to loan him to us for the day on the condition that we helped out with the afternoon rush.

First, Theo and I holed up in the bunk room to do a massive brainstorming session, coming up with as many details as we could about my dad's theory of Atlantis. Then we wrote a script and had Geoffrey practice it a few times, ironing out the spots that sounded too cheesy or over-the-top.

We spent most of the morning and part of the afternoon

in the cave recording Geoffrey, partially because the acoustics were good, but mostly because it was so crowded everywhere else. In between takes, we took turns helping out in the shop and fanning each other with a big pasteboard we found on top of a crate.

By the time we were finished, all three of us were bathed in sweat, and I never wanted to hear another word about *lost civilizations* or *pyroclastic flows* ever again. But the good news was, I'd been right. When Theo pasted a quick sound bite over some of the footage we already had, it did sound more professional. A *lot* more professional.

The bad news was that, despite my best efforts, the project had not taken my mind off my impending dinner plans with my dad. That had been too much to ask.

As promised, we worked during the afternoon rush; then Theo took off to work on some panoramic shots, while I ducked into the cave for a second shower and to figure out what constituted Yacht Appropriate Attire™. It was probably my nerves about spending time with my dad, but I couldn't decide what to wear. All of my understanding of yachts came from music videos. At some point would everyone start throwing dollar bills in the air while we all dove into the ocean?

It's possible I was overthinking this.

I tried on two different dresses, a skirt, and a jumpsuit

before settling on the first dress I'd put on: the V-neck maxi dress I'd worn to Dax's graduation. Next, I located a small, frenetic blow-dryer under the sink and actually styled my hair, then put on some makeup and my favorite wedged sandals. And because Coco Chanel said that "a woman who doesn't wear perfume has no future," I spritzed myself with a cloud of perfume and emerged from the cave coughing asthmatically.

If anyone needed a future, it was me. *Onward and upward.* I had no intention of talking about the past with my dad tonight. In fact, I hoped we wouldn't talk about much at all.

A part of me hoped my dad's business license trip had been extended, but as soon as I stepped into the bookstore, I saw him helping Ana at the register. His hair was wet and freshly combed, and he wore one of the button-up shirts I'd approved for filming, this time actually buttoned up. Also, shorts and flip-flops. He had his limits.

They both looked up as I walked in, and a smile took over my dad's face. "Liv, you look like your mother."

"Thanks." I didn't bother to tell him what we both knew—I didn't look a thing like my blond, long limbed mother. I looked like *him.*

A bouquet of fresh flowers sat on the counter, and he scooped them up and brought them over to me. "I saw these at my favorite flower stall in Athens; they reminded me of you."

It was a small bouquet, the colors arranged in a simple

mix of light pinks and whites. Something about them *did* feel like me, but I wasn't sure what. Also, was it just me, or was this starting to feel like a very awkward prom date? Was a dilapidated limo about to pull up outside the bookstore?

Ana hurried over. "Oh, how lovely! Liv, you are a vision."

"Should I go change?" I asked, gesturing to his flip-flops. "Because I thought you said it was more formal. . . ."

"Don't change a thing," Ana said quickly. "You look beautiful."

"Agreed," my dad said.

"Okay." I sank my nose into the bouquet, breathing in deeply. It smelled incredible, but I was mostly trying to hide the panic that was undoubtedly creeping over my face. We were going somewhere alone. The last time that had happened, I'd been *eight*. What if he tried to talk about the time period before he left, or what it had been like after he left, or . . . ?

Breathe, Liv.

I needed to keep this all under control. "How was Athens?" I managed. "Did you get it all worked out with the business license?"

I tried to keep the disappointment or whatever it was out of my voice. Or at least most of it.

He and Ana shot each other a brief look that was not lost on me. What was that? Regret? "Mostly," my dad said. "But

I heard *you* had quite the day of work. That voice-over idea was genius."

I nodded, enjoying the feeling of solid ground under my feet. As long as we talked about the documentary, we'd be fine. "Geoffrey did a really great job."

"I did, didn't I?" Geoffrey walked in from the second room, carrying a large stack of books, and when he saw me, he did a fake double take. "That dress! It reminds me so much of the one Mathilde was wearing for her headshot. Unfortunately, they haven't put it on the website yet, so I can't show it to you."

"Isn't that something," Ana said, giving me a little smile. She gestured to the clock. "You two had better go. The ship will dock when? At six?"

"Five fifty," my dad corrected her. He began fiddling with the sleeve of his shirt, and an alarming truth settled over me. He was as nervous and wobbly as I was. How would we possibly keep this night afloat?

"Well . . ." He glanced back around the room like he was also hoping for some sort of bookstore emergency to occur—a deadly paper cut? An avalanche of novels? But none came, so finally he settled on me.

"Shall we go?" My father extended his arm to me, and I gave Ana and Geoffrey a little wave.

"I'll take the flowers," Ana said, scooping them up from

me. I wanted to grab hold of her arm and make her come, but I doubted it would be particularly effective. And besides, I needed to get this over with. *"Au revoir,"* she sang. "Have a lovely evening."

If only.

My dad held open the bookstore door for me, and I stepped out into the clear, calm evening. It felt like walking the plank. Well, walking the plank in a pair of wedge sandals and the knowledge that fine cuisine awaited me on the other end.

But otherwise, exactly like that.

Chapter Fifteen

#15. HALF-FINISHED SUDOKU PUZZLE

My dad and I were full-time Atlantis hunters and part-time bench sitters. He said that was something that was missing in America—people never took the time to sit. There was a bench in Grant Park that should have had our names on it because we spent so many hours there. I'd bring a coloring book and a pack of crayons, and he'd bring the sudoku puzzle he was working on, but he almost never worked on it then. Instead, we sat side by side, silent and taking it all in.

He said that there are two types of silence, the silence that is empty and the silence that is full, and it's never hard to figure out which one you're dealing with. He was right about that.

WE TOOK THE SAME ROUTE DOWN TO THE WATER THAT WE always did. It should have felt easier without all the gear we normally carried, but the stilted conversation weighed at least double that of the filming equipment, and by the time we got to the castle I was positively out of breath. I was also having a difficult time moving like a regular person.

Was it inhale, then exhale? How did people normally swing their arms while they walked? Did three hundred people really have to come out to greet us every time we walked by?

Also, wedge sandals should not actually be allowed onto the island. What was I thinking?

While we picked our way down the stairs, me hanging on to the railing and trying to decide if I dared brave the stairs barefoot, my dad launched into a very long and detailed explanation of how the sunset cruises on the island worked while I made *uh-huh* noises like I thought it was the most interesting subject in the world. I mean, it wasn't *un*-interesting. Sunset cruises were big business in Santorini. Most of them were four- or five-hour affairs, starting in central Fira and then stopping at multiple destinations and swimming spots before culminating in Oia for dinner and sunset.

At least there would be other people on board. I latched on to that idea and held it tightly. We needed a buffer. Where was Theo and his giant camera when you needed him?

The ship looked more like a runaway pirate ship than the yacht I'd envisioned, with tall sails and polished wood interior that gleamed in the changing evening light. Something like two dozen guests were already on board, their ages ranging from old to positively ancient. Judging by their jubilant expressions and half-full wineglasses, they'd been partying for a while now. They stared at us with unabashed curiosity, and I wondered what we looked like. Did we look like a typical father and daughter? Or was the awkwardness exuding from us in a big ugly cloud? People love a train wreck. No wonder their expressions were so gleeful.

"Nico Varanakis!" the captain yelled, hurrying over to help us aboard. "Ladies and gentlemen, we have ourselves a stowaway of the finest caliber. The stories you have heard of him are true. At long last, may I present Nico, the Atlantis hunter!"

The captain must have given them quite the introduction to my father, because the entire ship broke out in a wild ruckus, cheering and yelling, a few of them clanging spoons against their glasses and shouting out *"OPA!"* My dad bowed, which was both embarrassing and the exact right move. Several more *opa*s rang out over the water, and when my dad straightened, his cheeks were flushed. If I weren't so terrified of the ocean, I would have taken this opportunity to throw myself into its depths. Were we really about to join this circus?

The captain theatrically made his way over to us, expertly managing the rocking boat and dock and holding his arms out welcomingly. He was in his late twenties or early thirties, with darkly tanned skin and a thick beard, and he was clearly working the yacht-captain angle. He wore a crisp white jacket fitted tightly around his arms, complementing his dark aviators, and a little cap with a gold braid running across the brim. It looked more like a costume than a uniform.

As if he could read my mind, he winked at me, his voice still loud enough to include the rest of the cruise. "Ah, the *daughter of Atlantis*. Let us begin with a test of Greek culture. The rest of you, no cheating." He turned and waggled a warning finger at them, and they broke out in applause again. He had them eating out of the palm of his hand. "Now we begin. Here in Greece, all men have one of five names." He held up one hand and pointed at each finger one by one. "This is an exaggeration, yes, but we are named for our grandfathers, and our grandfathers are named for their grandfathers, and so on, forever, and forever, amen. I only exaggerate a little. If you can guess my name, you win my *hat*."

He pulled it off, tossed it spinning into the air, then caught it one-handed behind his back and bowed to me with a flourish, earning himself another round of applause.

Ridiculous. But he was right. The people of Santorini clearly loved to name themselves after each other. In all the people my dad had introduced me to, I'd heard only a handful of the same Greek names: Marias and Anastasias and Christos all linking up to form a chain. And as embarrassing as this whole thing was, I was relieved, too. A cheesy cruise director may turn out to be a better buffer than even Theo. Either way, I was in.

The passengers smiled at me expectantly, and the yacht captain replaced his hat. "Well?"

"Giorgos," I said, spouting off the first name that came to mind.

The yacht captain grinned gleefully. "No! But this is a good guess. Try again."

"Dimitris?"

"Wrong!"

"Constantino?"

"Wrong once more!"

My mind scanned through the three hundred people my dad had introduced me to over the past few days. A gray-haired woman on the boat nodded at me encouragingly. "Kostas?"

Bingo. A smile broke out over Kostas's face, and the boat erupted into a cheer as the hat landed in my hands. "Well done. You are as clever as you are beautiful. Now please, make yourself comfortable."

"Good job," my dad said, following me onto the boat. For a moment everything felt fine. The boat felt luxurious and rich, and the deep azure water rocked us lazily. Everyone wanted to shake my dad's hand and say hello to me. But then

I saw where we were supposed to sit, and my entire mood came crashing down. Two cushioned seats sat positioned near the bow of the yacht, a solid ten feet away from the rest of the cruisers, who sat shoulder to shoulder, not an inch to spare between them. Meaning, I wouldn't be able to rely on them to get through the evening. Great. I settled into my seat, trying not to panic.

And so . . . more silence. Silence as Kostas called orders to the crew, and silence as the ship carefully pulled out into the water, music now blaring from the speakers. We'd clearly been given the VIP seating. The view from our perch was breathtaking, but I was so anxious that it was physically painful to hold still. I looked out at the water, up at the sails, back into the water, up at Oia, over to the cruisers, who were now playing a drinking game that seemed to revolve around the chorus of the Greek song booming at full blast. My dad, on the other hand, sat completely still, his shoulders tense, gaze out to sea. He almost never sat still. What was he thinking? Was he as uncomfortable as I was? Why couldn't we have stuck with the documentary-making? The seconds ticked by until I couldn't take it anymore. Finally, I gestured to Kostas, blurting out the first thing that came to mind. "Dad, are you named after your dad?"

He hesitated, and a quick wave of uneasiness passed over his face. I knew almost nothing about his family, only that he had lost both his parents by the time he came to America, meaning I had managed to upend an extremely personal can of worms in my attempt to keep things as un-wormy as possible.

Smooth, Liv.

Then, shockingly, a look of relief. Presumably because I had shown some interest in his life? He leaned in. "Yes, I am named for my father. And for his father. If you had been born a boy . . . you would be Nico." He smiled, the uneasiness gone. "You have chosen a lovely name for yourself, but do you know the story of your given name?"

My *given* name. It was such an odd expression, like I'd been handed a wrapped present with a bow. I looked longingly at the cruisers. "Olive? No. Mom never told me."

It was an unintentional dig, but a dig all the same. After I was eight, Mom was the only one who possibly could have told me where my name had come from.

He caught the barb, his face smooth. "Near my home growing up, we had an olive tree. It was very old. Maybe two hundred years old. I used to climb into it and imagine all the things it had seen and all the things it must know." He met my eyes. "And then, when I held you for the first time, I saw your eyes. They were so big and bright, I thought you must know things too, and I thought of that tree immediately. I could feel your strength already. I knew you would withstand anything. And here you are. You have withstood."

The ship went over a rough patch, sending spray and panic into my face. The salt water stung my eyes, and I rubbed at them fiercely. Why didn't I already know this story about myself? Did my mom know it? Had I ever heard it? The olive tree sounded slightly familiar, but he'd never talked much about his childhood home, so . . . Panic was building in incremental units, and when I dropped my eyes, they got snagged on the numbers tattooed on his arm, the one that meant *family*.

A wave of anger pulled me out of the despair enough for me to catch my breath. Who waited for a geriatric booze cruise to tell their child important stories like this? And why was he telling me now at all? Didn't he know how painful this would be?

"Dad . . . ," I started, but I didn't know where to go from there. How to tell him that our tie had been severed long ago. He must know that, right?

His voice rose, and I quickly realized he was misunderstanding my emotion. "Liv, I have so much to tell you, and explain, I almost don't know where to begin. When I left . . ." He took a deep breath, his eyes suddenly full of tears.

Oh no. *NO*. He had planned this to be an apology cruise. I had to stop it.

"*Dad.*" This time it came out as a hard stop, and he understood. His lips pursed together as he looked at me.

I took a deep breath, forcing my lungs to expand through all the conflicting feelings battling for space in my chest. "I've been fine. There were hard years, but my life is good now. Mom and I moved on; she got remarried. I have my little brother, and I have lots of friends, and a boyfriend, and a whole life. Everything turned out *fine.*"

With no help from you. I didn't say those words, but they were there anyway. I quickly added on, "I don't want to waste our time rehashing things. I want to enjoy this."

This. What did *this* mean? The cruise? The sunset? I guess it was open to interpretation.

He looked a little stunned. Eyes wide, his mouth slightly downturned. Silence stretched between us. One . . . two . . . three . . . and . . .

"Yes," my father finally said, nodding. "That is your choice." He nodded again. "I have enjoyed the last few days with you so much. Let's enjoy the sunset."

"Sounds great," I said, but my voice sounded half strangled, and he gave me a searching gaze that I pretended not to notice. I quickly turned to look out over the water.

And for the next fifteen minutes, that's what I did—if *enjoy the sunset* meant staring awkwardly into the glowing orb so as to fool everyone into thinking that I wasn't blinking back tears, fighting off a mild panic attack, while the rest of the ship rocked out to what sounded like a Greek knockoff of "My Sharona."

This was the literal worst.

Eventually, and to my everlasting relief, two servers appeared from the hull of the boat and presented us with plates piled high with food. Spiced souvlaki on wooden skewers, lemon-scented rice, and a salad made up of thick chunks of feta, tomato, and cucumber. They even set up small standing trays for us and poured a soda for me and wine for my dad.

"Enjoy," my father said, clinking his glass together with mine. His face took on a serious expression, and for a moment I thought he was going to try to press the issue again about why he'd left, but instead he tilted his head toward me. "Tell me about Dax."

Hearing my dad say his name was a startling collision of worlds. Of course Mom had told him about Dax. I braced myself against the edge of the boat. "Did Mom tell you to ask me?"

He cocked his head curiously. "No. Why? Should she have?" The boat was picking up speed now, skating over the ocean toward the setting sun, and my soda sloshed precariously in my glass. I had the odd sensation of both racing and holding still.

I shook my head. "No. I don't think Mom likes him very

much." Her words from back home echoed in my mind. *It can be easy to lose yourself in your first relationship.* No wonder she was so leery of Dax—her first relationship had cost her too much.

"She doesn't?" He tilted his head.

There was no good reason for me to elaborate about my dating situation, so of course I did. "Dax wants us to go to the same school, or at least schools that are close to each other. He's a year ahead of me, and he's going to Stanford."

"Stanford," my dad said. A smile stretched across his face. "So he is a good student."

He sounded admiring, and relief spread through my chest. My mom had never seemed to be able to see the good things in Dax. Or maybe it was that she wasn't nearly as impressed by them as everyone else was. I perked up a little, stabbing my fork into a chunk of feta. "Yes. And a good athlete. He was the captain for our school's water polo team. He's really great at it."

He carefully placed his napkin on his lap. "And what school do you want to go to, Liv?"

"RISD." The letters spilled out automatically. I hadn't said it to anyone but my mom yet. I hadn't even said it to myself all that much. Mostly I'd stalked the website, taken notes on which of my pieces would be best for the application, and pretended I didn't care, when in reality I cared so much it made me feel like I was in the center of a swarm of bees. I took a deep breath, my eyes focused on my salad. "It stands for—"

"Rhode Island School of Design?"

My gaze shot up to his, and when I looked up, he had his hands wrapped around his glass, a small smile on his face. "You've heard of it."

He smiled. "I once dreamed of applying there myself. But life took some unexpected turns."

"Wait, *what*?" I dropped my fork with a loud clatter, like I was tumbling, sliding, *something*. My dad had wanted to apply to RISD? Had my mom known that?

Of course she had. And she'd never once mentioned it. She'd kept encouraging me, and tacking up the brochures on our family bulletin board. This was too weird. Too *much*. I'd done everything possible to disentangle myself from my dad, and now his influence was going to follow me into college?

RISD suddenly felt as out of reach and insignificant as the tiny cave houses receding in the distance.

I tucked my hands under my legs, willing them to stop shaking. "It doesn't really matter anyway. It's difficult to get into. Extremely difficult."

He shook his head, his eyes bright. "No. Your grades are excellent. And so is your artwork."

Mom had told him about my grades? *Ugh.* She owed me a very serious talk. "It's still a long shot."

"Simply being alive is a long shot," he said. "And art isn't your future; it's your today. It's in the way you do everything."

He was right, but I also really wanted him to be wrong. I *needed* him to be wrong. "But being an artist . . ." I reached up and grabbed my fork forcefully. "It doesn't make a lot of sense financially. Going into debt over school is not very smart and—"

He slammed his palm against his tray, making me and his silverware jump. "What does making money have to do with art? You don't make art to make money. And you don't make it because it's convenient. You do it because it's what you're here to do, and if you don't do it, you are running from yourself. Liv, you are not here to fail. You are here to *create*."

The Impassioned Speech, starring Nico Varanakis. I'd once heard his speeches on a near-daily basis. I'd forgotten how they made things—life—appear so black-and-white. Was it black-and-white? Was art really my destiny? Okay, destiny was sort of a gross word, but was art who I was?

His words lingered in the air, and for one moment I couldn't help but believe him. And even more powerfully, I believed that *he* believed in me. Which made my mind spin in circles, because how could someone who believed in me also have left me? It was a contradiction. An unsolvable riddle. He couldn't get to do both, and yet I knew that, right at this second, he was.

My dad literally *made my head hurt*. And now I had my own questions bubbling up. Was he making a case for his life's passion? Was he trying to explain what had brought him back to Santorini?

We'd already dived a few hundred feet. What was a few more? I took a deep breath. "Is that why you look for Atlantis? If you weren't looking for it, you'd be running from yourself?"

He looked at me for a moment; then his shoulders rounded. "Running, yes. Atlantis has always been important to me. But sometimes more important than it should have been." He glanced down at his plate. "Theo told me to ask you about your thoughts on Atlantis. He said you had some strong opinions that you might want to discuss."

Theo! I mentally cursed him. "When did he tell you that?"

"The day after you arrived. He said you had something to tell me about Atlantis and that you would kill him if he told me."

My body tensed, gearing up for confrontation, but my dad wasn't fighting. He looked focused. And curious. Like he actually wanted to hear what I had to say. Maybe Theo was right. Maybe my dad did need to know how I really felt.

But could I do that to him? He must know that I didn't really believe in Atlantis anymore, but what would telling him explicitly do to him? At this point I didn't owe him anything, but . . .

Fine. I was going for it.

"To me . . ." My voice wobbled. "Dad, I know you've done all this work, and talked with an expert and all that. . . ." I'd thought all these things a million times, maybe two million, but saying them aloud to my dad was a completely different experience. "But I believe that Atlantis is a morality myth that was used to scare people out of being prideful. Plato talked about it because he was worried about the people of Athens. He thought they were getting too rich and proud, and he told them a story that was supposed to scare them into being good again. I don't think it's a place you—or anyone," I added quickly, "can actually find."

There.

The last few words came out in a wild gulp, and I could barely look at him because my heart was having a monumental freak-out.

But I'd said it. And I'd officially crossed the line from mutiny to betrayal.

I braced myself for whatever reaction he was about to have—anger, or sadness, maybe even a lecture on the veracity of Plato's dialogues—but when I looked up, he didn't look devastated. His eyes were shiny, and he had the crooked smile he'd always reserved for my mom and me. Pride. He was looking at me with *pride*.

He leaned forward, his shiny eyes on mine. "Liv, you have

your own mind. Your own *wonderful* mind. I always knew you would be a thinker."

Okay, not what I was expecting. Not even in the general vicinity of what I was expecting.

"Um . . . ," I stammered.

He bobbed his head enthusiastically, his plate forgotten. "Tell me more!"

Was he serious? I studied his face, my heartbeat smoothing out in rhythm with the bobbing of the boat. He was serious.

"Okay . . . well, there are some issues with Plato's story and Santorini."

"Yes. Tell me." He held his hand out in a beckoning gesture, his face still lit up.

"Plato talks about the volcano erupting nine thousand years before his time, but if it was the Santorini volcano, it would have been three thousand years before his time. That's a big difference." I'd learned this in my post-believing, pre-ignoring phase of Atlantis, better known as the Anger Phase.

He was nodding, fast, and then faster. "Yes. What else?"

"Plato said that Atlantis was bigger than Asia and Libya put together. Santorini isn't as big as either."

I couldn't tell if it was the sunset or pride, but his face managed to brighten even more. "Another good point. Liv, you have done your research. I am so proud."

"Not a *lot* of research," I said, but that wasn't true and we both knew it. You didn't know exact details about Plato's explanation without doing some digging.

"I will think on those things," my dad said. "Do some research. If there is really an inconsistency, then I would like to know about it."

Right then a loud blast of music erupted near my ear, so loud that I nearly dumped my plate into the ocean. It was Kostas, only now instead of a yacht captain, he was a musician. He'd replaced his yacht-captain jacket with a shiny button-up. A gold saxophone dangled heavily around his neck, and he had one foot propped up on the bench.

My brain had barely enough time to process these facts before he began blasting the kind of music you'd hear in the waiting room at the dentist.

"He plays the saxophone too?" I said.

"Not well." My dad fought back a smile. "But it brings him a lot of tips."

An elderly couple stood and began slow dancing, with a half dozen others joining in. The remaining cruisers pulled out their phones and began filming. The entire thing was unforgivably cheesy, but with the sunset splayed out all gorgeous and commanding in the background, it also kind of worked.

"So . . . you're okay? With me not believing?" I was still trying to wrap my mind around this.

"I am more than okay." His dark eyes met mine, startling me a bit. Color aside, we had the exact same eyes. *Exact.* Whenever I looked at pictures of myself, I could see it—the curiosity, the brightness, all of it. If it weren't for the lines around his eyes, it would be like looking in the mirror. "You were never under any obligation to believe. And I do have answers for those concerns, but I will leave them for now. But"—he swallowed hard—"do you think it's possible that you can believe in *me* for a bit? Even for a few days? I know it is a lot to ask. But, Liv, I believe I have found it this time. I really, really do."

A lump formed in my throat. The thought of believing in my dad again was such a big and bright idea, it hurt to look at. Maybe it was the stupid saxophone-and-sunset combination, but suddenly I was remembering what it felt like to be his daughter. To believe in him. It made me want to sing or cry, or something, but at the same time, how could he possibly think I could ever do that again?

"I-I don't know . . . ," I stammered.

He put his hand up reassuringly. "That is also more than okay," he said. The sun had already turned into its molten, golden mass. Dad was right—watching it from the water with the light splashing over everything was incredible. Like I was actually becoming a part of the sunset, rather than observing it.

"And the thing about Atlantis?" My dad's voice broke

through my thoughts. "Sometimes it's more about the hunt."

I nodded again, because I had no idea what else to do, and when I looked down, I realized his hand was pressed to his inner arm, right on the spot where I knew the tattoo of my geographic location was. I don't think he even realized he was doing it. And now I was wondering how many times he had done that while he was here and I was on the other side of the world.

He turned to me. "Tomorrow night, I will take you to one of my favorite places on the island. Kamari. Liv, you will love it."

And just like that, I was signed up for a second solo night with my dad. So long to avoiding the past. It was inked into our skin.

Chapter Sixteen

#16. MINIATURE SPIRAL NOTEBOOK, WITH NOTES WRITTEN IN GREEK

I was endlessly fascinated by my dad's ability to write in Greek. I heard him speak in Greek all the time, both to me and to his friends in Chicago's Greektown. I was used to that. But writing in Greek? Now, that was impressive.

I found the notebook tucked in the glove box of our car two weeks after he left, and when I saw the writing, I thought maybe it was a clue. I knew my mom couldn't read it, so one afternoon before she got home from work, I took it to Markos—the owner of our favorite Greek deli— and asked him to read it for me.

Markos must have already heard the news about my father, because his eyes darted apologetically toward me.

It was a grocery list.

MY OPTIMISM SET WITH THE SUN, AND BY THE TIME WE returned to the dock in Ammoudi Bay, my heart felt nearly as heavy. I wanted to believe in my dad, the same way I wanted to believe in Atlantis, but that would require ignoring reality, and I wasn't about to do that again.

Here were the actual facts. Even if my dad had wanted to chase Atlantis or end his marriage with my mom, he didn't have to leave *me*. He could have visited. Or called. I knew a lot of people with divorced parents, even people whose parents lived in different cities or states. They didn't fall off the edge of the earth when they left. They didn't disappear. This wasn't a trumped-up golden city we were talking about after all. This was a *father*.

The entire way up to the bookstore, it felt like a balloon was expanding in my chest, the pressure crowding out my ability to think or feel anything. I wanted to *escape*. Leave all this mess behind. I managed to keep it together until we reached the bookstore. Then, once my dad disappeared down the street, tears began spilling down my face, dragging all my eyeliner with it. Had I really gotten all dressed up just to have my heart broken all over again?

I needed to regroup. Focus. I thought of my phone charging up in the bunk room and felt a shot of hope. I needed to talk to Dax. He'd help me—*Liv*—remember my real life, not this alternate reality where my feelings about my dad still controlled everything.

I rushed back to the bookstore and found it unlocked but empty, a single lamp illuminating one corner. There must not be a lot of thieves intent on stealing romance novels. I clambered up into the bunks, reached for my phone, then dropped back down, dialing Dax, all in one smooth motion.

It rang and rang, then went to voicemail. Dammit.

"Answer," I said aloud, then hit dial again. Same thing. Only this time it went to voicemail after three rings. I pressed the phone tightly to my ear, willing the sound of his voice on the voicemail greeting to make me feel slightly more grounded. *Hey, it's Dax. Leave me a message and I'll probably call you back.* I needed that *probably* to be a definitely.

I cleared my throat. "Hey, Dax. Will you call me as soon as you can? It's been a rough day, and I really need to talk to you."

What was he doing right now? Surfing? Lying out on the beach? I couldn't help but wish that I was doing that too. After a few seconds I stumbled over to the travel section of the bookstore, running my hand along the covers, hoping to get my mind off things. *Finland. Japan. Turkey. Russia.* That stupid saxophone song was still in my head, and I couldn't stop thinking about what my dad had said. *Do you think it's possible that you can believe in* me *for a bit?* How do you believe in someone who left you when you were eight years old? And how was I supposed to manage the enormous chasm that existed between how he *said* he felt about me and what his actions said about how he felt about me?

I looked down at my phone, willing it to ring. "Dax, call me back *now*," I demanded.

"Rough night?"

I jumped about a foot, dropping my phone in the process. It clattered noisily at my feet.

Theo was sitting in the chair behind the register, and he spun around slowly like the villain from an old Bond movie. A marmalade-colored cat lay curled up on his lap, along with a red notebook and a pen.

"What are you doing?" I demanded. I couldn't decide if I was more embarrassed or angry. Had he heard my voice-mail to Dax? I studied his concerned eyes. Yeah. He definitely had.

He shook his head. "Sorry. That was a lot funnier in my head. I meant to startle you, not make you throw expensive gadgets."

"Mission *not* accomplished." I scooped up my phone and stuffed it into my pocket.

"How was the dinner cruise? Did you lower the average age?"

"By a lot." I sighed and crossed the room to pet the cat, who arched its back in annoyance. Despite my interest in them, cats never seemed to like me. "Who's this?" I asked.

"Purrnest Hemingway. Not to be confused with her sister, Margaret Catwood." Purrnest jumped off Theo's lap and hid behind a tower of books.

"Really?"

Theo shrugged. "Geoffrey is excellent at pun bookstore cat names. I think it's half the reason my mom keeps him around. And you aren't answering my question. How was the sunset cruise? It was with Kostas, right? Please tell me he played his saxophone."

"Did he ever." I sighed again, then remembered Theo's part in the whole debacle. "And my dad and I talked about Atlantis, thanks to you."

Theo spun lazily in his chair, clearly not at all concerned about the angry vibes heading his way. "Interesting. How did you feel about the conversation?"

I sank onto the desk, wilting like one of the houseplants I was always rescuing from my mother. "I don't know."

Theo held up his pen. "The subject has a difficult time discerning her emotions," he said, pretending to scribble on his notebook.

I swung my legs over, bumping them into his. "You're a punk."

He widened his eyes. "Really? No one has ever told me that. And I'm curious, do people usually call you back when you tell them to from a long distance?"

I kicked his kneecap lightly. "Sometimes. And here, I brought you this." I tossed him Kostas's hat.

"Always wanted one of these." He pulled it on, adjusting it so the brim was low over his eyes, then looked up at me thoughtfully. "My mom warned me that you looked gorgeous tonight. And you do."

My cheeks went hot, even hotter than they already were, but this time for an entirely different reason. "She warned you?" I said, reaching down to scoop up Purrnest in an attempt to hide my blush.

"She knows I have a weakness for girls in black dresses."

"*Any* girl in a black dress?" I tugged on the ends of my hair. I didn't have to see it to know that my hair had gone wavy in the humid, salty air.

"Not *any* girl." He cocked his head, studying me. "Anyway, are you okay? You seem kind of angry. And shouty."

"'Shouty' isn't a word. But yes. I am shouty."

He studied my face. "Besides the talk with your dad, what's wrong?"

What *wasn't* wrong? "I miss home. My mom and brother, and Dax . . . and then everything with my dad—" I grimaced. "This is a disaster."

He straightened. "Disaster. A severe disruption of the functioning of a human or community."

"Exactly," I said. "Also, why do you know that definition off the top of your head?"

"It's in the documentary," he said.

Ugh. The documentary. At least it provided a change in subject. "How did filming go tonight?" I'd suggested that he get some fill-in footage of the many businesses that paid homage to the mythical city.

"Great." Theo shrugged. "You were right. Fira has, like, a hundred shops with Atlantis in the title. I even interviewed a few people—tourists and locals—and asked them what they thought about Atlantis. Everyone seemed to be on board with the whole idea."

"Maybe because it didn't disrupt their entire lives." I hadn't meant to say it, but it tumbled out with the general anger I was feeling.

Theo's eyes lifted to mine. And I felt his hesitation. I knew what was coming. We were *so* not done talking about my dad.

"Oh no . . . ," I said, putting up a hand warningly. He didn't catch the gesture.

"What was it like when your dad left?"

I almost fell off the table. This was literally the first time anyone had ever asked me that question.

"I know. Serious lack of boundaries," he said, his hands up in surrender, eyes grave and thoughtful.

"Theo . . . do you even know how to do small talk?"

"Yes. I'm actually very good at it." He leaned back, adjusting the captain's hat. "But not with you. I told you, you're the one person I don't know how to read."

He was staring at me like I was an exotic parrot or a new species of salamander, but still, I felt weirdly flattered. A part of me liked that he couldn't figure me out, and that he was interested enough to try. Most people saw layer one, Liv, and were fine with it. Not Theo.

I let out a choked little laugh, and then, inexplicably, I was actually answering his question. "We cried a lot. And then we couldn't afford the apartment we were living in, and my mom couldn't find another job, so we moved, and then she lost that job, and we tried to live with her parents for a few months . . . but that didn't go well. And then we apartment hopped and stayed with friends of hers until she finally got a good job and was able to start law school. I was alone almost all of the time. I remember thinking that clocks slowed down in the afternoons after school. I still sometimes feel that way."

It all came out in a rush, all those details forming a cloud of sadness. I'd never told anyone what those years had been like, how chaotic and disorienting, and *sad*, and yet here I was telling someone who was practically a stranger.

Theo sat up and leaned toward me, resting his chin on his hand. "Have you ever asked your dad why Atlantis is so important to him?"

I closed my eyes, shaking my head. Asking my dad why he cared about Atlantis was like asking a fish why it cared about water. It was necessary to its survival. "Have you?"

He paused and blinked slowly. "No. And I think that's something we need to address in the documentary."

Always with the documentary. Heat flared through my chest. Did he think of my life as something to be entertained by? Ready with his camera? "We don't have time to add anything to the documentary, especially after losing all that time today," I said.

"No, we really don't," he agreed. "But I keep thinking about your dad at the volcano and how everyone gathered around him. Have you ever noticed how magnetic he is? It's like people are more interested in the Atlantis hunter than Atlantis itself. So why not incorporate more of your dad's story? I get the feeling that it's more to him than a city or some old ruins." His hands cupped the back of his head. "What do you think?"

I grabbed the yacht hat and pulled it on over my face. Digging deeper into my dad's obsession with Atlantis was not going to make any of this better. The thought of it made me want to charter a boat and get as far from this island as possible. A mixture of energy and anxiety pulsed through me, and I jumped to my feet. "Can we talk about something else? Anything else? Better yet, can we go somewhere?"

A slow smile spread across his face, and he reached for my hand, pulling himself to standing. "How about a swim?"

"Not in the ocean," I said quickly.

"Not in the ocean," he agreed. His hand was still on mine, and the warmth of it trickled up my arm, making me feel like I'd swallowed helium. It was a new feeling—one I couldn't recall ever having with Dax. It scared me. Instead of letting go, he moved in closer. "It's a place I haven't taken anyone before, but I think you'll really like it. Come with me?"

"Yes," I said, because what else are you supposed to say when someone holds your hand and you feel it right down to the tips of your toes?

Breathe. You have a boyfriend. You and Theo are friends.

It seemed like the sort of thing you shouldn't have to remind yourself. But Theo made me feel like I was on a life raft in the middle of a storm. I couldn't get my bearings.

Outside, the night was thick and velvety, the only sound coming from the gentle rolling of the ocean down below and murmuring voices from open windows and patios. I had no idea where Theo thought we were going swimming at this hour, but I couldn't think about that. I needed to stay grounded. Refocus. Get my *sea legs*, as my dad would say. The fact that I found Theo as attractive as I did didn't really matter. What mattered was how I reacted to said fact.

Theo met me on the front walkway. He'd changed back into his bathing suit and a black T-shirt, and his dark eyes shone brightly. "Ready?"

"Ready." Maybe if I didn't look at him, I'd be okay?

To my utter shock, Theo *walked*, me trailing a few steps behind him, sidestepping the occasional pedestrian and looking at all the closed storefronts. At first we headed through the maze of alleyways toward the cliffs, but eventually Theo changed direction, leading us farther into the darkness and away from the blue domes.

"Where are we going?" I finally asked. The night was so quiet I almost wanted to whisper.

He wrapped his arm around me, pulling me into a warm hug that scrambled my brain and made my cheeks go hot before releasing me. "Trust me, Kalamata."

Trusting him was easy; it was me that was the problem.

When we were about halfway down the cliffside, Theo stopped in front of a low white wall with a rounded wooden door blocking the entrance. It had a foreboding-looking padlock on it, but Theo picked it up and began jiggling it.

"What are you doing?" I watched Theo clank the lock around

noisily a few more times before it suddenly gave, popping open.

He unhooked the lock, then swung the door open in a long creaking motion. Soft light puddled out from behind the door, and I stood on my tiptoes to see over his shoulder. Through the door I could see a few lounge chairs strewn with white cushions and a cluster of potted plants. A wall reflected moving water.

"Theo, what is this?" I asked, louder this time.

"Paradise." He hooked his arm through mine. "Come on."

I don't know which made me more nervous, the touching or the extreme quiet, but I certainly wasn't going to turn down the promise of paradise. I followed him—warily—into what turned out to be the courtyard of a small cave house. A smooth infinity pool, lit up aqua in the night, occupied most of the space, extending to the edge of the property's ocean view. Water flowed over the side, creating the illusion of the pool merging with the sea. Stars pinned up the darkness, and the half-moon reflected brightly in the pool.

I'd never seen anything so beautiful. And the quiet stillness that hovered suddenly over us made my heart feel too big for my rib cage.

"Well?" He looked at me in his smug Theo way, but I couldn't help proving him right.

"It's perfect." I exhaled, feeling the uneasiness, anxiety, panic—all the things I'd been fighting since I'd arrived in Santorini—melt away into the darkness.

"You're welcome," he prompted, giving me one of his charming smiles.

"Theo . . . I . . ." My voice froze in my throat, nerves tingling my spine. "I needed this. Thank you."

The smile that washed over his face shone brighter than the moon's reflection in the still water. So bright, my knees wobbled. "I know. Let's go."

He steered me toward the edge of the patio so I had a full view of Oia. The dark sky melted into the even darker ocean, and the hillside lit up with other houses and glowing pools. Normally when I saw something this breathtaking, I wanted to paint it, but I knew there was no way I could capture this view. This was something you had to experience with all of your senses.

I glanced back at the cave house. The whitewashed walls looked freshly painted, and cobalt-blue shutters had been drawn against the dark windows. "Who lives here?"

He was already kicking off his shoes, pulling his T-shirt over his head. "It's a rental that doesn't get rented out very often. The owners stop by every few weeks or so. You can tell by whether or not they put their colorful cushions out."

I looked at the all-white patio furniture. "And they let you swim here?"

Theo shrugged. "I wouldn't say they *let* me, Kalamata, but they sure haven't stopped me."

Only disbelief could snatch my attention from this kind of view. "We don't have permission to be here? We're breaking in?"

He grinned, putting his hands on my shoulders. "Relax. No one broke into anything. You saw that latch was open. And don't worry about your criminal record. If anything, *I'm* breaking in. You're my unsuspecting guest."

His smile was hard to resist. And the *pool*. My rule-abiding soul wanted me to make a run for it, but instead I kicked off my flip-flops and dipped my left foot in, letting the water lap against my bare skin. It was the perfect temperature, and the hum of the pool's filter layered effortlessly against the sound of the rolling waves down below.

Forget rules. This was perfection.

I pulled off my T-shirt and shorts and carefully eased myself into the pool. The water was a degree or two below body temperature, but it cooled me from the inside out. I lowered down, allowing myself to spin, eyes closed, arms outstretched. When I opened my eyes, Theo was still on the ledge, his eyes wide.

"What?" Something was different about this look of his—it wasn't his usual *I'm trying to dissect your every move* stare. This was more surprise. Like the look he'd given me back at the airport when he'd first seen me. I stood, adjusting the strap of my favorite swimsuit—a black one-piece with a wrapped top and a cutout below my rib cage—and settled self-consciously back into the water.

"Nothing." But he didn't glance away.

"Okay . . ." I flipped onto my back so I could see the stars. There were so many that they looked more like a haze than separate lights. And the *moon*. Crisp and heavy and so very, very bright. It was probably overlooked in the land of sunset, but this moon was special.

When I righted myself, Theo had dropped down so his shoulders were in the water. He backed up against the edge, eyes still locked on me.

He was reading me again. "Why are you staring at me?" I demanded, sending a wave of water his way.

"I don't know. Sorry." He shrugged, wiping the water from his face. "Moonlight looks good on you, I guess." He sounded nervous.

It looked good on him, too. My heart leapfrogged. I opened my mouth, not sure what to say.

"Boyfriend," he said quickly, beating me to it.

That broke the tension. I smiled. "You're *so* funny."

"Aren't I?" His hands floated up to the surface, hovering in front of him, and he dropped his eyes down toward the water. "Why don't you ever swim? You obviously know how."

I glanced out into the darkness. I could lie, but it felt wrong to here. "I prefer pools over the ocean. The ocean is sort of . . . scary."

He nodded and, for once, did not insist that I elaborate.

Instead, he started clearing his throat. "That's a . . . uh . . . nice bathing suit you've got on there."

"Theo! Boyfriend!" This time I sent a wave of water his way, and he ducked, a huge smile on his face.

"Yeah, yeah. I know. All I'm saying"—he ducked under the water, then came up, water streaming—"is that's *not* what you were wearing on the boat with your dad."

I bit the inside of my cheek. Hopefully the darkness was masking how red my face was turning. "Yeah, because my dad was there."

"So, what, then? This is like your official breaking-into-a-cave-house suit?"

"Exactly." I swam to the pool wall, resting my arms up over the edge so my legs could flow freely behind me. Theo's attention felt . . . *Nice? Terrifying?* Like standing at the top of a particularly slippery slope. Theo's charm was massively inconvenient. "So how many times have you broken in here?"

"I still disagree with the term 'breaking in,' but . . ." He shrugged, then looked up at the sky as if tallying. "I don't know. Fifty times? A hundred?"

"A hundred? Seriously?" I shot him a look of disbelief.

He drifted up next to me, hooking his elbows over the edge of the pool so we were side by side. "It was really hard for me to move here. I'm happy to be here with Bapou, but I thought I'd finish high school in London, and I was really angry at first. Finding this place to escape to helped. Also, no one is ever here. And a pool is meant to be swam in. Its main purpose is to be filled with people. I'm doing whoever lives here a favor. Do you think this pool *wants* to be alone?"

"You realize you're talking about an inanimate object, right?" I said, but what I was really thinking about was that— like me—Theo had not chosen to come to Santorini. Yet another thing we had in common. And he was also right: the pool did look happy to have us here.

I rested my cheek on my arm, legs stretched behind me, water lapping in my ear. "So, Theo, what's your life plan?"

He turned back from the view to look at me. "Swim with a girl in Oia?"

I flicked water at him. "We aren't swimming; we're floating. And past that."

He shrugged. "Well, tomorrow I want to make a documentary about the lost city of Atlantis. And after that . . . I don't really have a plan. I'm mostly trying not to be a jerk."

I laughed before realizing he was serious. "Really? That's your plan?"

He shrugged again. "I know that probably sounds like I've set the bar really low. But I've seen it a lot. Like my dad, I don't think he started out a jerk. But he got so wrapped up in his work, and then it was like we didn't matter anymore. It was only about his ambition."

Hmm. Sounded familiar.

"We were one more thing that he had to move around." He continued, eyes out to the ocean. "He was so surprised when my mom told him she was leaving, but she'd been lonely for so long. Now I wonder if he really even notices that we're gone."

Things had gotten a lot deeper than I'd expected, and we were suddenly much closer than we had been a moment earlier. Who had moved? Him? Me? Both of us? His forehead beaded with water, and his hair was wet and tangled, water lapping his dark, wavy strands. "I'm sure he does," I said, but regretted it immediately. Why had I said that? I didn't know Theo's dad. I had no idea. And I'd always hated it when people told me how to feel about my own parental relationships. "Sorry. We have that in common. An absent dad who puts work over their families."

Theo's hand slipped off the edge, and he sank into the water, moving closer to me. "No. With your dad, it's different. It always felt to me like—" He stopped abruptly. Droplets of water clung to his eyelashes, and his eyes were so *serious*. Even when he was having fun, they were always so serious. "Oh no. I'm doing it again."

"Doing what?" My breath hitched in my chest, and I lowered myself into the water, my eyes level with his, mouth right above the surface. If I moved at all, I'd run into him.

His gaze studied mine. "Back at the domes, I promised not to talk about your dad anymore. Sorry."

Oh. *Right.* My stomach unclenched. "You can finish what you were going to say," I said, but I gripped the pool edge tighter, bracing myself.

"Okay." He took a deep breath. "It seems like . . . well, I always felt like he was trying to find Atlantis for you." The words spilled out, and he looked up at me plaintively.

"What?" I stood up quickly, my feet slipping on the pool bottom in my haste to move away. Spell broken. Whatever I'd felt a moment ago was gone. Now I felt defensive. "Theo, that doesn't make sense. Why would he find Atlantis for me? He *left* me for Atlantis."

Theo stood up too. "I'm not a mind reader. That's how it's always seemed to me."

We stared at each other in silence, the only noise coming from the pool hum-humming and the waves crashing below. Water dripped down Theo's chest and shoulders, but he stayed statue-still. If he thought I was going to make the first move, he was mistaken. Finally, he dropped his gaze. "Sorry. I know I probably shouldn't have said that, but I felt like you should know."

"Theo . . ." I clenched my fists under the water in frustration. "I know you really like my dad. But I don't understand why . . ." *You keep defending him. You can't see him. You don't get this.* So many ways to finish this sentence, but Theo looked so *sorry*, miserable really, the moonlight highlighting the earnestness in his eyes. Theo may not be able to see all the facets of the situation, but it wasn't his problem. I couldn't take this out on him.

I groaned, then fell back into the water, keeping my eyes on the sky. The stars looked even farther away than normal. "Never mind. Change of subject?"

Brief pause, then minor tidal wave as Theo launched himself over to my side of the pool. "No problem. I even have another subject in mind." He had a big smile on his face.

I sighed, but it was more theatrical than anything. He was still moving closer to me, and my heart seemed to think this called for an epic freak-out. "Great. What is it?"

His lips parted. "Kalamata. This boyfriend of yours, is he—"

Behind us a light flipped on, bright as a spotlight, and we both winced, covering our faces as panic flooded through me.

"Theo?" I finally managed. Maybe it was a motion detector? From another house? But Theo was looking over my shoulder, his gaze fixed worriedly on the house. "Theo, what?" I whispered.

"Shhhh."

"Poios eínai ekeí?" a male voice called. Oh no.

Theo's eyes moved calmly to mine. "Kalamata, listen to me. We are going to have to run."

My heart shot to my throat. "Run? But . . ."

"*Now.*"

"*Paravátes!*" a voice roared from much too close.

I was too startled to react. Before I realized what was happening, Theo was pulling me out of the water, his arm tight around my waist, and then we were sprinting for the door, dripping and sliding as we grabbed our stuff and *ran*.

I thought the homeowner would chase us off his property and leave it at that. I'd thought wrong. Once we'd spilled out onto the walkway, our clothes and shoes a wild jumble in our arms, Theo grabbed my hand. But instead of running up toward the bookstore, he pulled me down a flight of stairs, zigzagging into the darkness, our backs to the cliff.

"*Stamáta tóra!*" the man yelled, his voice reverberating in the quiet.

"Th-Theo . . . ," I stammered. My adrenaline was so high I felt liquid, my brain a useless mess. Theo was having no such issues. He must have been a pirate evader in another life, because he began darting into narrow alleyways, down staircases, leaping over walls, even jumping a four-foot drop over the edge of a walkway—and I just flapped behind him like a kite.

I slipped at least a dozen times, but whenever I tumbled, Theo managed to catch me, eventually tossing his armload of clothes to one side so he could steady me better. Did he have a plan? Were we mindlessly running? I wanted to ask, but my brain was too jumbled to form the words.

The man's footsteps echoed loudly over the ocean's hammering waves. My breath came in so short and fast, I was wheezing, and right when I thought my heart was going to explode, Theo hurried us onto an enclosed porch covered by a wooden pergola. Sun chairs sat grouped at one end, and a hot tub was tucked into one corner.

He rushed us over to the hot tub, then ducked around its side, squeezing between it and the wall. "Liv, come on!"

The man's footsteps and his angry voice boomed closer as I ducked down beside Theo. There was barely enough room for the two of us. We faced each other, our knees pulled up to our chests, separated by a few inches. We were both breathing hard.

I was a sweaty mess, my bathing suit sticking to me in all the wrong ways and my bangs plastered to my forehead. Theo, of course, looked amazing. Skin glowing, eyes bright, bare chest heaving. He was apparently made to be chased through Santorini's cliffs in a pair of swim trunks.

His shoulders were tan and smooth and . . .

Never mind.

"Thief!" the man yelled in a thick accent. He was really close now, maybe twenty feet away. At some point he'd figured we weren't locals, switching from yelling in Greek to yelling in English. "Swim in my pool? Americans! Thief!" Had the man seen us duck in here? And if he did find us, then what?

I reached out and grabbed Theo's hands, squeezing them tightly. Even though we were caught in a panicked game of cat and mouse, I had the sudden, inexplicable desire to laugh.

Theo and I locked eyes. His face was red, and I could feel that his chest and shoulders were still wet as they grazed my skin. My heart bounced against my rib cage.

"Don't laugh," I whispered.

"Huh?"

But it was no use. We were silent laughing, the kind of rolling laugh that absolutely cannot be controlled. The both of us with our shoulders heaving, faces buried in our knees. I don't even know what we were laughing at. The death sentence coming our way? The tickle of our breath on each other's knees? The fact that we smelled like two enormous chlorine tablets? At one point I snorted, and that made things much worse.

Stop, Theo mouthed. *Stop*. He buried his face in his knees, his shoulders shaking.

"I see. I see you!" the man yelled, but he sounded farther away now. "There it is now."

My stomach hurt from holding in laughter. Tears were running down my face.

"I *find* you." His voice was an echo, the sound fading under the noise of the ocean.

"He's leaving," I whispered, wiping my eyes.

My legs were starting to feel cramped, but I pulled them in tighter, resting my chin on my knees. Cold water dripped rhythmically from our hair and bathing suits, and when Theo looked up, he had a big smile on his face too.

"Outsmarted the pirate," Theo said, his mouth all of four inches from mine.

"Thanks to you." It was time to look away, but neither of us did. I could feel his breath on my cheeks as the water from his hair rolled down his arms and onto mine. Whatever was going on this moment, it was picking up speed, gathering momentum. I couldn't stop looking at his lips, and he couldn't stop looking at mine. Our breath was hot between us, my legs slippery on his. Was he about to kiss me?

Worse. I was about to kiss him.

A small string pulled me toward him, and then he reached up and touched my lower lip with the pad of his thumb and I was leaning in and every single one of my cells was on fire and I closed my eyes and—

Theo suddenly yanked backward, hitting his head on the hot tub cover with a loud thud and effectively ruining whatever trance we were under. A rush of conflicting emotions crashed through me—confusion, disappointment, relief, panic. But "Ohmygodareyouokay?" was all I was able to get out.

"Fine. You? I'm . . . uh, sorry about that. . . ." I'd never seen

Theo stumble for words before, and I attempted to get to my feet but succeeded only in falling back down, scraping both my elbows in the process and managing to wedge myself in even tighter. What was happening right now?

"Ow. My fault." I tried again, this time managing to get to my feet relatively unscathed. I was so embarrassed and exposed that I may as well have been fully naked instead of half naked. Had we really almost . . . ?

What was *wrong* with me? Theo pulled himself to his feet, his hand on the back of his head. "I think I'm going to have a bump on my head. What are those called in English? A duck egg?"

"A goose egg." I grimaced. "Theo . . . wow. I think it was, like, the excitement of it all? You know . . . being chased and then this tight space, it was kind of unavoidable."

Unavoidable? Had I really said that? A slow, knowing smile spread across his face, the sight of which made me want to throw myself off the edge of the cliff. "I mean—not unavoidable, just . . . understandable? Or—"This hole was just getting deeper. And his growing smile was not helping at all. Not one tiny bit.

My cheeks were like the fiery gates of hell. "Never mind. Forget I ever said it."

He crossed his arms over his chest, the teasing smile still firmly in place. "I don't know if I'm ever going to forget that you said that, but it's not a big deal, Kalamata. Don't worry about it."

Not a big deal? To whom? I crossed my arms too. The night air was warm, but not enough to keep me from shivering in my wet bathing suit. "Well, it's a big deal to *me*," I blurted out. *Why, oh why, can't I stop talking?*

"Kalamata . . ." He reached out to touch me, and I quickly darted away.

Run! my brain yelled. *Before you try to kiss him again.*

"I'll see you up there." I hurried to the edge of the porch but was immediately confronted with three different paths, all of which branched out into even more options. This place really was a maze. So much for making a clean exit.

"Staircase on the left," Theo supplied from behind me. "Then the second right. I'll guide you up."

"Thanks." I kept my eyes glued to the steps, ignoring his gaze on my back. My lips were still tingling from where he'd touched me.

This was not going to end well.

Chapter Seventeen

#17. TV GUIDE *MAGAZINE, EMMY PREVIEW EDITION*

We'd moved again, into an apartment that had apparently once been leased by a woman named Rose Walker, judging by the TV Guide magazine that arrived in our mailbox every month. My mom laughed when she saw the first one on our coffee table. TV Guide magazine was still around? But instead of putting them in the recycling bin and relying on the internet like the rest of the world, my dad started using them.

My dad wasn't a TV watcher. He was a reader, and an explorer, and an artist. But some days he'd turn on the television. It never lasted long. Five, six, once seven days, and then he'd stand up from the couch and ask about my homework before we'd go out into the sunshine again. I always knew not to talk about Atlantis on those days. It's funny what you don't know, but what you understand in your gut.

THERE'S AWKWARD LIKE, *CAN WE CONTINUE ON OUR merry little way and pretend this never happened?* and then there's awkward like, *Do you happen to know of any nondormant volcanoes that I could throw myself into, because that seems to be my only remaining option?* The walk back up to the bookstore was definitely hovering near option two. Or at least it was for me. Every time I looked at Theo, he was still smiling that horrifying smile. Good thing someone was endlessly amused by this whole scenario.

Once it had been established that I would not be fleeing the scene, it took us about twenty minutes of hunting to find all the shoes and clothes we'd strewn along the path and then another fifteen to sneak past the cave house and get back up to the bookstore so we could pretend to be asleep while listening to our French rap. And the whole time I could barely look at him because WE HAD ALMOST KISSED.

But having plenty of time to analyze it during our silent walk back to the bookstore, I told myself that I had been so tangled up after the cruise with my dad that I'd let my guard down and lost my head. Or maybe it was because Dax still hadn't called me back and I was getting more and more nervous about the thought of telling him about RISD. Or maybe it was the trifling fact that Theo made me feel like I was swimming through champagne bubbles. It was an extremely inconvenient realization, but that didn't mean it wasn't *true*. All I knew was that I really didn't need this extra complication in my life right now. All I wanted to do was fall asleep.

And once I was finally able to calm my racing head, which sprinted from thoughts of Theo to Dax to my dad, that's exactly what I did.

When I woke the next morning, Theo's bunk was empty, and I was relieved to see the day's call sheet taped to my bunk. It instructed me to meet at the bus stop. Today we were filming Akrotiri, the archaeological site of the Minoan ruins. I'd been excited to see the ruins, but now I couldn't rely on Theo to make the day's social interactions run smoothly. I needed a buffer for my buffer. And that's when a light bulb went off.

I studied the paper. *Archaeological site.* Henrik! Was it possible . . . ? I scrambled for my backpack and dumped the whole thing out, sending pens and notepads flying as I searched for the magazine scrap Henrik had written on, then grabbed my phone.

After showering and deflecting Geoffrey, who wanted to talk about Mathilde's request for "more emotional space," I headed out into the stark, hot sun, my backpack heavy on my shoulders.

I hadn't been to the bus stop since my first day, and I was surprised to realize I could find my own way there easily. It was funny how quickly the village had started to feel familiar, like a shoe that had needed some wearing in. Less than a week ago, it had looked like a blank canvas, an endless maze of white. But now I could see the nuance. Oia was full of its own quirks and charms: crooked doorways, plants growing from tomato cans on windowsills, mounds of cheap snow globes and stuffed donkeys lining shop windows. I was even beginning to distinguish between the different shades of white and recognize some of Oia's resident dogs.

It made my heart ache a little. Santorini was so baggage-laden for me, I'd never considered I might love it. I quickly shoved the thought and its accompanying feelings away, right in time to see Theo, my dad, and their mountain of gear waiting for me. They were speaking quickly in Greek, and when they turned to look at me, I braced for the onslaught of weirdness from Theo, but to my surprise it was my dad who drew my attention.

"Liv!" He hurried over to take my backpack, an act that was both kind and optimistic. He was already so weighed down with equipment he could stand in for one of the local donkeys.

I squinted at him. "Dad, are you okay?" He was nicely dressed, his hat pushed back on his forehead, but he had deep circles under his eyes, and his skin looked pale. More than that, his energy, which was always dialed too high, was noticeably low.

"I didn't sleep well," he admitted. "I think the food on the cruise did not sit well with me." He nodded toward my backpack. "I hope you brought the old man makeup. I need it today."

"Are you okay, boss?" Theo asked, his eyes skimming straight over me. "You shouldn't have to film if you have food poisoning."

"I'm fine," my dad insisted, winking at me. "So long as we have the makeup and some coffee, I am fine. Please do not worry so much."

He didn't look fine. Theo met my eye worriedly, and we had a quick nonverbal conversation. *Should we push back another day? Can we push back another day?* The answer to that was no, but Theo gave a little shrug as if to say, *Think we can talk him out of this?* And the answer to that was *Definitely not.* Also, communicating this way with Theo did make me feel better. Something unwound inside of me. Yes, we'd almost kissed, but Theo was right. A momentary lapse in judgment didn't have to be a big deal. We didn't have to make this awkward. "I'll do your makeup on the way," I said, turning back to my dad.

"And, Nico, you rest during the drive," Theo ordered. "Akrotiri is at least an hour away."

"Please do not *worry*," my dad repeated, putting his arms up in protest.

It turned out that we weren't taking the bus at all. Yiannis the Walrus was driving us in his cab, evidenced by him suddenly running full speed at us, a cigar in one hand and coffee in the other. "Nico!"

After the customary backslapping and Greek excitement yelling, we stuffed our gear into the trunk. Then the four of us, plus Yiannis's cigar, loaded up into the cab. To get to Akrotiri, we had to drive all the way down to the literal other end of the island, which would be simple except we were in *Santorini*, which meant traffic, donkeys wearing colorful harnesses, tourists driving ATVs, and buses swinging out recklessly on the narrow roads.

I never get carsick, but this was pushing me over the edge. Inside the cab, the conditions were even worse. Yiannis smoked the entire way, Theo's camera kept making an appearance, and I was shakily trying to apply my dad's makeup, so by the time we stopped in the parking lot in Akrotiri, I was ready to throw up at least three days' worth of food. My dad looked even worse. Maybe we did have food poisoning.

"Let's never do that again," I said, stepping shakily out of the cab. I checked my phone. Still no response from my top secret island contact. I needed him to come through.

"Akrotiri," my dad announced, taking a moment to collect himself. "This is where the ancient civilization of Minoa lived. Or as I like to call them, the original Atlanteans."

"That was good. Did you get that on film?" I asked Theo.

"Of course I did." He hesitated and quickly glanced toward my dad, who was unloading our gear with Yiannis. Theo nervously tugged at his hair, and I could feel the metaphorical wall he was building between us. Yeah, sure. No awkwardness here. The humid air felt fully saturated today, and my heart was clanging around like crazy. "Can we talk for a minute?" he said under his breath.

"Sure. What's up?" I asked in an obnoxiously chipper voice. *Why do I always do that when I'm nervous?*

His eyes finally met mine. "I wanted to apologize about last night, the whole pool and . . . um, hot tub thing. I thought about it some more, and you're right, it is a big deal. You have a boyfriend, and besides, I really like working with you. It was sort of a mistake."

Sort of? His eyes were liquid and oh so sincere, and now I was blushing again. "Completely my fault too. We can keep things professional. And friendly," I added quickly. "Also, it isn't only that I have a boyfriend. There's the no long-distance rule, right?"

I don't know what made me say it. Now I sounded like I was interested, which I definitely wasn't. *Couldn't* be. Theo's eyes flew up questioningly to mine. They lingered there for a moment before he took a small step back. "Right. So . . . we're good?"

"*So* good."

I hated myself.

* * *

Unfortunately, we weren't the only ones interested in the Minoan civilization. There were also about ten tour buses packed full of sunscreen-coated tourists, all waiting in line at the ticket counter. "This is going to be rough," I said to my still-carsick-looking father.

His eyes shone excitedly from his pale face. "But worth it. This will be important to the film. Can you believe we have a view into ground zero of Atlantis? Or as an Atlantis skeptic would call it, the Bronze Age Aegean civilization?"

He lifted his brows pointedly at me, and I couldn't help but smile. He was clearly referencing our conversation from the night before, setting my doubt alongside his belief. They seemed a lot more at home together than I'd thought they would. "Any progress on the Asia and Libya issue?"

"Working on it," he said.

"Oh *no*." Theo groaned. We turned to see him staring at the sign at the entrance. "Look."

I stood on my tiptoes. A large sign at the entrance to the site read NO COMMERCIAL FILMING.

"But . . . we're amateurs. Won't they let us bring it in? Or sneak it in?" We all looked at Theo's camera, which seemed to swell in proportion to our stress.

"I'm not sure," my father said. His face flashed with disappointment, making him look even sicker.

"How long do you think it would take to get a permit?"

Theo grimaced. "In Greece? Ninety years. Eighty if we're lucky."

My heart sank. Good point. My dad and Ana hadn't even managed to secure a business license for their year-old bookstore yet.

"Now what?" I said aloud. If I'd been unsure before, my feelings made it clear now. For better or for worse, I was invested in this film.

"Liv? Is that you?" The voice came from behind me, puncturing my despair, and I spun around to see a familiar face making its way through the crowd. "Henrik! You got my text." I hurried over to him.

"I did indeed." He took off his sunglasses, a wide grin spreading over his face. "Well, look at you. A few days in Santorini has done you some good."

"You too." He wore shorts and flip-flops and seemed relaxed and happy. Exactly like people on vacation should look. Aka the opposite of what I was currently looking like, which was a giant ball of stress. "How's your boyfriend?"

"Oh, him." He shook his head, but then his smile deepened. "The best. He's been on the site since five a.m. I wondered if you'd reach out, Liv. You picked a good day for it. I was already planning to bring him breakfast."

"So this is the site? This is where your boyfriend works?"

According to my few minutes of research on my phone, there was only one main Minoan excavation site; even so, it had seemed too good to be true.

"One and the same."

I pumped my fist triumphantly. *Hallelujah.*

"Hello." My father made his way toward us, approximately ninety bags strapped to his back. "I'm Nico Varanakis."

Oh. Right. Introduction time. "Henrik, this is my dad, Nico. Dad, this is Henrik. I met him on the airplane. He, uh . . . gave me a pep talk. And his boyfriend works here on the site. I texted him this morning to see if he could give us an in." *And distract me from all the awkwardness around here.*

This random interaction would faze most people, but not my dad. "Henrik!" he boomed. "Wonderful to meet you. Any friend of Liv's is a friend of mine." He reached out to shake Henrik's hand and managed to drop a rolled-up map and his Indiana Jones hat in the process. I was glad now that I'd told Henrik the entire Atlantis/Dad story. It made all of this less strange.

Henrik scooped up the map, then took my dad's hand in his. "So nice to meet you, too. Your work sounds . . . fascinating." He winked at me, then turned to Theo. "And you must be the budding documentarian. Liv told me all about you."

"Not *all* about you," I quickly countered. All I'd done was give Henrik a quick rundown of our project and living situation via text. Why was he making it sound like a big deal?

"Theo," Theo said, emerging from behind his camera long enough to shake Henrik's hand. He pointed to the site's sign. "Do you by chance know anything about the filming rule? We don't have time to get a permit."

Henrik studied the sign thoughtfully. "Hmmm. That shouldn't be problem. Let me call Hye."

He stepped away, leaving the three of us to watch the still growing crowd of people outside the site. A moment later he waved to us. "Hye says he can get you in early, and not to worry about the camera. We have about half an hour before the doors open, and he wants to give you the insider's tour. But we're going to have to be fast. Very fast."

"Take-no-prisoners touring," Theo said. "We can do that."

"Well done, Liv." My dad and I exchanged an excited look, so natural and spontaneous that it startled me. Had we bypassed our regular filter? Was he proud of me? More importantly, was I *happy* that he was proud of me?

I'd need to think about that later, because right now we were sprinting for the back entrance to the site. And before long, a Korean American man wearing a huge smile alongside what had to be the dustiest pair of jeans to ever exist swung the back door open. I liked him immediately.

"Hye," he said, reaching out to shake our hands. His eyes lit on my father. "You're the Atlantis hunter?"

My dad smiled confidently. "Nico Varanakis, very nice to meet you."

Hye took him in with one appraising look, and I felt a tinge of panic. Did he think he was delusional? Hye nodded, pausing for a moment before gesturing to the site. "If proof of Atlantis is your goal, my guess is you'll want to see what made the Minoans technologically advanced. I thought we'd start with the upper levels, see the structure of the buildings, and then we'll graduate to some of the details that made the Minoans stand out. Sound like a plan?"

"Beautiful," my dad said.

I could have kissed Hye on the lips. We marched dutifully behind Hye, making our way into the quiet site, the sound of the growing crowd fading behind us.

I'd been so worried about what the day would be like that I hadn't thought about the fact that the Akrotiri excavation site might actually be extremely interesting.

Inside, a rustic roof made of slats of wood stood overhead, keeping out the sun but inviting the sounds of birds and insects from outside. Dust and scaffolding and complicated-looking tools were everywhere. At first glance the site looked like a heap of modestly contained rubble, but as we followed Hye to the top of a walkway overlooking the site, the ruins below began to take shape.

"I think this is our best view. I'd recommend getting some

footage here," Hye suggested, but Theo was already doing that.

"Give me two minutes," Theo said.

I walked to the edge of the railing and caught my breath, my eyes slowly making sense of what I was seeing. Beyond the rubble, Akrotiri was a town—a city, really—that contained defined streets and tall, roofless buildings with stone walls reaching two, sometimes three, levels high. Artifacts such as benches and large ceramic pots resided in a few of the structures, and wooden supports had been built into the buildings' stone windows. If you squinted your eyes, it was easy to imagine a bustling city—one that had no idea of the destruction that was about to come.

Hye pointed to a nearby house. "These dozen houses are a small slice of what we believe Akrotiri once was, likely just 3 percent of what remains buried. Judging by the quality of the architecture as well as the items found inside, we think these homes belonged to wealthy merchants. Lower levels were used as storage, while the upper levels were where daily life took place."

Theo swung his camera at Hye.

"Tell them about the art," Henrik said. "Liv will like that."

Hye smiled, then gestured for me to follow him a few feet down the walkway. "One of the best indicators of Akrotiri's wealth is the abundance of art. Most of the structures contain colorful frescoes showing scenes of large towns and harbors full of boats. The subjects of the paintings give us a lot of insight into what their lives were like, and the attention to detail shows that they cared about beautifying their life." He pointed down toward a heavily pigmented fresco. We all leaned over the side to get a better look. "That's the Spring Fresco. It depicts the volcanic island along with flowers and swallows. Whoever painted it used local minerals, which accounts for it having survived for so long. That and the layer of pumice that coated the city."

The fresco covered three walls that stood intact on the building, and a wash of color decorated the fourth one. Something about the room being decorated made it so much more real to me. Had that been a family room? A dining room? What kind of life had gone on in there?

Suddenly I was thinking about the last apartment my family had lived in all together. The one with the sink that always leaked and the doorways that had swelled out of their frames. One minute the Minoans had been living their daily lives, cooking and making pottery, throwing open their windows, and the next a volcano had exploded, sending their world into darkness. My family had also had no idea what was to come. Or at least, I hadn't.

"They were real," my dad said, suddenly beside me. Despite

our rush into the site, he looked relaxed. "The Minoans, I mean. Isn't it amazing to think of that?"

My throat was tight, so I nodded. We had been real too, even if it was harder to see that these days. Had he known what I was thinking?

"Let's keep it moving, people," Theo said, making a shooing motion from behind his camera. "We only have twenty-six minutes until public admission."

Have you ever seen one of those game show contests where people run through grocery stores filling their carts with as much as possible? That's what the next twenty-six minutes were like. Hye and my dad really hit it off, and before long they were deep in discussion, blazing through the ground level of the site while the rest of us did our best to keep up.

Theo oscillated between getting shots of the site and directing impromptu interviews from Hye, who, despite having been given very little notice of our visit, was being a wonderfully good sport. Henrik and I kept falling behind because I was getting sidetracked every few minutes by all of the site's interesting details. The settlement looked rustic, but as my dad had said, it was actually very advanced, with earthquake-fortified homes and indoor plumbing.

By the time we'd made it to the center of the site, I was

out of breath, and I had dust streaked across my black romper and down my legs. There was no way to avoid it.

Henrik fell into step beside me, gesturing to Theo, who had cornered one of Hye's students, a petite undergrad with thick glasses and an armload of sediment. He gave a low whistle. "Is Theo always this . . . ?"

"Aggressive? Invasive?" The poor student looked positively terrified in front of the camera. *Should I save her?*

He raised an eyebrow at me. "I was going to say *curious*."

"Oh. Yes. Always."

"And those two," Henrik said, pointing to my dad and Hye, who stood staring up at an open doorway. "I have to say, it's nice to see Hye communicating with someone who speaks his language."

"—indoor plumbing is what really impresses me. This kind of technology wasn't seen again until the Romans," I overheard my dad explaining. All traces of illness had been erased from his face. It seemed as if the enjoyment of seeing these ancient ruins was the antidote to whatever he was fighting. He looked like a live firework, i.e., normal.

"Fifteen hundred years later," Hye added. "Incredible, isn't it? What I'm really interested in is the city's layout. Have you noticed the way . . . ?" They walked around the corner, their voices trailing off.

"God bless the seekers," Henrik said. "He's really great, isn't he?"

"Hye? He really is."

"I meant your father. I have to admit that he isn't quite what I pictured. How are things going with him?"

"Well . . ." I checked in with my body, and was surprised to find ease rather than the usual stress. "I think okay? Having a project has been helpful."

"Good." He rubbed some dust from his chin, his mouth widening in a slow smile. "And what about with your boyfriend? You didn't tell me he was coming on the trip."

"What?" I looked up and realized he was pointing to Theo. My equilibrium went up in flames. "We're not dating. Our parents own a business together, and Theo is the cameraman on this project, and . . ." My words were toppling all over each other, which was clearly making the situation worse.

Henrik laughed. "Relax. I know he isn't your boyfriend. But maybe you should remedy that whole 'not your boyfriend' thing. Because not only is he cute, but he also looks at you like you're the greatest thing that's ever happened to him." He peered into my face. "Oh my God, I've never seen anyone blush like you. Your entire face turns the color of a lobster."

I clamped my hands over my face. "Please stop."

"I'm not doing anything," Henrik said. "This is all you."

We ended up overshooting our thirty-minute goal by several hours, with my dad meeting and talking with almost every worker on the site, and even giving a brief speech about the similarities of Akrotiri and Atlantis to an enthusiastic group of bystanders before completing his own interviews. By the time we were finished, my dad had spent several hours on camera, and he was the kind of exhausted that not even concealer could manage to cover up. Filming really took it out of him.

"Back to Oia, boss?" Theo asked, looking at him worriedly. He had been very careful not to stand too close to me. I expected that, even after our morning conversation, but the strange part was that my dad seemed to be doing it too. It took me a while to catch on, because he kept talking to me like everything was normal, but a few hours in, I realized we were engaged in some sort of dance. When I took a step toward him, he stepped back. If I tried to touch up his makeup or help redirect him while he was filming, he never quite met me in the eye.

But why? I know our cruise wasn't the best dinner experience in the world, but I hadn't realized that the wall between us could grow even thicker. Was this trip going to make things worse?

After thanking Hye over and over again for the VIP experience, promising to keep in touch with Henrik, and getting a few final shots of the entrance to Akrotiri, we were finally done with the day. We found Yiannis napping in the front seat of his cab. Dad and Theo both dozed on the way back to Oia, and by the time we straggled back to the bookstore, we were 100 percent exhausted.

The bookstore didn't care that we were tired. It was packed, like always. Even Bapou seemed to be attempting to help out, although that mostly involved speaking in Greek to the English-speaking customers while jabbing at books with his cane.

When Ana saw us, she flew over to my dad. "Nico, you have overdone it." She switched to Greek, chastising him before turning to us. "You two also look terrible, but I need your help. This crowd is feisty today. One of the cruise ships has a problem with its electricity and everyone is grumpy, including our resident baker." She gestured over her shoulder. "He keeps trying to force tour books on the customers."

"Beautiful! Welcome to Santorini!" Bapou roared to a fleeing customer.

"I'll take over customer relations," Theo said. "Bapou! *Kse-xna to!*"

We worked, as Geoffrey would say, like *hedgehogs* until the customary shutdown at sunset, and then Theo, Ana, and I limped up to the roof to collapse and watch the sun settle over the horizon. My dad didn't even make it that long. After two hours in the store, he'd gone back to the apartment without mentioning our evening plans to go to Kamari. I'd expected him to show up around now, but so far there was no sign of him.

Things with Theo still felt like a bit of a tightrope walk, and I was glad for the lack of alone time. I glanced over at Ana. Her hair was up in high bun that had grown messier with each passing minute in the bookstore. For once she looked tired. "Where's Geoffrey?" I asked.

"Walking the streets. He and Mathilde are in an argument and he needed some time to think." She sighed heavily. "That man. His heart is pure, but what will we do with him?"

"Find him a real ballerina to love?" I suggested.

"Tell him that if he doesn't produce actual proof of Mathilde within twenty-four hours, he will be forced to read *Pride and Prejudice*?" Theo said.

I kicked my flip-flops off and set my feet on the ledge. My phone sat in my lap, several unopened text messages from Dax on the screen. He was sending me photos of the bonfire they'd had on the beach last night, but I was too tired to even open them. "Geoffrey doesn't like *Pride and Prejudice*?"

Theo lowered his voice, Geoffrey-style. "Too much prejudice and not enough pride. Also, that Mr. Darcy is a pompous jerk and Elizabeth could have done better."

"Heresy!" Ana said, her energy instantly returning. "Don't ever let me catch you saying those words again. Now. You two have been working so hard, you should have a night out."

"I actually have plans with my dad," I said quickly. "He's taking me somewhere. I think he said Kamari?" Though I was nervous about another dad-daughter night out, I was glad to have a solid excuse to keep me, Theo, and Santorini's moonlight out of each other's company. Whatever awkwardness we agreed not to have between us was still there, as large and inconvenient as a volcano.

"Kamari?" Ana made a few valiant attempts to stuff errant strands of hair back into her topknot, but it only seemed to make things worse. She gave up. "Oh, yes, how nice. It is quite a unique and charming village. But"—she avoided my eyes—"I'm afraid I received a text that he is not feeling well at all. So tonight, I think it would be better if he rests."

I whirled around to look at her. "He texted you? When?" As far as I could tell, she didn't have a phone on her, and besides, why would he text Ana and not me?

"Earlier," she said, producing a bobby pin from her pocket and stabbing it into her hair.

Was that what all the weird energy was at the site today? He'd been trying to figure out a way to tell me he was bailing on me tonight? If so, he could have just told me. Bitterness and sadness and all sorts of unpleasantness began swirling through my chest. Was he really standing me up without telling me? I mean, if he was sick, that was fine. But why couldn't he tell me himself?

Ana, clearly oblivious to what was going on in my mind, suddenly brightened. "Theo, you will take Liv to Kamari!"

"Um . . . he doesn't have to do that," I said quickly, and Theo let out a loud *"Maman!"* before rattling off some sort of protest in French. His voice dropped a hair lower in French than it did in English or in Greek, and I hated that I was noticing that. Also, would it hurt him to act like going out with me wouldn't be the worst thing on earth?

Ana was having none of it. "It is decided. The two of you will go to Kamari, and you will have a *wonderful* time. I will pack you your dinner." She jumped to her feet and then she was off in a whirl of perfume, leaving Theo and me in a stunned silence.

"Is your mom setting us up on a date?" I asked, pressing my fingers into my collarbone.

Theo sighed, tucking his hands behind his head. "Yes. Sorry. But if we're here when Geoffrey gets back, we're going to have to spend the rest of the night counseling him on his fake relationship while you continue to ignore whoever is texting you."

My face went red, and I quickly scooped up my dinging phone. More messages from Dax. Why couldn't I make myself open them?

Theo was right. Whatever awkwardness I had to endure on a coerced date with Theo, it had to be better than sitting around wondering why my dad would invite me all this way just to bail on me.

I still had no idea what Kamari was, but it must require sandwiches, sodas, and an armload of sweatshirts, all of which Ana provided in no short supply. I think she was a little worried we might not actually go, because she insisted on walking us to the bus stop and then waving to us once we were on board.

The ride wasn't *terrible*. The sky had faded to a dusky purple, and the bus was full of tired but contented tourists, all chatting quietly to each other, and before I knew it, we were having a semi-normal conversation while also devouring the food Ana had packed. It was a nice distraction. Before long, Kamari was announced as the next stop.

Kamari turned out to be a town, a pleasantly cluttered beach town. It was stuffed full of open-air restaurants and shops displaying eclectic assortments of bathing suits, snorkel gear, and inflatable pool toys. A long stretch of ocean appeared between buildings, and I caught a glimpse of rows of thatched umbrellas and white lounge chairs.

"Let's look at the beach first," Theo said once the bus had let us off. I followed him down to the boardwalk, and we stood at its edge, watching the waves roll in. Instead of sand, there were tiny black pebbles. To our right, a pair of high, pale cliffs overlooked the ocean.

"Well?" Theo asked, gesturing to the beach.

"Well what?" I looked down at all the small volcanic rocks, and suddenly Plato's words ran through my mind. *One kind of stone was white, another black, and a third red....* "Black Beach! Is this it?"

He already had his camera out. "Two birds with one rock, or whatever that American saying is. This isn't tonight's plan, but I do need footage." I stepped aside and let him do his work. But the beach made me think of my dad, and suddenly the uneasy feeling brewing in my chest was magnified. *Why hadn't he canceled our plans himself?*

Once Theo had some footage, we turned our backs on the water, and he led me uphill through town alongside a busy road, past buildings and open lots, until we arrived at a red stucco building with no roof. Music blared from inside, and a long line of people stood next to a row of potted plants. Strings of bulb lights lit an outdoor seating area, and a spoof sign of the MGM lion—this time featuring a donkey—hung at the entrance.

I looked up at the posters on the wall. "Is this a movie theater?"

"Better." After the ticket booth, we followed a short hallway lit with paper lanterns before stepping into a large, open-air space. My breath evaporated. It wasn't simply a movie theater—it was movie theater *heaven*. A giant screen stood freely in the perfumed air, surrounded by exotic plants, wire sculptures, colorful lighting, an entire garden of succulents, and rows of freestanding hammock chairs.

I spun around, my heart swelling with excitement. It felt like a collision between Old Hollywood and a tropical island. Big band music played from the speakers up front, and vines with fuchsia flowers crept over the walls. To top it all off, the sky had darkened to a deep midnight blue, and fragments of conversations, mostly in English with a variety of accents, filled the air. There was even a large snack bar featuring what looked like Swiss chocolates and mountains of freshly popped popcorn. My mouth immediately began watering from the smell.

"I love this." I spun toward him. "Theo, I *love* this."

He met my smile, his jaw twitching slightly. "That's on your dad. It was one of the top five things he wanted to show you while you're here. Go find us some seats and I'll get snacks."

"Done." I took my time choosing where we'd sit, finally settling on two sling-back chairs next to a small, bubbling water fountain featuring a cross-legged Buddha. Ever since I'd arrived in Oia, I'd been in constant motion, and it felt nice to sit and blend in for a moment.

My phone dinged and I looked down. Dax. You getting these? Wish you were here.

My stomach twisted guiltily. I'd meant to call him this morning, but I'd felt too uneasy about hearing his voice after the Theo incident. That and then the day had flown by in a blur of Henrik, the archaeological dig site, Dad avoiding me, Dad being sick, Dad canceling. *Dad. Dad. Dad.* Ugh. My finger hovered over the screen. I had no clue what to say. *Wish you were here? Have fun? Take lots of pics? Miss you too . . . ?*

The last thought stopped me. I hadn't been thinking about him nearly as much as when I'd first arrived. *Is that normal?*

"Kalamata?" I jumped up to see Theo looking for me, staggering under the load of a giant bucket of popcorn, two ice cream cones, and a half dozen candy bars.

"Over here. What is all of this?" I asked, off-loading the candy bars.

"I forgot to ask what you like, so I got one of everything."

My mouth twisted into a smile. "I love *everything*. How did you know?"

"Lucky guess." He smiled at me, and instantly the weirdness evaporated. *Poof.* "Dark chocolate or lemon? Or both?" Ice cream was already dripping down his hand.

I took the lemon from him. "What's the movie tonight?"

He adjusted his cone into his popcorn hand, fumbling for the ticket in his back pocket. "Something in black and white. I saw the title in Greek, but I don't know what it is in English. Something about liking things hot?"

"Hmmm." I grabbed a handful of hot, buttery popcorn. It still stung to be here without my dad, but Theo was making me feel a lot better. He had that effect on me.

"Sorry your dad couldn't make it," Theo said, as if he could read my mind. He hesitated. "It's not the same, but . . . I know what it's like to have your dad bail on you. It used to happen all the time. At some point I gave up."

"Oh." The popcorn stuck in my throat. "Do you see your dad much now?"

Theo shook his head. "Not if I can help it. I'm supposed to be with him for Christmas, but I'm lobbying pretty hard for that not to be the case. Hey, look."

He nodded toward the screen, where the same MGM donkey spoof had appeared. The rest of the crowd noticed too and began clapping, and then the lights flickered once, twice, and then dimmed. "Five-minute warning. Let's sit."

Excitement flooded through me. I couldn't think of a single other place I wanted to be right now. "Thanks for bringing me here." I bumped Theo in the shoulder.

"You're welcome." He hesitated, holding up his still dripping cone. But instead of eating it, he looked at me with big, worried eyes. Oh no. Now what? "Are you worried about your dad?"

I straightened in my chair. That wasn't what I was expecting. "Because he was sick today?"

He grabbed a handful of popcorn. "No, I mean about the documentary. This morning he told me he thinks it's missing something. He's worried that the evidence he has won't be enough for National Geographic. They e-mailed him that they're hoping he'll find some new piece to the story."

So that's what the stress was about. *Atlantis*. Always Atlantis. It was starting to make sense. How run-down he was. How sick he looked. Why he'd canceled on me. Did Atlantis always have to be the thing that drove us apart? A flash of pain worked its way under my rib cage, but I forced myself to ignore it.

"How is he supposed to find something new on an eleven-thousand-year-old story?"

He shrugged. "I know, it doesn't make sense. But I wanted to tell you in case you have any ideas. This means so much to your dad." And clearly to Theo, too. I was hit with a wave of jealousy. Theo and my dad have now what I used to have with him when I was young: looking at our map together, lining up clues, diving into Plato. Maybe it wasn't so bad to want to have that again.

I racked my brain, but nothing came to mind. "I'll think about it," I said. I didn't have a lot of hope that I actually would, but I knew how important the documentary was to Dad, and to Theo. I turned to him. "Between the three of us, we'll come up with something. Right?"

I wasn't entirely sure that was true, but the worry lines on Theo's forehead disappeared. "Right. Now no more talking about Atlantis. We need a night off."

The movie was an old one, and Theo had partially gotten the title right. It was an old black-and-white comedy called *Some Like It Hot.* The theater played it in English with Greek subtitles, and before long I was swept up into it. The film was about two male musicians who witness a crime and have to go into hiding, so they join a traveling all-female band featuring Marilyn Monroe, who they both immediately fall in love with (of course) and fight over while trying to maintain their disguises and outwit the mob.

I was a little bit distracted, partially because Theo and I kept grabbing popcorn at the same time and accidentally touching hands. Every time it happened, a small light turned on inside of me. If I had to say what it was I found so compelling about Theo, it was that he was so completely Theo. I'd never met anyone like him, and I doubted I ever would again. And if this were a different night under different circumstances . . .

Stop.

I held my phone tightly as a reminder. The sooner I got back to Dax, the better. Because whatever was going on between Theo and me, it wasn't going away.

Chapter Eighteen

#18. DRIED OREGANO AND ROSEMARY LEAVES

After my dad left, we couldn't afford rent anymore and we had to leave our apartment. He hadn't had a regular job in almost six months, but he had done a lot of odd jobs for the landlord in return for a lower rent. On his good days you could find him tightening one of the banisters or fishing a fork out of Mrs. Davis's disposal (again). On his bad days he had his shows.

Mom said we couldn't take the plants with us. We were moving into a basement apartment with an old classmate of hers. Plants needed light, and they'd be better off if we left them for the apartment's new owner.

I knew it was silly, but I cried when I said goodbye to the oregano and rosemary, and then wrote a note for the new owners with my dad's secret for growing plants: "PLANTS GROW FASTER IF YOU TALK TO THEM. THESE ONES LIKE KNOCK-KNOCK JOKES THE BEST." The talking thing is actually true. I read about it in a research article online because I didn't trust that my dad was right.

WHEN WE GOT BACK TO THE BOOKSTORE, ANA WAS curled up in one of the chairs reading a novel with her legs tucked under her.

"Ah, and here we have a wild bookstore owner in her natural habitat," Theo said, doing his best Australian accent.

"And how was it?" Ana asked, looking at us smugly over the top of her reading glasses. The cover of her book featured a large man with long hair and an open shirt holding a limp-looking damsel. *Forbidden Desert Love.* Ana really did read the books she sold.

"It was great. They played an old Marilyn Monroe movie," Theo said.

She sighed contentedly. "That woman was something. Perhaps not *happy*, but something."

"How's Nico?" Theo asked.

"Fine. He keeps saying that filmmaking is a young man's game."

"It isn't." Theo walked across the room, plucking a grumpy-looking Margaret Catwood from the top of the mystery section. "There was a Portuguese filmmaker who made his last film when he was 106."

"Impressive." She set her book aside. "You missed a very

long talk with Geoffrey. He and Mathilde are in a serious argument, and he's worried their relationship won't survive it."

"His fake relationship will definitely not survive this fake fight," Theo said, clutching Margaret to his chest. "Please tell me you didn't encourage him."

"He looked like a droopy puddle with arms. I had no choice but to take him seriously. I told him that all relationships ebb and flow, and if they're truly committed to each other, they will find a way to right themselves." Ana smiled ruefully and slid her glasses on top of her head. "I will see you both tomorrow. Sweet dreams." She blew us a kiss, then let herself out, closing the door behind her.

"Your mom's awesome," I said.

"*Ouf!*" Theo spun toward me. "I have an idea. For the film. Come with me!"

"No, Theo, I am not breaking into a cave house. *Again.*" I was only half kidding. But really, I wasn't going anywhere. I was exhausted.

"Relax, it's in here." Theo walked through the main room to the smaller room—the one that housed all the children's books—and I watched as he kicked off his shoes and climbed barefoot up onto the waist-high table. He stepped carefully over a sign on an easel that read FOR MOST OF HISTORY, ANONYMOUS WAS A WOMAN—VIRGINIA WOOLF, and then reached up, popping open a small door that until this moment had looked like a normal part of the wall.

Whatever flaws may be ascribed to the bookstore, it was never ever boring. "Another secret room?"

He reached in far, up on his tiptoes, his voice muffled. "This one's more like a cupboard. Now, where is it?"

"How many secret compartments are there in this place?" I asked, not even trying to hide the giddy explorer in me. There's something about a secret room. Or cupboard. I knocked on the wall closest to me. "How many of these panels pop open?"

"Nine? Ten? Something like that. Your dad wanted it to feel magical in here."

Mission accomplished. I glanced up at the ceiling. My dad had covered it in painted constellations, the stars slightly bigger than the ones he'd cut out for my sunset birthday party. Every detail of this place—from the walls to the soft, colorful rugs—screamed magic and twilight and the promise of extraordinary things.

"There it is." Theo jumped off the table, then straightened. When he held the item out to me, all the lightness evaporated. Not only did I recognize it, but I *knew* it. I knew exactly what the paper would feel like under my fingertips, how heavy it was. I even knew how it would smell.

A huge lump formed in my throat. "It's a map, isn't it?"

Theo's eyes met mine inquisitively. "How'd you know?"

"I'm a good guesser," I said weakly.

He pushed it into my hands, and I carefully removed the plastic, then unfolded it, taking my time to smooth out the wrinkles. My heart squeezed as I flattened it out. Except for the lack of crayons and cartoons, it was almost an exact replica of the one he'd left behind.

For a moment I couldn't do anything but stare at it. Finally, I turned to Theo. "What do you know about this map?"

"This is the first map he worked on when he arrived in Oia. He worked on it for something like five years, and he took it with him everywhere. It's where he developed the theory that he and the Egyptologist have been working on." He slid it over to me excitedly. "Look how worn out it is. He carried it on him for years."

I swallowed, hard. Because I'd carried the original map around too, tucked into my backpack or coat pockets—it was one-half of a friendship bracelet that I'd thought meant something. But our map had been replaceable. It felt like pressure on a forgotten bruise.

Theo, mistaking my stillness for interest, jabbed my shoulder excitedly. "*This* is what we're missing. The documentary isn't about Atlantis. It's about your dad's life. It's about why he cares so much about finding Atlantis. It's his story. It needs to be personal." He pointed to the map. "*This* is where it all began for him. Maybe he can't dig up new proof of Atlantis, but he can show how it affected his life.

We'll make the documentary more personal interest."

I waited for the thought to settle, to mean something. Almost immediately, I knew Theo was right. We did need to bring a personal element to the film—I knew it the way I knew which color of paint to reach for. The only issue was that this map *wasn't* the beginning.

"Wait right here." I stepped over a snoozing Purrnest Hemingway, making my way to the cave and my suitcase, and dug through it until I found the sketchbook I'd tucked my dad's map into. It had been a long time since I'd looked at it anywhere but inside my own bedroom, and I hesitated for a moment before forcing myself to carry it out to the eagerly awaiting Theo.

"*This* was his first map." I spread it out, watching it gleam in the lamp's pool of light.

"*Whoa.*" Theo reached out to touch it, but stopped himself. "Okay, this one is really old. And way more interesting-looking. Is this part . . . you?" He pointed to all the crayon scribbles marking up different sections of Santorini. I'd been so proud of my contributions, so sure that I was helping my dad on his mission to find Atlantis.

"It says my name, doesn't it?" OLIVE was written with the *L* and *E* backward across the top. "I found it. After he left."

A part of me wanted to spill the rest of it—*this was one of twenty-six items*—but I couldn't get myself to say it out loud. Also, I had an idea of my own. "You're right, we do need to make the documentary more personal. Has my dad ever told you about the lighthouse keeper?"

I knew he had by the way Theo's eyes lit up. According to my dad's stories, it was a local lighthouse keeper who had ignited my dad's interest in Atlantis. He'd loaned him his first copy of *Timaeus and Critias* and had helped him draw his first map of Santorini.

Theo put his hands on my shoulders, spinning me toward him. "Kalamata, you're *brilliant*. That's exactly what we need for the documentary. I'm sure the lighthouse keeper is long gone, but we'll go to the lighthouse tomorrow after the beaches and have your dad tell the story of how he first became interested in Atlantis. How was I doing this without you?"

He threw his arms around me, engulfing me in a tight bear hug that nearly knocked me over. Theo was so *physical*. Plus, his arms were so warm and comforting. Somehow I felt safe and relaxed, and maybe that's how a small detail from my past broke through my protective barriers.

While the rest of the items my dad had left behind had been scattered around the house, in drawers and on countertops, the map had been placed. I'd found it folded and tucked carefully beneath my pillow.

I hadn't found the map. I'd been *gifted* the map. And that was a big difference, wasn't it? A tiny window opened up in my chest. Not all the way, but enough to let some sunlight in.

Even with all the soothing enchantment French rap had to offer, I spent the night tossing and turning, and I woke feeling groggy, my bare legs tangled up in my sheets. I didn't even bother to look over at Theo's bed anymore. I knew exactly how I'd find it—sheets pulled up, pillows fluffed, last night's clothes folded at the foot of it. I looked to the wall for my call sheet, but there wasn't one.

I took a moment to rub my eyes, then carefully swung open the bunk's door. Down below, a despondent-looking Geoffrey stood holding a copy of Cormac McCarthy's *The Road*. He really *did* look like a droopy puddle with arms. When he saw me, he gave a weak nod. "Ah, Liv . . ."

"Problems with Mathilde?"

"How'd you know?"

"Lucky guess. Where are all the customers?"

He bobbed his head sadly. "Store's closed today. Ana and your dad had to go to Athens."

"Wait, what?" I sputtered, panic flowing through me. I jumped the last few rungs, my ankles tingling as I hit the floor. "But we only have a few more days left to film. We can't take today off."

"More business, more problems," he said despondently.

I ran straight up to the roof, pajamas and all, to find Theo sitting with his laptop balanced on his knees.

"Theo, what's going on?" I skidded to a stop in my bare feet. "Geoffrey said our parents went to Athens."

He pulled his headphones off. His face was set in a grim look of resolve. "Early this morning. It was a surprise to me, too."

"But . . ." I spun out toward the water, trying to tame the feelings in my chest. Disappointment? Frustration? Hurt?

No, it was spicier than that. *Anger.* We'd finally come up with the angle that the film needed, and now we might not have time to actually follow through on it. "What are we going to do? We're going to miss the deadline."

Theo rested his head back against his chair. "I've been sitting up here trying to figure that out. Should we ask for an extension? Film the rest without him? I don't know what to do. My mom said it was an emergency. They could get in serious trouble if they don't figure out the business license issue."

Wind ruffled up from the sea, sending my hair flying, and I shoved my bangs back angrily. "When will they be back?"

His shoulders rounded. "If they take the fastest ferries, then they could be home by seven tonight."

"Seven?" I fell into the chair next to him. How was this

happening? We couldn't afford to lose a whole day. Not when we had an unapologetic deadline hurtling our way. Now what? Also, I couldn't ignore the other thought tugging at me.

"Does something seem strange about this?"

Theo flicked his eyes to mine. "About what?"

"Does my dad go to Athens this often normally? And do you usually have this many business problems? It seems like a license is something you'd have figured out by now."

He leaned in toward me. "All I know is that it's been a mess trying to keep a business going here. When they first started, everyone told them it would be easy to set up shop, but it's been problem after problem."

I attempted to gather my hair into a ponytail. "It seems so sudden. Why didn't your mom say anything about this last night? We saw her right before midnight."

He twisted his lips to one side, thinking. "She must not have known then. Either way, we don't have a lot of options. I think we'd better spend the day working on editing. Sound okay?"

Why was Theo so calm about this? It did *not* sound okay. Questions roared in my ears: Why would my dad go to the trouble of inviting me to Greece if he was going to avoid me? Had our conversation on the cruise really been that bad? Because that's when things had started changing—when he'd started dodging me.

Was he really going to bail on me for the rest of the trip?

It's not like I had unlimited time here. I didn't even have a *lot* of time here.

And there was also the fact that time was not on our side to finish this documentary.

One of my mom's favorite sayings came to me. *Control what you can control.* Theo was right. My dad being gone was out of our control. We had to complete the film as best we could.

My mind flew back to the schedule in my filming binder. "We need to stick with the schedule. Let's do whatever you had planned for today, and then we'll go to the lighthouse and film without him."

My voice came out assured and commanding, and Theo blinked at me. "Film without your dad?"

I gave an exaggerated shoulder shrug. "Well, we can't go with him, so . . . yes."

Theo hesitated but then gave me the look I was always giving my mom. A *Fine, I guess there's no stopping you* sort of look. "Today is Red Beach. It isn't very far from the lighthouse." He glanced pointedly at my pajamas. "Meet you back here in twenty?"

"Ten." I headed straight for the cave and my CREW T-shirt.

The morning was particularly hot, and after an hour of riding massively overcrowded buses with sweaty, jostling people—

all of whom seemed to have forgotten to apply deodorant—I was beginning to regret my decision to carry on with filming. Wouldn't a day lounging down on Ammoudi Bay with my sketch pad have been better?

Dax texted. How's it going?

If I were telling the truth, I would have written something like, *I'm hot, grumpy, and my dad keeps bailing on me,* but instead I scrolled through my photos, then sent one I'd taken of the caldera a few days earlier. Another day in paradise! Immediately after I press send, the bus hit its brakes, causing a woman to put her elbow directly into my left eye. Theo looked at me sympathetically.

Once our bus screeched to our stop, Theo and I shouldered the equipment between the two of us, which was no easy feat, then made our way through a cluster of stands selling cold drinks and pool toys, the owners of which looked positively despondent. If the locals were this demolished by the heat, how was I supposed to manage it?

After the parking lot was a hike that required climbing over tumbled chunks of rock, my sandals slipping in the hot, soft dirt as sweat trickled down my back.

"Tell me again what's so special about Red Beach?" I groaned after sliding off a rock and nearly losing my balance.

Theo offered me a hand. "Well, it's red. And it's a beach."

"Thanks for that," I muttered, repositioning my over-stuffed backpack on my shoulders.

"You've never seen anything like it," Theo said.

"How do you know?"

He shrugged in his confident way. "Kalamata, I know *everything*."

"Mm-hmm," I mumbled, but I was glad to have the old Theo back.

Finally, *finally*, we rounded the corner, and then I saw the beach from afar . . . and, well, I hated to admit it, but Theo, as usual, was right. I'd never seen *anything* like it.

Red Beach was—shocking, I know—very, very red. But it was even more dramatic than I'd imagined. Orangey-red cliffs stood tall and commanding before dropping abruptly to a narrow strip of beach that crumbled almost immediately into pristine turquoise surf, the color contrast so stark and startling that it made my eyes water. Yellow striped umbrellas dotted the beach, and gleaming white boats lazily made their way through the cove.

Posted at the edge of a steep, winding path that led to the beach was a large weathered sign that had been translated into several languages.

DANGER—NO ENTRY

FALLING ROCKS, SERIOUS RISK OF INJURY

But either people hadn't read the sign or they didn't care,

because the beach was packed full of people. There was even a small shop set up at the far end with an ice cream freezer out front.

I pointed to the sign. "Are we going?"

Theo's hair was damp with sweat, and he had a streak of dirt across his cheek. "Kalamata, Santorini is an active volcano. Are we really going to let a few measly falling rocks stop us?"

I flexed menacingly at the cliffs, nearly dropping my bags in the process. "Bring it, falling rocks."

Theo nodded approvingly. "By the way, did you know olive trees can be classified as sensitive, moderate, or hardy?"

I wanted to ask which category he thought I fell into, but that would be admitting defeat to the whole Olive thing, so I rolled my eyes at him and carried on.

It took several more minutes of hiking to reach the actual beach, and when we got there, I had to stop to take it all in. Red Beach was all rock and no sand—a true volcanic beach—with the size of the rocks progressing from large to medium to small as we moved in toward the water, but what really interested me was the overall *vibe*. Two different sets of music blared from speakers set up by sunbathers, and towels were lined up almost end to end, accommodating all the people intent on enjoying a day at the beach. Out in the water, a group of kids attempted to knock each other off floaties shaped like slices of pizza.

These people were on vacation, enjoying a unique, albeit dangerous, day at the ocean. I wanted to feel that way, but I didn't. I felt panicky, and not because of the falling rock signs. Because my dad wasn't here, I couldn't help but feel let down.

I was working up my courage to take off my sandals, brave the rocks, and wade into the water, when Theo grabbed my sleeve. "Look at that." I turned to see him pointing toward the cliffs and what looked like a door that had been—inexplicably—built directly into them. The door was a soft pink color with a boarded-up window and a heavy padlock.

"Um, why is there a door built into the cliffs?"

"It's the Door to Nowhere. I forgot about it, but it will be perfect for the film. Come on."

"The door to *where*?" But he'd already taken off across the beach, weaving through all the scantily clad people on their towels, and I had no choice but to follow after him.

When I caught up, Theo was crouched down, getting an angled view of the door. "There are two stories to the door—the tourist version and the local version," he began. "Locals tell tourists that it's like a Narnia door, a magical portal to other worlds, but it's really a storage space. Fishermen used to use it to store their nets, and now the beach owners use it to store umbrellas when the tourists clear out for the season. This is a perfect example of local lore. It will be great on the documentary."

"Two stories," I repeated, placing my palm flat on the peeling paint. Did anyone really believe the Narnia one? And if so, why, when there was almost always a boring explanation eager to explain the magic away?

I felt the thought coming before it spelled itself out. *Dad is a Narnia person.* He'd always seen the magic in the mundane. Had my mom and I been the mundane? Is that why he'd left and why he was avoiding me now?

I wanted to be angry, let the tidal wave carry off the more complex emotions, but the sadness was too overwhelming. Being here with my dad only to experience him *not* being here for me again . . . It was so heavy. He'd left for Narnia, while my mom and I were stuck in a tangle of off-season umbrellas and fishermen nets. Bringing me here had only highlighted that fact.

I turned to see Theo filming me again, and even if I'd wanted to, I couldn't have disguised my expression. I was too low. "You get it?"

"Got it." He lowered his camera solemnly. "Let's go, Droopy Puddle."

The only way to get to White Beach was from Red Beach, and we waited at the dock for a water taxi, then spent an hour filming its off-white cliffs and crystal clear water.

Theo insisted on a swim break, and I sat with my feet in

the cold, trying my best to assuage the heaviness in my chest, but no dice. You can be in one of the most beautiful places in the world and still feel like a smoldering heap of garbage. I'm assuming the opposite is true too.

By the time we headed for the lighthouse, I was dragging more than walking, and Theo kept wrapping his arm around my shoulders to give me upbeat facts about our favorite fruit. *Did you know that ninety percent of all harvested olives are used to create olive oil? Did you know that the world's first eye shadow was created in Ancient Greece and was made of olive oil mixed with ground charcoal?*

No, Theo. I did not.

Lunch didn't work either. We stopped at a small restaurant for warm souvlaki pita wraps, but not even all that pillowy goodness could get me going again. How was it possible that I, of all people, was dreading going to a lighthouse? For my final art project last year, I'd done a series of drawings on Seattle lighthouses that my mom and I had spent several weekends driving to. But this lighthouse was one that I clearly should be seeing with my father. This trip had had some good times, but it had mostly confirmed what I already knew about my dad. He wasn't here for me.

Getting to the lighthouse not only required a cab ride, but another hike on a path lined with tumbled rocks and bushes until we reached the caramel-colored peninsula jutting out into the ocean. This was the very last bit of Santorini—we were as far from Oia as we could possibly get.

For a moment we stood out in the open, the wind hitting us back and forth from different angles, Theo filming like always. The lighthouse was small and simple, made of white stone with brown brick outlining its edges. A weather vane sat atop a green cap, and a cobalt-blue Greek flag waved in the unrelenting wind. The peninsula itself was a mishmash mound of rocks, which made the sturdy lighthouse stand out even more. It looked so out of place in its determined practicality. Beyond it, the entire caldera sparkled from the sun, highlighting all five of Santorini's islands.

"Let me film you walking all limp and dejected," Theo instructed. "I'll get some video and we'll set it to dramatic music. We can talk about all the poor wretched souls who have been forced to spend a day exploring one of the most beautiful islands on earth."

"Theo . . . ," I groaned, throwing my arms in the air, but I began a walk fit for the poorest and wretchedest, and Theo cheered behind me.

"Yes, like that. *Perfect*."

How did he make me smile so much?

As I headed out toward the cliff, I realized that we were far from alone. Several groups of picnickers had staked out spots in the rocks, and when I saw a father and his young daughter, I was hit with a wave of envy that I quickly replaced with self-reproach. Hadn't I trained myself *not* to miss my dad? Also, I was a teenager. I was supposed to be annoying him with my phone usage and scaring him to death from the passenger's seat of my first car, not trying to *reconnect* with him. This entire situation felt wrong.

After a while, Theo caught up to me, phone in hand. "Droop, listen to this. Akrotiri Lighthouse was built by a French company at the end of the 1800s and was one of the first in all of Greece. It stopped operation during World War II, but the Greek navy put it back to use in the 1940s. You see how it is shaped?"

I stood on my tiptoes to see over the top of the fence surrounding the structure. Along with the lighthouse tower, there was a full building, the back end shaped like a rectangle.

"Today the lighthouse is run by remote, but back in the day, this is where the lighthouse keeper and his family lived. That's who your dad met. Can't you imagine him here as a little kid?"

I sighed, resting my chin on the fence. Because yes, I really, really could. I'd seen photos of him as a child. He'd looked mischievous and energetic, and I could picture him scampering over these rocks, fearlessly approaching the edge, forming his early theories about Atlantis. He'd always been who he was, and I wished that that person had made space for me. But was he even capable of that?

"Why don't I get you on camera telling what you know about the lighthouse keeper?" Theo said. "It won't be the same as having your dad here, but it will give it a nice personal edge anyway."

Like usual, Theo's camera was collecting a lot of interested stares, and the weight of all those eyes dragged me down even further. "Hey, Theo, I'll be right back."

His dark eyes met mine sympathetically. "Sure, Kalamata. Take your time."

I spent the next few minutes exploring the little peninsula. Water crashed all around me, and for a moment I stood at the very edge, face to the water, willing the ocean and spray and all that blue sky to make me forget—even for a moment— about my dad, Dax, college, everything.

It didn't work. I felt exposed and all alone, exactly like this lighthouse.

My mom was wrong. Coming to Greece hadn't changed anything. This trip was yet another broken promise. I found a seat on a smooth-topped rock, then pulled my sketchbook out from my backpack and began to draw.

As my sketch took shape, my feelings clarified along with it. Here was the thing: regardless of the many reasons *not* to want it, I did want a relationship with my dad. I wanted someone to come to my art shows and games, and give my boyfriend a hard time, and nag me about finishing my schoolwork. And I didn't want any dad. I wanted *my* dad. I wanted our old friendship and easy talking and all of our adventures and the way he made boring things—grocery shopping, walking to school—interesting. I wanted it so badly that it made me feel dizzy and unsteady and achy all at once. Missing my dad *hurt*.

But was that ever going to be a possibility? As hard as I'd fought against the battalion of postcards marching their way into my life, the fact remained that I'd always hoped they meant something. That he felt the same way, and that maybe we'd find a bridge or some kind of common ground, something to bring us back together. For a moment on our sunset cruise, I'd thought he'd been thinking the same thing. I'd thought he'd been capable of coming back into my life. He'd asked me to believe in him, hadn't he? Had my hesitations slammed that door shut? And if so, could it really be considered an invitation at all?

I looked up toward the hazy outline of Oia and felt the truth solidify. No matter what I had or hadn't said on the sunset cruise, a true reconciliation would never happen. If this trip had proven anything, it was that my dad couldn't—or maybe wouldn't—be there for me. Our relationship was ancient history, and the sooner I could get past that, the better.

Things at home may not be perfect, but at least I'd know what the score was and how to fit in. At least I didn't have to hope for things that were never going to happen.

I clutched my pencil tightly in my hand. I'd drawn a lighthouse. Steady, capable, but all alone.

Chapter Nineteen

#19. DOODLE OF OUR LANDLORD, MACK

This one took me a while to find. It was stashed under a pile of bills in what my dad called our "drawer of requirement," which, despite the Harry Potter allusion, meant bills. Lots and lots of bills. That drawer was always packed full, but he kept everything in neat bundles, with rubber bands holding together the different piles. Red meant pay immediately. Yellow meant pay as soon as possible. And green meant no rush, we'll get to it. In the months before he went away, he stopped using the rubber band system, and the drawer overflowed.

I found the drawing on the back of a medical bill, and I knew who it was immediately: our landlord, Mack. Mack is sitting in his recliner, and his eyes are big behind his thick glasses, his hands resting neatly on his chest. This drawing looked more real than if Mack were standing in front of me. But what really got me about it was the expression on his face. You could see that things hadn't worked out for Mack the way he'd hoped they would, and it made you wish he'd had a better run.

AS I MADE MY WAY BACK TO THEO, I SAW THAT HE WAS IN a deep conversation with a balding, dark-bearded man wearing track pants and a gray T-shirt. I wasn't in the mood to interact, so I posted up next to the lighthouse fence, carefully out of eyesight, until I heard Theo yelling for me.

"Kalamata? Where are you? Please tell me you didn't throw your broody self into the depths of the ocean."

My sigh was swallowed up in the wind. This self-pitying thing was getting old, even to me. "Over here, Theo."

He came running, jumping over all the jagged pieces of rock with his backpack bouncing against his back. The man was now out of sight. "Kalamata! You'll never believe this!" In all of the exciting Theo moments, this was the most amped I'd ever seen him. If I poked him with a pin, he'd probably burst.

"Another door to nowhere?" I asked, leaning over to stretch my back. Maybe I could convince Theo to take me back to Cinekamari tonight. Another film would do wonders for my bad attitude.

"That man back there asked me what we were filming, and when I told him about our documentary, he said I need to go to a restaurant called Vasilios. The owner claims to have found a piece of Atlantis." He blurted out the words so quickly that it took me a moment to separate them from each other, and when I did, my enthusiasm definitely did not match Theo's.

I straightened. "A piece of Atlantis? What does that even mean?" I made sure to add a healthy dose of disdain to my tone. Was this entire island full of delusional people?

But he would not be deterred. Theo danced back and forth excitedly. "He said that back in the 1980s, a fisherman who lives nearby dove and found some remains of a golden city. He's been trying to get people to take him seriously ever since."

Who did that sound like? I bit my lower lip. "And let me guess. You want to track him down?"

Theo grabbed my shoulders, shaking me like a present on Christmas morning. "Of course I do. Best case, he actually has something for us; worst case, we have a good story and some footage of a local talking about his own Atlantis hunt. Kalamata, this is it!"

I couldn't help but feel a little bit over Atlantis at the moment, but the thought of going back to hang out in the empty bookstore feeling upset didn't sound all that great either. What could it hurt, besides my already battered, wind-swept heart?

Ha.

"Where's the restaurant?" I asked, carefully peeling Theo's hands from my shoulders. He smelled like salt water. Why had I never realized how good that smelled?

"It's a taverna on a beach called Kambia. He says it's a local favorite; we can't miss it. We can take a bus. Come on!" And then he was running again.

Kambia was a quiet, tucked-away beach that had somehow managed to avoid the crowds of Red Beach and Akrotiri. We ended up walking most of the way. It wasn't nearly as impossible to miss as Theo's informer had claimed, but after cornering a lot of innocent bystanders for informational shakedowns, Theo found someone to direct us to the correct beach, and we left the road, taking a warped staircase down to a small sandy cove. A narrow wooden dock led past the rocky beach out into the clear water.

The late-afternoon heat was finally beginning to let up, and there were only two people camped out on the rocks, both of whom looked baked to perfection. *That's what you'd be doing on Dax's senior trip*, my brain reminded me. Relaxing. Not chasing around leads with a hundred pounds of equipment on my back and a completely broken heart.

"*Kambia* means caterpillar," Theo said in what I now recognized as his Imparting Useless Facts voice. He pointed to the scrub of trees and bushes behind us.

"Interesting." He ignored my lack of enthusiasm.

"In the spring, thousands of butterflies hatch from their cocoons in the pines. It's a butterfly parade."

I put my hands on my hips and looked around, enjoying the warm breeze. The cove felt like it was holding its breath. Keeping a secret. "Santorini without crowds—who knew it existed?"

"Wait until winter," Theo said. "My first morning in December, I thought I was on the set of a zombie apocalypse movie. The entire place empties." He pointed behind me. "Taverna."

"Huh?" I turned and saw the small building camouflaged against the rock. I easily could have walked right past it. The taverna's walls were inlaid with mismatched rocks the exact color of the cliffs, and at least half of the structure consisted of an open patio. Pots full of overflowing succulents dotted the railing, and several small tables stood empty. A loose sign hanging over the doorway swayed lightly in the breeze: VASILIOS.

If I'd had my doubts before, now I was sure of it. You didn't find breaking evidence in tiny fish huts. I rocked back on my aching heels. Sandals had been the wrong choice today. "Now what? Ask for Vasilios, the man who claims to have a piece of Atlantis?"

"Sounds like a solid plan," Theo said from behind his

camera. If he didn't make it as a filmmaker, he should probably try for magician. He could make his camera appear out of thin air.

Fine. I made a face into the lens, then walked down the rest of the steps and crossed the sand to the taverna's porch. As we approached, a round, pink-cheeked woman appeared in the open doorway, a pencil tucked behind her ear. "Are you here for dinner?" Her voice was friendly, with the slightest hint of a Greek accent, but when she caught sight of Theo's camera, her smile faded. "How can I help?"

Theo nudged me, and I did my best to muster some enthusiasm. "Hi. We're documentarians, and we're here hoping to speak with Vasilios. Is he available?"

Her expression went blank, and I recognized the move for what it was. Defensiveness. "My father is resting. What is this in regard to?"

"Someone told us he has . . ." I trailed off, wishing with my entire heart that I did not have to say what I was about to say to this very practical-seeming woman. "Someone told us that he has information about the lost city of Atlantis. We would love to talk to him about it."

"Atlantis?" The woman's expression sharpened instantly. "Who told you this?"

"Um . . ." *Random man at the lighthouse* didn't quite carry the weight that this scenario needed. "Someone we met earlier."

"Also, we'd like to eat," Theo added, eyeing the coral-colored octopus hanging from the rafters.

She folded her arms over her apron. "You cannot speak to my father today. He is not well."

I could practically feel the animosity wafting off her. Then it hit me. I knew exactly what was going on here. "My dad is an Atlantis hunter too, and he's spent a lot of time working on his theory. We aren't here to make fun of your dad. Or you," I added quickly. "And if he can't meet with us, that's okay. But we'd really like to talk to him."

It was quite the speech. Theo looked at me wide-eyed, then stepped forward. "She's right. We're fellow seekers." He must have heard that word from Henrik.

The woman sighed, studying us for a moment, but instead of sending us away like I thought she would, she pointed to one of the tables. "Have a seat, please."

We made our way across the creaking porch, and I slid into a worn, silvery-gray chair, taking in the hand-crocheted tablecloth and carefully arranged vase of flowers. The smell of spiced meat floated through the restaurant's open door, making my mouth water. Theo took the seat across from me, then leaned forward, holding his hand up in front of me. "What do you think, Kalamata?"

I met my hand against his, matching our fingers. His palms were calloused, the tips of his fingers reaching at least an inch above mine. "I think we're never going to meet Vasilios, let alone see whatever proof he has."

"No, I mean what do you want to *order*." He plucked the menus from the stand on the side of the table and pushed one to me. It was written entirely in Greek, without even any pictures to give me hints.

"Order something for me?"

"Stuffed squid with feta? Ceviche sea bass?"

Our pita hadn't been all that long ago, but suddenly I was starving. "All of it." I checked my phone, half hoping to see something from my dad. Did he even have my number?

Theo's eyebrows lifted. "For someone who's so afraid of the ocean, you sure love to eat from it."

"Those two things are entirely unrelated."

A staccato of footsteps sounded from inside the restaurant, and when I looked up, an elderly man with flowing white hair was barreling toward us. He was short and wide, with wire-rimmed glasses and a large smile on his face. "Hello!" he called. "Hello, Americans! American teenagers!" His daughter had been lying about his health. This man could probably beat Theo in a race.

Theo and I quickly got to our feet, exchanging a look.

"I'm American, but this one's Greek," I said, gesturing to Theo. "Are you Vasilios?"

He struck his chest. "Yes, I am Vasilios. My restaurant!" He beamed at us, then gestured to Theo's equipment. "Hollywood! Yes? Hollywood!"

"Well . . . ," I started.

His eyes settled on me curiously. "Eh?"

Theo let off a series of rapid-fire Greek sentences, and Vasilios's face lit up like a strobe light. "Atlantis! Yes, I show." He pointed at me. "*You.*"

My face warmed up, he was looking at me so intensely. "Um . . . you'll show me?"

"Yes. You. You wait!" Vasilios took off down the porch, and soon he was running for the stairs like a sprinter going for the gold. Not quite the napping old man I'd pictured from his daughter's description. He looked faster than Julius. Faster than *Dax*. And sharp. But the thing about Santorini is that after a while you aren't really surprised by anything.

"How old do you think he is?"

"Not a day under a hundred and seven," Theo said. "It's the oleic acid derived from all of the olive oil we eat here. It reduces blood pressure and keeps us young. Did you know that the average Greek uses twenty-three liters of olive oil per year?"

"You are relentless," I said, keeping my eyes on Vasilios's disappearing form. "Does everyone move that fast in Greece? I thought you were supposed to be a relaxed culture."

Theo tipped back on his chair. "Relaxed? Who told you that? Have you ever spoken to a Greek?"

"I *am* Greek, remember?"

"Barely," Theo said. "You won't even drink the coffee. Don't get me started on the half cup of sugar you dumped into your cup at the bus stop this morning. You practically had to chew it."

"I was tired. And you leave my sugar coffee alone." I relaxed back into my chair, feeling a small nudge of relief. The waves were soothing sounding, and my mind desperately needed a break from everything with my dad.

Thirty minutes later, Theo was attempting to steal a piece of charred octopus off my plate, when the staccato footsteps appeared again, announcing Vasilios's return. His face was bright red and he was drenched through his T-shirt.

"Camera time," Theo said, dropping his fork and pulling his camera out of his backpack.

I jumped to my feet. "Vasilios?" He was breathing heavily, and from his red face he looked about a minute away from a heart attack, and my heart rate went up too. "Are you okay? Have you been running this whole time?"

Vasilios took a moment to catch his breath, doubled over with his hands on his knees. Then he popped up like a Toaster Strudel. "I am fisherman. I fish. For taverna. For family. One day in net, I see. I find . . ." He said a word in Greek, looking to Theo for help.

Theo's eyes widened, and he repeated the word back, and

then they spoke for what felt like forever, Theo rattling off questions and Vasilios responding nearly as quickly. Theo's face was brightening with every word, and despite my best intentions, anticipation was forming a tidal wave in my chest. When I couldn't stand it anymore, I grabbed Theo's arm. "Theo, what? What did he find?"

Theo's face was a cautious mixture of disbelief and awe. "Kalamata, what did Atlantis look like?"

He wanted me to spell it out? "Uh . . . well, it was an island, made up of concentric rings. Alternating land and ocean. And in the middle was a golden statue to Poseidon. Everything was covered in gold, and there were hundreds of statues."

"Covered in *gold*?" he prompted. "Or something else?"

"No." I thought back, mentally thumbing through my Atlantis knowledge. They'd had their own type of precious metal. What was it called? Oro something? The word flew to mind. "Orichalcum!"

"In English, orichalcum, yes!" Vasilios began spouting off words again, and Theo translated, keeping his eyes fixed on Vasilios.

"Orichalcum is a mixture of copper, zinc, nickel, lead, and iron. Plato wrote about it in the ancient texts; it was the currency of Atlantis. And the three outer walls of the Temple of Poseidon were coated in it."

All of those facts lined up with what I already knew. I

shifted antsily, my hands gripping the table. "Is that what you found? Theo, is that what he found?"

Another burst of Greek. Theo translated again. "Yes, that's what he found in his net. A piece of orichalcum."

My heart began thumping so loudly in my chest that it couldn't hear my brain's instructions to *calm down*. Consider the facts. The odds of whatever Vasilios had found being orichalcum ranged from virtually impossible to completely impossible. It could be a rusted tin can, or a piece of an old ship. It could be anything.

As if in answer to my question, Vasilios reached into his pocket and pulled out a small lump wrapped in a red cloth. He held it out to me eagerly, and I froze.

"Kalamata," Theo prompted, but all I could do was stare.

My hands were shaking. Or was the table shaking? *Something* was shaking. "Um . . . Is he . . . ? Is that . . . ?"

"*Koitázo*," Vasilios urged.

"Open it. Wait!" Theo lifted his camera to his eye, steadying it on his shoulder. "Now open it."

I took the object from Vasilios. Felt its weight. Felt the significance of it tunnel my vision and steady my breath. *This isn't it. This can't be it*, I instructed, but *maybe . . .*

I couldn't stop myself. I unwrapped the cloth quickly, nearly dropping the object in my haste, and then it was out in the open, the cloth bunched in my shaking hands and—

There.

Nestled in Vasilios's red-and-white checked napkin was a cell-phone-shaped piece of metal, scratched and irregular, with a definite metallic gold hue and rounded edges. On one end were several fine lines, the remains of etching, worn down by the sea, and on the other was a jagged edge, like something that had been broken off from something larger. Something *regal.*

Everything zoomed down to a tiny frame, the rest of the world disappearing, the way it did behind Theo's camera. "What . . . ? How . . . ?" I had no idea where I was going with that sentence. "What—are you sure? Are you sure this is orichalcum?"

It is, my heart insisted. But hearts didn't know things like this, did they?

"Yes, yes, yes," Vasilios said eagerly. It was heavier than it looked, and warm, almost as if it were alive.

A piece of Atlantis.

Liv, don't get ahead of yourself. I needed to ask the questions. The *right* questions. The ones that a real archaeologist or scientist or mythologist or whoever would ask. The ones Indiana Olive would ask. "Vasilios, how do you know this is the real thing?"

My voice sounded calm, but I was holding the orichalcum so tightly that it was hurting my fingers.

Vasilios launched eagerly into his explanation, and I

waited for Theo's translation as patiently as I could, my eyes glued to the metal.

"He had it tested, by a friend of his who is a scientist in Thessaloniki. He didn't want to take it to the authorities, because he thought they would take it from him. But his friend confirmed that it is the correct percentages of metal to make it orichalcum."

I sank into my chair, my heart on fire. How? Why? Could this possibly be for real? "Where did you find this?" I asked.

Another eruption from Vasilios. Only this time I recognized a word. *Aspronisi*. The volcanic island my dad had named that first day at Maria's. The one he claimed was the closest landmark to Poseidon's temple. The spot that my dad and Dr. Bilder had pinpointed as the most likely location of the center of Atlantis. *That* Aspronisi.

Theo and I quickly locked eyes. I don't know who looked more shocked. "Did he say *Aspronisi*?" My voice came out in a whisper. Now even Theo looked shaken. He set his camera down, eyes wide.

"Yes!" Vasilios said excitedly. *"Aspronisi."*

Vasilios spoke and Theo translated. "He found it thirty meters east of the island. He says he remembers it like it was yesterday."

My chest erupted in confetti. Fireworks. *Lava.* All of my

little-girl dreams were bursting in my chest, clamoring for a turn, jumping with their hands in the air.

I was holding a piece of Atlantis. The real Atlantis. I knew it the way I knew the tide would rise and the sun would set. *Proof*, the waves whispered.

"Call my dad," I said. "Call him right now."

Chapter Twenty

#20. BOX OF SHEET MUSIC, TITLES IN GREEK

None of us played the piano or any instruments at all, so when I found the sheet music in his closet, I was stumped. Did it belong to someone else? But then I saw the lightly penciled notes written in the margins in Greek, and I thought they must have something to do with us.

I thought my mom might notice if I took it all, so I looked through the yellowing, fragile pages until I found one with a title in Greek and English—"Moonlight Sonata," (Piano Sonata No. 14, First Movement)—and added it to my growing pile. The page was as thin and brittle as an autumn leaf, and something about it made me feel melancholy.

OUR CALLS WOULDN'T GO THROUGH TO MY DAD AND ANA, so we ended up sending a series of text messages, one every ten minutes or so until Ana texted that they were on the ferry and to hold tight. After that it took them more than four hours to get home, and by then I was a writhing mess of nerves.

The whole thing was so implausible, it made me feel like I was caught in a whirlpool. What were the chances that someone who had heard Vasilios's story would (a) see Theo filming, (b) ask him what we were doing, and then (c) point us to the one man who had the same theory my father did? Not even the most rational part of my brain could come up with an explanation for all those things happening. And then add to it that it had happened in the very place that my dad had first learned about Atlantis?

Brain explosion.

Theo and I waited up on the terrace, keeping watch for our parents while he attempted to edit the day's film and I scrolled obsessively on my phone, bouncing around between articles and websites devoted to Atlantis. It had been a long time since I'd truly studied Atlantis, and I was surprised to see all of the new theories and speculative articles that had bubbled up over the years. I was particularly interested in new speculation regarding some of Plato's word choices, and I took a few notes in my filming binder.

After a while, Theo gave up. He said it was impossible to focus on things like playback and color grading when a chunk of Atlantis sat perched in the six inches between us. It was hard to focus on anything.

Dax started calling before sunset, but I hit ignore all three times. I couldn't even consider taking his calls right now. If I answered, he'd hear my excitement, and then what would I say?

The sun had begun falling when Theo stood, shielding his eyes with his hand as he peered down Main Street.

"They're here!" He slung his camera onto his shoulder, pulled me to my feet, and we ran up the street to meet them. Ana looked frazzled, her hair a frizzy cloud around her face, her eyes tired. My dad looked even worse. His clothes were rumpled, and the dark circles were back under his eyes, but he was moving fast, energy darting off him in waves that I could feel from several feet away.

When he saw us, he pushed past a slow-moving crowd, his eyes focused on me. The sunset had caught his face, and he looked ablaze. "Liv? Liv, is it true?"

"Dad!" I ran the rest of the way to meet him. I'd left my shoes, sketchbook, and oil pastels in a messy pile, but the orichalcum was clutched tightly in my hand, the stone pavement warm and smooth under my feet. My heart was fluttering like a moth.

Theo had said I should be the one to show it to him. I still couldn't believe that Vasilios had allowed us to bring the orichalcum home with us. True, it had been physically difficult for me to let go of and I had promised *cross my heart and hope to die* that I would return it to him in perfect condition, but he hadn't acted worried. He'd seemed almost relieved, grateful that someone was taking it from him.

And now I got to be the one to give the evidence to my dad. I didn't waste a second. I pulled out the cloth napkin and pushed the whole thing into his waiting hands. The pathway was clogged, and people kept bumping into us, but none of us moved. We just watched as he unwrapped it. Me, Ana, and the camera. I couldn't breathe. Couldn't do anything except watch the way his face was transforming. He looked nine years old. Then twenty years old. Then forty. He looked more like my dad than I'd ever seen him.

"Liv . . ."

My heart felt like it was going to explode out of my chest. I couldn't stop thinking of how many times he'd drawn Atlantis. How he'd memorized the rings. How he knew exactly how many to create from the center. All that time I'd spent sitting next to him, drawing maps; I thought about all his piles of books. How we'd read every book there ever was, how the librarian let us keep some of the old ones because we were checking them out so often.

All the hours we'd spent reading and thinking and searching about Atlantis, it had culminated in this moment, a small island of people gathered around something I'd never believed would happen. Of something that no one but him had fully believed in. It made me ashamed. And grateful.

Proof.

Proof.

"Liv, how did you . . . ? How?"

I told him the whole story in a rush, not minding the commotion around us, not even minding the camera, and when we were done, he wasn't looking at the orichalcum anymore. He was looking at me, big tears welling up in his eyes. "This is more than a person can ask for. Liv, this is because of you. And, Theo, thank you."

"It was nothing, boss," Theo said, his voice a little choked behind the camera. Even Ana stopped wringing her hands for a moment and placed them on my father's back, her face shining. Regardless of what came next, this moment was special.

I didn't want to break the spell, but there was one more detail I had to tell my dad. "Vasilios, the man who found this, he said he'll take us to the exact location tomorrow. Theo and I talked; it can be the final scene in the documentary."

"And tomorrow I will dive." He said it almost to himself, and Ana and I exchanged a look before realizing what he meant.

"You'll dive the location?" I said. "But . . . I thought you said you needed better equipment."

"If I know the exact location, *exact*," he insisted, "then it is worth a try. And if we do it tomorrow, then we have time to submit the footage with the film. Right, Theo?"

He lowered his camera slowly, but instead of the excitement I expected, his features were laced with concern. "Right. But I'm not certified, so I can't go with you. You'll have to learn how to use the GoPro and—"

"Nico, *no*," Ana cut in. "It's too dangerous. You can't do this alone. Alone will not work."

"It will be a quick look," my father said. "I cannot miss this opportunity. Can you imagine if I saw something? What that would do for the documentary, what that would do for *us*?" He was looking at me as he said it.

"Not a good idea," Ana said.

"Liv, you will come with me!"

Theo nearly dropped his camera and had to scramble to save it.

All the excitement and nerves and adrenaline that had been pumping through me screeched to a sudden and painful halt. *"What?"* I broke eye contact with my dad.

"You're scuba certified—your mother told me! And you've spent so much time filming with us, you can be the one to do the camerawork." Mom again. She'd told him? Had she told him about the nightmares, too? Dizziness washed over me.

"Not a good idea," Ana reiterated.

Theo broke in hesitantly. "*Maman*, if a fisherman pulled

this up, then it is well within the recreational dive limits. As long as it's a sunny day, they will probably have great footage."

I had to break through my mental fog, stop this train before it picked up too much speed. "Dad . . . I can't . . . ," I started.

Ana spoke rapidly in Greek, her voice overlapping with mine.

My dad quickly reached for her arm, starting in Greek and then morphing to English. "Yes, I understand. But do you see? This is it. *This*. I have waited my entire life for this moment, and now my daughter is here to share it with me. It is a gift. A gift from Poseidon if you will. Ana, we must." He whirled on me. "Liv, we will do this together!"

It was like a spotlight had centered on me. For a moment, my heart was welling up, spilling over. It was like when I was little, when I was so sure of what Indiana Olive was capable of. When I knew that I would be the one to find Atlantis. But then the light turned too hot.

"N-no," I stammered. "No, I can't dive. Not here." I shook my head. "I'm certified, but I don't do it. Not anymore." *Not here, and definitely not with you.*

He closed his mouth, then opened it again. "But . . . you are certified? You have experience?"

"Well, yes. But . . ." His face was so hopeful, and panic

rose up in me, as cold and dense as seawater. Scuba diving at a resort with my mom and James was one thing. Scuba diving with my dad—here—well, that was not going to happen. "I'm out of practice," I blurted out.

His face blossomed in a relieved smile. "Santorini is an easy place to dive, and I am a master diver, certified even to take beginners. Once we are under, you can rely on me entirely."

"Dad, I'm not *going*." My voice came out way too loud, splitting the conversation in half. They all looked at me, surprised. It was me crying at the birthday party all over again. And I couldn't offer up an explanation, not without telling them about my nightmares. "I'm not going under the water. Not here."

Theo made a small noise in his throat, but whatever he wanted to say, he kept it to himself.

"It is entirely your decision," Ana said soothingly.

"But—" My dad quickly stopped himself. "Of course, Liv. I don't want you to do anything you don't want to. I can dive on my own. You'll stay above with Theo. Even an old dog like me can learn to use an underwater camera."

My face was still hot, but I nodded, dropping my gaze to my feet.

"But, Nico, what about the *asthma*?" Ana said, emphasizing the last word.

"I'll call my doctor. In the past he has told me that so long as I take the necessary precautions, I am fine to dive."

"But . . ." She didn't seem to have another argument for that, so she shook her head.

My dad rested his hand on her shoulder. "Let's not argue anymore. We have a lot to do tonight, and it is already late." He looked at Theo. "We need a plan."

It was lucky that my dad had so many favors racked up on the island, because we needed all of them. The owner of a nearby dive shop reopened to get my dad fitted for what he needed. Theo tracked down a local photographer friend of my dad's who agreed to loan us an underwater camera. Ana wrung her hands and snapped at everyone in Greek. I was put in charge of mapping out the next day's plan—where and when would we meet Vasilios? What questions did we need to ask him on camera? What would my dad say and do before diving in? Would we film him from up above or let him handle it? How could we ensure he got good footage while he was down below?

By the time we reconvened in the shop, it was after eleven o'clock, and I was so tired that I was wired. There was an electrical charge in the air, our collective energy making the shop feel like pre-storm.

My dad had already spent close to an hour on the phone

with Vasilios, and now he got out his maps and called the Egyptologist he'd been working with, then put her on speaker while we discussed exact location. I was right. The spot that Vasilios had told us was within five meters of the location that my dad and Dr. Bilder had pinpointed. My dad had insisted that I keep hold of the orichalcum, and as he spoke, I placed it on the map over the island of Aspronisi. White Island. In between calls, I'd done some research and now knew that it was half a mile long, with one small dock, a rocky beach, and very few visitors. According to internet lore it had been owned by the same family for seven generations, but no one seemed to know who that family was or why they cared to own it in the first place.

"The possibilities of finding something are of course very slim," Dr. Bilder said, but she kept trying, and failing, to conceal the excitement in her voice. "Even if we get the location correct, the chances are still small. But I will say, the possibility is rather exciting."

"Agreed," I said, and my dad looked up at me over the map and smiled. It felt like it had at the excavation site. Spontaneous. *Natural.* How could it not? We'd always said we'd do this.

Dr. Bilder continued. "Remember that nature is irregular. The goal is to look for anything that doesn't look irregular. Straight lines, circular formations, that sort of thing."

My imagination instantly produced a wealth of aqua-tinted images that I couldn't help but explore. The edge of a circular road. The corner of a golden door. Things that untrained eyes had overlooked but that we might be able to identify . . .

I know, I know. My delusional was showing. But also, *what if*?

My dad seemed to be imagining the same thing, and when he hung up, his eyes were shiny. "Now we need sleep. Tomorrow will be a big day."

"One more thing." Theo had been surprisingly quiet that night, doing his work without the usual banter. "Nico, every hero needs an origin story. And we need to film your personal history, like we'd planned."

"Now?" my father asked.

I felt as incredulous as he sounded. Despite how excited I was, every cell in my body wanted to *sleep*. "Theo, it's night. Where would we even film it?"

"Exactly," Theo said. "What better time to capture the beginnings of Nico's love for Atlantis than the night before his groundbreaking discovery? Think of the dramatic effect." He said "discovery" like it was a given, which of course it wasn't—but still, he had a point. "We could do it right here in the bookstore. Kalamata can help me re-create the setup we had last time we attempted this. Nico, you up for this?"

"*Fysiká,*" he said, nodding. If he was in, I was in too.

A burst of energy pulled me to my feet, and I spun around, taking in the long shadows playing across the bookstore walls. "Dad, you go change and get ready. You should wear one of your brighter shirts, something to make you stand out. Theo, you gather all the lights; we're going to want as many as we can get. I'll get the set ready. We want it to look perfect."

"Aye, aye, Captain." My father gave me a little salute.

"Did you know that olives are the very bossiest of all fruits?" Theo called over his shoulder, but my mind was already hard at work. We needed to set the scene.

First I dragged the antique desk in front of my favorite section of bookshelves; then I tacked some of my dad's old maps on the wall, arranged a pile of old leather books just so on the desk, positioned a few lamps, and shooed a few cats away. When I was finished, I stood back, satisfied. It looked like the kind of place someone about to have the biggest breakthrough of his career would sit to ponder. A space fit for an Atlantis hunter. Perfect.

Theo was adjusting his tripod when my dad stepped in, looking much more pulled together in a fresh shirt and combed hair.

"Makeup?" I asked.

But he shook his head and made his way to the desk. "Let's tell the real story, no covering up required."

Theo nodded. "Exactly."

My dad took a seat, resting his elbows on the desk, while Theo and I looked at the scene through his lens. "Perfect," Theo said.

"No. Something's missing. Hold on." Before I could talk myself out of it, I hurried up to the bunk to where I'd stashed our original map the night before. "You need to use this."

The map was rolled up, and as he unrolled it on the desk, I saw the moment when he recognized it. He froze, and for a moment I thought I'd made a mistake. Should I not have given it to him? Finally, he looked up slowly. "You still have this."

Not a question per se, but he was asking something. I could feel it. And now was not the time for sugarcoating. "I . . ." I tightened my hands, pressing my fingernails into my palms. "I kept it safe in case you needed it back."

Now his eyes were shiny. "I can't believe you've had it all these years."

Theo's camera was up of course. He could sense emotion like sharks could sense blood in the water, but without nearly as much tact. But to my surprise, he suddenly lowered his camera, dropping his eyes respectfully.

Even though I wanted to hide what I was feeling, I forced myself to stay present, because this moment, whatever it was, needed to happen at some point. Better now, when the possibility of finding something still loomed large. Who knew what tomorrow would bring?

I stared down at the map, willing myself to be brave, willing myself to be Indiana Olive, the girl who had known so many things for sure. I closed my eyes briefly, and there she was. Crayon in hand, Dad beside her, connecting dots and examining clues. She could handle this.

I took a deep breath, opening my eyes. "Dad . . . earlier tonight I did some research, about the things we talked about on the sunset cruise. About the problems with what Plato said? I read probably twenty articles, and I think I've figured it out." I caught sight of his raised eyebrows and had to look down quickly before I lost my nerve. "Before Plato, the story of Atlantis had only ever been passed along verbally, so there was probably a lot of human error before it ever got to Plato."

He looked intrigued, so I kept going. "Plato said that Santorini was greater than Libya and Asia, which obviously isn't true. But the Greek word for 'greater than' was 'mezon,' with a Z, and the word for 'between' was 'meson,' with an S. Santorini isn't larger than Libya and Asia, but it is *between* them."

His smile was overtaking the room. I kept going. "And as far as timing went, Plato said that Atlantis sank nine thousand years earlier, when Santorini's volcano happened more like nine hundred years earlier. But the Greek symbols for nine hundred and nine thousand are nearly identical.

He easily could have received mixed-up information."

I did my best to ignore Theo, whose eyes I could feel burning a hole into the back of my shirt as I focused entirely on my dad. I had never felt so vulnerable before. I was about to say the opposite of what I'd said on the sunset cruise. "Dad, why is Atlantis so important to you?"

I felt Theo's startled eyes on me. He'd been trying to get me to ask that question all along.

If I'd learned anything from the legend of Atlantis, it was this: stories evolved. They got passed down and twisted, and sometimes they came out okay and other times they quadrupled the size of continents or transported timelines to entirely different centuries. If Plato could have missed the mark so entirely, was it possible I had too? Was it possible I could learn something that maybe wouldn't change this whole situation, but could at least give it nuance?

Maybe.

My dad's eyes were thoughtful, his face determined. "I will tell you the beginning." He looked at Theo. "On film?"

Theo fumbled for his camera, his face still surprised. "Whatever you want, boss."

My dad took a seat, then carefully spread the map out in front of him. His body language was calm and composed, but he splayed his fingers a few times, a telltale sign I recognized from all those years ago. He was nervous. "Ready."

Theo gave me a thumbs-up, and then I held my breath.

My dad looked straight into the camera. "My name is Nico Varanakis, and I grew up in Santorini. I was born to my father, Nico, and my mother, Madalena. We lived in a beautiful house overlooking the ocean, and our home was filled with people and wonderful things. My father was intelligent and loved literature and philosophy. My mother was gentle and a classically trained pianist. She held many recitals in our home."

He paused for a moment, and I waited in the silence, my heart beating as if it could make up for all the quiet. I knew nothing about these people, hadn't even known their names.

"In many ways, my childhood was magic. I was given a lot of freedom, and I spent most of the time rowing my own small boat, exploring caves and hunting for treasure on the beaches. But the year I turned ten, my life changed suddenly."

Ten. I pictured myself at ten. It was both a lifetime and a moment away. By that age I already hadn't seen my dad for two years.

He continued. "My father owned a vineyard called Meraki, one of the most well-known that has ever been on this island. The vineyards in Santorini are famous for several things. The volcanic ash and lava make for a distinctive type of soil, and so a distinctive flavor of grape. And because of the strong winds, the grapevines are grown coiled near the earth instead of on trellises. Also, because there is not a lot of rain, the volcanic soil is kept moist by the sea air.

"The work on the vineyard was all done by hand, and it employed many, many people. Sometimes it felt we had a small army working for us. My father supplied wine to the majority of the restaurants and hotels on the island. He also had many investors, all of whom lived on the island. He was constantly evolving his process, stretching the limits of what he could create.

"But then there were the allegations." My father hesitated slightly but lifted his chin, determined to keep going. "He was accused of having committed investment fraud, and owing his employees tens of thousands of dollars. At first, we all believed he was innocent, but as time went on, we learned that he wasn't. To avoid being prosecuted, my father left the country, abandoned us. We lost everything. My mother lost her entire life. Her family disowned her, and she had no money and no connections to take us elsewhere, and even if she had, our name would follow us. We were trapped. She sold everything she could and tried to make a living off piano lessons. But Santorini is a small place, and people believed she had been in on the deception. Former employees had lost their homes and life savings because of my father. No one wanted to be associated with us."

The pain in his voice was almost tangible. "Eventually

she found work as a housekeeper for the lighthouse keeper in Akrotiri, a man named Giorgos who had no connection with the vineyard and was practical enough that he wouldn't have cared if he did. She did his cooking and cleaning and took in laundry when she could. My mother worked very hard and was deeply unhappy. It wasn't the work or the loss of all her nice things that bothered her; it was that she had lived her life as a lie."

He dropped his gaze down to our map, his voice suddenly quieter. "If he was feeling particularly generous, the lighthouse keeper, Giorgos, allowed me to follow after him while he did his work. One day, he told me a story. A smart and important man I'd never heard of before—Plato—had once written an account of a beautiful and idyllic island that had sunk into the sea after angering the gods. A paradise lost. The people had once had everything, but their pride had cost them. It had been their downfall."

His eyes moved to mine. "I recognized the story in my soul. It was my story. I also had lost a paradise. In the space of a few weeks, my mother and I had lost safety and contentment to a life of instability and fear."

His eyes returned to the camera, and I couldn't look away.

"I became obsessed with the story. If I could find Atlantis, then all would be well. My mother would stop crying. She would no longer suffer from pain. For years, I waited for my father to come back. I waited for someone to come save us. But no one ever did. And soon my mother's sadness became something more.

"By the time we found out what was wrong, it was too late. The disease had progressed too far. I dropped out of school, tried to find jobs, find a doctor to help us. But we had become outcasts on the island. I was only sixteen. I knew where my father was by then, and I wrote to him for help, but there was nothing." My dad's voice broke. "She died a few months later. That's when my love of Atlantis became a quest. I would find it. I would contribute to the world. I swore to her that I would find it. Paradise would be restored. What was lost would be found. And now I believe it has."

He shifted his gaze from the camera to me. I couldn't move. Could hardly breathe. I'd forgotten we were filming. I'd forgotten everything, only that my father had once been a child who had been hurt, the same way I had. A child who had waited and waited for his father to come home. A child who had wanted to make things *right*.

Theo slipped his arm around my shoulders, and I was grateful for its weight, the way it kept me glued to the earth.

"Finished," my dad said, and then he looked down, like he couldn't bear to see my reaction.

I was seeing a little boy at the lighthouse. After his family fell apart, he'd needed something to hold on to, something to get him through all those difficult years. A magical, peaceful city with a hundred golden statues and a god keeping everyone safe was as good a thing to hold on to as any. I understood that. I'd done the exact same thing.

His loneliness was an ocean. A vast body of water as heavy as it was frightening. When my dad left, I'd had my mother and grandparents, and then later James and Julius, plus countless friends and neighbors all along the way. When his dad left, he'd had his mother, and then he'd had no one. Regardless of the fact that he had put me in a similar scenario, he hadn't deserved that experience. Neither of us had.

And I knew, with a ferocity that surprised me, that he would not do this next part alone. Not while I was around to make it otherwise.

The words appeared on their own. "Dad, I'm diving with you."

Chapter Twenty-One

#21. HOMEMADE SCARF, BLUE AND CLUMSY-LOOKING

For a while my dad was in bed a lot, and my mom told me I had to spend my after-school time with Mrs. Douglas, who lived upstairs. Mrs. Douglas claimed to have once been a third-grade teacher, but I found that hard to believe because she had no idea what to do with children. After a lot of trial and error, we eventually fell into a routine. The routine went like this: graham crackers, Jeopardy! and my knitting kit.

She found the kit in one of her overstuffed closets, and when I saw the color of the yarn snarled inside, I was over the moon. Knitting was not easy, and Mrs. Douglas was not particularly patient, but after three weeks I had a vaguely scarflike creation.

I managed to wait an extra two weeks until his birthday, and when I gave him the present, I was so excited I had to tear the paper off with him. As soon as he held it up, I

told him, "It's to keep your neck warm! That way you won't
get sick anymore and I won't have to go to Mrs. Douglas's
apartment!" He was quiet for a long time after that. I knew
I'd gotten it wrong, but I didn't know how.

I DON'T THINK I SLEPT MORE THAN TWO HOURS. EVERY
time I closed my eyes, the water was rising up to meet me
and I struggled to surface, my body on fire with adrenaline.
Eventually, I gave up on sleeping and stared up at the dark
ceiling, my mind whirring.

My mom once told me that it's difficult for kids to recognize their parents as anything but supporting cast members in their own feature films, and here it was true. I'd been
so wrapped up in my own story with my father that I hadn't
stopped to think about what his story was. So many things
were clicking into place—everything from my dad's constant service to his neighbors on the island (Had he been
trying to make amends for the people his father had hurt?)
to why he'd left Santorini so abruptly in the first place.

But for every *aha* moment, there was a *WTF* as well.
Because if my dad knew what it was like to have a parent
leave, how could he possibly have turned around and done
it to me? And if Santorini had been terrible enough for
him to flee, what had convinced him to come back when
he did?

A nagging feeling pulled at me. His story explained why he loved Atlantis so much, but it didn't explain why he'd built and then abandoned a family on an entirely different continent.

His pre-filming words came back to me. *I will tell you the beginning.* The beginning wasn't all of it. The beginning was just . . . the beginning. My dad's childhood wasn't the whole story. I was almost positive of it.

I called my mom again, but her phone went straight to voicemail, so I left her a vague message. *Mom, I have something important to tell you; call me back.* But what I really had were questions. Something was still buried.

Theo stumbled down from his bunk around six a.m. and patted my face clumsily before heading to the cave. We both got ready in silence before my dad and Ana showed up soon afterward, packed and ready, followed by a puffy-eyed Geoffrey, who had spent the night arguing via phone with Mathilde. Emotionally distressed or not, he would man the store single-handedly today.

While Ana set Geoffrey up for the day, Theo went to beg for coffee from Maria's, leaving my dad and me alone up on the roof, a pile of bags at our feet. After last night's filming, I hadn't known what to say and he hadn't seemed to either, and now it all sat in a heap between us.

"Indiana Olive's day has finally come," he said, breaking into a smile. According to his face, he'd gotten roughly the same amount of sleep I had.

"Dad, about last night . . . ," I started, and he put a reassuring hand on my shoulder.

"We'll speak later. Today we'll focus on the task."

I nodded, a lump forming in my throat. But then Theo appeared with coffee that was twice as terrible as usual, and then it was really time to go.

Yiannis drove us there, and after a few unsuccessful attempts at listening in on their Greek conversations, I turned to my window, watching as the island woke up, the sun pouring out onto the water before making its way to land.

I couldn't stop looking at my dad. This had to be the most important day of his life. How did he look this calm? A few times he caught me looking and winked. I guess this day was important to me, too.

The plan was to meet Vasilios at the dock in front of the tavern. We would use his boat, and he would lead us to the exact location. I was a little worried he wouldn't show, but when we arrived at the staircase leading down to the taverna's cove, Vasilios was standing on the dock wearing a thick sweater, a floppy fisherman's hat, and a smile that could light up the entire caldera.

"Nico!" he bellowed into the quiet morning air. My father

hurried down, and the two of them shook hands, then hugged and slapped each other's backs, instantly becoming friends, because that is what Atlantis hunting does to people, I guess.

The beach was completely empty, and besides the water, the only sounds came from us. Ana elected to stay on the dock rather than spend the next few hours "seasick and useless" as she put it, and as we loaded up the gear onto Vasilios's boat, she reached out and held my hand tightly. "Be careful, Liv. You are both very special to me."

I nodded, but her kind look made my vision go wavy around the edges. I missed my mom so much I felt untethered. I had no practice with missing my mom—she had always been there. And doing this dive without her even knowing felt very wrong. I'd have so much to catch her up on, including the fact that she'd been right about the scuba diving certification—it had come in handy.

On the dock I pulled on the wet suit my dad had managed to track down and climbed shakily onto the boat, Theo and my dad right behind me.

Was I ready? Absolutely not.

And then Ana waved, and we waved, and the engine coughed, and away we went.

If I believed in a sea-god capable of ruining plans and stirring up the ocean with a massive pitchfork, then that is exactly what I'd think had happened. Instead of the bright, satisfying emerald I'd grown used to, the water was a moody darker color and the surface choppy. Unsettled.

Angry.

My stomach was one massive knot. It wasn't terribly cold, but I couldn't stop my teeth from chattering. I was excited, yes, but the feeling was spiked with dread. I knew I could back out at any moment, but I also knew that I wouldn't let myself.

While Vasilios and my dad spent the ride in boisterous conversation, I spent the entire ride repeating everything I knew to be true. *My dad is a master diver. Vasilios is a life-long fisherman. The dive is not particularly deep.* Theo seemed to know exactly what was going on in my head because he sat right next to me offering facts that were even less relevant than normal. *It takes between three and twelve years for an olive tree to produce olives. In Ancient Rome, women used olive oil as sunscreen and perfume. Olives have to be cured in brine or salt to become edible.*

I leaned into him, shoving all thoughts of Dax aside. My regular life felt as shrouded and faraway as a golden city.

Santorini shrank steadily into the distance, the ocean churning beneath our boat, and as we reached Aspronisi, I was surprised by how small it really was. It looked more like an accident than an island: a rock dropped in the center of a vast ocean, the top smoothed out into a plateau. It clearly told the story of Santorini's volcano, forming a geological layer cake, dark gray on the bottom, courtesy of the lava, chalky white on top, thanks to the pumice. My dad was right. Evidence of Atlantis was everywhere.

Vasilios navigated his way expertly around to the eastern side of the island, then killed his engine, allowing us to drift into a makeshift dock.

This was happening.

I was so nervous that my head felt detached from my body. We needed to get moving. Now. I began gathering my equipment. *Fins, mask, regulator, buoyancy compensator.* My hands were shaking so hard it was difficult to even hold anything.

"Liv?" my dad asked, concern darkening his face.

"I'm feeling cold, but I'm sure I'll warm up." I held his gaze for a few seconds, and either he believed me or saw my determination. Shaking or not, we were doing this.

I pulled my flippers on; then my dad helped me put on my vest with the buoyancy control device and attached my air cylinder while Theo filmed us. I'd done this before, lots of times, but I was starting to feel light-headed, and my dad had to keep reminding me how to do everything. Finally, I was ready. I straightened up, pushing my shoulders back as I faced my dad. He was smiling. "You were born for this, Liv. You're a natural." He smiled, but his fingers were flexing over and over.

"You too," I said quietly.

"Ready for this?" Theo asked, passing me the GoPro. Last night, he had given me a quick tutorial on underwater filming. It was all about light. The more light we had, the more color we had. But looking down into the dense swirling gray, I couldn't imagine that I'd get anything worth using.

"Do your best," Theo said, reading my mind. "Filming won't be great, but try to get a few good shots of your dad. Worst case, we'll come back another day."

We didn't have another day, and we both knew it. Not if we were going to get the footage to National Geographic on time.

Theo went up to the front of the boat to talk to Vasilios, and as soon as we were alone, my dad leaned in, his face serious. "Liv, I'd like you to stay close to the boat. I know you've dived before, but visibility does not look good today. Too much sediment."

"But, Dad . . . aren't you supposed to stay with your diving buddy?" "Diving buddy" sounded cute, but it was the first rule our instructor had pushed on us. *Never dive alone.*

He set his hand on my shoulder. "Normally, yes. But I plan to stay down there as long as possible, and I don't want to put you in a dangerous position. Stay shallow, and if I want you to come down, I'll flash my flashlight at you. Watch closely. Okay?"

I wanted to protest. Push back. Tell him I could do this.

Make him proud, but . . . my hands. *Why won't they stop shaking?* My scuba instructor's second most important rule came to mind. *A nervous diver is a compromised diver.* What if I actually did endanger him?

"I can do that," I said.

"Let's go," my dad called. He sat on the edge of the boat, adjusting his gear until he was ready. Then, after giving my hand an excited squeeze, he rolled in backward. Which meant . . . my turn.

For a moment I didn't think my legs would move, but then Theo was next to me, his camera resting on Vasilios's shoulder. "You're next, Kalamata."

His voice was like a starting gun. *I can do this.* I moved clumsily toward the edge of the boat, sitting on the lip while I struggled with my mask. I was already feeling a bit lightheaded, but I had to keep it together. For my dad's sake. Theo handed me my air regulator and helped me adjust my goggles.

He wore a thick sweatshirt over his swim trunks, his hat flipped backward over his tangled hair. He was so close that I could have counted every single one of his long, straight eyelashes if I wanted to.

A part of me did want to.

When I was ready, he grabbed my right hand, rubbing it between his. "You're shaking. Are you okay?"

"I'm just cold. And nervous. And . . ." I dropped my

head, forcing my breath to be even. "This is a big deal."

He moved in closer, his bare legs grazing mine. "No, Kalamata. A big deal would be coming to an island you've never been to in order to see someone you haven't seen in nine years. This?" He pointed his chin at the water. "This is *nothing*."

A grateful smile worked its way through my panic. "You're right."

"Of course I'm right," he said, grabbing my other hand. "Remember to keep moving when you're in the water. If you ball up, you'll just get colder and colder. And that is literally the only scuba diving tip I know." He moved his hands to my waist, helping me to my feet. Even through my nerves, I felt warmth spill through the rest of my body, and when I looked up at him, I saw how close his face was to mine—so close I could kiss him if I wanted to. But now wasn't the time for such thoughts. "Hey, Kalamata, it's going to be okay. If you need anything, just surface and I'll help you. And remember, your dad knows what he's doing. He's done so many dives, this is *nothing*."

He was basically giving me the reverse talk that Ana had given me. I wanted to thank him, hug him, tell him that he made me feel safe—safer than any emergency equipment or diving protocol ever could—but how to even start that?

I was eventually going to have to deal with this Theo thing. But first, Atlantis.

He hesitated. "After this . . . after today. We should talk." His eyes met mine, and a deep flush moved through me. Was he saying what I thought he was saying?

"I'd like that."

He looked down at my wet suit, cracking a smile.

"What's so funny?"

"I haven't seen you get in the ocean once, and now you're scuba diving. It's kind of extreme. Also, you look like a mermaid."

"No, I don't." I gestured to where my dad had jumped in. "Where do you think I got the extreme from?"

"Good point. You ready?"

"Ready." I scooted back on the edge of the boat and placed the regulator in my mouth. Theo gave my hand one last squeeze, and I looked up, catching one quick glimpse of the thick gray clouds overhead as I rolled backward, the ocean enveloping me in an icy hug.

Hello, Poseidon.

Chapter Twenty-Two

#22. RECEIPT FROM JANE ADDAMS MEMORIAL TOLLWAY

I thought all dads went on trips. Every few months my dad would sit me down to tell me he needed to get on the road again, get some research done, and ask me to be a big help to my mom until he got back. Then he'd take the car and we wouldn't see him for a while. Usually it was a few days, but once it was two weeks. My mom never knew when he'd be back either, and if I asked her, she'd just say soon. It was never soon enough.

Once, I was playing at a neighbor's house, and I asked her where her dad went on his trips. She had no idea what I was talking about. That's the first time I realized that not all dads leave. So why had mine?

AT FIRST I FELT LIKE I ALWAYS DID IN SCUBA GEAR—AS effortless and graceful as an elephant wearing roller skates.

My mask felt too tight, my fins too loose. I fiddled with my equipment, wiggling my mask and pulling my knees up to adjust my heel straps. You'd think underwater would be a quiet place, but it isn't. When I was certifying, James had explained to me that sound waves travel much faster underwater than they do in air, and it was even more apparent to me here than in Mexico. Crackling, snapping, and creaking noises came at me from all directions, and to combat it, I focused on the sound of my breath moving through the regulator, the steady whooshing eventually putting the other sounds back into their places.

Deep breathing helped more than just my ears. After a few minutes my body adjusted, giving me the supported, effortless feeling scuba divers must live for. My dad appeared next to me, a cloud of bubbles over his head, and he gave me the *OK* sign. I signed it back, and he pointed his fingers, one in front of the other. *You lead, I'll follow.*

We spent a few unrushed minutes filming the area while I acclimated, kicking with long, even strokes, my toes pointed backward. I'd forgotten how being underwater felt like being on an entirely different planet. The water bent light, coloring everything in deep blue-green shades that I knew would only get darker the deeper we went. Little bits of seaweed and other ocean debris spread around us like confetti. The fish were camera shy, darting away from our lights. Visi-

bility wasn't great, but it wasn't as bad as the surface had suggested, and besides the uninterested sea creatures, everything
was cool and blue and still, and—best of all—not nearly as
tumultuous as it had looked on the surface. If I didn't know
better, I'd almost think I was *enjoying* the ocean.

My dad swam up to me, and we met eyes through our
masks. I could tell he was smiling. He turned on his dive light,
aiming it downward, then signaled *go down* with a thumbs-
down and another *OK*. I okayed back. Then he tented his
hand into an upside-down *V*, resting the tips of his fingers
onto his opposite palm. It took me a second to realize what
he meant. It wasn't a dive signal. It was *our* signal. It was a
volcano, code for "I lava you." He'd come up with it when I
started elementary school—when it was too embarrassing for
him to tell me he loved me in front of my friends.

My hands immediately made the sign back, my throat
tightening, and he tapped the tips of his fingers on mine. I
aimed the GoPro at him, and he waved a few times before
diving toward the darkness.

Dad. So much had changed, and yet so much hadn't.

It didn't take long for his figure to disappear from view,
and soon I couldn't see his light, either. I turned off the
GoPro and focused on staying calm. The boat was a comforting presence up above, and I made sure to keep it in the
corner of my eye.

I deflated my buoyancy control device, dropping six feet or so, but still keeping the boat in my line of vision as I swam in small, careful circles, enjoying the feeling of my body twisting through the water. This wasn't so bad, was it?

After a while, I wished I had a watch. According to my dad's calculations, it should take him less than ten minutes of slow movement to get to the bottom, and once he was down there he could stay for as long as his air allowed him to, which would likely be another thirty to forty minutes. That meant about a hundred circles before he'd come back to the surface.

With proof? My heart jumped at the thought. Even if there was something, would he be able to see it? For a blissful few seconds, I allowed myself to imagine what it would be like if he found something. I doubted it would be parades at the White House and our names written in the sky like my dad had said it would be, but what if we actually found something solid enough to link Atlantis to Santorini once and for all? One piece of orichalcum may not be enough, but what if there was more?

I checked my oxygen tank. I had plenty. I could stay down here all day if I wanted to. I rolled faceup, turning my attention to the boat. Vasilios had set up a diving light, a flashing strobe attached to the bottom that felt like a security blanket. All I had to do was swim a few feet up, and I'd be with Theo.

Theo, who I was taking a brief underwater break from thinking about. Never mind the underwater butterflies. *What does he want to talk about?* His eyes had looked so serious when he'd said that. The thought sent goose bumps rippling down my body.

As usual, thinking about him threw me off.

I rolled downward again, my eyes focused into the space where my father had gone. His light winking in the darkness, a reassuring firefly letting me know that everything was fine. Better than fine. I dove a little deeper, letting the water carry me, support me in this moment. I was in Santorini with my father. We were looking for Atlantis. Things weren't just fine. They were good.

That was the last thought I had before, just like in my dreams, the ocean went dark.

For a moment I froze, my body instinctively coiling into a ball, my heart racing as my mind caught up. *The diving light.* The ocean hadn't gone dark. It just wasn't lit up by the boat anymore. Vasilios had just turned off the diving light, or maybe it had turned off on its own. But without it, the water suddenly seemed so much hazier than before. I adjusted my mask, squinting. The water looked and felt thicker, like driving through fog. Was it really just the diving light? Or had something shifted? Was my dad's visibility okay?

I scanned the floor below me, looking for my dad's light, but . . . nothing. Where had I seen him last? I spun, looking one direction, then the other, my concern steadily ticking upward. He wouldn't have turned his light off, would he?

Where is he? Even as I tried to talk myself out of it, a horrible panic gripped my chest. Everything below me was so dark. *Too* dark. What would possibly have caused him to turn off his light, especially when the water was thickening with each passing second?

Maybe I should look for him. Or go for help? But all my spinning had left me disoriented, water sloshing in my mask, and when I looked up, I had one crystalized thought. *Where did the boat go?*

That's when I lost control. I was flailing. Spinning. Panic lit me up in the darkness. My body couldn't stop moving; I didn't know where to go. *Which way is up?* Bubbles. I was supposed to watch for the direction that the bubbles went, but I couldn't see anything and I couldn't slow my mind down enough to look for them. My wet suit was too tight around my neck. It was constricting me, squeezing me. My head was so fuzzy I couldn't think. I could only *feel*.

Where was my dad? I'd lost my *dad*. Where was the boat?

I had to get out. Get up. But the surface was so far, I was flailing, struggling, sobbing behind my mask. Then my regulator was out. I inhaled salt water, my hands desperately trying to find the mouthpiece, but I ripped through empty water. Every moment of this trip, every moment of my life, had led to this. Me drowning, within swimming distance of Atlantis. Within swimming distance of my *father*. I tried to scream, but it was no use.

I closed my eyes and let the ocean swallow me.

Chapter Twenty-Three

#23. PACK OF MARLBORO SMOOTH CIGARETTES

I know cigarettes are sticks of death and do all kinds of horrible things to your lungs and kill unicorns and all that, but I really, really love the smell of Marlboro Smooths. Right after my mom and I moved to Seattle—which felt like an entire lifetime after my dad had left—we were walking down Pike Street when someone walked by smoking one. Instantly, I was transported to our tiny Chicago apartment, and it made my heart hurt so much that I had to stop to catch my breath.

Dad had been working at a bar that summer, and most nights he didn't get home until one or two a.m. My mom put me to bed at nine, but every night I'd lie awake until the front door opened and I smelled his cigarette smoke wafting in from the patio. That was when I could finally fall asleep.

It took so little to feel safe then.

OLIVE. OLIVE.

My head hurt so much it felt like it was being squeezed through a sieve. Where was I? Why did my chest feel so heavy?

OLIVE.

I opened my eyes. I was lying on the bottom of the boat. Theo was crouched over me, shirtless, his hair dripping with water, his face panicked. I sat up, and what felt like a vat of salt water came up out of my stomach, and I was throwing up all over the inside of the boat, my body heaving. I couldn't breathe.

"Get this off me! Get it off!" I yelled, struggling with my wet suit. I fought against Theo, my head too confused. Was he helping me? Harming me? "Where's my dad? Theo, where's my dad?"

"Olive, look at me!" Theo grabbed my shoulders, forcing me to look into his eyes. "Breathe, okay. Olive, just breathe. I think you had a panic attack. The boat's dive light reset, and then part of your suit came up. I dove in. Olive, you're okay, okay? You're okay now." Tears were welling up in his eyes, making the edges of his eyelashes sparkle. "I didn't know if you were going to wake up. But now I need to talk to you about your dad, okay? Because we need to decide what to do. Did you two get separated?"

I shook my head, fighting through the fog in my brain.

Separated? We hadn't been together, had we? Vasilios was crouched down next to me too, speaking rapidly into his phone. Finally, it came back to me. "He went down without me. He wanted me to stay by the boat, and he'd signal me if he wanted me to come down."

"What?" The sharpness in Theo's voice made my heart leap into my throat. "What do you mean? I thought you two were going to stay together."

I shook my head. "Before I dove, he told me to stay by the boat. Didn't you hear that?"

Theo's expression shifted. He looked so panicked that it set my heart on fire. "Theo, what? What's wrong?"

"Olive, he shouldn't be down there. He shouldn't be diving at all. He's had some health issues. His kidneys . . ." He exhaled, his eyes locked on mine. "That's why my mom didn't want him to dive. He's in kidney failure."

"*Kidney failure?*" Instantly I was on my knees, trying to stand, but black dots appeared in front of me, sending me tilting, and Theo quickly grabbed my shoulders, gently pressing me back down to sitting. "What are you talking about?" I demanded.

"That's why he's been going to the mainland so much. Earlier this summer he got set up to do dialysis at home with my mom so he could be ready for when you got here. It's been okay, but this week his numbers were bad. He had to keep going into the clinic. He made me promise not to tell you. I didn't know how serious it was until last night, and now . . ."

My shoulders were shaking violently. "Theo, his light went out."

Theo's face snapped to attention. "It went out? Or you lost sight of it?"

They've been lying to me. All of them. Even *Theo.* The weight of it hit me with almost as much force as the panic I felt over my dad's scuba light disappearing. "Why didn't you tell me?" I yelled, shoving myself backward. If my dad was that sick and something went wrong . . . "Theo, I have to go back in there. I have to make sure he's okay."

"Olive, you can't," Theo said, his eyes wide. "Do you really think you could stay calm enough to go look? What if it happens again? Kalamata, you're shaking."

He was right. I didn't want him to be right, but he was right. I was shaking so hard I could barely form words. Vasilios said something in Greek, and Theo quickly translated. "The water ambulance is on its way. Just in case. I'm sure he's fine, but . . ." Theo reached out like he wanted to touch me, and I flinched, adrenaline kicking me backward.

We should talk. "Theo, is that what you needed to tell me? That my dad's sick?" I demanded.

He hesitated, but when he looked at me, the guilt in his eyes said it all. It hadn't been about us. It had been about my *dad.* I exhaled sharply. If anyone had told me, we wouldn't be in this mess to begin with. I wouldn't have endangered my dad.

He stepped toward me quickly, his hands up in surrender. "Olive, I'm sure he's fine. He's a great diver. He probably just turned off his light to explore something. And maybe when the boat's light went out it panicked you, so you lost sight of his and—"

"His light was *off.*" I was having a hard time controlling the volume of my voice. How could they have done this to me? I would have talked him out of it, would have come up with another way. How could they all have lied?

"The water ambulance will be here soon," Theo repeated, and Vasilios nodded nervously behind him.

I thought I knew what it felt like to wait long periods of time. I'd sat through tests and bad news. I'd waited years for my dad to call or show up. But none of those experiences meant anything in comparison to how this felt. Vasilios kept clumsily patting my back and murmuring things in Greek that I'm sure were comforting, but I couldn't even try to understand them.

I couldn't tell if I was crying steadily or if it was salt water dripping from my hair. Either way, it wouldn't let up. If he was in trouble down there, then every second mattered. I was completely numb. How was it possible to be this scared of losing something I'd already lost so many years before?

Theo stayed close, but not touching. I couldn't even look at him. *He'd known.*

After what felt like a million years, the water ambulance appeared, its pointed wide front moving quickly toward us, a man poised at the front. Vasilios yelled to them, and before long a man in red shorts and a hat had boarded our boat and was asking us questions in Greek, then English when he realized I couldn't understand him. I did my best to answer, but all I could really tell them was that my dad was scuba diving, he was in kidney failure, and he might be in trouble.

"How long has he been down?" He was probably around Geoffrey's age, and his skin was a dark even brown, his voice calm.

Days? Decades? "How long?" I asked Theo.

He glanced at his watch. "About thirty-five minutes."

"Okay," the man said. "A typical diver on a typical tank can swim forty-five minutes. This is nothing to worry. Was he in good health this morning?"

Theo and I looked at each other, both of us thinking about the deep circles under my dad's eyes, the puffiness in his face. The signs had been there the entire time; I'd just been too wrapped up in myself to notice them. Whatever self-control I still had dissolved, and tears began pouring down my face. "I don't think so."

The man put a kind hand on my arm. "I have called a professional diver. He is coming now. We will prepare for a rescue dive, okay? No need to worry. This is just a precaution. We will prepare."

I was past worrying. I was numb. The only thing I could feel was Theo's arm around my shoulder. When had that happened? "Please find him," I pleaded.

"Here!" Vasilios suddenly yelled. "Is here!"

Relief shot me forward, and we all ran to the side of the boat. Down below, I saw an orb of light. He was coming up.

"Help him, help him!" I said.

Theo and the rescue worker both reached in to pull him aboard. My dad looked a bit woozy, but mostly he looked worried, and he pushed through the others to get to me. "Olive, are you okay? I saw the GoPro fall. I thought . . ." He grabbed my face, as if trying to convince himself I was really here.

I hadn't even realized I'd dropped it. "Dad, I'm fine. I had a panic attack, but Theo pulled me out. Your light went out. . . ." I shook my head, trying to see through the tears. "Dad, why didn't you tell me you were sick? Why didn't—" And then the edges of my vision pulled inward, and Theo was trying to help me to the floor, and then I was hot, then cold, then hot again, and there were arms on me, catching me, and I had one last glimpse of the sky before I couldn't see anything.

* * *

The next two hours were a blur.

The ambulance couldn't decide who needed help more—my dad, whose blood pressure was low and who also began vomiting shortly after his summit, or his daughter, who kept blacking out every time she tried to stand. We were both taken to the hospital in Fira, where we were set up in separate rooms for monitoring—my dad on the upper level, where they'd check his blood levels post-dive, and me on the main floor in an innocuous little room, where they monitored my blood pressure and oxygen levels and told me over and over that I would be just fine. It was my body's reaction to *stress*.

Stress wasn't the right word for it. Betrayal? Abandonment? Guilt? That was a bit closer.

Post-dive, my thoughts were about as cohesive and focused as a handful of confetti, but I managed to pick up most of the story on our way to the hospital. According to what I could understand from the Greek conversation Theo had with the medical professionals, my dad had been in kidney failure for almost five years. And although he had been actively treating it with dialysis, this past year he'd suffered a steady decline in his health. He'd had to make several emergency trips to a hospital in Athens over the past week, which made his decision to dive all the more dangerous.

As I listened, I felt my body tighten up over and over. This was all information that I'd had a right to know, not just as his visitor and collaborator in Santorini, but as his daughter. And it wasn't just my dad who had let me down. It was Ana. And Theo. Maybe even Geoffrey the Canadian. All those conversations we'd had, all those days on the water, they'd all known. Rage overtook me, eventually turning on me. If I hadn't been so distracted by Theo and my overall desire to flee, would I have noticed that my dad was sick?

Maybe.

And then there was the grief. It lapped up over the edges of my rage, reviving the sinking, heavy feeling I'd carried with me through my childhood. This was why I'd worked so hard to keep my father at bay. Losing someone once is miserable. Losing them twice is cruel.

As they were strapping a blood pressure cuff around my arm, a horrible thought hit me. Did my mom know? Is that why she'd been so adamant about me coming here? *No.* She wouldn't do that to me, would she? My thoughts spiraled into darkness. Someone had made sure I had my phone with me, and as soon as I was alone I tried calling her, but when I dialed, my call went straight to voicemail. Again. Why wasn't she answering my phone calls? Why wasn't she calling me back? I called James. Nothing.

It was just me, a rotation of nurses attempting to communicate with me in a mixture of Greek and English, and the angry hornet's nest that had overtaken my body.

I'd done grief and sadness and loneliness. I'd managed anger. But this? This was unprecedented.

A few hours later, when the nurses decided I was sufficiently stable for a visitor, Theo came bursting into my tiny hospital room, not even bothering to knock. My expression stopped him dead in his tracks because he froze midway, his mouth set in a worried line.

"You okay, Kalamata?" His voice was penitent, which just made me angrier. He'd spent the last week trying to convince me to give my dad a chance, all the while knowing that my dad had been lying. Not to mention *he* had been lying to me. It must have made for great filming.

I scowled at him. "Where's your camera?"

My tone was hardly friendly, but he took it as an invitation, closing the door behind him and bounding toward me. "Confiscated. They won't allow me to film here." He dragged a chair noisily up next to me, then took a seat. "Not that I would. So," he said.

I crossed my arms. I wasn't about to help him out.

We sat in awkward silence, the machine next to me beeping every so often. They'd made me change into a light blue hospital gown, and my bare legs stuck out the bottom. My pedicure was chipped and fading, and who knew what my hair and face looked like, but for once I didn't care. My breath felt shaky and raggedy in my chest. The air was thick.

Finally, Theo crossed his ankle over his knee, jiggling his foot anxiously. "I'm guessing you have some questions for me?"

Pressure formed in the space between my eyebrows, and my words shot out like arrows from a bow. "Like, how did it feel for you to know that you were lying to me this entire time?"

His mouth dropped open in what looked like genuine surprise. "What? I wasn't lying to you. Your dad asked me not to tell you. I had to honor his wishes."

Honor his wishes? I could feel my heart rate increasing, a fact that the machine I was connected to instantly alerted us to.

"Is that okay?" Theo asked, pointing to the screen.

"Ignore it." I struggled through my wires to sit up, locking eyes with him. "Theo, you've spent this entire time trying to convince me what a great guy my dad is and how he's changed. But this whole time he was lying, and you were too. He brought me here because he's dying, isn't he?"

The realization had been lurking under the surface, murky and miserable. He wanted to reconnect because it was his last chance. Meaning, if he weren't sick, would he have even reached out? The thought made me hurt from the top of my head to the tips of my toes.

For once, Theo was quiet, his dark eyes studying me. "He isn't dying." But his voice lacked resolve. A part of him was mourning already. I knew that because I was too.

I held up my phone. "But people can only expect to live five or ten years on dialysis. And in the ambulance you said it's been five years already."

"Some people live for much longer when it's going well," Theo quickly said.

My breath was coming in hot and fast, my fists clenched. Why couldn't he just tell the truth? "But, Theo, it's *not* going well."

He looked like I'd slapped him, and as I stared at his indignant expression, I realized what I was seeing. Theo was in denial about losing my dad. He'd never experienced the loss of Nico Varanakis. I had. My heart crumpled, this time for him.

He reached for my hand but stopped himself, grabbing the railing on my bed instead. "Kalamata, you *can* trust me. I didn't tell you about your dad's illness because he asked me not to. He didn't want the trip to be overshadowed by it, or for you to have any extra pressure because he wasn't well." He studied me again, this time his mouth twisted. "Are you angry at him for being sick?"

All my soft feelings went up in a puff of smoke. Was I angry at my dad for being sick? Who did Theo think he was?

I gripped the sheets tightly, my stomach condensing into a knot.

"No, Theo. I'm angry at him for not *telling* me what was going on all this time. I'm angry at him for endangering himself and me for some stupid tip about Atlantis. I'm angry at him for deciding to keep me out of his life until the very last second."

Theo reached for me again, but quickly thought better of it. "But that was the point of this trip. He wanted you here before it was too late, before he was too sick to have this time with you."

Lava was building in my chest, my heart hammering as I stared at Theo. Yes, the situation was complicated in some ways, but in other ways it wasn't at all. My dad had brought me back just in time for me to lose him again. If it wasn't so horrible, it would be funny.

"Theo, it was already too late." My voice was high-pitched and raggedy, but I couldn't stop it. Why was no one getting this? Why did no one seem to understand that my *dad*, the sun I had orbited around, had left me in a darkness that no human should have to endure? Did they really expect me to welcome him back into my life just because this could be my last chance? The time period when my dad and I could have reconciled, formed a new relationship, had passed. The train hadn't just left the station. It had jumped the tracks and headed for the other side of the world.

I wanted to explain all of that, but what was the point? Yes, a part of me had once thought—hoped—that Theo was someone who could understand the experience of losing my dad. Understand what it was like to have been left with pieces of something that never added up to a whole. But he didn't. No one had ever understood, and I needed to get used to that.

"Theo, I . . ." But I didn't know how to finish the sentence. I was too angry, and I knew I'd be saying things I couldn't take back. Maybe I didn't want to take them back. But his dark eyes met mine, and I felt a pang in my chest. I'd liked those eyes so much. I'd trusted them. And now that it was all out in the open—yes, I *had* been falling for those eyes, despite the many, many reasons why I shouldn't be. It had all been a lie.

He dropped his gaze. "National Geographic doesn't want the film anymore. They said we don't have enough original material."

His words felt so heavy. I didn't want them to, but they did. It was time to let all of this go. "Well, what did we expect? It's not like we were actually going to find something."

Sadness splayed across his face, and I had to fight off the regret. It was true, wasn't it? "I'm really sorry," he said quietly. "I wasn't trying to hurt you. I'd never hurt you. I—I—" And then his eyes locked on to mine, searching for something.

Hoping for something. I knew what he wanted because I had wanted it too. And now here we were. "If all this hadn't happened . . ." He waved his hand vaguely toward where my dad's room must be. "Maybe—"

A surge of anger hit my chest. "But it *did* happen."

He looked away. We'd been dancing around this for a week now, but the safety I had felt with Theo was slowly drifting. He'd been lying just like my dad had.

"I think you should go."

I could see the pain physically ripping through him, and I quickly dropped my eyes to his shoulders, trying to ignore the same feeling running through me.

He waited for a moment, his stance begging me to take it back. Ask him to stay. I didn't.

"Bye, Liv," he said quietly.

Liv.

It hit me like a ton of bricks. He crossed the room and disappeared out the door. I watched him leave me alone, realizing the truth. You can't always trust the people you hope you can: they are always going to disappoint you in the end.

Chapter Twenty-Four

**#24. SHRINK-WRAPPED DEMO CD OF A BAND
CALLED GIFT HORSE**

We were supposed to use the money for groceries.

*Our cupboards were pretty empty. My dad had been
spending long hours out job hunting, leaving no time to
shop, which meant we'd been living off peanut butter and
jam sandwiches. That night he'd promised to make me
spaghetti with garlic bread.*

*As we approached the street, my dad stopped to
listen to some performers, a trio who had set up a little
sign that read GIFT HORSE. No one else was listening,
but my dad said they were great, and bought several of
their CDs to pass out to people walking by. Then he took
me to Navy Pier, where he let me ride the carousel three
times in a row.*

*I was always begging to go on the carousel, but that
day it wasn't like the other times. His eyes were too bright*

and he was talking too loudly to the attendant, and I knew that there would be no garlic bread that night.

I CRIED FOR WHAT FELT LIKE THE ONE BILLIONTH TIME since receiving my dad's postcard; then I curled up with my phone, running my fingers across the screen. I got a text from Dax: **You alive?** If I weren't so miserable, I would have laughed. I forced myself to reply. **Soo busy. Call you tonight?**

The hospital insisted that I needed to stay overnight, which felt ridiculous but was definitely preferable to the bunk room with Theo. As soon as I got ahold of my mom, I would make plans to go home. I just needed her to answer. So I tried my mom again, then James, leaving what felt like my hundredth voicemail. Finally, I gave up and tried to sleep.

I tossed and turned on the hard bed, listening to beeps and fending off visitors. Around dinnertime, Ana tried to stop by, but I told the nurses I needed to rest. The nurses told me that my dad had asked if he could come down to my room for a talk, and no way was I up for that. Theo didn't try to visit again, but I felt no relief over that. I missed him. Horribly. Which made no sense given the fact that he had been in my life for such a short—and painful—amount of time.

Sleeping felt impossible, but when I woke it was much too early. Pale, gray light trickled under the curtains of my tiny window and the mumbling of several voices just out-side my room found their way to my bed. . . .

The muscles in my arms and back were sore from all the churning I'd done the day before, and I smelled like the ocean. Maybe they would let me shower?

"Hello?" I called, and the talking stopped. My voice felt scratchy, and I touched my hand to my throat.

I sat up just as the door cracked open. "Good morning." It was a new nurse, one I hadn't seen yet. "We are ready to discharge you from the hospital. But first—"

"Liv?" The interrupting voice made me freeze. Was I hal-lucinating? Still fuzzy? And then she sailed in, looking tired and windblown and so very, very pregnant. *Mom.*

I nearly blacked out again, this time from relief. She made it over to me in three giant steps, and then I was all wrapped up in her, her hair in my face, her long arms draping around me. The relief consumed me, swept me off my feet. I was sob-bing again, holding on as tightly to her as she was to me.

"Tell. Me. Everything," she said.

And so I did. I told her about the documentary, and Theo, and the bookstore, and Vasilios's orichalcum, and how we'd dived even though the conditions were terrible. When I got to the part about me having a panic attack underwater and Theo saving me, she could barely listen long enough for me to finish.

"Oh my God. Oh my God, Liv," she said over and over. "What if Theo hadn't been there? What if—"

"He was there," I said. "And Dad didn't let me dive very deep, so I'm sure I would have made it up." I wasn't so sure at all, but there was no use in terrifying her. Not when it was all over and done with. "Are you breathing?"

She looked stunned. Then angry. Then stunned again. "It isn't *my* breathing I'm worried about. I think I need to sit down. . . ." She looked around for a chair, but then apparently decided it was too far away and just climbed onto the bed with me.

I needed to ask The Question. The one I wasn't sure I wanted the answer to. I gripped a handful of blankets. "Mom, you didn't know about Dad being sick, did you? Because if you knew and didn't tell me . . ."

"I had no idea about the kidney failure," she said quickly, and my heart slowed. "I would have told you if I'd known. But I did know something was wrong. When you told me about how he was leaving every few days . . . something didn't add up. I called Ana and she wouldn't tell me, but, well . . ." She rubbed her hand over her tired face. "Call it mother's intuition, but I felt that I needed to be here just in case I was right. I didn't tell you I was coming because I didn't want to worry you. But I know him. He wouldn't have kept leaving you like that unless something was wrong."

There was a rushing in my ears, a heaviness that not even my mom could make disappear. "He did last time," I blurted out.

I immediately felt vulnerable, exposed. Her expression turned grave. "Have you talked to him about that?"

"Well..." My mind scanned the last eight days, my breath catching as I landed on the sunset cruise. He'd tried to, and I'd shut him down. "No. Not... really."

She rested her hand on mine, meeting my eyes seriously. "Liv, I'm going to tell you something, and I need you to listen, because I think it will change some things for you. And then I need you to go talk to your dad, okay?"

I nodded, but my throat felt so tight that I put my hand up to it, testing that it was still working. My heart was sprinting without me. What could she possibly tell me that would change things?

She tucked my hair back from my face, her blue eyes glistening. "Your dad didn't leave to look for Atlantis."

I waited for all of the air to get sucked out of the room. For disbelief to hit me. But it didn't. Instead I felt... relief? But over what? *Recognition*, my brain supplied. *You know this.* But I didn't. How could my brain know something my memory didn't?

"What are you talking about?" Now my heart felt like a drum, steadily marching onward.

She inhaled, then exhaled slowly, moving her hand to her

belly. "Do you remember when he went to the hospital? You were in first grade."

I shook my head, but instantly a series of images traveled to the front of my brain: a long bright corridor full of doors, low-pile carpet with interconnected hexagons, my mom's hand tight in mine. My dad was behind one of those doors. I just didn't know which one. Or why.

She was watching my face carefully. "He went twice, once for two weeks, once for almost a month. Do you remember?"

I didn't, but my body recognized it. There was a tender spot, a tangle of emotion that blossomed and grew the moment I looked at it. Why had he been there? "Was he having kidney issues then?"

She reached down and squeezed my hand, and the movement made the bed creak. "No. Remember how Dad was always up or down? There was never an in-between. Some days he was on top of the world; other days he could barely get out of bed. He was diagnosed with bipolar disorder during that first hospitalization. He'd had . . ." She hesitated. "An episode. He lost his job and spent most of our money buying a car that he crashed late one night. He was arrested and then hospitalized. Do you remember?"

A rush of cold was working its way up my body, a slow-moving tidal wave. My hands were shaking, blood rushing in my ears.

"I don't remember that," I said, but my voice shook, and even as the words left my mouth, I knew they were not true. A part of me did remember. I might not have it accessible in my thinking brain, but the experience had imprinted itself on my DNA. I could feel the instability, the confusion. The fear. *He'd left before.* Lots of times. But he'd been looking for Atlantis, hadn't he?

My mom was watching me carefully. "A lot of people don't begin to show signs until they're in their early twenties. Your father was one of those people. At first he just experienced what's called hypomania—he'd go on kicks of staying up all night working on projects, his paintings and woodworking, all of that. But then the episodes began to get more severe. He wouldn't sleep for days at a time, and his projects became more extreme. Do you remember when he tried to rebuild our kitchen cupboards?"

The memory came to me, images strung together in bits and pieces. I'd come home from school one day and found my dad in an argument with the landlord. My dad was insisting he could build better cupboards than the ones that were in place, but once he removed them, he never put new ones up.

My mom let me sit in silence, not rushing me in the slightest. "Yes," I said finally. Another memory pulled at me, insisted I take a look. There was something about the car, too. I lifted my chin. "He used to go on . . . explorations."

Explorations appeared unbidden on my tongue. It was his word. It was what he called those days and weeks when he disappeared. For one unguarded moment I saw the pain in my mother's eyes, saw what that experience must have been like for her.

"Yes. That's what he called it when he was in a downswing. He'd take the car and live out of it for a few days. He'd drive to the ocean, and I wouldn't know where he was or when he was going to come back." Her voice caught. "You'd sit by the window, watching for him for hours at a time."

She closed her eyes briefly. "Things got bad enough that he began having incidents in public, fighting with clerks, things like that. I began to feel worried about leaving you with him. After the diagnosis, he was able to get on medication and was stabilized for a while, but he struggled to remain consistent. I started to notice a pattern: whenever he became obsessed with talking about Atlantis, I knew he was headed for another manic episode."

Memories were rushing me, filling me up and emptying me out. My dad talking too fast. People yelling at us on the streets. His hands shaking. The packages full of Atlantis maps and supplies that would build up on our stoop, bought with money we didn't have.

She exhaled, slipping her fingers into mine, her eyes serious. "And then there was the Easter dress incident." Panic was slowly building in my chest, flashes of memory looping through my mind. There were people yelling—at me? At my dad?—horns honking, and most of all the *eyes*.

"I remember some of that." *Stop stop STOP*, my brain ordered. But I had to look, had to remember. "What . . . ?"

That was as far as I could get, and she understood, jumping in. "It was the Saturday before Easter, and he took you to the Loop to buy you a dress. You two were crossing the street, and a cab almost hit you in the crosswalk." She spoke slowly, her eyes carefully focused on mine. "It stopped in time, but it scared your dad, and he lost it. He'd been up and down for weeks, and the stress really set him off. He started yelling, and kicked the car repeatedly until he'd dented the door. A crowd gathered, and someone called the police. Your dad was arrested."

I was breathing, but none of the oxygen seemed to be making it to my head. I felt just as light-headed as I had underwater, and just as untethered. I remembered the dress, yellow when I wanted pink and too frilly for anything we ever went to. What had happened to it? Had I dropped it in the street? But most of all I remembered my confusion. My dad was taking care of me, but I knew there was something wrong with the way he was doing it. I could tell by the way people looked at us. "Then what happened?" I managed.

She squeezed my hand. "This time he went to the hospital

for several weeks. I tried to tell you why, and explain, but you told me I was wrong. Then you took all his maps to school for show-and-tell and told everyone your dad had gone to the Sahara desert to look for Atlantis."

My throat caught. I'd brought a map of the world, one I'd spent all night drawing with markers on a poster board. The teacher had cut me off midway through my show-and-tell, and I'd gotten so upset that I'd thrown the board. She'd acted like she didn't believe me. Because she hadn't. Obviously.

I realized I was clenching my teeth, but I didn't stop because the pressure in my jaw took away some of the ache in my chest. I'd been a kid trying to make sense of the world, my mind coming up with reasons that hurt less than the ones I was being presented with. As painful as the thought of him leaving to search for Atlantis had been, it had been less painful to Child Me than what was actually happening—my dad, who I relied on more than anyone in the world, had been struggling with something inside of himself. Something I didn't understand.

You knew all along.

The thought rose quietly, and I looked at it long and hard. *Truth.* Because I wasn't just learning all of this. I was *recognizing* it. Maybe I hadn't known all the details of my dad's mental illness, but some deep part of me had known he hadn't left to find Atlantis.

I dropped my head, pressing my fingers to my temples. My mind was swirling, moments and memories locking into place. And then I was thinking about my mom. A question pulled at my mind, made my lungs constrict. I looked up at her. "Why didn't you just tell me the truth? Why did you let me believe that?"

I didn't want to be angry with her, but I was. I'd been a child; she'd been the adult. It had been her job to guide me through that experience.

Her mouth twisted with regret. "I didn't handle it well, Liv. You were so adamant about what you wanted to believe, and after a while, I started to think that maybe it was better for you to have your story to help you cope. As you got older, I thought you must know. But then you started having those nightmares. . . ." She exhaled. "If I'm being honest, I struggled with the stigma of mental illness. I didn't want you to see him differently, or for others to look at us differently. I know now that I was wrong. Mental illness has nothing to do with what kind of person you are. And not being open about your father's challenges was wrong and caused you pain, and I am so, so sorry for that."

Her eyes were welling up, and so were mine. It was a lot to digest and go over. What I did know was that she was sincere.

"I don't know what to say," I said.

"How could you?" She wiped my cheek with the palm of

her hand, which only made more tears spill out. Then a horrible thought struck me. I'd spent years obsessed with Atlantis, just like my dad. Even now, anytime a story or movie popped up online, I couldn't help but read it. "Mom, is it hereditary? You said Atlantis was his trigger. Do I have bipolar disorder too?"

She shook her head. "According to Ali, you've never had any of the early signs. Your obsession with Atlantis . . . That was about missing your dad."

I nodded, letting the information pool in my chest. I pulled my knees up, hugging them tightly. It was as if my mom had just put a spotlight on my dad, suddenly bringing him into focus. I felt disoriented and relieved and guilty all at once, the emotions crashing and competing in my chest. I'd misjudged so much.

"Does he know I didn't know?" I managed.

"Yes," she said firmly. She scooted in, her belly pressing into me. "And he understands. That was part of the reason for this trip. He wanted to make good on some old promises and show you that he was someone you could trust again. And not telling you about the kidney failure . . ." She sighed. "My guess is that he didn't want to let you down again."

It made a terrible kind of sense. But trusting my dad again . . . Would that ever happen? *Could* that ever happen?

I looked down at my mom's wedding ring. It was several times larger than the one she'd worn when she was married to my dad, but I knew she kept her first one in her jewelry stand. I'd gone to check on it several times over the years. "Do you regret marrying Dad?" I asked, my fingers clenching.

She didn't hesitate for one single second. "Never. I regret a lot of things I did afterward, but I will never regret your father, and of course I have never regretted you." She paused. "I love James, and I'm sorry for the pain you've been through. But if I had to do it all over again—marry that smart, quirky Greek just a few months after I met him? I'd do it in a heartbeat."

I let her words spread over me, tears flooding my eyes. I'd needed to hear that, that our early life together hadn't been a mistake to her. I had a million questions, but one kept rising to the top. "Mom, if he didn't leave for Atlantis, then why are we looking for it now?"

"That's a question for him. I think it's time for you to go talk to your father."

"Now?" The thought set my chest on fire. I looked in panic at the weak morning sunlight. "He might not even be awake yet. What if—"

"Now," she said firmly.

There was no arguing with her. This was just like when I'd gotten the invitation to come to Greece in the first place. Besides, I knew I could be brave. I already had been for a very long time.

I took a deep breath. "Which room is he in?"

* * *

My dad's hospital room was even smaller than mine—nothing but a bed, a worn rocking chair, and a whole lot of machines. I found him lying back with his eyes closed, not connected to any of the machines, which alarmed me. Shouldn't something be monitoring his heart and oxygen? What about his kidneys? How did they monitor those?

He must have felt my gaze on him, because his eyes flew open and he sat up quickly. "Liv! How are you feeling?"

He'd gone from a dead sleep to asking how I was. I couldn't decide if I should laugh or cry, and a mixture of both came out. His face had more color than it had the day before, but it was still swollen, and his legs and ankles were puffy below his hospital gown. But what I really noticed was how tired he looked. Now that he wasn't trying to hide it anymore, I could see the deep exhaustion etched into his face, the hospital's fluorescent lights highlighting every line. Over the course of my trip he'd spent countless hours out filming in the sun. Had every minute of it been a struggle?

As I studied him, his expression turned to alarm. "Liv? Are you okay? You look nervous."

Accurate. He tried to get out of his bed, but I held one hand out to stop him. "I'm okay. Can I sit?"

"Of course." He gestured to the chair, falling back heavily into the bed. For a moment I stared at my lap, trying to figure out which questions needed asking, but there were so many of them, and where to even begin? "Dad . . . I have some things to ask you."

"Yes." His voice was relieved. Then he smiled slightly, gesturing to the hospital bed. "Take your time. I have nowhere to be."

My smile matched his, but I was too nervous to look at him for long. What I needed right now was strength. My mom had given me a good push, but I needed an extra nudge, something to get me up and over the hill. But maybe there wasn't a right way to do this. Maybe I just had to start. "Dad . . ." *Deep breath.* "You didn't . . . You didn't leave to find Atlantis."

There.

"No." He shook his head, his eyes searching mine. "I always loved to tell you stories." He twirled his fingers, hesitation floating around him, settling heavily between us. "And I-I'd like to tell you the rest of mine."

"Yes, please." I dragged the rocking chair in slightly, so I was within arm's distance. I was having a hard time looking at him, but I did it anyway, preparing myself for what might be coming.

He folded his hands in his lap, his face composed. "After my mother died, I spent several years alone on Santorini, working and studying. It was lonely, and I found no joy except in my studies of Atlantis, but that felt like a dead end. So the summer I turned twenty, I decided it was time to leave the island. I had no future here, so I went to the United States, for no reason other than I heard it is a good place to begin a life." His eyes crinkled around the edges. "When I met your mother, I believed it to be true."

In my mind I saw the photograph of them from that first summer, and I felt both lighter and heavier somehow.

"I'd never believed in love at first sight, but that's exactly what it was. We married, and those first few years were more than I'd ever expected. Of course, we had our problems. As an immigrant, work was always difficult, and her family was not happy to know me. They had hoped for someone more like them. And I began to struggle with steadiness." He held his arms out, miming balance. "I was a man walking on a rope, you know, in the circus?"

"A tightrope walker." I nodded, my throat tight. His struggles had begun much earlier than I'd imagined.

"For years I had problems, with sleep and keeping jobs. But I was able to manage. And then there was you." His hand flew to the tattoo on his inner arm. My coordinates.

"I loved your mother so much, but nothing had ever mattered as much as you did. You were so perfect. I promised myself I would make everything steady. I didn't have a name for it yet, only that I must keep steady. But no matter how hard I tried, I struggled, more and more as the years went on.

I couldn't sleep. I couldn't keep a job. Other days, no matter how much I wanted to, I couldn't get out of bed. And then, when you were only six, your mother miscarried. Do you remember?"

I nodded. I remembered her in the hospital, remembered my father beside me and his tears that just wouldn't stop. I hadn't thought of that in a long time.

"Things became extremely difficult after that. I began having episodes, doing things I believed to be right in the moment. One second I was high in the sky. Nothing could touch me. And the next I would see what I had done, how I had hurt you and your mother, and I thought I could not go on." His tears caught up to his voice, weakening it. "Your mother couldn't go to school. Our bills began piling up. I could not see a way out; all I could do was dream, and those dreams were always about Atlantis. I escaped to Atlantis in my mind, and I brought you with me. Our future together, what we would do when we found the lost city . . . It was the only place that felt real to me anymore." His voice cracked again, but he rubbed his eyes, determined to continue. "I began hearing lies in my head, believing that you were both better off without me and that you needed to be free of me."

The logic of that hurt my brain. He thought we'd be better off if he left? Heat rushed down my neck, flushed my cheeks. "Dad . . . ," I started, and he nodded, anticipating my objection.

"It was not correct, I know. That is the problem with mental illness. It can be like looking into a foggy mirror. You no longer see clearly. Liv, do you recall the years before I left?"

Pain was moving through my body in waves now, and soon I was a ship taking on water, memories flooding me almost faster than I could handle.

I remembered waking up in the middle of the night to find him cooking three-course meals or playing music too loudly. I remembered a neighbor waiting for me outside my school, because my mother didn't know where he was and was afraid he wouldn't show up to get me. And then there were the other memories I'd recalled when talking to Mom—him arguing with strangers, or neighbors, over small things. All things that I had not understood, had to tuck away because they didn't fit with the other side of my dad—the one who took me to the playground and went to a braiding class so he could style my hair. How could he be both those people at once?

"I . . ." I took a deep breath. I wanted to tell him to stop, that we didn't need to go over all of this, but I'd been carrying these things for too long. I needed to know what had happened. "I do remember. At least some of it."

He nodded, his shoulders rounding. "I could no longer bear to see what I was doing to you or your mother. I thought I must start over where I began. If I went back to the beginning, maybe I could make it all right. At first it was the same. I lost jobs. I struggled. But every day I promised myself that I would figure this out. Eventually I found a doctor, a woman in Athens, who helped me find the right balance of medications. Slowly, slowly I found stability. *Peace.* But it was never right, not without you."

My throat was constricting the way it always did, and my eyes burned with tears.

"I thought I'd come back. But every time I tried to, I thought of you sitting with me over our maps. I thought of how you trusted me and how I had not been who you needed. But when I missed you, I would read about Atlantis. And then earlier this year I found an article written by an Egyptologist, Dr. Bilder. She had many of the same ideas I did. And I thought *maybe*, maybe this time I could finally give you Atlantis. But, Liv . . ."

His voice choked, and he waited for me to look up, to meet his eyes. "This time we have had together . . . I know it's been difficult, but thank you. I am not asking for forgiveness, but I am telling you that I love you. And I wish I could go back to the beginning."

I dropped my head into my hands, my breath hot on my wrists.

I'd needed to believe that my father had left me for a perfect golden city that only he could find, because the alternatives—that he was struggling and unsafe—were too frightening for my child mind to manage. But I wasn't a child anymore. He didn't have to be perfect for me to be safe.

"Me too," I finally said. "I mean, I wish we could go back to the beginning. And this trip, it's been . . ."

"Difficult," he supplied.

"Well, yes," I admitted, because that was true. This had been hard. But a lot of other things were flooding my mind. The sunsets, the birthday party, the Lost Bookstore of Atlantis, all those hours sweating under the sun while I listened to his stories. Something my mom had once told me sprang to mind. "Difficult isn't the opposite of good."

"No, it isn't," he said. His eyes were clear.

"Dad, was there anything down there?" The question was suddenly burning a hole through the center of my chest. "In the water. Did you see anything?"

This time he hung his head, sounding sorrier about this than about anything. "Nothing, Liv. I'm sorry."

I waited for the news to percolate into my subconscious, for the picture to go from distorted to clear. *We didn't find it.* It took only a few seconds. I unclenched my fists, and the gleaming city—its concentric rings and golden statues and gilded walls—fell from my outstretched palms. It went easily, sinking into the darkness like it had never existed at all.

"Okay," I said, and as I looked at him, my nightmares

sprang to mind, the images adding up to something they never had before. In all those dreams, I hadn't been looking for Atlantis. I'd been looking for my dad. And here he was. He wasn't gilded or impermeable, but he was *here*.

I didn't have any words, so I reached for his hands—rough and cold feeling—and squeezed them tightly in mine. He squeezed back. I think it was enough.

A small knock echoed from the door, breaking our gaze, and when my mom walked into the room, my dad inhaled sharply. "Ellen." A long, tense moment fell over them as they stared at each other. My mom seemed sad, but hopeful, and my dad . . . If I'd ever wondered if he truly missed her, well, I had my answer. He looked sucker punched. Gutted.

"Hi, Nico," she said quietly. Her eyes were shiny.

The air between them was charged, electric, and for one horrible second I wondered if this was going to go badly. But then my dad pulled himself to his feet and hurried over to her, and then they were hugging, both of them crying, my mom's blond head pressed against his shoulder, her pregnant belly making everything awkward and disjointed looking. Even so, exactly two lifetimes came and went in that hug. I'd forgotten what they looked like together. How she was just a hair taller than he was, how his shoulders relaxed when she was around.

I felt like my heart was going to burst out of my body.

These were people who had really, truly loved each other—who still loved each other. Life, and all its trappings, had gotten in the way. It happened sometimes.

Also, in the history of third wheels, I was currently in the running for first place. I cleared my throat, but neither of them seemed to notice.

"She's amazing. She's so amazing. You did such a good job. Thank you, Ellen," he said, over and over.

"You're welcome," she said, her eyes shut tightly. They released each other, but neither of them looked away.

My mom wiped her eyes, streaking mascara and tears across her face in a gray rainbow. "You look just the same."

"And you look . . . completely different," he said, reaching for a lock of her short hair, and they both burst out laughing and hugged again.

Seeing them together felt so strange and yet so *right*. How was it possible that my mom could be here, married to someone else, and pregnant, and still be the same person who loved him so much? It was like the collision of two entirely different dimensions. Her words came to me. *Once you've truly loved someone, you never stop.*

"When will the baby be here?" my dad said, looking down at her bump.

She rested her hand on the small of her back. "In two months. I worried they wouldn't let me on the plane. James

came with me. And Julius. The flight over was a nightmare."
She smiled at me. "We had to keep giving him ninja breaks
in the aisles."

My heart jumpcd. "Julius is here?"

"James checked into a hotel in Fira so Julius could sleep.
They'll call us when they wake up." Her eyes landed on me
for just a moment before going back to my dad. "Nico, I want
to hear everything."

"It's been too long," he said, grinning.

The sparse room felt tight and cramped, packed full of all
the things they needed to say and reconcile. The moment was
no longer mine. It was theirs.

"So, I'm just going to . . ." I made it out of the room in
record time.

After I'd spoken with my nurse and changed into my regular
clothes, I found Ana camped out in the lobby with a sultry-
looking stack of romance novels and an even sultrier-looking
cup of coffee, and she nearly dropped both when she saw me.
"Your mother found you? She is with your father?"

I nodded, still overwhelmed by everything the last few
hours had brought. "I think they needed some time to talk."

"Of course they did. Oh, Liv."

She leaned forward like she was preparing to scoop me
up in one of her big hugs, but if she did that, I was pretty

sure I would dissolve again, and I wasn't entirely sure my tear ducts could handle another crying session. Also, seeing her was making me think about my last conversation with Theo, and I was most definitely not ready to add that to the heap of worries in my mind.

I moved toward the door. "I think I could use some time on my own."

"Of *course*," she said again. "I will stay here with your father and mother. His levels are looking better, but the staff said they would like to keep him for another day for observation. Theo has gone to get us some proper breakfast. He'll be back soon."

My heart quickened. "I think I'll just . . . head back up to the bookstore. I'll take the bus."

"Theo will go with you!" she said.

It took everything not to actually sprint for the door. "Thank you, but no, I can find my way on my own."

"I will send Theo to check on you later," she called.

"Not necessary," I said.

The walk to the bus stop was long. I was exhausted and sticky in the shorts and T-shirt I'd originally worn to Akrotiri. I desperately needed a shower, and some real sleep, but my mind was too full to think about that. I was circling on my family's story and the way I'd twisted it to include the lost city of Atlantis, when, really, it hadn't been about Atlantis at all.

Here's the thing I really couldn't get over: how hard my dad had worked. He'd fought for his life. He'd done the work to get healthy. He'd built me a bookstore on the most magical island I'd ever seen, and he'd figured out a way to make good on all the adventures we'd planned. But most of all, he'd *tried*. Even when the chances of rejection were unbelievably high.

Could we possibly find what we'd lost?

I needed to think. *Unravel.* I had so much to piece together and work through, but what I really had was a story. My story.

Once upon a time there was an island so perfect and beautiful that it angered the gods.

Once upon a time there was an island.

Once upon a time.

I needed a way to process this. To record it. Maybe I needed to tell my dad my side of the story, the same way he'd told me his. *What was lost is now found.* My thoughts drifted to the shoebox, all those items piecing together a story.

And that's when I had the idea.

Chapter Twenty-Five

#25. THE LAST PAGE OF PLATO'S TIMAEUS AND CRITIAS, TORN OUT OF A BOOK, THE FINAL PASSAGE HIGHLIGHTED

"Zeus, the god of gods, who rules according to law, and is able to see into such things, perceiving that an honorable race was in a woeful plight, and wanting to inflict punishment on them, that they might be chastened and improve, collected all the gods into their most holy habitation, which, being placed at the center of the world, beholds all created things. And when he had called them together, he spake as follows—"

It cuts off after that; the rest of Plato's words were lost. We'll never know what Zeus said to all those gods. I guess the rest was left up to us.

I RAN STRAIGHT BACK TO ANA, TOLD HER I ACTUALLY would be needing Theo's services after all and to have him meet me at the bookstore, and then sprinted back to the bus stop for what had to be the longest, twistiest ride of my riding-the-bus-in-Santorini career so far. My head was thick with ideas. How long did I have to pull this off? One day? Two? The time constraints were ridiculous, but if I could talk Theo into helping me, I might just be able to make it work.

The bookstore was shuttered and lonesome feeling, but once I was inside I ignored all that, gathering my sketch pad and oil pastels and setting up shop right in the center of the store. I taped a row of papers across the main wall of the bookstore, divided them into little squares, then went to work filling them in, drawing, then writing, then drawing some more, until finally my idea began to take shape. By the time I finished two hours later, my entire arm was on fire from all the work, and my head buzzed with exhaustion, but I could see the summit.

When I finally heard Theo at the door, my chest exploded in a combination of excitement and panic. He may say no, and I'd have to be okay with that. But if he said yes . . .

I'd been up checking my phone in the bunk room, and I dropped out, spider-monkey style. "Theo?"

"AAAH!" He stumbled backward, gripping his chest.

"Sorry. So, so sorry," I said quickly. "I didn't mean to scare you. Although, I guess now we're even?"

"My mom said you need help with something." His hair

was strangely tame, and he put his hands in his pockets, a move designed to look casual, but that in all our time together, I hadn't seen him do once. He wasn't quite looking at me, but he was talking to me, and I was going to count that as a win.

"Theo . . ." I took a deep breath. If I was going to pull this off, we'd have to start immediately. We didn't have time to address the giant pink elephant standing between us. Hopefully there would be time for that later.

"Theo, I have an idea. It's something for my dad, and I have to get it done fast. Will you help?" I pointed to my drawings, and he walked over to give them a closer look. He looked at them for what felt like an eternity, moving piece by piece through the layout. By the time he turned around, he still looked distant but also impressed. "I'm in," he said.

We went through what felt like ninety hours of footage. A hundred hours of footage? It was difficult to watch my interactions with my dad, because it highlighted all the ways I'd misjudged him. But what I hadn't prepared for was how difficult it would be to watch myself through Theo's camera—through his eyes.

From the moment he'd begun his interrogation at the airport, Theo had truly seen me, capturing me in a way that was so raw and unfiltered that it hurt to look at. I'd thought I was so invincible, with my smooth bangs and carefully applied eyeliner, but you could see my fear and worry, all that vulnerability I'd dragged right alongside my overstuffed suitcase. What was even more surprising to watch was the way the images of me evolved. It was like witnessing a butterfly transforming in reverse. Slowly but surely, I'd let go of my perfectly constructed persona, physically, but emotionally as well. As the days wore on, I'd stopped looking so polished and careful and started looking more like *me*. It was like I had finally given myself permission to sink into my skin.

At dinnertime, Bapou brought us a covered plate of spanakopita and two honey-sweet *kataïfi* pastries made from shredded phyllo dough. He and Theo exchanged a few words, and then he patted my head softly. "Beautiful. Welcome to Santorini."

His voice was uncharacteristically subdued, and I saw the meaning in his eyes. *I'm sorry your father is ill.*

"Thank you, Bapou," I said, and he cupped my cheek in his hand before heading for the door.

We worked straight through sunset, the light through the windows fading from golden to dusky to black, until finally, there was just one last piece to do. The most important part. By then it was the middle of the night, so I went into the cave to splash some water on my face to make it look like I was awake. Then we turned on every light we could find, and I carried my shoebox to the desk I'd set up for my dad what felt like millions of years ago. My hands shook lightly. If I didn't get this part right, then the rest didn't matter.

Theo trained his camera on me, for what was likely the last time. "Ready?"

"Almost," I said.

I closed my eyes and thought about my list, *26 Things My Dad Left Behind, by Indiana Olive.* I thought about my maps and all of my nightmares. I thought about *what was lost is now found.* And then I opened my eyes, stared into that blinking light, and began talking.

By the time we finished, I'd gone an alarming amount of time without sleep. My eyeballs felt shriveled up, and if I had to look at a computer screen for even one more minute, I was probably going to disintegrate into a pile of dust. But the final product was good. Not perfect, but *good,* and at some point, I knew it was finished.

"Preview?" Theo asked.

We watched the entire thing in silence, me, Theo, and Catticus Finch. Or was it David Pawster Wallace? I wasn't sure. There were about a million things I wanted to correct about the video, but I also knew that the point I'd been trying to make—I'd made it. And I couldn't have done it without Theo.

"*Thank you,*" I said. My words were minuscule compared to what he had done for me, but they were all I had to give.

"It's nothing." He pointed to the screen, where an image of my dad was frozen. "You're like him. A natural." He turned to look at me, and my eyes got snagged on his full lips, his dark eyes. . . . Now that I was letting myself see how gorgeous he was, it almost hurt my eyes to look at.

He yawned, reaching his arms over his head. He didn't seem exhausted by any stretch, only a tad worn, but still, it was a new look on him. I wanted to collapse into him or at least lay my head on his shoulder, but I knew I couldn't do that.

According to the dozens of texts that had gone back and forth between me and my mom, my dad was doing much, much better, and the relief combined with my exhaustion made my whole body feel weighted down and numb. But the night wasn't over for me yet.

I gestured to the bunks. "You should get some sleep. See you up there?"

He shook his head slightly, then slowly made his way to his feet. "I'm going to sleep at my mom's. Maybe get a little more work done. I want to go over the opening one more time."

"Right. Of course." I was horribly disappointed to not have one last bunk sleepover, but it was probably for the best. I quickly scrambled to my feet. "So you'll call your mom? Have her arrange the details?"

"She's already started. Events are her thing. I don't know who is going to love this more, my mom or your dad."

"All of the above?" He gathered the rest of his belongings, then walked to the door, and I followed after him, catching sight of my reflection in the glass window. My hair was half pulled up, exposing my ears in all their sticking-out glory, and my skin felt dry and tight from the salt water, not a single speck of makeup on my face. But my eyes were clear. Focused. Like the girl I'd seen on camera.

"Theo, thanks again," I said, and this time he met my eyes and smiled. It was like the sun peeking out from behind a cloud. I hadn't quite realized how warm it was until it was gone.

He held my gaze for a moment, and a spark that felt an awful lot like hope formed in my center, raising my pulse and making me stand up a little bit straighter. "I'm happy to," he said carefully. "Anything for your dad."

The spark instantly extinguished. Point taken. *I didn't do this for you. I did it for your dad.* I swallowed back my disappointment. "See you tomorrow?"

"I wouldn't miss it. Good night, Kalamata." And then he was gone.

His absence made the air feel heavy. I desperately wanted to climb up into the bunks and close my eyes, but there was one more hurdle I had to cross. I pulled out my phone and made my way over to bookstore's armchair. This call wasn't going to

be easy, but it had to happen. And if I was honest with myself, I'd known, even before coming to Santorini—before hiking up a volcano, trespassing in a pool, watching an outdoor movie in Kamari, scuba diving for a piece of Atlantean treasure—that this decision was always going to be inevitable. Sometimes moving forward is as simple as admitting what you already know.

Summoning my final shred of resolve, I hovered my finger over Dax's name and pressed call.

When I finally woke up, I had no idea what time it was. I checked my phone and was met with two dozen phone calls and at least as many texts, mostly from my mom. Five p.m. OMG. Was it really five? I'd slept for almost an entire day.

I tumbled out of bed, nearly falling out of the loft and onto Theo, who was standing below wearing—was that a suit? His hair was brushed and he was wearing proper shoes and he was so painfully handsome that it made me want to throw myself into the depths of the ocean.

"Theo! Wow, you look . . ." *Unbelievable. Devastating.* ". . . nice," I finished lamely.

"Thanks." His eyebrows arched, and I swear I saw a hint of the old Theo appear, the one I hadn't *hurt.* "I was about to wake you up. Yiannis is picking your dad up from the hospital and will meet us in Kamari. I told him we'd take the bus, but that means we'll have to leave here in an hour. Is that okay with you?"

"An hour? That's nothing."

He smiled, a tiny ghost of a smile, but a smile.

And then, before I could embarrass myself even more, I told Theo I'd be right back and ran for the cave. *And now for my next trick, making myself look presentable!*

I washed my hair three times, unearthed every beauty supply I'd brought, and went to work. When I finally stepped out of the cave, Theo was sitting under a circle of light in the corner, a paperback tucked open. When he saw me, he stumbled to his feet, his mouth slightly open. I couldn't tell what his expression meant.

"Do I look okay?" I asked, suddenly self-conscious. Had I gone overboard? I was wearing the one dress-up dress I'd brought, a black floral minidress with a square neckline and shirred bodice, plus gold strappy sandals and my favorite red lipstick. I'd even tried something new with my hair, letting my natural wave show through with one side tucked back to expose—gasp!—my left ear.

"More than okay." He looked like he was about to say something else, but he quickly changed gears. "My mom went all out on invitations. Almost everyone RSVP'd, which is really impressive given that they only had one day's notice. We should have a really good turnout tonight."

He was stumbling over his words, and I couldn't help the hope it sent ricocheting through me. Maybe we'd get a

chance to start over too? "Then I guess we're set." His eyes were locked on mine. Would it be too much to ask if they stayed that way forever? But they slid away.

Behind me, the bell on the shop door jingled. "Hello?" a female voice called into the bookstore.

"Sorry, we're closed for the night," Theo said.

"I'm actually looking for someone. An employee." We both turned, and I was surprised to see a woman close to six feet tall, with an elegant neck, long legs, and thick black hair gathered into a high ponytail. She smiled, showing off perfectly sculpted cheekbones. "Hello, I'm Phaedra."

Theo and I exchanged a quick glance. The bookstore wasn't exactly teeming with employees. "Are you Ana's friend?" I guessed.

Her smile broadened, and she straightened her shoulders, emphasizing her perfect posture. "No, I'm looking for Geoffrey. I'm his girlfriend. Or . . ." Her brow wrinkled. "Or at least I hope I am. We've been in a bit of an argument."

An *argument*? Theo and I exchanged a glance and I took a step forward, my head buzzing. "But . . . you said your name is Phaedra?"

She laughed lightly. "Oh, he calls me Mathilde. After a character in my favorite short story."

"*Holy. Fried. Souvlaki*," Theo said.

Except that's not actually what he said.

Once we'd scraped our jaws off the ground, it was time to go. Geoffrey was already at the Cinekamari, assisting with setup while Ana checked my dad out of the hospital. That meant Phaedra rode with us on the bus, answering the nine thousand questions we had, mainly related to the fact that yes, she really did exist, and yes, she was here to try to win back Geoffrey (Her! Trying to win him back!) because he was the love of her life and she couldn't bear the thought of life without him.

I shouldn't have been so surprised. Geoffrey really was a catch. And yes, Phaedra was featured on the Greek National Opera's website. She was a principal dancer and was currently preparing for her starring role in her company's upcoming performance of *Coppélia*.

Theo and I kept shooting each other surprised goldfish eyes, and it was . . . nice. Eye contact and all. It felt familiar and a touch of what we used to be. Mathilde said she knew who I was and why I was in Santorini, but we needed to fill her in on nearly everything else, including the event we were currently barreling toward. And by barreling, I mean sort of slowly creeping toward while every donkey in Santorini leisurely ambled in front of us.

Near Fira, we got stuck in traffic, and then there was a large commotion involving the bus driver telling off a group of beach-going tourists who were attempting to board wearing wet clothes, and by the time we made it to Kamari, my stomach was a mess of knots, but it was almost showtime.

As the bus crept into the town, I began to worry that no one would actually show up, but when we arrived, Cinekamari was packed. I recognized a lot of the faces: Maria the bakery owner, Hugo the artist, Kostas the saxophone-playing yacht captain, Vasilios and his daughter—Vasilios looking considerably less shaken—even Henrik and Hye were there, plus about a hundred more. And the guests I didn't recognize all seemed to recognize me. People kept patting me and saying things in Greek that I didn't understand, and I smiled and said things in English they didn't understand. The vibe was even better than I'd imagined—festive and celebratory, a night that screamed *We did something*. The screen was lit up with the simple title screen Theo and I had made, FINDING ATLANTIS.

"Are they here yet?" I asked Theo, who was checking his phone.

"Three minutes." He tilted his head toward the bar, flashing me a mischievous grin. "Want a snack? I could get you one of everything."

I shook my head. "I'm too nervous."

Suddenly a small warm object landed on my back, nearly knocking me to the ground and messing up my hair in the process. "I am the ninja your friends warned you about!"

"Julius!" I grabbed his arms and swung him forward in front of me, giving him a tight squeeze. He wore sneakers and a T-shirt with a tie, and the sight of him made my heart spill over. I'd been more than homesick. I'd been Julius-sick. "Julius, I'm so happy you're here! I missed you so much."

"You are SMASHING ME," he yelled, squeezing out of my grasp. "Did you know I saw a donkey and a lot of boats today? And I need to tell you something important."

I set him down and he stared up at me grimly. "Liv, I think a bad guy snuck into your room. He knocked over your sparkly eye shadow and broke it. I don't know who!"

I bit back a laugh. "Thank you for telling me. We can figure that out later. I'm very happy to see you."

"Me too," he said with obvious relief. "Mom said your dad lives here. She went to get some flowers for you, but it's a surprise, so don't tell her I told you."

"Cross my heart," I said.

"You must be Julius." Theo moved up next to me, his arm brushing mine.

Julius eyed him suspiciously, taking in Theo's suit and shiny shoes. "Who are you?"

"I'm your sister's friend. My name is Theo." He crouched down so he was eye level with Julius. "Hey, Julius, what do you call an angry ninja?"

Julius scrunched up his face in concentration. "What?"

"Nothing. You run."

Julius's face lit up like a Christmas tree. "Let's battle, Theo. Okay? You versus me. I'll be the good guy. You can be the bad guy. Now *fight*." He instantly began karate chopping and kicking with his dusty shoes, and I swooped him up before he could ruin Theo's suit.

"We'll do that after the movie, okay? How about you go find your dad and order some popcorn?"

"Prepare for an epic battle," Theo said.

"Yes!" He launched one more roundhouse kick at Theo, then turned to find James.

"Thanks for that. I forgot how *much* he is." I watched the top of Julius's head disappear into the crowd.

"Exactly as described. I think he'll find me to be a worthy opponent," Theo said. He looked over the top of my head. "And look who it is. The man of the hour. You ready?"

"Ready." My heart kicked things up a notch as I spun around. There he was. Dad 2.0. Ana had done some work on him. He'd gotten a haircut, and he wore a navy-blue suit that fit him perfectly. Without his regular baggy clothes, he looked slim and strong, and for a moment I forgot how sick he was. People had already begun to swarm him. My heart ached.

"You said ten years?" I didn't have to tell Theo what I meant.

"People have been known to live on dialysis for twenty

to thirty years. And knowing your dad, he'll squeeze at least twenty to thirty thousand years' worth of living in there."

"Yeah," I whispered. My chest was heavy, but I needed to get moving. Time to get this show going. It took me a moment to cut through the crowd, but as soon as he saw me, my dad's face beamed brightly. "Liv!" He pointed to the screen. "Is it true? You really finished the documentary?"

"Well . . . ," I said.

"Honey, you look beautiful. So beautiful." His eyes were already tearing up, which made mine do the same. If we weren't careful, we might flood the entire island.

"Good evening to all of our distinguished guests." Geoffrey's deep voice rumbled through the microphone. "We would like to invite you to be seated for our presentation tonight."

"Let's get you to your seats," Theo said, appearing at my side. "Ready?"

The garden's lights flashed once, then twice. Excitement flared through my center. "Come on, Dad. Let's go."

We hurried my dad to the front-and-center seats marked with a rope that said RESERVED. Behind us, the atmosphere hummed with excitement. I caught sight of James, who was wearing Julius on his shoulders, and he waved and gave me a thumbs-up. I waved back.

"Liv!" my mom called from the theater's entryway. She

was holding an enormous bouquet of pink flowers, and she pointed to Julius and James. "I'll sit with the boys. Good luck!"

I blew her a kiss, and she caught it with one hand.

I took the seat next to my dad's, carefully arranging my skirt and crossing my legs so my foot was inches from Theo's. Theo and I exchanged nervous smiles. I was so excited it felt like fireworks were going off under my skin.

"Were you able to submit the film to National Geographic?" my dad asked Theo.

"You'll see," Theo said.

Once the crowd had more or less settled, Geoffrey continued the introduction, holding the sheet of paper we'd typed up for him. "Welcome, friends and family, enemies and friends, to a very special evening in honor of a very special man. As many of you know, Nico Varanakis has been an ardent Atlantis hunter for many years now. He has overcome many obstacles, and tonight we want to celebrate him. So without further ado, please enjoy *Finding Atlantis*, a Kalamata production."

"Ready?" Theo said into my ear.

"Ready."

He met my eyes for a few heart-fluttering seconds, twisting my stomach. *Later, Liv,* I reminded myself. But later seemed both terribly long and terribly short.

The lights went out, and then the screen lit up. Theo

had made a second title page overlaid on mine and my dad's map with the words FINDING ATLANTIS, STARRING NICO VARANAKIS. It looked fantastic, and everyone else must have thought so too, because several cries of *opa!* mingled with applause.

"Perfect." I sighed.

"Thanks."

The volume started out too high. We had chosen big, soaring instrumental music to begin the film, and it took a moment for whoever was controlling the film to get it settled down, but finally everyone stilled.

The first scene opened to my dad, the day before I'd arrived in Santorini. He was on his boat, docked in Ammoudi Bay, and his hair whipped around in the wind. I'd seen this already, obviously, but seeing him on his boat looking so hopeful and *Dad*-like got to me anyway.

"What's tomorrow?" Theo's voice asked, off camera.

"Olive gets here," my dad said. His smile was so big you could hardly see his eyes. "And then I get to take her on an adventure."

I heard my dad exhale. "But, Liv, this isn't the National Geographic—"

"Just watch," I whispered back.

We'd used a lot of material Theo had filmed of my dad that had nothing to do with Atlantis, like him and Ana at the ribbon-cutting ceremony of the Lost Bookstore of Atlantis and him and Bapou having a coffee at Maria's. There were even a few impromptu interviews of Theo asking my dad about where he'd grown up and about his time in America. If I hadn't known any better, I would have thought Theo had been planning for this film all along.

And then there were the months leading up to my arrival. Theo was right. My dad had really kicked his research and work into gear, pouring all his extra energy into finding a way to make Atlantis real for me. Theo had clips starting from the day my dad had sent me that first postcard, all the way to the day they got the news about National Geographic accepting their documentary proposal. My on-screen dad had teared up at that part, then told Theo he needed to go; he had a post-card to write. In almost every scene, regardless of what he was doing—boating around the bay, studying yet another transla-tion of the Egyptian *Book of the Dead*—my dad explained why he was doing what he was doing: *to give Olive Atlantis.*

I'd watched this all about a dozen times by now, but I couldn't help crying.

About ten minutes into the film, I showed up, confused and annoyed, at the airport. My obvious suspicion of Theo got a good laugh, and at one point the real Theo reached over and squeezed my arm, which eased some of the tightness in my chest.

A lot of it was painful to watch again, like how clearly terrified I was to see my dad, and then the awkwardness of that reunion, us standing frozen on the roof. And then there was me crying at my birthday party, my dad's pain and helplessness so evident now that I wasn't living it.

From there we moved on to searching for Atlantis. But in this new version of our documentary, we'd left out most of the footage we'd worked so hard to film. Instead of my dad's explanations about Plato or the Minoan civilization, we'd focused on the peripheral filming: me putting makeup on my dad, him staring out at the water, us looking at Hugo's painting in the Venetian watchtower.

It reminded me of making sugar cookies with Julius—instead of using the shapes we'd cut out from the dough, we used all the scraps, and in doing so, showed the actual story. The movie wasn't about finding a golden city. It was about *us*.

I kept sneaking looks over at my dad. He was staring at the screen, his entire body focused and alert.

And then, finally, the final scene, filmed last night. The shot opened to me sitting in the desk at the bookstore, my dad's maps spread out in front of me, my shoebox front and center. I looked nervous and tired, and clearly hadn't thought to brush my hair or put on something that didn't look like it had come from the bottom of a suitcase, but my eyes were focused, like my dad's always were on camera.

My voice rang out over the theater. "When my dad left, he left twenty-six things behind. Most of them were throwaways, but I kept them anyway." My voice sounded strange to me, and seeing myself up there made me feel more vulnerable than I ever had. It was a mirror that I had no control over, my every move amplified. I saw the way I pulled at my hair whenever I was self-conscious, or the way I bit my lower lip when I was trying not to cry.

I'd shown our maps, all the spots that I'd drawn in, all the things that I'd cared about because my dad had cared about them first. I spoke about what it was like when he left, how confused I'd been, and how hurt, and about the twenty-six things my father had left behind, each documenting a piece of our story.

When I got to item number twenty-six, I began struggling for words. All twenty-six were laid out on the desk in front of me, and when I looked into the camera, I was fighting against tears.

"The last item on my list was always the hardest for me to reconcile, because it was personal, and it was something I knew he cared about, maybe more than anything. The other items, it was easy to pick out their flaws, or what was wrong with them. I understood why he'd left them behind. But this one was different." I held up my list, and Theo zoomed in so you could see the writing. #26. ME.

I continued on-screen. "Number twenty-six was me. I didn't understand why he'd left her behind with all the other things. He thought he had to. And I understand that now. I thought we'd lost each other. But sometimes lost things can be found."

And then, unexpectedly, the film cut to my dad. He was standing by the ocean, his hands in his pockets, like he hadn't realized Theo was sneaking up on him.

I looked questioningly at Theo. "You added something?"

He shrugged, a mischievous smile pulling at his lips. "It was missing something."

"Nico," On-Camera Theo called. "You've been looking for the lost city your entire life. In a recent article, you were quoted as saying, 'Atlantis means different things to different people. Island or not, it's a symbol of the things we care about most.' So tell me this, Nico. What is *your* Atlantis?"

He turned and smiled, his arms outstretched so you could see the tattoo on his inner arm. "It's Olive. She's my Atlantis."

I couldn't see the screen anymore; my eyes were too blurry. My dad's hand was in mine. I hadn't even noticed him reach over.

And then there was the film's final line, the one I'd chosen. It was me looking out like I could see the audience, like I could see my dad.

We found it, Dad. We finally found Atlantis.

Chapter Twenty-Six

#26. ME

WHEN THE SCREEN WENT DARK, MY DAD GATHERED ME into a tight, crushing hug, the armrest stabbing into me, and we stayed that way for a while, both of us making the other's shoulder soggy. "Wow," he said.

"Was that true?" I asked. "What you said up there?"

"It was always true." He pulled back, dabbing at his eyes. "Well, we've found Atlantis. Now what will we do?"

I laughed too, wiping at all the tears and makeup melting off my face. "Now I think you should greet your fans. This is your moment." I pointed at the back of the theater. Caterers were already setting up the elaborate buffet, overseen by an extremely bossy Bapou, looking extra dapper in a three-piece suit, and Geoffrey, who had a certain ballerina clinging to his arm. The theater's speakers crackled, and colorful lights lit up the garden as big band music began playing. Perfect timing.

"Wow," he said again.

His eyes shone, and as I watched him take it all in, emotions poured through me, all mixed and sloshing. I was glad for this moment, but I also felt completely overwhelmed. The crowd's energy was palpable. They were ready to pounce, offer their congratulations and love. And I was grateful for it, but I was already overflowing. One more drop and I would topple over. I needed air. Or water. Something.

There was also one more thing on my agenda for tonight. An important thing. Before I could lose my courage, I grabbed Theo's sleeve. "Can we go somewhere? You and me?"

His eyes moved to mine, and I winced at their surprise. "Where?"

I gestured toward the theater's exit. "Outside?" He hesitated, glancing back at the crowd.

People were already making their way toward us. Ten more seconds and they'd hook their claws into us and we'd never be able to get away. I caught sight of his camera bag and had a brilliant idea. "I want to do one last interview."

"Okay," he said, his voice rising in interest.

I knew he wouldn't turn down the possibility of an interview. Relief flooded me and I exhaled, knotting my fingers into the skirt of my dress. "Come on."

We darted out the side entrance, bursting out of all the light and chaos and into the cool stillness of Kamari at night.

I thought I'd know exactly what to say the second I left all the chaos behind, but I didn't. I had no idea. Instead it got all quiet and awkward, and Theo looked at me expectantly. "Where do you want to do the interview?"

"How about down by the water?" I said. And then I took off down the dark street, not looking back, because if he didn't come with me, I didn't know what I'd do.

Luckily, he followed.

It was a long, quiet walk, and I was way too nervous to try to make conversation. Kamari didn't have much by way of street lighting, and by the time we reached the beach, the dark sky blended seamlessly with the deep purple ocean, the stars pinning the sky into place. The seaside restaurants were going strong, but everything past the boardwalk was dark and quiet. My hands were shaking.

"Keep going?" Theo asked, eyeing my outfit.

"Yes." I pulled off my sandals, then wound the edge of my dress around my hand and stepped out onto the cool sand. I needed the ocean for this.

As we made our way to the water, I looked up at the stars. Each one was tiny, but urgent in its own job. Tonight mattered. I knew it did. It was very possible that I was going to regret what I was about to do, but I also knew I would definitely regret *not* doing it. I couldn't bear to carry the words home with me. I had to take the chance.

When I finally reached the edge of the tide, I tossed my sandals aside, then turned to face him. Theo had taken off his shoes too, and his pant legs were rolled up. As usual, the moonlight was doing him all kinds of favors. If I looked at him for too long, I was going to lose my nerve. Instead, I stared down at the water bubbling around my bare feet, reminding myself to breathe.

"Are you sure you want to film here?" Theo unzipped his camera bag. "It's pretty dark."

My hands were shaking, but I nodded. "I think it will be perfect. Ready whenever you are."

"Okay." He knelt down and pulled out his camera, turning it on before setting it atop his shoulder.

Am I really about to do this? Can I really ask for one measly night?

But I only had tonight. After this, I'd go back to the hotel with my mom, and the day after that I'd leave, and whatever chance I had with Theo would be gone. Which meant *now*. I had to act now.

"Three . . . two . . . one," Theo said, and then the time for decisions was over.

A cold wave hit my calves, and I took a deep breath of the salty air. I hadn't planned to do this on camera, and now I felt all kinds of pressure to improv. I needed to start talking. I'd start with . . . olives. Why not?

I cleared my throat, my heart hammering, as I stared into

the camera lens. "There's a story of how olive trees came to Greece. It's part of a legend. When the city of Athens was first formed, there was a contest between the gods. Whoever gave the people the best gift would have the honor of being the city's protector. Poseidon went first. He hit a rock with his trident, and water rushed out. If they chose him, they'd have the power of the sea."

I'd sunk ankle-deep into the sand, water lapping at my legs, but I was too nervous to move. Theo shifted from one foot to the other. I could feel the question in his posture. *Why are we here doing this?*

Because I had to. *Stick with me, Theo.*

"Athena, the goddess of wisdom, went next. She hit a rock with her spear, and an olive tree appeared. It was a symbol of peace and wealth. The citizens chose her gift, and named Athens after her. Legend says that all of the olive trees in Greece are descendants of that first tree."

"Interesting fact," Theo said from behind his camera.

I was too nervous to smile. The hard part was next. Right then the moon shifted from behind the clouds, shining down on the water like a spotlight.

Not helpful.

I yanked one foot out of the sand, gripping the edges of my dress. "This is the actual important part. I'm going to reintroduce myself, okay?"

His face poked up from behind his camera. "I know who you are, Kalamata."

"I know. This is for me." The water was so cold my ankles felt numb, but I held still, making my voice loud and clear. "My dad's name is Nico Varanakis. He's Greek, and he studies the lost city of Atlantis. He also struggles with mental health issues. When I was eight, he left my mom and me and went back to Greece. Afterward, my mom and I struggled. We had to move constantly, and I was so lonely and heartbroken that I decided that the only way to survive was to become someone else." I was overwhelmed with affection, thinking about that girl. She'd done what she had to, to make it through.

"But I was pretending, sometimes even forgetting the things I care about. I like drawing and old movies and makeup. I hate running. *Hate* it. I want to go to art school. I have a new thing for French rap." A small laugh trickled from behind the camera. "What I mean to say is, hi. My name is Olive. You can call me that now. Also . . ."

I dug my toes into the sand, willing the words to come out right. "I met someone here in Santorini. Someone who knows too much about olives and the worst times to stick a camera in a person's face. But I like this someone. A lot. He doesn't do long-distance so that means it's only for tonight, but I have to tell him anyway. I really like him, and I want to be with him."

There, I'd said it. Sort of. A congratulatory wave hit me at shin level, but I stood my ground against a very . . .

Very.

Very.

Very.

Long pause.

The camera lowered slowly, and we stared at each other. The lit-up boardwalk made a perfect background for him, the moonlight softening his features. For once I couldn't read his expression. Was he surprised? Upset? Trying to figure out how to let me down? My heart was attempting to break out of my chest. "I already was calling you Olive," he finally said.

Not exactly what I'd had in mind.

"Theo," I wailed. "Are you not going to acknowledge what I said?"

"I'm getting there," he said.

I covered my face with my hands. This was a disaster. Maybe this confession thing wasn't such a good idea, but this ship had already set sail. I had to keep going. *Don't think, just talk.*

I dropped my hands, forcing myself to look at his perfect face. There was a question there. What was it?

"Dax and I broke up," I blurted out. He flinched. Yikes, that one maybe required a bit of forethought. "Last night. We broke up last night after you left."

"Oh." Theo's shoulders sagged slightly. "I'm sorry to hear that." Again, no encouragement whatsoever. *Keep going.*

"I'm the one who broke up with him." I shifted forward onto my tippy-toes, gathering myself. "He didn't really know me. And honestly, that wasn't his fault. I'd made up this new version of myself so I could fit in. It was a survival technique."

"Sometimes those are helpful." His eyes finally met mine, and I felt a tiny shiver move through me. I couldn't stand it anymore.

"Theo! What are you thinking right now?"

He moved forward slightly, a move I felt more than saw. "Are you supposed to yell at people during these sorts of things?"

I groaned. "No. Maybe. I've never done this before."

"Hmm," he said.

Two more waves came and went. Ten more seconds of this silence and I was going to have to fall back into the water and let it carry me away. I needed him to give me *something*.

"Theo?" I said.

"Tell me more about this other guy," he finally said.

A large wave rushed in around me, and I nearly fell over in relief. "I've never met anyone like him. I wasn't sure at first; he was kind of nosy, and annoyingly persistent. But he's also very smart and brave and really, really loyal. He's also pretty funny."

Was that a smile? I couldn't tell. Theo shoved his non-camera hand into his pocket. "*How* funny?"

"Not as funny as he thinks he is," I said quickly.

"Hmm. What about his physical appearance? Is he good-looking?"

"*Annoyingly* good-looking."

"He sounds . . . annoying." Theo bit his lower lip, and I gripped my dress tighter.

"Sometimes," I said. "But it's usually in the right ways. He doesn't let me get away with things, and as much as I hate that, I also think I needed it in my life."

"Hmmm," he said again. "You aren't really selling him. What about his hair? Does he have good hair?"

"Needs work."

"Abs? General physique?" Theo extended his arm. "Does he have good fashion sense?"

"Don't push it." But now I was smiling, and my panic was morphing into something else. Hope? We were staring at each other. Like a dare. I exhaled slowly. "There's one big problem. He lives in Greece, and I live in the States, and he has some pretty ironclad rules about how he lives his life, and he most definitely does *not* do long-distance dating, which means that if this is going to work, he will either have to make an exception or I will have to make do with . . ." I made a big show of checking my phone. "The forty-eight hours I have left."

"Forty-eight hours isn't very long." He looked at me thoughtfully. "I'm obviously speculating here, but it's possible that he came up with those rules before meeting you. And no matter how much he thinks he knows everything, he doesn't. This *is* the age of the internet, Olive. He could get on a plane. Or visit you during the holidays. Maybe you'd even start spending more time in Santorini with your dad, although I doubt your parents would let you stay in the bunks anymore. Worst case, you'll write each other old-fashioned letters and pine away miserably like every other couple in a long-distance relationship. It's not like it's *that* bad."

My laugh stuck in my throat. He was saying all the right things, but he still hadn't moved. Why was he so far away?

"So . . . ," I prompted.

He picked up his camera. "Okay if we do one more interview?"

My jaw dropped. *"Now?"*

"Last one." He adjusted the camera, angling it toward my face. "Olive. How does it feel to be the daughter of an Atlantis hunter and the girlfriend of a noted National Geographic filmmaker?"

Since the last time Theo had asked me a question similar to this, an entire lifetime had come and gone. Relief poured over me, dousing all remaining fear. This was actually happening. "It feels . . ."

I tried hard to keep my face serious, but no amount of biting my cheeks could stop my smile. The ocean sighed behind me, deep and surprising, with me right at the edge of it. To get to the bottom would take a very long time, but I had time. Time I was due.

The breeze picked up, blowing the ends of my hair into my face. Then I turned to Theo. "It feels right. Now please turn that thing off."

He met me in the water. And then my mouth was on his, and I could feel him smiling, even while he was kissing me, and I was smiling too, because I'd had no idea what it would be like to kiss someone as Olive, let alone kiss *Theo* as Olive. He circled his arms around my waist, lifting me until the tips of my toes left the shore. I wanted to kiss him for the next eleven thousand years, until a volcano collapsed and an entire civilization sank into the sea.

My hand found his and our fingers laced together—locking into place. And we didn't let go, not when we dragged lounge chairs out into the surf so we could stare up at the moon, or when the biggest wave of the night tried to carry us out to sea, and not when we climbed, dripping, back up to the party to join my newly rejoined family.

I still had a lot more finding to do. Not everything that had been lost had been found, but there was one thing I knew with absolute clarity. I'd keep looking. No matter what happened, I'd keep searching until every piece had been found.

Olive had always been good at that.

Acknowledgments

IF YOU'VE BEEN WITHIN A TEN-MILE RADIUS OF ME OVER the past year, then you know that the fact that this book exists is a personal miracle. Thank you for witnessing it.

A volcano-size thank-you to my dad, Richard Paul Evans, for that hour we spent in my coffee shop talking about where this story was trying to go—I could not have written this without you. Thank you for always believing I could.

I also want to thank:

Atlantis Books in Oia for being so downright magical and for showing me their hidden bunk room.

Nicole Ellul for all of the amazing suggestions and enthusiasm, and for not allowing me to use the word "just" five hundred times in the final draft.

The team at Simon Pulse, thank you for being my first writing home and for all of the work and care you poured into my books. This includes Rebecca Vitkus, Nicole Russo, Caitlin Sweeny, Alissa Nigro, Jessi Smith, Sarah Creech,

Tom Daly, Thandi Jackson, Savannah Breckenridge, Elizabeth Mims, Penina Lopez, Sara Berko, and Karina Granda for her artwork on this cover.

Mara Anastas for being lovely and committed and really fun to talk to. Five years ago you took a big chance on me, and I will never ever forget it.

Laurie Liss for the hundreds of phone calls and long-distance tear drying.

Garrett Despain for sneaking me onto a film set.

Anastasia Berco for giving me a glimpse of what life is like as a Greek teenager.

Chrystal Checketts for a lot of wisdom and love and that one smelly cigar, and most especially for the night of our backyard moon ceremony where it all became very clear.

Amanda Davis for telling me the perfect story and for loving our buddy.

Dr. Bilder for seeing what no one else did.

Rachelle at Scuba Utah for answering a lot of intense questions when she probably just wanted me to focus on breathing through my regulator.

The fabulously interesting community of people who write articles and books about finding Atlantis.

The friends and family who formed the net that made this book possible during an extremely difficult time. I'll try to send you fewer Kermit the Frog desperation memes in the future. (No promises.)

David. This was really, really, really not easy on you. Thank you for every sacrifice you made to help me create this. When you read this, we will have officially crossed the mark of having spent more of our life together than not. Huzzah!

Sam and Nora, golden cities in their own right.

My readers—your existence is another personal miracle. I gave more than I had to give on this book, and I hope it lifts you up and brings you joy.

The Universe, for sending me a map and twenty-six things. Thank you, and please send me another story!

And finally, thank you to me, for being the only person who knows what it took to not give up.

Author's Note

IT'S SAFE TO SAY THAT I SPENT A LOT MORE TIME researching Atlantis than was strictly necessary, and by that I mean I spent three months in full-blown obsession mode and even underwent a brief time period in which I was telling everyone around me that not only did the lost city exist, but that I was pretty sure that I knew where it was.

I have some very lovely, very patient friends. Also Trader Joe's clerks.

Although I consumed a truly shocking amount of information (Thanks, internet!), there were a few resources that I found myself coming back to on a near-daily basis, and I would be remiss if I did not call them out here in order to express my undying gratitude and affection. I could not have sent my characters on their own Atlantis hunt without the following.

"Can Santorini Be Atlantis?" is a video posted to YouTube by Harry Coote in 2015. If you were to check my computer for the number of times I watched this charming and informational sketch, you might worry about me. Watch it here and realize that Nico Varanakis really knew what he was talking about: https://www.youtube.com /watch?v=vbuHQR7URe0

"Lost City of Atlantis" is a documentary from the *World of Mysteries* series and the only show I've watched twice in a row (in a coffee shop) while also scribbling frantically in a notebook. My love for this documentary runs deep. (The geology! The archaeology! The late-nineties fashion!) I most especially loved Don Pastras's contributions. I couldn't track him down, but if anyone knows Don, will you please tell me so I can send him my book and possibly a bouquet of olive leaves? Thank you. And if you'd like to watch the documentary, you can find it here: https://www.youtube .com/watch?v=MScbhEYUgB0

Meet Me in Atlantis: Across Three Continents in Search of the Legendary Sunken City, a book by Mark Adams. Mr. Adams was clearly suffering from the same Atlantis-induced fever I was, and his book was not only highly educational but highly entertaining. Readers, you should read his book next.

And of course, if you really want to go to the source, then you'd better pick up Plato. I suggest *Timaeus and Critias* (Oxford World's Classics), a new translation by

Robin Waterfield, and might I suggest you pair it with a very large cup of coffee and your comfiest sweats?

And to the many, many other people who wrote blogs and posted in forums and published articles about Atlantis, thank you. I was completely charmed and intrigued by your community, and I'm so glad you're out looking for magic. I hope you find your golden cities, but if you don't, I hope you have a great time looking.